ONE VIRGIN TOO MANY

Lindsey Davis has written over twenty historical novels, beginning with *The Course of Honour*. Her bestselling mystery series features laid-back First Century detective Marcus Didius Falco and his partner Helena Justina, plus friends, relations, pets and bitter enemy the Chief Spy.

After an English degree at Oxford University Lindsey joined the Civil Service, but became a professional author in 1989. Her books are translated into many languages and have been dramatized on BBC Radio 4. Her many prizes include the Premio Colosseo, awarded by the Mayor of Rome 'for enhancing the image of Rome', the Sherlock award for Falco as Best Comic Detective and the Crimewriters' Association Cartier Diamond Dagger for lifetime achievement. She was born in Birmingham but now lives in Greenwich, London.

ONE VIRGIN TOO MANY

TOO MANY

LINDSEY

DAVIS

arrow books

Reissued by Arrow Books 2013

5 7 9 10 8 6

Copyright © Lindsey Davis 1999

Lindsey Davis has asserted her right under the Copyright, Designs
and Patents Act 1988 to be identified as the author of this work

First published in Great Britain in 1999 by Century

Arrow Books
Random House, 20 Vauxhall Bridge Road,
London SW1V 2SA

www.randomhouse.co.uk

Addresses for companies within The Random House Group Limited can be found at:
www.randomhouse.co.uk/offices.htm

The Random House Group Limited Reg. No. 954009

A CIP catalogue record for this book
is available from the British Library

ISBN 9780099515166

The Random House Group Limited supports the Forest Stewardship Council®
(FSC®), the leading international forest-certification organisation. Our books carrying
the FSC label are printed on FSC®-certified paper. FSC is the only forest-certification
scheme supported by the leading environmental organisations, including Greenpeace.
Our paper procurement policy can be found at:
www.randomhouse.co.uk/environment

Typeset by SX Composing DTP, Rayleigh, Essex
Printed and bound in Great Britain by Clays Ltd, St Ives plc

PRINCIPAL CHARACTERS

M. Didius Falco	the man they love to blame
Helena Justina	a girl with a secret; hoping for a better bathroom
Julia Junilla	a dear little treasure
Nux	a dog, not quite so dear
The Sacred Geese of Juno and the Augurs' Sacred Chickens	protected species
Ma	a down-to-earth commentator
Pa (Geminus)	up to no good as usual
Maia Favonia	Falco's sister; inconveniently widowed
Cloelia (Maia's daughter)	hoping to become a Virgin
Marius (Maia's son)	wanting to stay on at school (a miracle)
Uncle Fabius (the dopey one)	a chicken-fancier, safely in the country
Petronius Longus	Falco's first partner; the one who pulled out
Rubella	awkward tribune of the Fourth Cohort of vigiles
Vespasian	Emperor of Rome; as high as you can get
Titus Caesar	a Romantic Prince
Berenice	a Queen of Hearts
Rutilius Gallicus	poet and ex-consul, on the up (getting Falco down)
Anacrites	Falco's second partner; the one who was pushed
Laelius Numentinus	an eminent chief priest (a wicked old basket)
Laelius Scaurus	a priest by rights (inactive)
Caecilia Paeta	a devoted mother (giving up her little darling)
Gaia Laelia	the next Vestal; a willing sacrifice?

Statilia Laelia	a devoted auntie (nothing wrong with that)
Ariminius Modullus	a devoted husband (wanting a divorce, of course)
Terentia Paulla	a married Virgin; another widow (convenient?)
Meldina	a beautiful part of the scenery (dangerous)
Athene	a reluctant nursemaid (safe with children?)
Ventidius Silanus	an Arval Brother, too dead to contribute
The Master of the Arval Brethren	a gourmet, too devious to comment
D. Camillus Verus	Helena's father; trying to do his best
Julia Justa	her mother; fearing the worst
A. Camillus Aelianus	a temporary scene-of-crime expert
Q. Camillus Justinus	Falco's new partner (permanently off the scene)
The *camillus* (no relation)	an Arval acolyte; a spotty youth
Constantia	a Virgin; a thriller
Gloccus and Cotta	contractors of distinction (absolutely terrible)

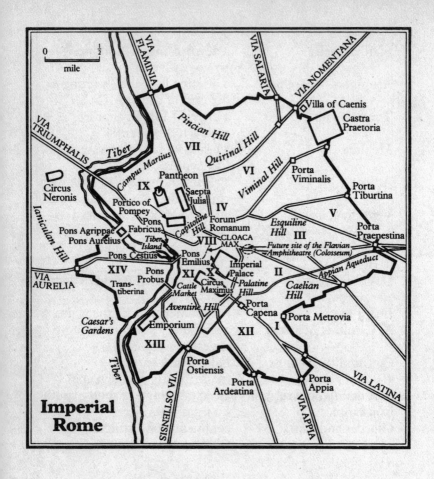

Imperial Rome

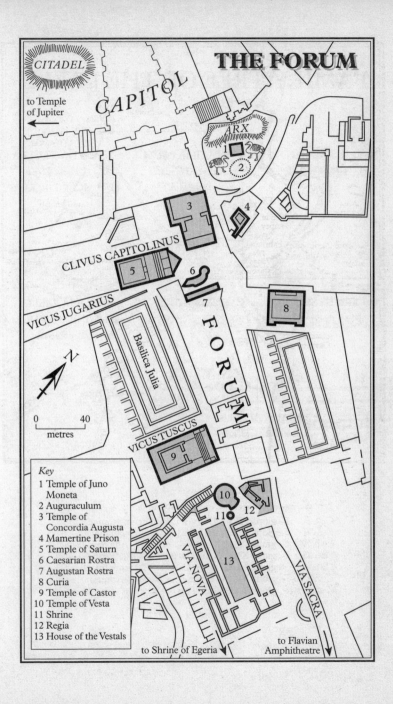

THE FORUM

CITADEL

to Temple
of Jupiter

CAPITOL

ARX

CLIVUS CAPITOLINUS

VICUS JUGARIUS

FORUM

Basilica Julia

N

0   40
metres

VICUS TUSCUS

VIA NOVA

VIA SACRA

Key
1 Temple of Juno
  Moneta
2 Auguraculum
3 Temple of
  Concordia Augusta
4 Mamertine Prison
5 Temple of Saturn
6 Caesarian Rostra
7 Augustan Rostra
8 Curia
9 Temple of Castor
10 Temple of Vesta
11 Shrine
12 Regia
13 House of the Vestals

to Shrine of Egeria ↓

to Flavian
Amphitheatre ↓

FAMILY TREE OF THE LAELII

P. LAELIUS NUMENTINUS m. STATILIA PAULLA   TERENTIA PAULLA
the ex Flamen Dialis   *the ex Flaminica*   *the ex Vestal Virgin*
                                  (deceased)   m. 'UNCLE TIBERIUS'
                                                             the family friend
                                                               (deceased)

P. LAELIUS SCAURUS m. CAECILIA PAETA   STATILIA LAELIA
Not a flamen   m. ARIMINIUS MODULLUS
                                                  the Flamen Pomonalis

GAIA LAELIA
Presumed the next Vesta

ROME: 27 MAY–7 JUNE, AD74

I

I had just come home after telling my favourite sister that her husband had been eaten by a lion. I was in no mood for greeting a new client.

Some informers might welcome any chance to flourish their schedule of charges. I wanted silence, darkness, oblivion. Not much hope, since we were on the Aventine Hill, in the noisiest hour of a warm May evening, with all Rome opening up for commerce and connivance. Well if I couldn't expect peace, at least I deserved a drink. But the child was waiting for me outside my apartment halfway down Fountain Court, and as soon as I spotted her on the balcony I guessed that refreshments would have to wait.

My girlfriend Helena was always suspicious of anything too pretty that arrived in a very short tunic. Had she made the would-be customer wait outside? Or had the smart little girl taken one look at our apartment and refused to venture indoors? She was probably linked to the luxurious carrying chair with a Medusa boss on its smoothly painted half-door that was parked below the balcony. Our meagre home might strike her as highly undesirable. I hated it myself.

On what passed for a portico, she had found herself the stool that I used for watching the world go by. As I came up the worn steps from the alley, my first acquaintance was with a pair of petite, well-manicured white feet in gold-strapped sandals, kicking disconsolately against the balcony rail. With the thought of Maia's four children, frightened and tearful, still burning my memory, that was all the acquaintance I wanted. I had too many problems of my own.

Even so, I noticed that the little person on my stool had qualities I would once have welcomed in a client. She was female. She looked attractive, confident, clean and well dressed. She appeared to be good for a fat fee too. A profusion of bangles was clamped on her plump arms. Green glass beads with glinting spacers tangled in the four-colour braid on the neck of her finely woven tunic. Adept boudoir maids must have helped to arrange the circle of dark curls around her face and to position the gold net that pegged them in place. If she was showing a lot of leg below the tunic, that was because it was such a short tunic. She handled her smooth emerald stole with unflustered ease when it slid off her shoulders. She looked as if she assumed she could handle me as easily.

There was one problem. My ideal client, assuming Helena Justina permitted me to assist such a person nowadays, would be a pert widow aged somewhere between seventeen and twenty. I placed this little gem in a far less dangerous bracket. She was only five or six.

I leaned on the balcony newel post, a rotting timber the landlord should have replaced years ago. When I spoke my voice sounded weary even to me. 'Hello, princess. Can't you find the door porter to let you in?' She stared at me scornfully, aware that grimy plebeian apartments did not possess slaves to welcome visitors. 'When your family tutor starts to teach you about rhetoric, you will discover that that was a feeble attempt at irony. Can I help you?'

'I was told an informer lives here.' Her accent said she was upper class. I had worked that out. I tried not to let it prejudice me. Well, not too much. 'If you are Falco, I want to consult you.' It came out clear and surprisingly assured. Chin up and self-confident, the prospective client had the bright address of a star trapeze artiste. She knew what she wanted and expected to be listened to.

'Sorry, I am not available for hire.' Still upset by my visit to Maia, I took a sterner line than I should have done.

The client tried to win me over. She hung her head and looked down at her toes pathetically. She was accustomed to wheedling sweetmeats out of somebody. Big brown eyes begged for favours, confident of receiving what she asked. I simply gave her the hard stare of a man who had returned from imparting tragic news to people who then decided to blame him for the tragedy.

4

Helena appeared. She cast a frowning gaze over the cutesy wearing the bangles, then she smiled ruefully at me from behind the slatted half-door that Petronius and I had built to stop my one-year-old daughter crawling outside. Julia, my athletic heir, was now pressing her face through the slats at knee level, desperate to know what was going on even if it left her with grazed cheeks, a squashed mouth and a distorted nose. She greeted me with a wordless gurgle. Nux, my dog, leapt over the half-door, showing Julia how to escape. The client was knocked from her stool by the crazy bundle of rank fur and she shrank back while Nux performed her routine exuberant dance to celebrate my homecoming and the chance that she might now be fed.

'This is Gaia Laelia.' Helena gestured to the would-be client, like a seedy conjurer producing from a tarnished casket a rabbit who was known to kick. I could not quite tell whether the disapproval in her tone related to me or to the child. 'She has some troubles regarding her family.'

I burst into bitter laughter. 'Then don't look to me for comfort! I have those troubles myself. Listen, Gaia, my family view me as a murderer, a wastrel, and a general all-round unreliable bastard – added to which, when I can get into my apartment I have to bath the baby, cook the dinner, and catch two baby birds who keep crapping everywhere, running under people's feet and pecking the dog.'

On cue, a tiny bright yellow fledgling with webbed feet ran out through the gaps in the half-door. I managed to field it, wondering where the other was, then I grabbed Nux by her collar before she could lunge at it, and pushed her down the steps; she scrabbled against the backs of my legs, hoping to eat the birdie.

Bangles clonked angrily like goatbells as Gaia Laelia stamped her little gold-clad foot. She lost some of her previous air of maturity. 'You're horrid! I hope your duckling dies!'

'The duckling's a gosling,' I informed her coolly. 'When it grows up' – If ever I managed to nurse it from egg to adulthood without Nux or Julia frightening it to death – 'it will be a guardian of Rome on the Capitol. Don't insult a creature with a lifelong sacred destiny.'

'Oh that's nothing,' scoffed the angry little madam. 'Lots of people have destinies –' She stopped.

'Well?' I enquired patiently.

'I am not allowed to say.'

Sometimes a secret persuades you to take the job. Today mysteries held no charm for me. The terrible afternoon that I had just spent at my sister's had killed any curiosity.

'Why have you got it here, anyway?' demanded Gaia, nodding at the gosling.

Despite my depression, I tried to sound proud. 'I am the Procurator of Poultry for the Senate and People of Rome.'

My new job. I had only had it a day. It was still unfamiliar – but I already knew that it was not what I would have chosen for myself.

'Flunkey for Feathers,' giggled Helena from inside the door. She thought it was hilarious.

Gaia was dismissive too: 'That sounds like a title you made up.'

'No, the Emperor invented it, the clever old boy.'

Vespasian had wanted me in a position which would look like a reward but which would not cost him much in salary. He thought this up while I was in North Africa. At his summons I had sailed all the way home from Tripolitania, eagerly hoping for position and influence. Geese were what the imperial joker inflicted on me instead. And yes, I had been awarded the augurs' Sacred Chickens too. Life stinks.

Gaia, who knew how to be persistent, still wanted me to explain why the yellow bird was living in my house. 'Why have you got it here?'

'Upon receipt of my honoured post, Gaia Laelia, I rushed to inspect my charges. Juno's geese are not supposed to hatch their own eggs on the Capitol – their offspring are normally fostered under some wormy hens on a farm. Two goslings who didn't know the system had hatched out – and on arrival at the Temple of Juno Moneta I found the duty priest about to wring their sacred little necks.'

'Why?'

'Somebody complained. The sight of scampering goslings had annoyed some ancient retired old Flamen Dialis.' The

Flamen Dialis was the Chief Priest of Jupiter, top greaser to the top god in the great Olympian Triad. This menace who loathed fledglings must be a humourless traditionalist of the worst type.

Maybe he had slipped on their mess, which the goslings frequently deposited in large quantities. You can imagine the problems we now had at home.

Gaia blinked. 'You must not upset the Flamen!' she commented, in a rather strange tone.

'I shall treat this Flamen as he deserves.' I had managed not to meet him face to face; I just heard his moans from a harassed acolyte. I meant to avoid him. Otherwise, I would end up telling some powerful bastard where he could shove his wand of office. As a state procurator, I was no longer free to do that.

'He is very important,' the girlie insisted. She seemed nervous of something. It was obvious the Flamen thought too much of himself. I hate members of ancient priesthoods, with their snobbery and ridiculous taboos. Most of all I hate their undercover influence in Rome.

'You speak as if you know him, Gaia!' I was being satirical.

That was when she floored me: 'If his name is Laelius Numentinus, he's my grandfather.'

My heart sank. This was serious. Tangling with some hidebound king of the cult priesthoods over a couple of ill-placed goslings was a bad enough start to my new post, without him finding out his darling grandchild had approached me, wanting me to act for her. I could see Helena raising her eyebrows and wincing with alarm. Time to get out of this.

'Right. How do you come to be here, Gaia? Who told you about me?'

'I met somebody yesterday who said that you help people.'

'Olympus! Who made that wild claim?'

'It doesn't matter.'

'Who knows you are here?' asked Helena in a concerned voice.

'Nobody.'

'Don't leave home without telling people where you are

going,' I rebuked the child. 'Where do you live? Is it far?'

'No.'

From indoors came a sudden loud cry from Julia. She had crawled away and disappeared, but was now in some urgent trouble. Helena hesitated, then went to her quickly in case the crisis involved hot water or sharp objects.

There was nothing that a child of six could need from an informer. I dealt with divorce and financial double-dealing; art theft; political scandal; lost heirs and missing lovers; unexplained deaths.

'Look, I work for grown-ups, Gaia – and you ought to go home before your mother misses you. Is that your transport in the street?'

The child looked less sure of herself and seemed willing to descend to the elaborate conveyance that I had seen waiting below. Automatically I started wondering. A rich and richly spoiled infant, borrowing Mama's fine litter and bearers. Did this happen often? And did Mama know that Gaia had pinched the litter today? Where was Mama? Where was the nursemaid Gaia ought to have attached to her even inside the family home, let alone when she left it? Where, thought the father in me without much hope of a serious answer, was Gaia's anxiety-burdened Papa?

'Nobody listens to me,' she commented. From most children of her age it would have been petulance; from this one it sounded simply resigned. She was too young to be so certain that she did not count.

I relented. 'All right. Do you want to tell me quickly what you came for?'

She had lost faith. Assuming she ever had any in me. 'No,' said Gaia.

I was several steps down from her but I could still look her in the eye. Her young age would have been a novelty if I had been prepared to take her commission – but my time for pointless risks was past. With my new post from Vespasian, ludicrous though it was, my social status had improved dramatically; I could no longer indulge in eccentric decisions.

I managed to find the patience you are supposed to lavish

8

on a child. 'We all have quarrels with our relatives, Gaia. Sometimes it matters, but mostly it comes to nothing. When you calm down, and when whoever offended you has had time to do the same, just apologise quietly.'

'I haven't done anything to apologise for!'

'Neither have I, Gaia – but take my word, with your family, it's best just to give in.'

She marched past me, head in the air. Encumbered by Nux and the gosling, I could only stand aside. But I leaned over the railing as she reached street level, and within hearing of the litter-bearers (who ought to have known better than to bring her) I ordered her in a fatherly manner to go straight home.

Helena Justina came out to me, as I was watching the litter move off. She regarded me with her fine brown eyes, eyes full of quiet intelligence and only half-hidden mockery. I straightened up, stroking the gosling. It let out a loud, appealing squeak at which Helena humphed. I doubted that I impressed my beloved too much either.

'You let her go, Marcus?'

'She decided of her own accord.' Helena obviously knew something. She was looking concerned. Immediately I regretted my rebuff. 'So what wonderful job from this Gaia have I just cruelly turned down?'

'Didn't she tell you? She thinks her family want to kill her,' said Helena.

'Oh that's all right then. I was worried it might have been a real emergency.'

Helena raised an eyebrow. 'You don't believe it?'

'Granddaughter of a chief priest of Jupiter? That would be a high-profile scandal and no mistake.' I sighed. The litter had already vanished, and there was nothing I could do now. 'She'll get used to it. My family feel like that about me most of the time.'

II

Let's go back a day and get things straight.

Helena and I had just returned from Tripolitania. It was a rushed sea trip, hastily taken after Famia's ghastly death and funeral. My first task after the journey had to be breaking the bad news to my sister. She must have expected the worst from her husband, but his being eaten by a lion in the arena would be more than even Maia could have foreseen.

I needed to hurry, because I wanted to tell Maia quietly myself. Since we had brought back with us my partner Anacrites, who was lodging with my mother, Ma was bound to discover what had happened pretty quickly. My sister would never forgive me if anyone else heard the news before she did. Anacrites had promised to maintain silence on the subject for as long as he could, but Ma was notorious for worming out secrets. Anyway, I had never trusted Anacrites.

Burdened by my responsibilities, I rushed off to my sister's house immediately we arrived in Rome. Maia was out.

All I could do then was slink back home, hoping I could find her later. As it turned out, Anacrites was removed from any danger of gossiping with Ma because both he and I were sent messages summoning us to a meeting on the Palatine to consider the Census results. By coincidence, I later discovered that Maia herself was missing from home because she too was attending a function with a royal connection – not that I would ever have expected it from my soundly republican sister – though her fancy do was at the Golden House on the other side of the Forum, whereas we went in search of the narrow pleasures of bureaucracy at the old imperial offices in the Palace of the Claudian Caesars.

The reception that Maia was attending would be relevant

10

to all that happened subsequently. It would have been handy for me to have warned her to do some eavesdropping. Still, you rarely know that in advance.

*   *   *

For once, I was visiting Vespasian in full confidence that he had nothing to complain about.

I had worked on the Census for the best part of a year. It was my most lucrative employment ever and I had myself identified the opportunity. Anacrites, previously the Emperor's Chief Spy, had been my temporary partner. This had proved an oddly successful arrangement – given that he had once tried to have me killed, and that I had always hated his profession in general and him in particular. We had been an excellent team, screwing cash out of lying taxpayers. His meanness complemented my scepticism. He took a filthy line with the feeble; I charmed the tough. The Secretariat we reported to, not realising how good we would be, had promised us a substantial percentage of all underpayments we identified. Since we knew the Census had a short time-scale, we had worked flat out. Laeta, our contact, tried to renege as usual, but we now possessed a scroll confirming that Vespasian loved what we had done for him, and that we were rich.

Somehow, at the end of our commission Anacrites and I had ended up without killing each other. Even so, he had done his best to come to a sticky end. In Tripolitania, the idiot had managed to get himself nearly killed in the arena. Fighting as a gladiator for real would damn him to social disgrace and harsh legal penalties if anyone in Rome ever found out. When he recovered from his wounds, he had to face life knowing I had acquired a permanent hold over him.

He had reached the meeting ahead of me. As soon as I entered the high, vaulted audience chamber, I was annoyed to see his pale face. His pallor was natural, but there were bandages under the long sleeves of his tunic and I, in the know, could see him holding his body very carefully. He was still in pain. That cheered me up.

He knew I was supposed to be visiting Maia that day. Had

11

I missed the palace messenger, I wondered whether dear Anacrites would have kept me in the dark about this meeting.

I grinned at him. He never knew how to take that.

I made no effort to join him across the room. He had plonked himself alongside Claudius Laeta, the papyrus bug we had outflanked over our fee scale. Now our Census work was over, Anacrites wanted to edge himself back into his old job. Throughout this meeting, he stuck close to Laeta; they continually exchanged little pleasantries in an undertone. In reality, they were locked in a struggle for the same top position. Outside the individual offices where they plotted against one another, they put on an urbane act as best friends. But if either ever followed the other down a dark alley, one would be found dead in the gutter next day. Fortunately perhaps, palaces tend to be well lit.

The meeting room had been set out in a square with cushioned thrones for the Emperor and his son Titus, the two official Censors; there were scroll-armed seats which meant we were expecting senators, and hard stools for the lower orders. Scribes lined the walls, standing up. Most of the large assembly had bald heads and bad eyesight. Until Vespasian came in with Titus, who was in his thirties, Anacrites, Laeta and myself stood out, younger even than the secretaries on the sidelines. We were amongst hard-bitten Treasury of Saturn types, the wizened mixtures of priestliness and money-collecting who had now gleefully counted the Census revenue into ironbound strongboxes in the basement of their temple. Jostling them were envoys of senatorial status who had been sent to the provinces to extract taxes from the loyal members of the Empire overseas who had so gratefully accepted Roman rule and so reluctantly agreed to pay for it.

Later in his reign Vespasian openly called these envoys his 'sponges', placed abroad to soak up money for him, with the implication that he did not care too much what methods they used. No doubt they had balanced their natural inclinations to use bullying and brutality against his clear wish to be known as a 'good' emperor.

I knew one of the envoys – Rutilius Gallicus, assigned to

arbitrate in a land dispute between Lepcis Magna and Oea. I met him out there. Somehow, between his first conversation with me and his departure he augmented his title until he was no longer a mere desert land surveyor but the Emperor's special agent of the Census in Tripolitania. Far be it from me to suspect this noble fellow of engineering his remit. Obviously, as an ex-consul, he was well in at the Palace. In Lepcis, we had enjoyed the close social bonds of two Romans trapped far from home amongst tricky foreigners, but now I felt myself starting to regard him cautiously. He was more influential than I had previously realised. I guessed his rise had nowhere reached its zenith. He could be a friend – but I would not bank on it.

I saluted him unobtrusively; Rutilius nodded back. He was sitting quietly, not attached to any particular group. Knowing that he came to Rome as a first generation senator from Augusta Taurinorum in the despised north of Italy, I sensed that he carried the outsider's whiff. I reckoned it did not bother him.

Being a new man, sneered at by the patrician class, no longer served as a handicap since Vespasian, the ultimate rustic upstart whom nobody had ever taken seriously, had surprised the world and made himself Emperor. He now entered the chamber with the air of a curious sightseer, but he went straight to his throne. He wore the purple on his solid frame with visible enjoyment and without making any effort he dominated the room. The old man took his place centrally, a sturdy figure, forehead lined as if with a lifetime's effort. That was deceptive. Satirists could make sport with his constipated appearance but he had Rome and the whole Establishment just where he wanted them, and his grim smile said that he knew it.

At his side eventually was Titus, similarly thickset but half his father's age and twice as cheerful. He delayed taking his seat as he gave affable greetings to those who had only recently returned to Rome from the provinces. Titus had a reputation as a nice soft-hearted darling – always a sign of a nasty bastard who could be bloody dangerous. He was providing the new Flavian court with vigour and talent – and

13

with Queen Berenice of Judaea, an exotic beauty ten years his senior who, having failed to entrap Vespasian, had turned her blowsy charms on the next-best thing. After only one day back in the Forum, I already knew that the hot news was that she had recently followed her handsome plaything to Rome.

Titus himself was supposed to be overjoyed by this dubious good fortune, but I was damned sure Vespasian would handle it. The father had built his imperial claim on high-minded traditional values; a would-be empress with a history of incest and interference in politics could never make a suitable portrait for the next young Caesar's bedroom wall, not even if she sat for the artist sucking a stylus and looking like a stay-at-home virgin whose only thoughts were of kitchen inventories. Somebody should tell her: Berenice would get the push.

Titus, friendly fellow, smiled benignly when he noticed me. Vespasian noticed Titus smiling and scowled. Being a realist, I preferred the scowl.

The details of the ensuing meeting are probably subject to official rules for secrecy. The results are fully visible anyway. At the start of his reign, Vespasian had announced he needed four hundred million sesterces to put Rome on its feet. Shortly after concluding the Census, he was building and rebuilding on every plot in sight, with the astonishing Flavian Amphitheatre at the end of the Forum to set the seal on his achievements. That he achieved his huge fiscal target is hardly news.

Even with a chairman who hated dawdling and the smartest officials in the world to steer the agenda through, the budget for an empire is extensive. It took us four hours to appraise all the figures.

Vespasian never appeared to notice that he had grounds for extreme satisfaction with his new funds, though Titus raised complimentary eyebrows a couple of times. Even the Treasury men looked relaxed, which was unheard of. Eventually the Emperor made a short, surprisingly gracious speech thanking everyone for their efforts, then he was gone, followed by Titus.

14

The meeting was over, and I would have been out of there at a fast march had not a spruce slave shuffled Anacrites and me into a sideroom unexpectedly. There we kicked our heels and sweated amongst a group of nervous senators until we were shunted on to a private interview with Vespasian. He should have been lying down for a nap like a respectable pensioner; instead, he was still hard at work. We finally grasped that rewards were being handed out.

We had ended up in a much smaller throne room. Titus was missing, but as we had joked during our wait, Titus looked tired; Berenice must be sapping his strength. Vespasian used both his sons as public props but that was to accustom the public to their pink little imperial faces for when he passed on; he never really needed a sidekick. He could certainly manage a few brisk thanks for a pair of low characters like Anacrites and me.

Vespasian made it seem as if he was genuinely grateful. In return, he said, he was adding both our names to the equestrian list. This came out so casually I nearly missed it. I had been watching a woodlouse scurry along a painted dado and only woke up when I heard Anacrites express an unpleasantly suave murmur of gratitude.

To be bumped up to the middle rank required land holdings worth four hundred thousand sesterces. Do not imagine our trusty old emperor was donating the collateral. He pointed out with a snort that we had screwed so much money from him in fees that he expected us to put aside the qualifying amount; he just bestowed on us the formal right to wear the middle rank's gold ring. There was no ceremony; that would have required gold rings for Vespasian to hand out. He of course preferred people to buy their own. I did not intend wearing one. Where I lived, some thief would steal it the first time I went out.

In order to make a distinction between me, the freeborn conniver, and Anacrites, a publicly employed ex-slave, Vespasian then told Anacrites that he was still valued in intelligence work. I, on the other hand, was honoured with the kind of horrible sinecure that the middle ranks traditionally crave. While working on the Census, I had prevented a fatal accident to the Sacred Geese on the Capitol. As a reward, Vespasian had created for me the post of Procurator of Poultry for the Senate and People of Rome.

'Thanks,' I said. Smarming was expected.

'You deserve it,' grinned the Emperor. The job was rubbish, we both knew that. A snob might be thrilled to be associated with the great temples on the Capitol, but I hated the idea.

'Congratulations,' smirked Anacrites. In case he planned to annoy me any more, and to remind him I could ruin him, I gave him the traditional gladiators' salute. He fell silent. I let it go there; he was already enough of an enemy.

'Was I recommended for this position by some kind friend, Caesar?' Antonia Caenis, the Emperor's long-term mistress, had before her death given me a hint that she might ask him to look again at my prospects. His gaze was direct. After forty or fifty years of respecting Antonia Caenis, past advice from her would always count with Vespasian.

'I know your worth, Falco.' Sometimes I wondered whether he ever remembered that I held some damning evidence against his son Domitian. I had never yet tried blackmail, though they knew I could.

'Thanks, Caesar!'

'You will go on to worthy things.'

I was hamstrung, and we both knew it.

Anacrites and I walked from the Palace together in silence.

For him, there was probably little change in store. He was expected to continue his career in state service, simply enhanced by his new rank. It might do him some good materially. I had always suspected that after a career in spying Anacrites had already stashed away a secret fortune. He owned a villa in Campania, for one thing. I had learned of its existence from Momus, a carefully cultivated nark.

Anacrites never discussed his origins, but he was undoubtedly an ex-slave; even a freedman at the Palace only acquired a luxury villa legitimately as a reward for an exceptional lifetime's service. I had never worked out his age, but Anacrites was not looking at retirement yet; he was vigorous enough to have survived a head wound that ought to have finished him, he had quite a few teeth left and most of his sleeked-back black hair. Well, the other way Palace slaves collected pretty things was straightforward: bribery. Now he was in the middle rank, he would expect the bribes to be bigger.

We parted still in silence. He was not the type to offer a celebratory drink. I could never have swallowed it.

For me, the future looked dreary. I was freeborn, but plebeian. Today I had risen above generations of rascally Didii – to what? To being a rascal who had lost his natural place in life.

I left the Palace, exhausted and gloomy, knowing that I now had to explain my terrible fate to Helena Justina. Her fate too: a senator's daughter, she had left her patrician home for the thrills and the risks of living with a low-down rogue. Helena might seem reserved, but she was passionate and self-willed. With me, she had faced danger and disgrace. We had struggled against poverty and failure, though we were for the most part free to enjoy our lives in our own way. It was a bid for independence that many of her status might envy but few would dare to choose. I believed she had been happy. I know I had been.

Now, after being promised equestrian status for the past three years, I had finally acquired it – together with all its restrictions. I would have to engage in refined branches of commerce, the lower reaches of local priesthoods, and the less-well-remunerated administrative posts. With the approval of my social equals and a nod from the gods, my future was settled: M. Didius Falco, former private informer, would have three children, no scandals, and a small statue put up in his honour in forty years' time. Suddenly that did not sound much fun.

Helena Justina was stuck with permanent, boring, respectable mediocrity. As a source of scandal, I had definitely failed her.

III

So my first day back in Rome was trying enough. I spent the evening privately at home with Helena, adjusting to our new status and what it might mean for us.

Next day I found Maia and broke her terrible news. Things were not improved by the fact that the trip which killed her husband had now brought special rewards for me. Of course I felt guilty. When Maia said I had no reason to reproach myself, I felt even worse.

I stayed with my sister most of the day. After that harrowing experience, I came home to find I had to deal with the child-client, Gaia Laelia. Then all I wanted was to go in and close the door.

The world, however, had now heard I was back. Indoors, there were no more clients, and for once neither creditors nor pathetic loan-seekers. Instead, members of my intimate circle were lounging at my plain board table, hoping I would cook for them. One friend; one relative. The friend was Petronius Longus, who might have been welcome had he not been chatting like a crony to the relative I could least tolerate: my father, Geminus.

'I told them about Famia,' said Helena in an undertone. She meant the cleaned-up version.

We had agreed that only Maia herself was to know the full story. Famia had been sent overseas by the faction of charioteers for whom he had worked as a horse vet, looking for new stock in the Libyan stud farms. The remote locale enabled us to blur the details. Officially, he had been killed in an 'accident' with a wild animal.

It was up to Maia when, if ever, she let it be known that Famia, a loud and bigoted drunk, had raucously insulted the Tripolitanian gods and heroes in the Forum at Lepcis

Magna, to the point where hospitality to strangers had faltered and the inhabitants had beaten him up, thrown him before a visiting magistrate, and charged him with blasphemy. The traditional Tripolitanian penalty was to be torn apart by wild beasts.

The arena in Lepcis was awaiting a series of Games – normal in Africa where blood sports to assuage the anger of insulted gods are regular even when the harsh Punic gods have not been insulted at all. The locals had a lion ready starved. Famia was dispatched the next day, before I even knew he had landed at Lepcis, before I realised what was happening or could attempt to prevent it. I had scrupulously told Maia the cause and manner of her husband's death, while advising her to protect her children from the full horror at this stage. But the one thing I was not telling even her was that the magistrate who had sanctioned the execution in order to keep the peace in Lepcis had been my Census colleague, the Emperor's senatorial envoy, Rutilius Gallicus. I had been staying in his house at the time. I was sitting alongside him when I found myself watching Famia die. Even without knowing that, Maia had blamed me.

Petronius and my father both eyed me curiously as if they too somehow suspected I was implicated up to my neck.

Helena relieved me of the gosling, which she placed in its basket alongside its squeaky sibling. Luckily our apartment was above the shop of a basket-weaver and Ennianus was always eager to sell us a new container. We had not told him I was fostering geese. I was already regarded as a clown in this neighbourhood.

'Where did you rustle the fledgelings?' scoffed Pa. 'Bit skinny for roasting. By the time they can go in the pot, they'll see you as their mother!'

I grinned, gamely. Helena must have told him about my new rank and the fine job that came with it. He would waste days thinking up bad jokes.

Petronius shoved Nux between his boots under the table. Julia was handed to her doting grandfather. Pa was hopeless with children, having abandoned his own to run off with a girlfriend. He loved Julia, however, preening himself

19

because her other grandfather was a senator. She loved him back without needing a reason. The next generation all seemed eager to revere Pa even before they reached the age when they could sneakily visit him at his antiques emporium and be bribed with trinkets and titbits.

Fighting my irritation, I found a stool and sat down.

'Drink?' offered Petronius, hoping to get one himself. I shook my head. Remembering Famia temporarily spoiled my taste for it. That's the most poisonous aspect of drunkards. They cease to enjoy their own liquor – while observing the results of their excess kills its pleasures for the rest of us.

Petro and Pa exchanged raised eyebrows.

'Hard business,' commented Pa.

'You always like to be obvious.'

Helena laid a hand on my shoulder, then removed it. I had come home a hunched, miserable bastard who needed to be comforted but would not allow it. She knew the signs. 'You saw Maia this time?' she asked, though my filthy mood surely confirmed it. 'Where had she gone yesterday?'

'She took one of her daughters to some function where young girls were being introduced to Queen Berenice.'

Helena looked surprised. 'That doesn't sound like Maia!' Rather like me, my sister despised establishment formality. Being asked to attend on Titus' exotic ladyfriend would normally make Maia as rebellious as Spartacus.

Petronius seemed to know about it: 'Something to do with the lottery for a new Vestal Virgin.'

Again, not like Maia.

'I had no chance for smalltalk,' I said. 'You know Maia. As soon as she saw me, she worked out that I had bad news. I was home – yet where was Famia? Even he would normally have dropped his luggage at his own apartment before heading for a wine bar. She guessed.'

'How is she taking things?' asked Pa.

'Too well.'

'What does that mean? She's a sensible type. She won't make a fuss.' He knew nothing about his younger children, Maia and me. How could he? When he absconded from responsibility I was seven, Maia only six. He saw neither of us for over twenty years.

When I first told Maia her husband was dead, she fell into my arms. Then, she backed off at once and demanded the details. I had rehearsed the story enough times, on the sea trip home. I kept it brief. That made it seem even more bleak. Maia became very still. She stopped asking questions. She ignored what I said to her. She was thinking. She had four children and no income. There would be a funeral fund to which the Green chariot faction had made Famia contribute, which would pay for an urn and an inscription which she did not want but which she would have to accept to give the children a memorial of their disreputable sire. Maybe the Greens would come up with a small pension. She would qualify for the pauper's corn dole. But she would have to work.

Her family would help. She would not ask us to do it, and when we offered we would always have to say it was for the children. The children, who ranged from nine to three, were already frightened, bewildered, inconsolable. But they were all very bright. After Maia and I carefully explained that they had lost their father, I reckoned they sensed there was a secret we were keeping back.

My sister had known tragedy before. There had been a firstborn daughter who had died of some childhood disease at about the age the elder son, Marius, was now. I had been away in Germany when it happened, and to my shame I tended to forget. Maia would never forget. But she had borne her grief alone; Famia was never any use.

Petronius took Julia from Pa and handed her to Helena, giving Pa the nudge that they should leave. Pa, typically, failed to respond. 'Well, she'll remarry of course.'

'Don't be so certain,' Helena disagreed quietly. It was a rebuke to men. Pa failed to take this hint too. I buried my face in my hands for a moment, reflecting that an attractive, unprotected woman like my sister would indeed have to fend off a rash of propositions, many of them repulsive. That must be just one aspect of her despair in her new situation. Still, removing predators was one thing I could help her with.

'I bet –' Pa had been struck by one of his terrible mischievous ideas. 'I bet your mother,' he suggested to me portentously, 'will try to set her up with somebody we know!'

I could not bring myself even to try thinking up who he meant.

'Somebody else who's been given a nice station in life – congratulations, by the way, Marcus, and not before time; we must celebrate, son – on some better occasion, of course,' he conceded reluctantly.

Belatedly I caught on. 'You don't mean –'

'He has a good position with a sound employer, plenty of loot, prime of life, well known to us all – I reckon he's obvious,' crowed Pa. 'Your mother's precious lodger!'

I kicked back my stool, stood, then walked off to my bedroom, slamming the door like an offended child. It had been a bad day, but now I felt truly sickened. Like all my father's wild remarks, this had a deadly air of probability. If you ignored the fact the lodger was a poisonous, parasitic fungus with the ethics of a politically devious slug, here indeed was a salaried, propertied, recently elevated man who was longing to be part of the family.

Oh gods: Anacrites!

IV

What's the true story about Famia then?' asked Petro, running into me in Fountain Court the next morning. I shrugged and said nothing. He gave me a sour look. I avoided his eye, once again cursing Famia for putting me in this position. 'Bastard!' Despite his annoyance, Petronius was looking forward to trying to force it out of me.

'Thanks for taking Pa off last night.'

He knew I was trying to change the subject. 'You owe me for that. I had to let him drag me to Flora's and drink half my week's salary.'

'You can afford a long night in a caupona then?' I asked narrowly, as a way in to probing where he stood with his wife.

Arria Silvia had left him, over what Petro regarded as a minor infringement of the marital code: his crazy affair with a dim daughter of a prime gangster, which had cost him suspension from the vigiles and much scorn from those who knew him. The threat to his job had been temporary, like the affair, but the loss of his wife – which meant the virtual loss of his three children – looked likely to be permanent. For some reason, Silvia's angry response had come as a surprise to Petronius. My guess was, he had been unfaithful before and Silvia had often known it, but this time she also had to live with the unpalatable fact that half the population of the Aventine were grinning over what had been going on.

'I afford what I like.'

We were both dodging. I hoped this was not some fatal result of our attempted partnership. That had been just before I shackled myself to Anacrites. As friends since the army, Petronius and I had expected to be ideal colleagues, yet we had cut across one another from the start, each wanting his own way of doing things. We parted company after I found a chance to make a spectacular arrest without him; Petro reckoned I had kept him out of it deliberately. Since he was my best friend, breaking up with him had hurt.

When we fell out, Petro went back to the vigiles. It was where he belonged. He was enquiry chief of the Fourth Cohort, and even his po-faced hard-man tribune had to admit Petronius was damned good at it. He had thought he was going back to his wife too. But once Arria Silvia gave up on him, she had wasted no time finding herself a boyfriend – a potted-salad seller, to Petro's complete disgust. Their children, all girls, were still youngsters, and although Petronius was entitled to keep them with him, it would be stupid to attempt to do so unless he remarried smartish. Naturally, like most men who throw away a happy situation for a trifle when they think they can get away with it, he now believed that all he wanted was his wife back. Silvia was settling for her beetroot-moulder instead.

Helena thought that, with his record, Petronius Longus might find it just as hard to acquire a new wife as to reclaim the old one. I disagreed. He was well built and decent looking, a quiet, intelligent, affable type; he had a salaried position and had shown himself to be a handy homemaker. It was true that at present he was living in my squalid old bachelor apartment, drinking too much, cursing too openly, and flirting with anything that moved. But he had fate on his side. Looking bitter and wounded would work the right charms. Women love a man with a history. Well, it had worked for me, hadn't it?

If I could not give him the whole story about Famia yet, I had plenty of other news. 'I have a lot to tell you.' I had no compunction about exposing Anacrites' dalliance with the gladiatorial sword. Petro would settle for that scandal, until the fuss died down and I could explain the Famia fiasco confidentially.

'Free for dinner?' he offered.

I had to shake my head. 'In-laws.'

'Oh of course!' he retorted, with an edge. My in-laws, now I tentatively called them that, were senatorial – a swanky alliance for an informer. Petronius still did not quite know whether to mock my good luck or throw up in a gutter. 'Jupiter, Falco; don't apologise to me – You must be dying to present yourself as the wonderboy imperial favourite with the new middle-class credentials.'

It seemed tactful to find a joke: 'Up to my bootstraps in putrid goose-shit.'

He accepted it. 'Nice, on their expensive marble floors.' I noticed his eyes narrow slightly. He had seen something. Without appearing to break off our casual banter, he told me, 'Your ma has just turned the corner from Tailors' Lane.'

'Thanks!' I murmured. 'This could be a moment to nip off and officiate over some sacred beaks –'

'No need,' returned Petronius, in a changed tone, which carried real admiration. 'Looks as if your important new role has just come to you.'

I turned to follow his gaze. At the foot of the steps that led wonkily up to my apartment stood a smart litter. I recognised its white and purple striped curtains, and the distinctive Medusa head boss on the front: the same one that brought little Gaia yesterday.

Descending from it was a man in ridiculous clothing, whose snooty attendants and wincing demeanour filled me with horror. He wore a shaggy double-sided cloak and on his head a birchwood prong set in a wisp of wool; this contraption was held on by a round hat with ear-flaps, tied under his chin with two strings, rather like an item that my baby daughter used to pull off and throw on the floor. The cloak was supposed to be the garb of a hero, but the pointy-headed visitor belonged to a caste I had always reviled. In my new position, I would be forced to treat him with fake politeness. He was a flamen, one of the hidebound priests of the ancient Latin cults.

Two days in the job, and the bastards had already found out where I lived. I had known landlords' enforcers who gave a man more grace.

V

After a few words with the basket-weaver on the ground floor, the flamen's attendants preceded him up the decaying steps towards my apartment. Outside on the tiny landing where Gaia had broached me yesterday, Nux was now gnawing a large raw knucklebone. She was a small dog, but the way she growled stopped the cavalcade dead.

There was a short confrontation.

Nux gripped the bone, which was almost too heavy to lift. I had seen it – and smelt it – when I went out, a decayed monster she must have retrieved after letting it mature for weeks. A couple of flies buzzed off it. Since the half-door had been shut behind her to keep Julia in and away from the dog while it was dangerous, Nux had limited options. Her ears went back and she showed the whites of her eyes. Even I would not have approached her. Continually growling she advanced down the steps, lugging the bone, which thudded on each stone tread. The attendants retreated, stepping on the flamen's toes. Back at the foot of the stairs they squashed into a scared huddle as my dog stalked past them with her precious cargo, all the way subjecting them to a ferocious rolling growl.

The flamen clutched his cloak around him and sneaked up the steps. His attendants, four in all, reluctantly formed up at the foot of the stairs to protect his back, then when he disappeared indoors they stood at ease beside the litter. Nuxie dropped her bone in the road. Head down, she went around in a circle, pushing imaginary earth over the bone with her nose. Then, convinced her treasure was now invisible, she strolled off looking for something more interesting.

Petronius, a cat man, guffawed silently. I clapped him on

the shoulder; I waved violently to Ma to say this official business should not be interrupted for her usual loving enquiry about my family's bowels; I winked at the basket-weaver as I passed his shop. I walked upstairs quietly. The attendants ignored me. Ma called out, but I was used to not hearing my mother when she wanted me.

Indoors, I captured Julia as she crawled headlong for the half-door, which the flamen had left swinging open. Holding the baby on my shoulder and hoping she would keep quiet, I settled my backside against the new turquoise paint of the corridor wall, to overhear the fun.

I wondered what the flamen had expected. What he got was the girl I had left at home a few minutes before I met Petronius: a fairly domesticated treasure – with a volatile, rebellious streak. She had kissed me goodbye with a sensual hug and beguiling lips. Only her faraway eyes had revealed to a man who knew her well that she would like to see the back of me; she was dying to read some scrolls Pa had brought for her last night, lifted from an auction in which he was involved. By now she would have delved around in the scroll-box and been happily unrolling the first discovery. She would be furious when the priest interrupted.

She would see he was a flamen. The cap and prong were unmistakable. Senators' daughters know how to behave. But informers' wives say what they think.

'I want a man named Falco.'

'You are in his house. Unfortunately, he is not here.' Under her naturally pleasant approach, I could tell she had immediately taken against him.

Helena's accent was more refined than the flamen's. He spoke with unattractive vowels, which were pretending to be better than they were. 'I shall wait.'

'He may be a long time. He has gone to see his mother.' Despite the fact that I had dodged Ma in Fountain Court, telling her about Famia was indeed supposed to have been my errand.

If he had heard I was an informer, the flamen probably thought Helena was a hangover from some past adventure of mine. True. He would have assumed he was trying to contact a hard man in a squalid location whose female accomplice would own all the wrinkled charm of an old shoestrap. A bad mistake.

He would be realising now that Helena Justina was younger, fiercer and more refined than he had expected. His pinched nose must register that he stood in a small but scrupulously clean room (swept daily by Ma while we were abroad). It was typical of the Aventine, in that despite an open shutter it smelt of baby, pets, and last night's supper, but through it that morning was issuing a richer, more exotic, much more *expensive* perfume from the rare balsam on the warm skin beneath the light dress that Helena wore. She was in blue. Without paint, without jewellery. Needing neither. When completely unadorned she could startle and trouble an unwary man.

'I need to speak to the informer,' he whined again.

'Oh I know that feeling!' I could imagine how Helena's great brown eyes were dancing as she stalled the priest. 'But his speciality is dodging. He will turn up in his own time.'

'And you are?' the man demanded snootily.

'Who am I?' she mused, still teasing. 'The daughter of Camillus Verus, senator and friend of Vespasian; the wife and partner of Didius Falco, agent of Vespasian and Procurator of the Sacred Poultry; the mother of Julia Junilla, who is too young to have social relevance. Those are my formal definitions. My name, should you be keeping a daily diary of the interesting people you meet, is Helena Justina –'

'You are a senator's daughter – and you live *here*?' He must be looking round at our bare decorations and furniture. We coped. We had each other. (Plus various tasty artefacts waiting in store for better days.)

'Certainly not,' Helena rattled back promptly. 'This is merely an office where we meet members of the public. We live in a spacious villa on the Janiculan.' First I heard of it. Still, I was only the head of the household. With a practical young woman in charge of my private life (and in possession of her own bank box), if my home address changed overnight I would be the last to be notified.

28

Helena was picking on the prong-bearer now. 'I see you are a flamen. Obviously not the Flamen Dialis.' The top man, Jupiter's priest, wore an even more ludicrous uniform and kept the public at a distance with a long wand. 'The Flamen Quirinalis is my father's second cousin.' As far as I knew, this was pure invention. Being related to the priest of Quirinus, the deified Romulus, would place Helena in high circles, if true, and was designed to intimidate. 'The Flamen Martialis is ninety and renowned for groping women.' Not many people would know the unsavoury habits of the priest of Mars. 'I believe the Emperor is very concerned about how to deal with it . . .' Incorrigible girl. 'So you are not one of the patrician group,' Helena's cool voice concluded, insulting the man if he was at all sensitive about his status. 'Which, then, shall I tell Falco has called on him?' she cooed.

'I am the Flamen Pomonalis.'

'Oh poor you! That's the lowest of all, isn't it?' Excluding the novelty newcomers who honoured the deified emperors, there were fifteen priests in the College of Flamens, three culled from the aristocracy to attend the major deities and the rest, who sacrificed to gods most people had never heard of and who were recruited from the plebeian ranks. No one I knew had ever been selected; you had to be a pleb whose face fitted. 'Do you have a name?' demanded Helena.

'Ariminius Modullus.' I could have guessed it would be an awkward mouthful.

'Well, if this is about the goslings, Falco has the matter well in hand.'

'The goslings?'

'The Flamen Dialis has some objection to small birds, I believe.'

This made little sense to Pomona's pointy head. He sounded so wound up that his birchwood prong must be shooting right out of his bonnet. 'I have come about Gaia Laelia!'

'Well so I assumed.' Helena knew how to reply to an over-excited supplicant with maddening calm. 'The child came here with an intriguing complaint. You need to know what was said.'

29

The flamen must be biting his lip as he worried about what had been discussed yesterday.

'And you want to know what Didius Falco is intending to do,' Helena added ominously. If the child really were being threatened at home, it would do no harm to let her people know that we were aware of it. 'Is Gaia Laelia a relation?'

'I am her uncle – by marriage.' Where, I wondered, were Gaia's parents in this? Why had they sent this rather stiff mediator? Distracted, I leaned my head sideways, to try to discourage Julia from eating my earlobe.

'And you are acting for Gaia's parents?' Helena asked, barely hiding her scepticism. I dried Julia's dribble off my ear, using my tunic sleeve. She burped, messily. I wiped her face on the same bunch of sleeve.

'Gaia is in the guardianship of her grandfather. The family holds to tradition. My father-in-law will remain head of the household while he lives.' This meant Gaia's father had not been legally emancipated from the grandfather's control – a situation so old-fashioned that most modern men would regard it as untenable. The scope for causing friction in the family was huge.

'Gaia Laelia belongs to a family who have a long history of the highest religious service. Her grandfather is Publius Laelius Numentinus, the recently retired Flamen Dialis –'

Yes, that was the fool who had been complaining about my goslings. Interesting that he had in fact retired from office; everyone on the Capitol had still seemed to regard him with active terror.

'I thought a priesthood was for life? Some dereliction of his duties?' Helena chuckled, ignoring the speaker's pomposity. Priests who disgraced their office might be asked to resign, but it was rare. For one thing, the priests of the official cult had the power to cover up their crimes and the wherewithal to control critics. They could be absolute bastards yet the truth would never get out. Let's be honest: they could be bastards and everybody knew it, but still no controls would be applied.

The Flamen Pomonalis was stiff: 'The Flaminica, his wife, had died. Since the Flaminica partakes officially in many ceremonies, it is necessary for a widowed Flamen Dialis to step down. Otherwise, essential rites would be incomplete.'

Helena's own voice grew cold. 'Hard, I always thought, for a man to lose both his wife and his position at a stroke. Especially when the position is so significant, and its rituals are so demanding. Gaia's grandfather must now find his life rather empty. Is this part of the problem?'

'There is no problem.'

'Well, I am relieved to hear it.' She had the knack of seeming to engage in mere polite conversation, whilst she doggedly pursued a point. She wanted to know what had been happening in this family to make a young child take the unusual step of seeking outside help. A thwarted six-year-old would normally slam doors, scream herself into convulsions, and throw her wooden doll through a window, but then be pacified in a few seconds with just a bowl of honeyed nuts. 'Even so, your young niece came here with a tale of woe, and now you too are here to discuss it . . . What puzzled us was how Gaia chose Falco to confide in? How would she have known who he was?'

'She may have heard his name mentioned in connection with his appointment as Procurator of the Sacred Birds.' It gave me a thrill to imagine some crusty old ex-priest of Jupiter exploding with rage over his breakfast while he heard that the Emperor had given ancient responsibilities to an upstart informer – who would now be allowed to poke around with impunity amongst the temple enclosures. Was that why Vespasian had done it? 'And I believe,' conceded the Flamen Pomonalis, 'Gaia Laelia met a relative of yours at the reception when certain promising young ladies were introduced to Queen Berenice.'

His significant tone seemed rather overdone. The only link I had with Berenice was my sister Maia's uncharacteristic foray to the Palace, the day I had first tried to find her. Had the function Maia attended been stuffed with female relatives of priests? I controlled a snigger, wondering what my sister had made of that.

Helena must have decided to pursue the mystery with

Maia later. 'Well I suggest,' she said so crisply that it seemed like a rebuke, 'you tell me exactly what your family's concerns are.'

'Our concerns should be obvious!' the flamen snapped. Bluffing. Hoping little Gaia had never said whatever it was her precious family was hoping to keep quiet. Or, if Gaia *had* revealed too many secrets, trying to play down their importance.

'Don't worry. Falco and I know how to regard the complaints of an unhappy child. So embarrassing, is it not?'

'Children exaggerate,' he declared, relieved that she seemed to understand.

'I hope that's the case!' agreed Helena, with feeling. Then she faced him with it: 'Gaia says someone in her family threatened to kill her.'

'Ridiculous!'

'Not you, then?'

'How dare you!'

'So who was it?'

'Nobody!'

'I do want to believe that is true.'

'Whatever you were told . . .' He paused, hoping Helena would tell him more details. No chance.

'You are requesting us not to interfere.' Helena's tone was quiet. I knew what that meant: for her, this visit from the flamen made it look as if the child's appeal for help might be justified.

'I am glad we understand each other.'

'Oh yes,' she said. *Oh yes!* She understood him all right.

'No one could possibly wish her harm. There are high hopes of Gaia Laelia,' concluded the Flamen Pomonalis. 'When the ballot for the new Vestal Virgin is drawn . . .' He tailed off.

So a new Vestal was needed, and the little girl I met on my front doorstep had been put forward for the privilege. Could her uncle be suggesting to Helena that Gaia's name was certain to be drawn by the Pontifex Maximus in the formal lottery? Impossible! Vespasian's hand would have to dig around in an urn among a whole bunch of tablets. How could anyone know in advance which one would be gripped by the pontifical paw? I felt my face screw up in disgust, as I saw that the Vestal Virgins' lottery must be fixed.

How could they do it? Easy as wink. Only one name written on all of the tablets. Or one tablet loaded, like a bad dice. Or quite simply, Vespasian would just announce the pre-selected name, without looking at the tablets at all.

Pointy-head was still enthusing. 'It would be a new departure in the family – but a great honour. We are all absolutely delighted.'

'Does that include Gaia herself?' asked Helena coolly.

'Gaia is passionate about being entered.'

'Little girls do have such quaint ideas.' The Vestals were not Helena's favourite women, apparently. I was surprised. I thought she would have approved of their honoured role and status. 'Well, let us hope she is successful,' Helena went on. 'Then she will be taken straight to the House of the Vestals and handed into the control of the Pontifex Maximus.'

'Er – quite,' agreed the flamen, belatedly sensing an undercurrent. Presuming, however, that his appeals had been successful, he seemed to be about to leave. Taking a firm hold on Julia, I slid down the corridor and towards another room where I could conceal myself. I glimpsed Pomona's priest, in his cloak and birchwood prong, with his back to me as he bade Helena farewell; he hid me from her view as I crept past.

I waited until I was sure he had left, before I emerged.

As I opened the door behind which I had been hiding, a small determined figure blocked my way. Julia was whipped from my grasp. I groaned, but only quietly.

I was facing a tiny, frail old woman whose black eyes bored like bradawls. A bad conscience – for which I had no damned reason – pinned me to the spot.

'I suppose you have a good explanation,' announced the new arrival fiercely, 'why you failed to come home for the little one's birthday?' I did have. Famia's funeral rites, such as they were for the few scraps that had been left of him by the lion: an explanation, though not good. 'And I do know what happened to Famia – though I had to hear it from dear Anacrites!'

'Hello, Mother,' I said. I made it sound meek. 'We were forced to spend Julia's first birthday becalmed off Ostia . . . Are you going to congratulate me on my new status as a pillar of the state religion?'

'Don't give me any of your silly nonsense,' scoffed Ma.

As usual, I had done what I thought she wanted, only to find her unimpressed.

VI

This had turned into a tiring day. First, I had had to dance around Petronius Longus while he showed his pique; now here was Ma. She had various complaints: primarily why I had let her favourite, Anacrites, come home from Tripolitania half dead from the wounds he acquired in the arena. Playing gladiators had been his own idea, but I would get the blame for it. Luckily, it meant he was back as a lodger at Ma's house for further nursing, so she was not entirely upset.

'Why are you letting the poor thing go back to his job at the Palace?'

'Anacrites is grown up, Ma. His career decisions are nothing to do with me.'

'You two worked so well together.'

'We made a good pairing for the Census. That's over now.'

'You could find other work to share.'

'Neither of us wanted to remain in partnership. I showed him up.'

'You didn't like him, you mean.' Ma kept insisting that I did not really know Anacrites; that I had missed his fine sensitivity; that I belittled his talent. My own theory was that anyone who had tried to persuade an exotic foreign potentate to murder me should be allowed to run his own life – after being sealed in a barrel and dumped a thousand feet under the sea. Somewhere rough off Britain, preferably. 'You never gave him a chance. Listen, Anacrites has his sights set on running a new branch of the security services. You could help him with that, Marcus –'

'Alternatively, I could rot in the Pontine Marshes, eaten by leeches and infected with fever. That would be a whole lot more fun.'

'And what about Petronius?' demanded Ma, changing tack to catch me out.

'Petronius belongs in the vigiles.'

'He belongs with his wife!'

'The wife who has decided that she now belongs with a potted-salad seller.'

'I blame you,' said Ma.

'Not guilty. I wouldn't shove even Silvia into a life of pressed tripe and lettuce leaves. Petronius looks respectable, but he's a wandering dog who never saw where his best interests lay until it was too late. Of course the mere fact that I told him all along that he was stupid need not prevent people placing the blame on me!'

'I don't dare ask what you did to poor Famia,' Ma muttered darkly.

'He did it to himself. I brought home the remains, I'll be a good uncle to the children, and I'll try to look after Maia.'

'She won't thank you.'

'No, Ma.'

My mother's eyes narrowed and we shared one of our rare moments of sense: 'So how is she, son?'

'Too quiet. When I told her the news, she showed almost no emotion.'

'That won't last.'

'I'm keeping an eye out for when she breaks down.'

'Just don't you go upsetting her!'

Helena Justina, who had observed this conversation in silence from her wicker chair, holding the dog on her lap while allowing Julia Junilla to sit on her feet, smiled at me tenderly.

She was no help. What was more, I faced dinner with her parents that evening, where I would have to stand up to further inquisition about *their* family problems.

'You ought to be round at your sister's instead of loafing here,' ordered my mother. I intended it; I wanted to ask Maia about the reception for Queen Berenice and how would-be little Vestal Virgins fitted into it. 'Oh don't bother – I'll go!'

Ma had forestalled me. The Virgins would have to wait.

Petronius Longus would say virgins never do that. Still, the kind of virgins Petro joked about were never just six years old.

After Ma had gone, I waited for Helena to tell me about the Flamen Pomonalis visiting. I had to pretend that I came home right at the end of it, not that I overheard the whole interview. Helena could play up to me as a hidden accomplice if a conspiracy had been agreed beforehand, but she hated to be spied on secretly. For one thing, she resented being supervised.

She gave me a succinct report, obviously now deeply troubled.

'What exactly was Gaia's story yesterday when you saw her alone before I came home, Helena?'

'She said, "One of my relations threatened to kill me." And that it had frightened her,' Helena told me, looking thoughtful. 'She had got it into her head that she needed to see an informer, so I left it for you to deal with.'

'I'm starting to regret sending her away without asking more questions. I know you thought I should have gone into it more thoroughly.'

'You had your own troubles, Marcus.'

'This little girl may have worse.'

'She has grown up in a most peculiar home, that's for certain,' said Helena with some force. 'Her grandparents will have been married by a strange old formal ceremony, and as the Flamen Dialis and the Flaminica even their house itself had ritual significance. No child in such a home knows a normal upbringing. The daily life of the priest and priestess is proscribed by ridiculous taboos and rituals at every turn. It leaves little time for family matters. Even the children formally take part in religious ceremonies – presumably, Gaia's father went through all that. And now Gaia, the poor mite, is being pushed into becoming a Vestal Virgin –'

'An escape, by the sound of it!' I grinned.

'She is six,' growled Helena. She was right. That was no age to be removed from home and subjected to thirty years of sanctity.

37

'Do I take it, Helena, you intend to investigate?'

'I want to.' She felt wretched, which always unsettled me. 'I just don't see how to go about it yet.'

She was broody all day, not ready yet to share her further thoughts. I applied myself to clearing up goose droppings. Helena had made it clear that this was a daily rite which ancient traditions decreed could only be carried out by the Procurator of Poultry.

Dinner that evening came as a relief. The one thing to say for the noble Camilli was that despite their financial problems, they dined well. In that, they far excelled most Roman millionaires.

Their money was tied up in land (in order to protect their right to remain on the senatorial list) but a delicately poised tier of mortgages allowed them to live in a tolerable style. For instance, when they had invited us to dinner, they sent their carrying chair for Helena and the baby. We stuffed it full of presents and Julia's toys. I carried the baby. Helena was bringing letters from her brother, a bright sprig called Quintus Camillus Justinus whom I knew fairly well.

Helena had two brothers, both younger than her and both heavily bossed by her when they strayed too close. The elder, Aelianus, had been betrothed to an heiress from Baetica in southern Spain. The younger, Justinus, ran off with her. I had gone to Tripolitania, funded by the senator, with a brief to find the eloping pair. I knew it was thought to be my fault that Claudia Rufina had decided to swap brothers. Untrue, of course: she fell for the one with better looks and a more attractive character. But I had been involved in first bringing her to Rome as a prospective bride for Aelianus and the senator's wife had long held the opinion that anything touched by M. Didius Falco was bound to go wrong. In that, Julia Justa was following the views of my own family, so I made no attempt to disprove her theory. May as well live with the grief you know.

Helena and I had found that under the stress of desert conditions the young lovers had fallen out, but we ignored their finer feelings and cobbled them back together. We persuaded Justinus to cut his losses and marry Claudia (and her money), first sending the couple on a visit to Spain in order to reconcile her wealthy grandparents.

Justinus had been searching for silphium, the extinct luxury condiment. He had hoped to rediscover it and make millions. Once that mad plan had failed, the only way I could prevent him running off to be a hermit was to lure him into replacing Anacrites as my partner. He had no qualifications, and since he had now gone off to Spain indefinitely, at my third attempt to find a partner I had stuck myself with one who knew absolutely nothing – and who was not even available.

Helena had decided we could all share a house (which might explain why she had told the Flamen Pomonalis that we lived on the Janiculan). Knowing her, she had probably bought a place already. Watching her work around to telling me would give me hours of secret fun.

You might think that securing a Baetican olive oil fortune and a pleasant wife for their talented boy would earn me laurel wreaths from Justinus' parents. Unfortunately, it still left them with the problem of their disgruntled elder son. Aelianus had lost the money, lost his bride, and had to stand down from the senate elections for a year, all because his brother had made him look a fool. Whatever his parents felt about the resolution to his brother's life, Aelianus was the one they now had sulking at home. A young man in his twenties, with no occupation and very few manners, can dominate a household even if he spends most of his time out on the town.

'It seems best to let him alarm the neighbours with his rowdy friends,' murmured the senator on our arrival. 'So far he has not actually been arrested or brought home on a trestle covered in blood.'

'Is Aulus joining us for dinner?' asked Helena, using Aelianus' family name yet trying to disguise the fact that she hoped not. The dutiful elder sister, she always wanted to be fair but of the two boys, Justinus was much more like her in temperament and attitude.

'Probably not,' Camillus Verus, her father, replied. He

was a tall, shrewd, humorous man with sprouting grey-tinged hair that his barber had still not successfully tamed. I noticed a hunted air when he spoke of his sons.

'At a party?' I asked.

'This may sound hard to believe, but I have been trying to get him into one of the priesthoods – give him some honours to his name. If he is where he is supposed to be, it's the Sacred Grove of the Arval Brothers. This is the main day of their annual ceremonial.'

I whistled approvingly. It seemed the polite thing to do. The chosen clique presided over festivals and religious holidays, with an additional remit to pray for the good fortune of the imperial family. The Arval Brothers' activities derived from the dawn of history, when they had prayed for the health and fruitfulness of crops – in token of which, they all wore chaplets of corn tied on with white ribbons. The thought of the rather gruff Aelianus bedecked with a corn-ear crown made a hilarious climax to a good dinner. But frankly, if a son of mine wanted to join the corn-dolly brethren, I would lock him in the broom cupboard until the fantasy sweated out of him.

'So – tell us your news, Marcus.'

I announced my elevation and brushed aside con-gratulations like a good modest Roman. 'I warn you, sir, my conversation is limited nowadays to ways of worming poultry. My life is now fixed by the ritual events of the goddess Juno's calendar.'

'What – no more informing?' I caught his eye briefly. Decimus, as I was sometimes emboldened to call him, was a close friend of Vespasian and I never knew quite how much he knew about my official work.

'Stuck with the birds.'

He grinned frankly. 'You deserve the status but can't you ditch the aviary?'

'I am supposed to feel honoured.'

'Bugger that!'

Helena's mother gave him a sad look, and decided to lead me to my dining couch before her rude husband infected her newly respectable son-in-law with disreputable views. Until now, I had been the dangerous republican and Decimus the conventional Curia hack. I felt slightly unnerved.

As we reclined, Julia Justa placed olive bowls and saffron prawns before me with her long beringed hands. Helena leaned over and stole the prawns. 'Tell me, Marcus,' said her mother, resplendent in white and gold that glittered almost as much as her new, worrying friendliness. 'I have always wondered – how exactly do they persuade the Sacred Geese to stay on their purple cushion when they are being transported in a procession?'

'I'll find out for you. I suspect they make them hungry first, then a man walks alongside with a fistful of grain to bribe them to sit still.'

'Like taking a child to a party,' said Helena. Her mother looked approvingly at ours, who was sitting quietly in the arms of a slave, chewing her pottery rattle; she had even tactfully chosen to gnaw a toy her grandparents had bought for her.

Planning her moment. Little Julia knew how to disrupt mealtimes. She had learned new skills since the estimable Camilli last had a chance to dote on her.

'Isn't she good!'

Helena and I smiled the shameless public smiles of experienced parents. We had had a year to learn never to confess that our cute-looking dimpled baby could be a screaming troublemaker. We had dressed her nicely in white, combed her soft dark hair into a sweet curl, and now we were waiting with our nerves on edge for the inevitable moment when she decided to roar and rampage.

It was, as always, a good dinner, one which would have been more enjoyable had I felt able to relax. I liked Helena's father and no longer disliked her mother. They seemed to have accepted that they were stuck with me. Perhaps they had also noticed that I had not yet lived up to expectations and made their daughter unhappy, nor had I been thrown in jail (well, not lately), barred from any public buildings, lampooned in any scurrilous satires or featured in the rogues' gallery in the *Daily Gazette*. Even so, at these gatherings there was always a risk somebody would say something offensive. Sometimes I thought Decimus secretly hoped for the thrill of it. He had a wicked streak. I knew it well; he had passed it on intact to Helena.

'Papa and Mama, you can help us with something,' said Helena over the dessert course. 'Do either of you know anything about Laelius Numentinus, the Flamen Dialis, and his family?'

'What's your problem with a Flamen?' her father demanded.

'Well, I have had an early run-in with the silly old bastard,' I hedged, 'though it was not face to face.'

'Naturally. You'd be at arm's length, held off with his precious wand.'

'No, he has been retired; his wife died and he had to stand down. Not that it stops him complaining, apparently. The first thing that greeted me in my new post was a crisis caused by his displeasure at unwanted goslings scampering about the Capitol. I managed to avoid meeting him, or I would have been very brusque.'

'After a lifetime of being protected from close contact with the real world, he can't be good with people – or birds.' Decimus had a definite scorn for the flaminical caste. I had always liked him. He had no time for hypocrisy. And although he was a senator, I reckoned he was politically straight. No one could buy him. That was why he had no money, of course.

He knew few of the right people either; he admitted that Laelius Numentinus was simply a figure glimpsed at public ceremonies.

'What happened to the goslings, Marcus?' asked his wife with amusement.

'I found them a good home,' I answered soberly, not mentioning that the home was ours. Helena eyed me trickily.

'And are you expecting more trouble from the man – or is there some other reason for enquiring?'

'There's a child in his family whom they expect to be chosen as the next Vestal. I gather the Laelii can mystically influence the lottery.' I aimed the last comment at Decimus.

He raised an eyebrow, this time pretending to be shocked

42

at the imputation of fixing. 'Well,' he scoffed. 'We wouldn't want any little unscrubbed plebeian to emerge as the winner, when there are maidens with mile-long patrician pedigrees yearning to carry the water from the shrine of Egeria.'

'Famous for their antique chastity?'

'Absolutely notorious for their purity and simplicity!' concluded Helena dryly.

'No, no. It cannot be,' Julia Justa corrected me. 'Being a daughter of a flamen counts as an exemption from the lottery.'

'She is the Flamen's granddaughter, actually.'

'Then the father must have opted out of the priesthood.' Julia Justa laughed briefly. For a moment, she sounded like Helena. 'I bet that went down well!' In explanation she went on, 'That family are known for regarding the priesthood as their personal prerogative. The late Flaminica was notorious for her snobbery about it. My mother was a keen attendant at the rites of the Good Goddess – remember she took you once, Helena.'

'Yes. I've told Marcus it was just a sewing circle with dainty almond cakes.'

'Oh of course!'

They were teasing Decimus and me. The festival of the Bona Dea was a famously secretive gathering of matrons, nocturnal and forbidden to men. All sorts of suspicions circulated about what went on there. Women took over the house of the senior magistrate – turfing him out – and then enjoyed letting their menfolk sweat over what kind of orgy they had organised.

'I seem to remember,' I challenged Helena, 'you always made out that you disliked the Bona Dea festival – why was that, beloved? Too staid for you?' I smiled, playing the tolerant type and turning back to Julia Justa. 'So the Flaminica would have been a regular at the festival in her official capacity?'

'And her overbearing sister too,' answered Julia Justa, with an unaccustomed smirk. 'The sister, Terentia Paulla, was a Vestal Virgin.'

'A Vestal presides, if rumour is correct?'

'Well, she tries!' Julia Justa laughed. 'A group of women does not necessarily succumb to leadership as a group of men would – especially once the refreshments arrive.' Out of control, eh? That confirmed the worst fears of our masculine citizenship. Not to mention suggestions that wine played a major part in the girls' giggling rites. 'My mother, who was a shrewd woman –'

'Bound to be!' I grinned, including both Helena and Julia Justa in the compliment.

'Yes, Marcus dear.' *Marcus dear?* I gulped back my disquiet. 'Mama held that the Flaminica was very loose living.'

'Oho! On what evidence?'

'She had a lover. Everyone knew. It was more or less open. She and her ghastly sister were always arguing about it. The affair went on for years.'

'I am shocked.'

'You are not,' said Helena, flipping me with her dinner napkin. 'You are a hard-bitten and cynical private informer; you expect adultery at every turn. Mind you, *I* am shocked, Mama.'

'Of course you are, darling; I brought you up in a very sheltered way . . . Well, being Flaminica is a difficult role,' Julia Justa returned. Like Helena, she could be fair. She was a sophisticated woman: nowadays she even managed to be fair to me. 'The Flamen Dialis and his wife are selected from a very narrow circle – they have to fulfil strict traditional criteria. She has to be a virgin –'

'That's surely no trouble!' inserted Decimus satirically.

'They both have to be born of parents who have been married by *confarreatio*, the old-fashioned religious ceremony in front of ten witnesses, with the Pontifex Maximus and the Flamen Dialis present. Then, Marcus, they have to be married themselves with those ceremonies and can never divorce. The chances of them finding each other tolerable are remote to begin with, and if things go wrong they are trapped for life.'

'Plus the pressure of constantly appearing in public together to carry out their official functions –' I suggested.

'Oh anyone can go through the motions in public!' Julia Justa disagreed. 'It would be back at home that the tension would show.'

We all nodded sagely, while pretending to consider the concept of domestic disagreement as something remote from our own experience. As one does.

'So, what is the problem with the little girl?' asked the senator.

'Nothing at all, according to the family,' I said. 'The child herself told Helena she has been threatened with serious harm. She came to see us with this tale, and I confess, I failed to take it seriously. I should have asked more questions.'

'If she really is earmarked as the next Vestal,' Julia Justa commented, 'hers are the kind of people who would glory in it. What could cause conflict? Is she playing up about being selected?'

'Overjoyed, apparently.'

'I rather suspect,' said Helena, 'my grandmother would say, Gaia must be glad of a chance to be taken away from her relatives.'

'They do sound a grim lot.'

'Fossils!' muttered Decimus.

We had insulted the Laelii for long enough. Since dinner was over Helena buzzed off with her mother to talk about what had happened in North Africa with Justinus and Claudia. Her father and I occupied the senator's study, a squashed glory-hole full of scrolls that Decimus had started to read then forgotten about. We lit lamps and threw cushions off the reading couch, trying to pretend there was room to recline in some elegance. In fact, although the Camillus house was spacious, its master had been allocated a poky nook, as he ruefully liked to acknowledge.

It was, however, roomy enough for a pair of friendly fellows to let themselves relax when left unsupervised.

VII

To make it a manly symposium we had brought a fine glass
bottle of decanted Alban wine. Helena's mother had
instructed us to look after the baby; apparently, the grim-
faced slaves in her retinue had too much work of their own.
We had boasted that childcare fell well within our expertise.
The senator placed Julia on a rug and let her grab whatever
came to hand. Allowed to play amongst the grown-ups, she
was no trouble; she settled to playing spillikins with equipment from his stylus tray. I was a realistic father; I intended
to equip her for life. Even a year and four days could not be
too young for a girl to familiarise herself with men's
behaviour when they are let loose with a good flagon.

'So! Tell me about Aelianus singing the ancient hymn of
the Arval Brothers?'

His father sighed. 'Time to garner a few embellishments
on his social record.'

'I seem to be hearing about nothing but religious cults this
week. As far as I remember, the Brethren are the oldest in
Rome – a lineage all the way from our agricultural fore-
fathers? And don't they celebrate fertility by way of
energetic feasting? Sounds like your son made a good
choice.'

Decimus grinned, though rather distractedly. He must
prefer to think of this as a sober move.

'And what about selection, sir? Is it another lottery?'

'No. Co-option from within the serving Brothers.'

'Ah! So Aelianus has to infiltrate the corn-wreaths and
impress them with his convivial nature, specifically his skill
at worshipping good horticultural practice while guzzling
for the love of Rome?'

I could see some problems here.

Aulus Camillus Aelianus was two years younger than Helena, so about twenty-four, maybe twenty-five already if he was heading for the Senate. They must have been born pretty close. It suggested an unnerving period of passion in their parents' marriage, which I preferred not to contemplate. Aelianus had survived modest career postings in the army and in the civilian governor's office in Baetica, and was all set to stand for election. The process was expensive, which always causes family friction.

It also required Aelianus to approach those who might vote him in with conciliatory smiles, which was where I saw the difficulty; it was not his natural talent. He was of a slightly grumpy disposition, a little too self-centred and lacking the fake warmth to ingratiate him with the smelly old senators he needed to flatter. His father would shove him on to the Curia benches eventually, but at present it might be for the best that his brother's elopement with Claudia Rufina had delayed everything. Aelianus needed polish. Failing that, it might do him no harm at least to gain a reputation as a lad about town. Playboys gather clusters of votes without any need for bribes.

Everything is relative. As an apprentice in a copper shop on the Aventine, this young grouser would have seemed smooth and elegant. Perhaps not enough to fool the girls. But sufficient to become a leader of men.

'Mind you,' I said, as his father and I reflectively savoured our wine, 'people nowadays reckon the voting in most elections takes the line approved by the Emperor.'

'That was what we rather relied on!' admitted Decimus, for once alluding to his friendship with Vespasian.

'So what's Aelianus up to with these characters today?'

Decimus explained in his typically dry way: 'The Arval Brothers – we have learned this as we applied ourselves in a grovelling manner to winning them over – are busy in May. They hold their annual election for their leader and celebrate the rites of their special deity over a period of four days – on the second of which nothing significant happens, in fact. My theory is that after the first bout of unrestrained feasting they have to take a break; subdued

47

by a day with a bad hangover, they proceed more carefully.'

'These are grown-up boys! Who is the deity?'

'Dea Dia, the lady otherwise known as Ops.'

'In charge of crops since time began?'

'Since Romulus ploughed the city boundary.'

I glanced down at Julia, but she was contentedly examining one of her own tiny sandals. She had gripped her little fat ankle and pulled up her toes, with an interested expression that meant she was thinking about eating her own foot. I decided to let her learn from empirical research.

Decimus continued his tale: 'The first day of the rites takes place in Rome at the house of the Master of the Arvals – the chief Brother for that year. They offer fruits, wine and incense at sunrise to the Dea Dia, anoint her statue, then hold a formal feast at which further offerings are made and the Brothers receive gifts in return for attending.'

Travel and subsistence, eh? A nice clique to join.

'The most important rites – today's – see the election of the next Master in the Sacred Grove of the Dea Dia. I am hoping this will be the cue for them to hint at whether Aulus has been successful. I expect that the newly elected Master has some say in who will be taken on under his leadership.'

'I wish you well. It would be a great coup. Being an Arval Brother is one of the honours given to the highest in society.'

I did not exaggerate. Young males in the imperial family, for instance, would expect automatic co-option to the Arvals as supernumeraries. Probably our current princes, Titus and Domitian, had joined already. Normal membership totalled twelve only. Vacancies must be keenly sought after. I reckoned the Camilli were probably over-stretching when they put up Aelianus for this, but it was not the moment to criticise.

Mildly affected by the wine, even the senator seemed ready to admit the real situation. 'We don't stand much chance, Marcus. Bloody snobs!'

'Have they actually voted?' I asked carefully.

'No. That takes place in the Temple of Concord in the Forum and seems to be kept separate.'

We perused our cups and thought about the inequalities of life.

It was at this point that, against expectations, the young man under discussion appeared in the study doorway. His white festival outfit was badly crumpled, and he looked flushed. He was probably tipsy, but his face never gave away much.

Aelianus was more sturdily built and less fine featured than his sister and younger brother. A good chunk of Roman manhood, in his way: athletic and possessing good reflexes. He left his sister to be the reader in the family, while his brother was the linguist. Straight sprouting hair, cut rather longer than suited him; dark eyes; a sallow complexion at present: too many nights out with the boys. I would have envied him his lifestyle, but even though he was given too much freedom, he was plainly not happy.

'Yes, I'm here! Still, cheer up, Aulus.' He hated his sister living with an informer. Now Helena and I had made it permanent, I enjoyed teasing him.

Aelianus just stood there, neither coming in to join us nor storming off in annoyance. His father demanded to know any news about his co-option.

'I didn't get in.' He could hardly bear to say it.

Decimus asked who was elected. His son forced out a name I did not know; Decimus exclaimed in disgust.

'Oh he's a good fellow,' Aelianus managed to mutter, surprisingly mildly.

I murmured sympathy. 'Helena will be very sorry to hear this.' She would realise that it was one more slap down for a brother who might be spoiled for good unless he soon bagged some public achievements.

More than his failure with the Arvals was bothering him. Both his father and I belatedly stared harder at Aelianus. He looked as if he was going to throw up. 'Buried your face in too many goblets?' He shook his head. I grabbed a tasteful ceramic from a shelf with a vase collection and proffered it anyway. Just in time.

It was an Athenian cup, featuring a boy with his tutor, a nice didactic subject for one who seemed to have overindulged himself. The vessel had decent proportions for a sick-bowl, and two handles to grip. Wonderful antique art.

After he stopped retching, Aelianus made an effort to apologise.

'Don't worry; we've all done it.'

'I'm not drunk.'

His father hauled him to a couch. 'And we have all produced that finely honed poetic line as well!'

Aelianus stayed lost in a heavy silence. While Decimus fielded the Athenianware and shunted it elsewhere for some poor slave to find tomorrow, his son sat, oddly hunched. Experience told me he had passed the risk of being ill again.

'What's up, Aulus?'

His voice was strained. 'Something you know all about, Marcus Didius.' Decimus moved abruptly. I lifted an eyebrow, signalling that we should let the lad take his time. 'I found something.' Aelianus now looked up and wanted to talk. 'I stumbled over something horrible.'

He closed his eyes. His face told me the worst. In the grim business of informing, I had seen more than enough people wearing this expression. 'There has been an accident?' I was being optimistic.

Aelianus braced himself. 'Not exactly. I fell over a corpse. But whoever it is, it's very clear he did not die by accident.'

VIII

All right; take your time, son.' The senator had found a jug of water and a beaker. Aelianus rinsed his teeth and spat into the beaker. Patiently I emptied it into the Athenianware he had already used, rinsed the beaker, then poured fresh water, which I made him drink.

'So,' I asked firmly. 'Your father told me you went to partake in the main day of worship amidst the corn wreaths and dinner napkins? Stuffing your face in the cause of new growth at the Arval Brothers' Sacred Grove – was that where this happened?'

Aelianus sat up straighter and nodded. I chivvied him, brisk as a legionary commander taking details from a scout: 'The Grove is where?'

'Five miles outside the city on the Via Portuensis.' He had served in the army and civil government. He could give a reliable report when he chose.

'Are we talking about some verdant circle of venerable trees?'

'No. It is more like a forum complex. It has a circus, several temples, and a Caesarium for the deified emperors.'

'How modern! Silly me, I had expected some rustic haven.'

'The Emperor Augustus brought the rites up to date. The cult had fallen into abeyance rather –'

'Of course! He interfered in everything. So just set the scene for me.'

'There has been a day of worship, followed by games and races.'

'Members of the public?'

'Yes.'

'All men?'

'No.'

'Is the revelry over?'

'People are hanging on. Most of the Brothers have returned to Rome for another feast at the house of the current Master.' He paused. 'Well, except for one of them.' I noted that remark, but let him carry on. 'I came home early. People who had been at the Games were still enjoying themselves in the Grove.'

'What made you leave early?'

Aelianus sighed. 'One of the Brothers had taken me aside and warned me that they felt I was "not quite ready for the burdens of election to such a demanding cult". He obviously meant I was not important enough.' Aelianus dropped his gaze; his father compressed his mouth. 'I felt low. I tried to continue with a brave face but I kept hearing the snide bastard saying what a good impression I had made, and how sincerely the Brothers hoped I would find some other way to apply my supposed talents . . . I could not bear the way people looked at me. I know I should have braved it out . . .'

He paused for a moment, leaning on his elbow with one palm covering his mouth. The splayed fingers had bitten nails. I put a hand on his shoulder. Where my thumb touched skin under the edge of his tunic it felt cold. He was in shock.

Aelianus continued in a quiet voice, 'My horse was just outside the Grove, where they had set up a picket line. To get back there I had to walk past a pavilion for the Master, a big temporary tent. I heard a group of people coming out, so I dodged quickly around the back to avoid them. I stumbled over one of the guy ropes, then I literally fell on to the body.'

He stopped again briefly. 'I assumed the man was drunk. I don't know what made me anxious. But I felt my heart race even before I looked properly. The people I had heard all went off in another direction. Silence fell. Nobody was about. I could hardly take in what I saw. It was horrible. He was lying in his own blood. His clothing was drenched in it. His head had been covered with some kind of cloth, which was sopping too. His wounds looked terrible – one great gash across the neck especially. He had been cut down with a sacrificial knife. It was still lying alongside him.'

'He was definitely dead?' asked Decimus.

'No doubt.'

'Did you know him?' I murmured.

'No. But a corn chaplet with the white ribbons was lying by him, dragged off in the struggle presumably – he was one of the Arval Brothers.'

'Well, that creates another vacancy!' I sucked in air through my teeth. 'I take it you then reported your find?'

A narrow look crossed the young man's face.

'Oh Aulus!' groaned the senator.

'Papa, I was badly shaken. There was nothing I could do for him. It was a ghastly scene. There was no sign of the killer or I would genuinely have made an effort to apprehend him. One worry I had was that if anyone turned up and found me alone with the body I might be suspected of killing him myself.'

At once I asked, 'Could the corpse have been the man who told you that you were unacceptable to the Arvals?'

Aelianus met my gaze, wide-eyed. He considered this. 'No. No, Falco. Wrong build, I'm sure of it.'

'Good! So what did you do?'

'Got out of there fast. Ran for my horse. Rode back here as quickly as I could.'

'And came to ask our advice,' I suggested, guessing he had hoped to forget the whole incident.

He pulled a face. 'All right. I'm a fool.'

'Not entirely. You have reported your grim find to your father, a senator, and to me . . . That's acceptable.' Acceptable – but not enough. I tightened my belt and pushed my tunic down under it. 'We have two choices. We can pretend we know nothing about it – or behave like reputable citizens.'

Aelianus knew what I meant. He stood up. He wavered a little, but was probably fit for the job: 'I have to go back there.'

I grinned at him. 'Don't imagine you get all the fun. You will have to take me too. Catch me sitting here with a flagon when I can jump on a horse and give myself indigestion pounding five miles into the countryside – all to learn that somebody else has by now found your piece of butchery and nobody thanks us for reporting it a second time.' I turned to his father. 'I can handle this. But you will have the awkward job: explaining to Helena and your wife why we have bunked off –'

'I think I can distract them,' Decimus said, springing up with a start. He bent down and led out my baby daughter from behind his couch, holding her by her chubby little arms as she proudly demonstrated how she could now be walked along.

What a sight. I had known she could stand. It was a new trick. I had completely forgotten that it put her within reach of new attractions and dangers. I winced. Julia had somehow laid hands on the senator's inkstand – a two-tone job apparently; her face, arms, legs and her smart little white tunic were now covered with great stains in black and red. There was ink around her mouth. She even had ink in her hair.

She grabbed at her noble grandfather so he had to pick her up, immediately covering himself in red and black as well. Then, sensing trouble, her eyes filled with tears, she began to wail, at first just mournfully but with a steadily increasing volume that would soon bring all the women of the household rushing to see what tragedy had befallen her.

Aelianus and I got out of it and left the senator to cope.

IX

It was still light. Helena and I had dined early with her parents so we could return home with the baby before the streets became too dangerous. By the time her brother and I rode off, however, dusk was starting to fall. Time was not on our side.

The Via Portuensis travels out towards the new harbour at Ostia on the north bank of the Tiber. We had to cut into the city first, in order to cross the river on the Probus Bridge. Anacrites and I had started our Census inspections out this way and had usually been ferried over from beside the Emporium, but with horses that was impossible. I hate riding, though I noticed Aelianus had a good seat and seemed at ease. We could have borrowed the senator's carriage, but in view of the hour we required speed. I had declined an escort too. It would only attract attention. We were armed with swords under our cloaks, and would have to rely on our own good sense.

As we passed Caesar's Gardens, there were already suspicious characters abroad. Soon we were trotting by the menagerie where, six months ago, my social rise began as I investigated Census cheats among the arena suppliers. The establishment was locked and silent, no longer echoing to the bustle of gladiators after their evening meal or the unexpected roars of lions. Further out in the country we passed one or two travellers who had misjudged their timing, making a late arrival from the coast. When they ambled into town they would fetch up in the Transtiberina, a quarter that seasoned locals avoided, and for strangers bound to end in robbery or worse. Later still, we met occasional corn-bedecked members of the public who had been to the Games in the Sacred Grove. Aelianus reckoned most people had

55

either left much earlier or would stay until dawn. That seemed wise.

As best he could while riding he had told me of the day's events: early morning sacrifices by the Master; the Brethren's ritual search outside the goddess' temple for ears of corn; sharing laureate bread (whatever that was) and turnips (at least the Arvals were not snobs when they chose their vegetable side dishes); anointing the image of the Dea Dia. Then the temple was cleared and its doors closed while the Brothers tucked up their tunics and performed a traditional dance to the strains of their ancient hymn (which was so obscure they all had to be handed sets of instructions). Next came the election of a new Master for the following year, a distribution of prizes and roses, and an afternoon of Games over which the Arval Master presided in ceremonial garb. With good appetites by then, the Brethren returned to Rome to change into dinner robes for more feasting.

'At what point did the supercilious corn dolly take you aside and dismiss your talents?'

'During a break in the Games. I met him at the latrines, actually.'

'Nice timing.'

'Oh I am the sophisticated one in our family!'

'Yes; your life is assuming remarkable elegance.' I was smiling over his bitter quip, which had a wry note that was typical of all the Camilli. 'So tell me, Aulus: at that point there had been a lot of noise, and folk milling about the complex?'

'Yes.' Aelianus immediately saw what I meant. 'There were trumpets and applause from the Games too – a scuffle behind the pavilion would have been well muffled.'

We spoke no more until we arrived at the Grove.

There were trees. Over the centuries these had been reduced to a straggly windbreak around the complex. The Arval Brothers were not keen foresters. Even routine lopping of the sacred boughs called for elaborate religious procedures; whenever decay or lightning strikes necessitated felling and replanting, major solemn sacrifices had to be performed. This was inconvenient and had had the result that the trees which stood around the sanctuary were in a gnarled, half-rotted condition. The Brethren might worship fertility but they should have been ashamed of their arboretum.

Its buildings were a different matter. In decor and taste, the temples with their clean styling could have leapt straight from an architect's classical pattern book. The most refined lines and crispest details belonged to the Caesarium, the shrine for the deified emperors; every triglyph and antefix had a superior Augustan smirk. It looked as if the imperial family had plied the edifice with imperial money to ensure they were sufficiently honoured. Very astute.

Aelianus led me straight to the Master's pavilion. It was a lavish marquee erected once a year on festival days, a far cry from the ten-man leather tents used by the legions in what I called camping. This large, fanciful party piece boasted prong-topped poles and tasselled ropes. Its roof was formed from stitched sheets the size of cornship sails; elaborate side walls were attached all round and there was a porch, above which hung wreaths of corn and laurel leaves. New torches had just been set up outside the entrance, though nothing was going on inside.

I crossed the porch extension and glanced into the tent. The air temperature rose sharply. The hot, humid atmosphere took me straight back to the army. There was the familiar suffocating smell of warm, trodden grass. A few oil lamps were lit. A portable throne stood opposite the entrance. Before it, fine cloths covered a low table where only crumbs remained. Cushions were piled against the back wall of the tent, behind the throne. Attracted in by the light, moths and long-legged insects knocked against the roof. Nobody else was there.

I pulled out one of the torches. Dew dampened our bootstraps as we made our way behind the tent. Aelianus was starting to look apprehensive. Whatever he had seen earlier, he wanted never to see again.

As it happened, somebody had obliged him. When we turned around the corner to where he told me the corpse had been lying, it was no longer there.

*

I left him at the pavilion entrance while I tried to find attendants. Eventually I learned that there was nobody with any authority left at the Grove. All the Arval Brothers had returned to Rome. Oddly, nobody seemed to know anything about any man who had been terribly knifed under the guy ropes. There should be a commotion over the sudden death of one of the twelve Brothers. I saw no signs of consternation. The murder must have been hushed up.

I made Aelianus return with me to where the body had been. I had no doubts about his story, though I was beginning to fear that other people might be sceptical. I put one hand on the grass; it was very wet, far wetter than dew alone would cause. By torchlight, no traces of blood were now visible. On the skirts of the pavilion, however, I found a distinct spray of blood splashes. Whoever sluiced the ground had overlooked them.

The knife that had been with the body was gone too. There seemed to be no other evidence. Aelianus pushed his hand under the bottom edge of the tent; its side wall had once been pegged to the ground with wooden stays but they were pulled out. It may have been an oversight; the side walls were probably looped up earlier that day to air the interior.

With some difficulty we dragged up the wall of the tent, finding that the cushions I had seen were piled just here. We shoved some of them aside. Moving the torch closer, I discovered that the grass inside the pavilion, under the cushions, was stained with the rusty red of blood.

'Believe me now?' Aelianus demanded defensively.

'Oh, I always believed you.'

'Whoever cleaned up outside failed to realise there was more work to be done inside the tent.'

'Yes. If it's a cover-up, they will have been in a rush. I am seeing what happened now. Looks like the fight started inside the pavilion. A good place to ambush somebody – it would have given the killer privacy. At the first assault, the victim may have fallen against the tent wall. Since it isn't pegged, it gave way under his weight. He would have half fallen outside, then probably struggled right under the tent, trying to flee.'

I ducked under the flap myself, going in. On the inner surface of the tenting there were more smears of blood, long marks like dragging, which had not soaked through to the outside. They could have been made by a man falling.

'The trouble started inside. The desperate victim somehow made it outside, probably got caught up in the guy ropes in his panic, and was finished off. Ceremonially, with the sacrificial knife –' We both winced. 'The killer then pulled the tent wall down straight, piling the cushions up to cover the blood inside.'

'Why bother?'

'To delay discovery. You heard people, you said?'

'It sounded like attendants, clearing the interior.'

'Maybe the killer had also heard them coming. There was time for a few swift adjustments to make the scene look normal.' I wondered if the killer then walked out, passing the attendants or ducked back under the tent wall again. Either way, an encounter with Aelianus must have been only narrowly avoided. 'The corpse, behind the tent, could safely have been left.'

'Right, Falco. It might not have been discovered until the pavilion was taken down. That's not going to happen until at least tomorrow – or even the day afterwards when the festival formally ends.'

Thinking about this, Aelianus was staring at the area next to the throne where the assault must have begun. He gave a start. He had seen something glint under the cushions. Flinging the tasselled soft furnishings further aside, he retrieved a decorative holder of some sort. It was a flat tube, with one open end, the other closed in a curved shape. As a scabbard, it would be too short for a sword and too big for a dagger. It formed a distinctive, short, broad-bladed shape. We both knew what it was: a priest's fancy holder for a sacrificial knife.

'Well, somebody committed sacrilege,' Aelianus exclaimed dryly. 'It is forbidden to bring any kind of blade into the Sacred Grove!'

X

Dawn over the Arx.

Here, on the least high of the Seven Hills, stood the Temple of Juno Moneta. Juno the Admonisher. Juno of the Mint. Juno the Moneybags.

Before her temple stood M. Didius Falco. Falco the ex-informer. Falco the Procurator. Falco, dutifully working in his new post – and looking for a get-out clause.

Juno's temple on the Arx possessed the now-pampered geese whose ancestors had once saved Rome from marauding Gauls by honking when the guard dogs failed to bark. (It said little for the military commanders of the time that they had failed to post sentries.) Now once a year hapless dogs were rounded up to be ritually crucified whilst the geese looked on from a litter with purple cushions. I had to ensure proper treatment was being meted out to the geese. I had no remit for dogs. And nobody ever had a remit for correcting military incompetence.

Crying birds caught my attention. Two swallows were wheeling, pursued by a predator – broad wings, distinctive tail, short bursts of flapping flight interspersed with hovering and quick fluttering displays: a sparrow hawk.

This was the place of augury. It was the most ancient heart of Rome. Between the two peaks lay the Saddle, which Romulus had decreed a place of refuge for fugitives – establishing from the very first that whatever austere old men in togas liked to think, Rome would succour social rejects and criminals. On the second peak, the Citadel, rose the huge new Temple of Jupiter Best and Greatest, the largest temple ever built, and once it was completed in full decorative splendour with its statuary and gilding, the most magnificent in the Empire. There was a fine view of it from the Arx, and from there too another view looking eastwards to Mons Albanus whence the augurs sought inspiration from the gods. Here, especially at dawn, a man with a religious soul could convince himself he was close to the chief divinities.

I did not have a religious soul. I had come to see the Sacred Chicks.

Alongside the Temple of Juno Moneta lay the Auguraculum. This was a consecrated platform which formed a practical, permanent augury site. I had always avoided the mystical lore of divination, but I knew broadly that an augur was supposed to mark out with a special curly stick the area of sky he intended to watch, then the area of ground from which he would operate and within which he pitched his observation tent. He sat inside from midnight to dawn, gazing out southwards or eastwards through the open doorway until he spied lightning or a significant flight of birds.

I wondered idly just how he was supposed to see birds before dawn, in the dark.

Today no auspice-taker was in action. Just as well, because I looked inside the booth to say hello – forgetting that any interruption would negate the whole night's watch.

The Sacred Chickens had a different role from the Sacred Geese, but being used in augury they too lived on the Arx, and so it had seemed convenient to Vespasian to bundle them in with my main job. I found the chicken-keeper, one of the few people about. 'You're early, Falco.'

'Had a late night.'

Preferring to remain a man of mystery, I did not explain. Going to bed late after a crisis makes me stay awake, brooding over the excitement. Then it's a choice of nodding off at dawn and feeling terrible when you wake up late, or getting up early and still feeling terrible but having time to do something. Anyway, Helena and I had stayed the night at the Camillus residence after I returned with her brother. I could not face breakfast being polite to people I hardly knew.

The keeper showed me the hen-coops. They stood on legs to keep out vermin. Double doors with lattice fronts kept the hens in and gave protection from dogs, weasels and raptors.

'I see you keep them good and clean.'

'I don't want them dying on me. I'd get the blame.'

If I wanted to be pedantic, now that I was the procurator in charge of poultry management, it was my job to answer questions if too many of the precious pullets popped off, but I was not giving him an excuse to slack. 'Plenty of water?' I had been in the army. I knew how to be irritating when people were doing a perfectly adequate job without my supervision.

'And plenty of food,' the keeper said patiently (he had met my type before). 'Except when I've been tipped the wink.'

'The wink?'

'Well you know how it works, Falco. When the augur wants to see the signs, we open the cage and feed the chicks with special dumplings. If they refuse to eat, or to come out of the coop – or if they come out and fly off – it's a bad omen. But if they eat greedily, spilling crumbs on the ground, that's good luck.'

'You are telling me you starve the chickens in advance, I suppose? And I imagine,' I suggested, 'you could make the dumplings crumbly, to help things along?'

The chicken-keeper sucked his teeth. 'Far be it from me!' he lied.

One reason I despised the College of Augurs was that they could manipulate state business by choosing when the auspices should turn out favourable. Lofty personages who held opinions that I hated could affect or delay important issues. I don't suggest bribery took place. Just everyday perversions of democracy.

The Sacred Chickens' main function was to confirm good omens for military purposes. Army commanders needed their blessing before leaving Rome. In fact, they usually took Roman chickens to consult before manoeuvres, rather than relying on local birds who might not understand what was required of them.

'I always like the story of the consul, Clodius Pulcher, who received a bad augury when he was at sea, chafing to sail against the Carthaginians; the irascible old bastard threw the chickens overboard.'

'*If they won't eat, let them drink!*' quoted the chicken-keeper.

'So he lost the battle, and his whole fleet. It shows you should respect the Sacred Birds.'

'You're just saying that because of your new job, Falco.'

'No, I'm famous for being kind to hens.'

I made notes on a tablet, so it looked good. My instructions as procurator were typically vague but I would prepare a report even though nobody had asked for one. That always makes officialdom jump.

My plan was to suggest making the coop legs one inch longer. I would enjoy thinking up a spurious scientific reason for this. *(Experience suggests that since the time of King Numa Pompilius the average length of weasels' legs has increased, so they can now reach higher than when the statutory Sacred Chicken coop was first designed . . .)*

Duty done there, I sought out the Sacred Geese, my other charges. They rushed up, hissing in a way that reminded me that *their* keeper's specialist lore included warnings that they could break my arm if they turned nasty. Unlikely. Juno's geese had learned that humans might be bringing food. After I checked them out, they waddled after me relentlessly. I was returning to Helena, whom I had left feeding the baby in a secluded spot. A retinue of feather pillows on legs did not help my dignity.

She was waiting back at the Auguraculum, tall and stately. Even after being with her for four years, the sight of her made me catch my breath. My girl. Unbelievable.

Julia was now wide awake; last night, after being scrubbed and scolded about the ink episode, she and her grandfather had fallen asleep together. We crept away to a spare bedroom, leaving him in charge. There were plenty of slaves in the household to help him out if necessary. We had made love that morning without the risk of a nosy little witness appearing at the bedside.

'Lightly stained with woad!' Helena giggled. 'She and Papa were rather well tattooed.'

I put my arms around her, still yearning with intimate affection. 'You know how laundries bleach things – maybe somebody should have peed on them.'

'Papa pre-empted you with that joke.'

We were facing east, squinting into the pale morning sun. Behind us was the temple; to our left, the vista across the Field of Mars and grey-silver hints of the river; more to the right, the augurs' long scan towards the distant misty hills.

'You don't seem a happy gooseboy,' said Helena.

'I'm happy.' I nuzzled her neck lasciviously.

'I think you are planning to make trouble.'

'I'll be the most efficient procurator Rome has ever had.'

'That's exactly what I meant – they don't know what they have done appointing you!'

'Should be fun, then.' I leaned back, turned her round to look at me, and grinned. 'Do you want me to be respectable but useless, like all the rest?'

Helena Justina grinned back wickedly. I could handle becoming pious, so long as she was prepared to stick it out with me.

The city was stirring. Below in the Cattle Market Forum we could hear beasts bellowing. I caught a faint whiff from a tannery that must offend the refined nostrils of the gods – or at least their snooty antiquated priests. It reminded me of the ex-Flamen Dialis who had complained about the goslings. That reminded me of his troubled granddaughter.

'What are you planning to do about Gaia Laelia and her family?'

Helena pulled a face at the suggestion that it was her responsibility, but she was ready: 'Invite Maia to lunch – I have not seen her yet, in any case – and ask her about that royal reception.'

'Am I supposed to come home for lunch too?'

'It's not necessary.' She knew I was dying to be in on what Maia said. 'So,' she retaliated, 'what are *you* intending to do about that body Aelianus found and lost?'

'Not my problem.'

'Oh I see.' Appearing to accept it (I should have known better), Helena mused slowly, 'I don't know that I approved of my brother being set up for the Arval Brethren. I can see why he thought it would do him good socially, but the appointment is for life. He may enjoy feasting and dancing in a corn wreath for a few years, but he can be rather staid and serious. He won't endure it for ever.'

'You know what I think.'

'That all the colleges of priests are élite cliques, where power is traditionally wielded by non-elected, jobs-for-life patricians, all dressing up in silly clothes for reasons no better than witchcraft and carrying out dubious, secretive manipulation of the state?'

'You old cynic.'

'I am quoting you,' said Helena.

'What a misery!'

'No.' Helena pulled a dour face. 'You are an astute observer of the political truth, Marcus Didius.' Then she changed tack: 'In my opinion, unless it is already known who killed the man Aelianus found, then my brother should make it his business – with your technical help – to discover the murderer.'

'Why's this? So that he can inform the rest of the Arval Brothers and in gratitude they will elect dear Aulus to fill the vacancy?'

'No again,' scoffed Helena. 'I told you he is better off without them. So that when those snobs gratefully offer him membership he can make himself feel better by crying "No thank you!" and marching out on them.'

Sometimes people suggested that I was the hot-headed one.

'So you will be investigating this with him?' she grilled me.

'I have no time for unpaid private commissions. Helena my darling, I am very busy making recommendations for the care of things that honk and cluck.'

'What have you suggested to Aulus?'

'That he trots back to the Sacred Grove this morning and pretends to be making official enquiries.'

'So you *are* helping him!'

Well, I had said he could use my name as a cover, if it persuaded people to take him seriously. 'It's up to him. If he wants to know the truth about his mysterious corpse, he has plenty of free time and a good reason to be asking questions.

He'll have to find all the attendants who were working at the pavilion yesterday, and speak to the priests at the various temples; that will take him all day and prove whether he's serious. I bet he discovers nothing. The experience will douse his ardour and perhaps be the end of it.'

'My brother can be very stubborn,' warned Helena in a dark voice.

As far as I was concerned, Aelianus could play with this curiosity as long as he liked. I might even give him a steer or two. But the swift removal of the body and the secrecy with which it had happened looked ominous. If the Arval Brothers had decided to hush up the incident, now that I was loosely attached to the state religion myself, I had to hold back. Once I had been a fearless, interfering informer; now the damned Establishment had bought me off. I had held this post for just two days and already I was cursing it.

'What can he do then?' insisted my darling, being stubborn herself.

'Aelianus ought to present himself at the house of the Arval Master when the Brothers start assembling for today's feast. He should declare what he saw, making his involvement known at least to their chief, and if possible to the whole group. While he is there, he must keep his eyes open. If he notices any particular Brother is missing, he can deduce the identity of the corpse.'

Helena Justina seemed satisfied. In fact, she seemed to believe I was helping her brother rather more than I had agreed to do.

'That's wonderful, Marcus. So while Justinus is away in Spain, you have somebody to work as your partner after all!'

I shook my head but she just laughed at me. Before we left the Arx, we shared a moment surveying the city. This was Rome. We were home again.

If anyone has heard that a procurator attached to the cult of Juno once kissed a girl on the sacred ground of the Auguraculum, it's just winged rumour flitting around with her usual distaste for truth. Anyway, legate, that girl was my wife.

XI

Maia was being far too careful to look normal. She shrank from being hugged as if it seemed an unnecessary display. She was pale but neatly dressed as always, with her dark curls combed back from her face. She wore a dress that I knew was her favourite. She had taken trouble to reassure us; she was certainly making an effort. But her mouth was tight.

With her came all her four children, and when I took them into the other room to show them my goslings, Maia's eyes followed her little ones over-protectively. Always well behaved, they were even quieter than before, all intelligent enough to know their father's death would have drastic consequences, the elder ones secretly shouldering responsibility for bringing everyone through the tragedy.

'They make a lot of mess,' said Ancus, now six, as he carefully handled one of the fledgelings. He looked very worried. 'What are you supposed to do about clearing up?'

'I have to find them somewhere else to live, Ancus. I made arrangements this morning for them to go to Lenia's laundry over the road. They can waddle round the yard and forage in the back lane.'

'But don't they belong on the Arx?'

'There are enough geese on the Arx at the moment.'

'So you can keep the spare ones?'

'Perk of my new job.'

Ancus noted that gravely, seeing it as a career inducement.

'It doesn't seem a good idea to have geese pooping in a place where clothes are being nicely cleaned,' remarked Cloelia. She was about seven or eight, and believed herself frightened of creatures, but it had taken her no time to get the hang of shovelling their porridge and mashed nasturtium leaves into my charges. The practical one.

Lenia's laundry had never been salubrious. I only went there because it was handy and she pretended she gave me cheap rates. She was hoping that geese would guard the laundry from the evil attentions of her recently divorced husband. Having failed to wrest the property from her, Smaractus was trying to drive her out of it. 'Lenia hasn't thought of the mess, so we won't mention it. Do you want to help me take them to their new home?'

We all went in procession, carrying the little birds, their basket, and their porridge pot. This gave Helena and Maia a chance to talk alone.

'We'd like the pot back eventually,' I told Lenia.

She threw back her ghastly fox-red hair and croaked, 'Not too soon, Falco! I'll be wanting the pot for cooking these geese when they get big enough.'

'She doesn't mean that, does she?' Ancus whispered in my ear nervously. Knowing Lenia, I was pretty sure she did.

'Of course not, Ancus. They are sacred. Lenia will be looking after them very carefully.'

Lenia laughed.

We found Petronius outside the laundry, on his lunch break, so he invited himself to join us, bringing a melon as his entrance fee.

Helena gave me a private scowl when she saw Petro, but it seemed to me he would be a great help in jollying Maia. His idea of doing this was to wink at her and leer, 'The new widow's looking spruce!'

'Grow up,' said Maia. Her gaze followed Cloelia who was handing out food bowls rather precariously. 'And that does not mean you can drive me mad being nice to me. Just act normally!'

'Whoops. I thought you'd be sick of normal people murmuring "However will you cope?" You will, don't worry.'

My sister gave him a tart look. 'Is it true what I hear – that Arria Silvia and her potted-food man have decamped to live in Ostia?'

Petronius was milder than I had expected as he confirmed

this new disaster in his own life. 'Apparently, the gelatinous clown reckons there is a great market for his ghastly produce on the quays. And yes, Silvia has taken my daughters. And no, I do not expect to see the girls more than once a year in future.'

'I am sorry,' commented Maia briefly. We all knew he would miss his daughters; but at least he would be there if they really needed him. Her children could no longer say the same about their father.

Petronius, who had installed himself on a bench at the table, stretched his long legs in front of him, leaned back, folded his arms, and returned quietly, 'Sole purpose of presenting myself – to give you somebody else to feel sorry for.'

Maia, who thought Petro an even worse scoundrel than me, took it well, at least for her: 'Petronius and Falco: always the boys who had to be different. Now listen carefully, you two. The official set speech runs like this: my husband was a ne'er-do-well whose death may turn out to be the best thing that happened to me; if I want anything I have only to ask – though of course it means don't ask for anything that requires money or time, or causes embarrassment; most important, you have to tell me that I am still young and attractive – all right, you can say "fairly attractive" – and that somebody else will soon turn up to take Famia's place.'

Petronius Longus lifted Rhea, the silent three-year-old, on to his lap and started filling her bowl for her. He had been a good father and Rhea accepted him trustingly. 'Take Famia's place in being a ne'er-do-well, is that?'

'What else?' said Maia, grudgingly allowing herself a half-smile.

'Has enough time passed for us to tell you that you should never have married him?'

'No, Petro.'

'Right. We'll keep that one in reserve.'

'Don't worry; I can dwell on it for myself . . . Isn't it rich – how eagerly people want to tell you that the person you chose was not worth it! As if you were not already wondering what life was for, and why you seem to have wasted half of it? All, of course, preceded by, "I feel I have to say this, Maia!" So thoughtful!'

'You have to remember,' Petronius advised in a dark voice, like one who knew, 'that it all seemed to be what you wanted, at the time.'

Helena had been placing various serving dishes on the table; now she joined in, taking up their ironic tone, 'I'm sure there must be plenty of pious souls explaining that you have four beautiful children who will be your consolation, Maia? And that what you must do is devote yourself to them?'

'But not let myself go!' Maia growled. ' "In case something comes along". Meaning, oh Juno, let's hope Maia fixes herself up quickly with a new man, so we don't have to worry about her for too long.'

'Your words have a horrible resonance of Allia and Galla,' I commented, referring to two of our elder sisters who were particular mistresses of tact. 'And does that mean,' I asked her hollowly, 'that our mother has started plaguing you to be nice to poor Anacrites?'

This time Maia snapped. 'Oh don't be so ridiculous! Marcus darling, mother would never do that. She has already been warning me not to bat my eyelids that way because Anacrites is far too good for me –'

It was at this point that her control gave way and she started to cry. Helena went and held her while Petro and I distracted the children. I glared at him; he shrugged unrepentantly. Perhaps he was right. It was good for her to let go. Perhaps I was just annoyed with him for achieving it with crass remarks today where I had earlier failed.

Eventually Maia stopped weeping into Helena's girdle and dried her face on her own stole. She reached for Cloelia and Ancus and held one in each arm. Over their heads, she looked at me. The strain was showing now. 'That's better. Marcus, I have a confession. When you first told me what had happened I had an angry turn and poured every drop of wine we had in the house down the drain outside . . .' She forced a wan smile. 'Big brother, if you have any that's fit to offer, I would like a drink with my lunch.'

XII

Once everyone had eaten, I wanted to broach the subject of Maia's visit to the Palace to meet the fabulous Queen Berenice. I suggested that the children should take Nux for a walk in Fountain Court. Obediently they let themselves be shooed off, though since they were Maia's outspoken brood, they all knew what was happening. 'The grown-ups want to talk about things we are not to overhear.'

I had attached a rope to Nux' collar. When I gave the end of it to Marius, the nine-year-old eldest, he asked me anxiously, 'Is your dog likely to run away and get lost?'

'No, Marius. Nux won't ever get lost. We spoil her and overfeed her and pet her far too much. The rope is so that if *you* get lost, Nux will drag you safely back.'

We were on the streetside landing, out of earshot of his mother. Encouraged by this shared joke, Marius suddenly tugged my arm and confided what must have been bothering him: 'Uncle Marcus, if there is no money now, do you think I shall have to stop going to school?'

He wanted to be a rhetoric teacher, or so he had decided a couple of years ago. It might happen, or he might end up ranching cows. I knelt down and gave him a strong hug. 'Marius, I promise you that when the next term's fees are due they will be found.'

He accepted the reassurance though he still looked anxious. 'I hope you didn't mind me asking.'

'No. I realise your mother has probably said, don't go bothering Uncle Marcus.'

The boy grinned shyly. 'Oh we don't always do what Mama says. Today her orders were "Make sure you keep telling them how lovely their baby is – and don't complain if

71

Uncle Marcus insists that we all have some out of his awful old amphora of Spanish fish pickle".'

'So Ancus and you pulled faces and refused even a taste?'

'Yes, but we do think your baby is nicer than the one Aunt Junia has.'

I could tell Marius believed he had to be the man of their household now. I would have to stop that. It could cripple his childhood. At the very least, Maia needed her money worries ended, even if it meant dragging assistance out of Pa.

I returned thoughtfully to the others. Helena had been making enquiries without waiting for me. 'Marcus, listen to this: Cloelia's name has been entered in the Vestal Virgins' lottery.'

I swore, more out of surprise than rudeness. Petronius added a lewd comment.

'Don't blame me,' answered Maia, with a heavy sigh. 'Famia put her forward before he left for Africa.'

'Well he never told me or I'd have said he was an idiot. How old is she?'

'Eight. He never told me either,' Maia returned wearily. 'Not until it was too late and Cloelia had convinced herself it's a wonderful idea.'

'She's barred,' Petronius told us, shaking his head. 'I went through this business with my girls; they were all crazy to be entered until I had to insist that as a father of three I could exempt them from the lottery. It's wicked,' he complained. 'Six Vestals; they serve for thirty years and replacements are called for, on average, every five years. That fills Rome with dreamy little lasses, all desperately wanting to be the chosen one.'

'I wonder why?' retorted Helena dryly. 'Can they really all think how wonderful it would be to ride in a carriage, to have even consuls give way to them, to sit in the best seats in the theatres, to be revered throughout the Empire? All in return for a few light duties carrying waterpots and blowing up the Sacred Fire . . .'

Petro turned to Maia. 'Famia had the three children let-out –'

'I know, I know,' Maia groaned. 'He only did this because

he was such an awkward cuss. Even if Cloelia were chosen, it would be impossible anyway, now her father has been killed. A new Virgin must have both parents living. It's just one more upsetting consequence that I have to explain to my children –'

'Don't,' said Helena. Her tone was crisp. 'Tell the College of Pontiffs, so they can withdraw her. Just let Cloelia think somebody else has won the lottery by chance.'

'And believe me, there was never any doubt that somebody else will!' Maia muttered, now sounding annoyed.

She settled down and told us the story.

'My wonderful husband decided that if plebeians really are eligible, the honour of becoming a Vestal was just right for our eldest daughter. He did not consult me – probably because he knew what I would say.' It *was* supposed to be an honour, one that brought enormous respect to the girl during the thirty years she held the office, but Maia was not the kind of mother who would hand over a young, unformed child into the control of an institution. Her family was taught to respect Rome and its traditions – but to avoid daft schemes like devoting their lives to the state. 'So I am stuck with pretending it's a grand idea. I have Cloelia constantly over-excited, the others secretly jealous of her receiving so much attention, Ma furious, Famia not even in the country to help me cope with it . . .'

She fell silent. Petronius mused wickedly, 'I know we can assume the little darlings are virgins when the Pontifex first accepts them, but how can anyone tell that the pretty things stay chaste? Do they have to submit to ritual testing once a week?'

'Lucius Petronius,' Helena suggested, 'don't you have work to return to this afternoon?'

Petro leaned his elbow on the table with a grin. 'Helena Justina, talking about virgins is much more interesting.'

'You surprise me. But we are talking about would-be Virgins – which is not the same thing.'

'One virgin too many, in the case of Maia's Cloelia!' He was determined to cause trouble today. I would not have minded, but I foresaw that Helena would blame me.

'So tell us about the luscious Berenice,' I intervened. 'She's no virgin, and that's a certainty.'

'Ah well,' said Maia. 'She's definitely very beautiful – if you like that style.' She did not say what style it was, and this time both Petronius and I kept mum. 'If I had an exotic face and a small legion of hairdressers, I wouldn't care if my reputation was slightly soiled.'

'It would not be,' I assured her. 'Berenice is carrying the slur that she married her own uncle. You would never do that with Uncles Fabius or Junius!'

My mother's two brothers were farm clods with notoriously odd habits and, like me, Maia had no patience with their eccentricities. 'I suppose if the Queen's uncle was as mad as ours are, we should feel some sympathy,' she said. 'Anyway, the reason I had to go to the Palace was that all the little charmers whose names are in the urn to become Vestals, and all of us suffering mothers, were invited to a reception for Titus Caesar's ladyfriend. This was set up as an occasion where the female population of Rome would welcome the lovely one into our midst. But I imagine something formal is always arranged by those in charge of the lottery, so the little girls can be inspected and unsuitable ones weeded out.'

'Of course it is blasphemous to say this,' Helena smiled.

'Wash my mouth out!' Maia breathed. 'One of the Vestals was very obviously present anyway.'

'Austerely observing?'

'Not too austere; it was one of the younger ones. Constantia.' Maia paused, but if she had been thinking up an insult she refrained. 'Anyway, if anyone wants to place bets, I soon had the form book sorted – it's so bloody obvious what the result will be, the rest of us could just have gone home straight away. We all trooped up at the appointed time, and natural groups formed at once according to our class. All the mothers were introduced to the ravishing royalty – yes, Marcus and Petro, you would call her ravishing, though I thought her a bit cold –'

'Nervous,' Helena pretended to defend the Queen. 'Probably afraid she may be shouldered out.'

'I wonder why! As if by chance,' Maia sneered, 'she ended up surrounded on her dais by the mothers of patrician rank, while the rest of us talked amongst ourselves. And at the same time, one little girl had been selected to present the Queen with a chaplet of roses, which meant that little brat was cuddled on the silken lap of Berenice for half the afternoon, while Constantia – the Vestal Virgin – sat alongside. Those of us from less fortunate areas of life were struck by a sudden mysterious intuition as to which name will surface when the Pontifex dunks in the lottery urn.'

'This name would not be Gaia Laelia?' asked Helena.

Maia rolled her eyes. 'Dear gods, sweetheart! I never cease to be amazed at how you and my brother are at the forefront of the gossip! You have only been back in the city three days, and you know *everything*!'

'Just a knack.'

'Actually, we know charming, self-confident, dear little patrician Gaia,' I said.

'Through your family?' Maia asked Helena.

'One of my clients,' I returned smoothly. Maia and Petro guffawed. 'She looks ideal for the Vestal's job. All her relatives specialise in holding priestly posts. She has grown up in the house of a Flamen Dialis.'

'Well, dear me, I heard all about that. The child is perfect for the role!' quipped Maia sourly. 'So I don't want to be rude, Marcus, but what does she need you for?'

'That, I admit, is a puzzle. Did she talk at all to Cloelia?'

'Afraid so. I may lack social climbing skills but my strange ambitious baby goes straight to make friends with the people who matter.'

'Cloelia cannot be yours,' said Helena. 'Famia must have found her under an arch. Tell us about Gaia Laelia; did she look happy being favoured by Berenice and the Vestal?'

Maia paused. 'Mostly. She was one of the youngest and after a long time in the royal embrace I thought she probably got bored – anyway, there was a little flurry. It was handled very smoothly, and most people never noticed.'

'What kind of flurry?' I asked.

'How should I know? It seemed as if she said something

embarrassing, the way children do. Berenice looked startled. Gaia was whisked off the Queen's lap, her mother grabbed her, looking as if she wanted to be swallowed by a chasm opening up, and you could see everyone nearby laughing and pretending nothing had happened. Next time I saw Gaia, she was playing with my Cloelia and they both gave me a glare that said nobody should interrupt.'

'Playing?' Helena demanded.

'Yes, they spent over an hour carrying imaginary water vessels from one of the fountains.'

'What did you think of Gaia?'

'Too good mannered. Too nice natured. Too pretty and well favoured. Don't say it: I know I'm just a rude grouse.'

'We love you for it,' I assured my sister affectionately. I now explained how Gaia had come to see me, and what she had said about her family. 'I don't know what it's all about, but she was asking me for help. So what did you think of Gaia's mother? If someone on the family has it in for the child, could it be her?'

'Doubt it,' said Maia. 'She was far too proud of her little mite.'

'We only met an uncle,' Helena contributed. 'Is the mother downtrodden?'

'Not noticeably, at least not when she is out in female company.'

'But at home, who knows? . . . Did Cloelia tell Gaia she has an uncle who is an informer?'

'No idea. She could well have done.'

'And on the other side, I suppose you don't know if Gaia told Cloelia anything about her family?'

'Helena, when Julia is older you will learn about this: I,' said Maia, 'was merely the chaperon who enabled my daughter to mingle with elevated people and dream that she herself was ludicrously important. I hired the litter that took us to the Palatine. I caused embarrassment by wearing too bright a gown and by making jokes about the occasion in a rather loud undertone. Other than that, I was superfluous. I was not allowed to know anything that Cloelia got up to when the girls were let loose together. My only other role was later at home, mopping her brow and holding the bowl when the excitement made her throw up all night.'

'You are a wonderful mother,' Helena assured her.

'Do mention it to my children some time.'

'They know,' I said.

'Well, Cloelia won't think so when I have to break the news that she won't be chosen.'

'Mothers all over Rome will have the same problem,' Petro reminded her.

'All except the self-satisfied piece with the squint who produced Gaia Laelia.' The child's mother had really offended Maia. But I reckoned it was merely by existing.

'It may not be so simple. Something is definitely amiss there. The child came to ask for help for a reason.'

'She came to see you because she had a wild imagination and no sense of judgement,' said Maia. 'Not to mention a family who allow her to steal the litter and to traipse around town without her nurse.'

'I feel there may be more to it,' Helena demurred. 'It's no use. We cannot just forget it – Marcus, one of us will have to look into this further.'

However, we had to stop there because of a commotion at the street door when the children returned. The little ones were whimpering and even Marius looked white.

'Oh Uncle Marcus, a big dog jumped on Nux and would not get off again.' He was curling up with embarrassment, knowing what the beast had been up to yet not wanting to say.

'Well, that's wonderful,' I beamed, as Nux shot under the table with a sheepish and dishevelled appearance. 'If we end up having dear little scruffy puppies, Marius, you can have first pick!'

As my sister shuddered with horror, Petronius murmured in a hollow aside, 'It's very appropriate, Maia. Their father was a horse vet; you have to allow your dear children to develop their inherited affinity with animals.'

But Maia had decided she had to save them from the bad influence of Petro and me, so she jumped up and bustled them all off home.

XIII

'Well, that was a waste of time!'

I had allowed myself to forget temporarily that Camillus
Aelianus had somehow lost a corpse. He pounded up our
steps and burst into the apartment, scowling with annoyance. I hid a smile. The aristocratic young hero would
normally despise everything connected with the role of an
informer, yet he had fallen straight into the old trap: faced
with an enigma, he felt compelled to pursue it. He would
carry on even after he made himself exhausted and furious.

He was both. 'Oh Hades, Falco! You packed me off on a
wild errand. Everyone I questioned responded with suspicion, most were rude, some tried to bully me, and one even
ran away.'

I would have given him a drink, the traditional restorative,
but we had consumed my whole stock that day at lunch. As
Helena nudged him to a bench, his mid-brown eyes
wandered vaguely as if he were looking for a jug and beaker.
All the right instincts were working, though he lacked the
sheer cheek to ask for a goblet openly.

'Did you chase him?'

'Who?'

'The one who ran away. This was, almost certainly, the
person you needed to speak to.'

He thought about it. Then he saw what I meant. He
banged a clenched fist on his forehead. 'Oh rats, Falco!'

'Would you know him again?'

'A lad. The Brothers have youngsters assigned to them as
attendants at their feasts – called *camilli*, coincidentally.
There are only four. I could pick him out.'

'You'll have to get into a feast first,' I pointed out, perhaps
unnecessarily.

He dropped his head on to the table and covered his face, groaning. 'Another day. I cannot face any more. I'm whacked.'

'Pity,' I grinned, dragging him upright. The crass, snooty article had behaved abominably in the past over Helena and me; I loved paying him back. 'Because if you really want to get anywhere, you and I have to make ourselves presentable and take a stroll to the house of the Master of the Arval Brothers – *now*, Aulus!'

It was the final day of the festival. This would be his last chance. My youthful apprentice had to accept that his mission was governed by a time constraint. Like me, he was astute enough to see that if we were to tackle the slippery intendant of a cult that was hiding something, we would need all our wits and energy – and we had to act fast. His day's work had hardly begun.

'Men's games,' I apologised to Helena.

'Boys!' she commented. 'Be careful, both.'

I kissed her. After a momentary hesitation, her brother showed he was learning, and forced himself to do the same.

Aelianus knew how to find the Master's house; he had been invited to the feasting as an observer on the first day of the festival. It was a substantial mock-seaside villa on its own property island, somewhere off the Via Tusculana. A profusion of stone dolphins provided salty character and looked cheerful and unpretentious, though in the urban centre of Rome the rows of open-sided balconies on every wing gave a twee effect. On the Bay of Neapolis the owners could have gone fishing off their boarded verandas, but here their nostalgia for long-gone August holidays was way out of place. Nobody fishes in the gutters in Rome. Well, not if they know what I do about things that float in the city water supply.

As we arrived, it was clear from the disgorging palanquins that the élite members of the college were just assembling for that night's feast. There was a special buzz. I wondered if these men in corn-ear wreaths were greeting each other with extra excitement, knowing of the death the night before.

One man was leaving, however. Tall, gaunt, elderly,

haughty as Hades. Eyes that were careful never to alight on anyone. Flyaway white hair around a bald pate.

He had paused at the top of the entrance steps, as if waiting for some flunkey to clear a free path. When Aelianus leapt up the steps athletically, his cloak brushed very slightly against this old man, who flinched as if he had been touched by a leprous beggar. Sensing a patrician who might own a senate election vote, Aelianus apologised briefly. The only answer was an impatient humph.

The man seemed vaguely familiar. Perhaps he held some position of honour, or I might have seen him lounging in the good seats at the theatre. Jove knows who he was.

We marched boldly inside the main porch. I found a chamberlain. Our manner had warned him we were trouble, but we proved quiet enough to win him over. 'I apologise; this is very urgent. Before the fun begins this evening, we need to see the Master on a confidential matter. Didius Falco and Camillus Aelianus. It concerns an unfortunate occurrence yesterday.'

The chamberlain was suave, expressionless – and without doubt apprised of the scandal in the Grove. To the disbelief of my companion, we got straight in.

That was bad. The Master must be playing this the clever way.

At first it was not the Master himself we met, but his vice – a flustered barnacle covered with warts from whom, had he been a commoner instead of a pedigreed noble, I would not have bought a fresh fish in case it gave me bellyache. He was accompanied by the college's vice-flamen – a pallid cheese with a drip on his nose who must be the main source of this month's summer cold in Rome. These two stand-ins greeted us nervously, explained who they were, and mumbled a lot about having to officiate at that day's rites in the temple because the real Master and flamen had been called away. They were spared embarrassment when their principals turned up in travelling clothes.

I stood to attention deferentially. So, at this cue, did Helena's brother.

'Camillus Aelianus!' Washing his hands in a bowl held by a slave, the Master nodded congenially to show that he recognised him. 'And you are – ?'

'Didius Falco.' It was probably convention in such company to name your own association with religion, but I was not prepared to admit being the guardian of the geese. 'I have worked for the Emperor.' They could guess how. 'I am here as a friend to this young man. Aelianus had a rather unpleasant experience in the late hours of yesterday. We do feel that he should report it formally, should you be unaware of what occurred.'

'I am so sorry to keep you waiting; we had extra business at the Sacred Grove.' The Master was a huge-bellied man whose size must have been enormous long before he took office in a post with compulsory feasting. Dogging him, the cult's sacrificing flamen had neither girth nor height, but made his presence felt by a harsh laugh at inappropriate moments.

'A purification rite?' I asked quietly.

The efficient chamberlain must have warned his head of household what we had said we wanted. 'Exactly. The Grove has been polluted by an iron blade – but due solemnities have now been offered – a *suovetaurilia*.'

Major expiation by swine, ram and bull. Sorted. Three perfect animals rounded up and their throats cut, the very next day.

Would a bloody corpse be dealt with just as briskly? In this cult, yes.

The three subsidiary officers had found seats. The ears of grain in their head-dresses nodded gently in the light from a bank of suspended oil lamps; shadows passed across their faces. They were used to the effect. Aelianus, who had hoped to join them, must have trained himself to accept the sight. I managed to contain a smirk. Just.

'So, young man! Tell me what happened to you,' offered the Master, so graciously that my teeth set. He was now changing into a flowing white dinner gown, like those the others already wore. Over one shoulder was placed a folded vestment. The feast must have been delayed; still assisted by the discreet slave, he dressed hurriedly. The pressure on us rose. Well, nobody wanted the Arval cook to start bewailing a burnt roast.

Aelianus exhibited his least attractive scowl and said bluntly, 'I fell over a corpse at the back of your pavilion, sir.'

'Ah.' The big man revealed no surprise, only delicate concern. Garbed for the feast now, he gestured to the slave to leave us. 'That must have been a terrible experience.'

'You saw the body?' I slipped in.

'I did.' He was making no attempt at subterfuge. Normally in my job you meet head-on resistance, but this was a familiar scenario too; I knew it was far worse. To deal with complete openness is like falling into a grain storage pit. It can very quickly suffocate.

'The body subsequently disappeared.' Still upset, Aelianus spoke too harshly. If I let him continue in this style we would lose any grip on the conversation that we still possessed.

The Master looked from one to the other of us. It was a fine display of gentle reproach. 'Oh dear. You are suspecting dark deeds!' I felt my cheek twitch. We could have been discussing a few missing denarii from their petty cash, instead of a man who had been honouring the old religion, hacked to death in a tent.

'You tidied up?' I posed the question without exaggerated disapproval. These people were intelligent. They knew that I knew they wished that their secret had remained within the cult.

The Master immediately increased his air of deep apology. 'I am afraid we did. It was, after all, the main night of our annual festival and we hoped to avoid panic among the attendant staff and members of the public who were visiting the Games. The Sacred Grove of the Dea Dia had been polluted too, so there were considerations of how to reconsecrate it as swiftly as possible . . . Well, this is a most dreadful business, but there is no untoward secrecy. I am grateful that you have come to me with your concerns. Let me explain what has happened, as far as we know it –'

'The dead man was one of the Brethren?' I asked.

'Unhappily, yes.' I noticed he made no attempt to give a name. 'A sad domestic incident. The woman responsible was found wandering in the Grove immediately afterwards, covered with blood and weeping hysterically, totally deranged.'

'You call it a "domestic incident"; do you mean she is a relative of her victim?'

'Sadly, yes. Is it not true, Falco, that people are most likely to be murdered by members of their families?'

I acknowledged it. 'Men get killed by their wives, usually. You saw the woman yourself?'

For the first time he did appear to be overcome by the grim story. 'Yes. Yes, I did.' He was silent for a second, then went on, 'She became calmer, seeming bemused. I spoke to her gently and she admitted what had happened.'

'Was she capable of giving any rational explanation?'

'No.'

'Difficult!' I said dryly.

'These things happen. It was quite unexpected, or the ghastly consequences might have been averted. Our member, it now transpires, had been troubled by the woman's bouts of mental stress but was attempting to protect her by concealing them. People do that, you know.' I made a face that said I knew. 'I have made further enquiries, and I am satisfied that this is the truth. Her mind went. Whether it was under some great burden that cannot now be discovered or some unfortunate natural illness, we may never know.'

'Official action?'

'No, Falco. I have consulted the Emperor today, but there is nothing to gain by a court case. It would only add to the immense distress of those involved. Nothing remained for us to do but arrange for the body to be given reverently into the care of his relatives for burial. The poor woman has been assigned to her own close family, on the promise she will be nursed and constantly guarded.'

At this, the two deputy officials we had first met seemed to shift slightly in their seats. Glances passed between them and the Master, then the Vice-Master told him, 'We were just discussing the arrangements before you returned.'

'Good, good!'

I thought that exchange contained more meaning than the mere words implied. Was some sort of warning being given?

The Master was gazing at me, as if waiting to see if I pressed the issue. I decided to oblige. 'Of course there will be no publicity?'

He assented in silence.

'What was the name of the Brother who died?' Aelianus put in.

The Master gave him a narrow look from under his eyebrows. 'I am afraid I cannot tell you. It has been agreed –' He spoke heavily and his tone implied the agreement had been granted by Vespasian, at the consultation which the Master had claimed to have had. 'The name of the family involved in this terrible tragedy will not be released.'

The three other Brothers shifted in their seats. I was now in no doubt that they knew the whole story. They were rapt by the way their chief romanced us with the official version.

I pursed my lips, drawing in a long, slow breath. Once, I would have made myself unpleasant, insisting on further information – and I would have got nowhere. When the Establishment closes ranks, the personnel know just how to do it. Aelianus was hopping and eager to pursue it, but I shook my head slightly, warning him not to make a fuss.

'Young man,' sympathised the Master, 'I am most perturbed that you should have been drawn into this sad episode while attending on our rites. It must have been an appalling shock. I will speak to your father, but do pass on to him my sincere regrets – and you, Didius Falco, thank you – thank you most heartily for your help and support.'

'Rely on our discretion,' I smiled, trying not to make it grim. The big man in the dinner robe had not asked us to keep quiet; still, it was understood that we would be thoughtful towards the distraught family involved. 'I am a trusted imperial agent, and Aelianus, as you know, regards the Arval Brethren with the greatest respect.'

To ask who was in line for the unexpected new vacancy would have been crass. I tipped Aelianus the wink, and we saluted all round, then left.

Almost before we were out of the room, there was a murmur of conversation behind us. The Master's deputy began saying, as if he could hardly contain himself, 'We had a visitation from himself just before all that –' Then the door closed firmly.

I gazed at young Camillus, searching to see how he interpreted our interview. He was Helena's brother all right. He was angry at how we had been led along and finessed with stonewall courtesy. In view of the antipathy he had already harboured, he was blaming me for the lack of results.

His mouth tightened in distaste. 'Well, as I said at the start of this evening, Falco – *that was a waste of time!*'

XIV

We took three strides. Between the exit and us, the Brethren were processing into the Master's dining room. We stopped.

Behind us, the Master and his cronies came out from the room we had left. The big man paused, clapped Aelianus on the shoulder, then apologised that since the feast was to take place in his private house, where couches were limited, he could not invite us. The ordinary members had slowed, so the Master and other officers could now join the head of their group and lead the way. Aelianus and I stayed where we were to watch the corn dollies all process to their last formal meal of the festival.

'Aulus, I thought on the first day they squeezed you in to watch?'

'Yes.'

'But today the Master reckons they are pushed for space! Dining room must have shrunk.'

'You see conspiracies everywhere, Falco.'

'No. Just two unwanted enquirers who have been fed a very sticky porridge of half-truths.'

Probably all the Master was doing was covering up a tragic incident that would hurt those involved if it became a public scandal. I sympathised with the stricken family; after all, my own had troubles we preferred to veil. But I hated to be patronised.

Tripping over the hems of their white robes, the Brothers jostled past us. They were the pride of the patrician ranks, so half were tipsy and some senile. I counted them under my breath. There were one or two extras but the corn wreaths stood out. All twelve. Wrong; eleven. One had been carved up last night by a mad wife. At least, I supposed it was a wife, though on reflection the

Master had not specifically said so. (I was doubting him on every aspect now.)

'Full complement. Tell me, would-be noviciate, do they usually all make the effort to attend?'

'No. They reckon to muster between three and nine. A full quorum occurred once at the end of Nero's reign, and is still spoken of with awe.'

'That Master must have owned a spectacular cook.'

'I expect they were going to debate the crazy emperor.'

'Surprise me!'

The party had all crammed into the triclinium. We could hear mutters as they vied for the best couches and groans as the old men among them struggled to recline their raddled bodies encumbered with the clinging folds of their robes. I could imagine their eagerness to hear salacious details of the murder and to know how bad a scandal affected their order.

'Well, time to go, Falco.' Aelianus had the concentration of a gnat. 'There's nothing for us here.'

'That's what they want you to think. The Master of your admired order has turned us inside out. Now I know how a skinned rabbit feels as its fur is peeled.'

'I stumbled across a ghastly domestic incident. Don't you believe that?'

'Oh yes.'

'So the Master told us the truth.'

'Partially – probably.'

'He seemed perfectly open and reasonable.'

'A lovely fellow. But I bet he cheats at draughts.'

Four youths emerged from a side door. They wore matching white tunics and all carried salvers.

Aelianus, who had been on the verge of abandoning any pretence of comradeship with me, turned slightly. Despite himself, he caught my eye. Once again, curiosity had won and he was suddenly back in the game.

'Which was it?' I muttered.

He signalled to the third boy. I bounded across and grabbed him, whipped the salver away from him, dragged one arm up his back, and marched him into an alcove behind a statue. Aelianus blocked escape and confirmed aloud that this was the young man who ran away from questioning at the Grove earlier.

He was about thirteen. A few spots and stubbles. A pigeon-chested young lout who reckoned he could do as he liked and we had to put up with it. Aelianus wrinkled his nose. The pristine white uniform covered a body that shunned bathing in a routine adolescent way.

'Let me go! I have my duties at the feast –'

'This is the *camillus* with the runaway legs?' I asked Aelianus. 'I wonder why? What's he hiding?'

'Obviously something!' Aelianus leaned on the lad, squashing him up against the statue.

'Something bad, I'd say. What's your name, Speedy?'

'Find out. I've done nothing.'

'Can you prove that? There has been a murder, clever. So what did you see of it?'

'Nothing!' He glared back, acting dumb. He was cocky, but I could play the official line. We were in somebody's house, however; we might be discovered and thrown out at any minute. I had to act fast.

'What shall we do?' I mused to Aelianus. 'The vigiles would be the nearest who own a set of thumbscrews, but it's not my favourite district cohort. Why should they get all the fun? No, leave the esparto mat boys to comb the streets for arsonists. I reckon we'll haul this little beggar to the Palace.'

'The Praetorians?'

'No – they're far too soft.' Any lad in Rome would know the Praetorian Guard were vicious. 'I'll give him to Anacrites.'

'The Chief Spy?' Aelianus was playing along with me. 'Oh have a heart, Falco!'

'Well of course he's a brute; I can't stand his dirty methods. Still, he's got the best equipment. Speedy won't last long in the underground torture cell.'

While Aelianus was shuddering dramatically, the boy squealed in panic. 'I done nothing, I done nothing!'

One thing he had done was to make too much noise. I glanced over my shoulder, but despite his cries, the household staff were all absorbed in serving the first course at the feast. The Brothers were raising quite a din too, as they fell on their ceremonial hors-d'oeuvres and gossiped with their mouths full about last night's grim events. 'Answer my questions then, son. A man was killed, rather unpleasantly. What did you see in the Sacred Grove of the Dea Dia?'

'I didn't see him killed.'

'Well then? Do you know who he was?'

'One of the Brothers. They all look alike once they get dressed up. I don't know all their names.'

'Did you see the corpse?'

'No. Someone else found it; one of the temple priests, I think. He went off sick today.' The priest's own choice, or the Master's decision? 'I only saw the Master's attendants taking the body away on a trestle, covered up.'

'What else?' asked Aelianus quietly. Without any training, he now fell into the role of the friendly, well-spoken interrogator – the less brutal one. I could live with that.

'I saw her,' gasped Speedy, gratefully turning to this more sympathetic fellow. 'The woman who did it. I saw her.'

Suddenly he was less sure of himself, and looked more his age. A boy. An extremely frightened one.

'Will you tell us about her?'

'The men who were moving the body didn't want people hanging about. I was having a good gawp, but they ordered me to move away. As I was going, she appeared in front of me.'

'Can you describe her?'

The *camillus* was too young to have started taking mental notes of women's attributes. He looked helpless.

'What was she wearing?' I suggested.

'White. With her hair all tied up. White – but the front of her dress was covered with blood. That was how I knew she did it.'

'Of course. You must have been terrified,' Aelianus sympathised.

'I was all right,' he bragged, comforting himself in retrospect. He had probably had no time for real fear.

I stuck with the job in hand: 'Was she a young woman?'

'Oh no.' To a boy his age that could mean anyone over twenty-five.

'A grey-haired granny?'

'Oh no.'

'A matron? Was she high class? Did she wear jewellery?'

'I don't know – I was just staring at her. She had a wild look. And –' He stopped.

'And what?' asked Aelianus patiently.

'She was holding a bowl.' The boy's voice had dropped. This seemed to be the source of his hidden terror. 'She was holding a bowl like this –' He demonstrated, miming the action of carrying a vessel lodged on the hip, with one hand on the far rim. We were silent. He struggled. 'It was full of blood. Like in a temple sacrifice.'

'Dear gods!' Shocked himself, Aelianus set a hand on the boy's shoulder to steady him. Aelianus had told his father and me that the dead man had a large throat wound. Now we knew why. He shot me a look, then drew breath carefully. 'So what happened?'

'She did something horrible.'

'What?'

'Other people had seen her. I could hear them coming towards us, and I thought I was safe.'

'But?'

'Maybe she heard the people coming. She began to weep, crazily. She seemed to start awake from a dream, and she saw me. Then it was strange. At an altar, when they cut the beast's throat and catch the blood, they have a boy to hold the ritual bowl sometimes. She seemed to think I was there for that.' The *camillus* braced himself. 'She said, "Oh, there you are!" – and then she gave the bowl of the dead man's blood to me.'

XV

We crossed the hall in silence and were making our way from the house. A latecomer rushed up the steps towards us, a senator in full fig and to my surprise a man I recognised. 'Rutilius Gallicus!'

'Falco! What brings you here?'

'I could ask the same, sir.'

He paused, catching his breath. 'Duty.'

'Well, you can't be one of the Arval Brothers, or you would be prettied up with corn tonight! – This is Camillus Aelianus, by the way – the brother of Justinus whom you met with me in Africa.'

Just in time Gallicus remembered not to exclaim, *Ah, the one who ought to have married that rich Spanish girl his brother pinched!* 'I heard a lot about you,' he uttered instead. A mistake, as usual. Aelianus looked peeved. Embarrassed, Rutilius Gallicus dashed into his excuses for being here: 'I may not have told you, Falco, I am a priest of the Cult of the Deified Emperors. I took over directly after Nero, actually –'

I whistled. This was a top-flight honour, with close imperial connections, which he would hold for life and then have carved very large on his tombstone. Even Aelianus forced himself to look impressed. 'So you are attached to the Arvals after all, sir?'

'No more than I can help!' shuddered Gallicus, still at heart the straightforward north Italian. 'I hold no brief for them, Falco. But in view of their role in praying for the health of the imperial house, I am automatically invited to their festivals.'

'A free meal never comes amiss. I have heard a theory that election to be the new Master actually depends on a kitchen inspection, rather than the man's religious qualities.'

'I can believe that,' Rutilius smiled. 'Look, are you two going in to the feast? I am sure I can arrange it –'

'Not tactful, I'm afraid.' Taking a chance that he belonged to the inner circle who knew all about the murder in the Grove, I added, 'My young friend Camillus had the misfortune to discover a bloody corpse last night. You may have heard the story. We were just here asking some awkward questions. The Brothers are clearly sensitive about the incident; our faces won't fit at the party.'

Rutilius glanced about, as if making sure we were not overheard. 'Yes. I just came from the Palace; we were talking about exactly that. It's why I am late. Titus and Domitian Caesar would normally have been here –'

'Policy decision? It's tricky protocol,' I sympathised. 'If they stay at home over a tragedy that nobody could help, it looks cold-blooded. But if this murder blows up into a scandal on the lurid page of the *Daily Gazette*, the princes will not want their names linked . . . Let me guess: the lads in purple have been struck with an inexplicable stomach upset, and you are bringing their sincere apologies?'

'Domitian has a stomach upset,' Rutilius agreed. 'Titus elected for suddenly remembering the birthday of a very ancient aunt.'

'Ah well, he gets a quiet evening in the arms of the phenomenal Berenice.'

'Wonderful for both of them! Falco, I must dash inside –'

We bade him good evening and left the marine-style villa. After a while Aelianus asked, 'So what did you make of all that?'

'Intriguing. A woman goes mad and knifes a relative – only she dresses it up as a religious sacrifice.' I paused. 'It must have taken some doing. The killing would have been difficult, even in a frenzy – but then, after that strenuous effort, she had to manoeuvre the corpse to drain out the blood . . .' We both grimaced.

'Is this murder just an act of sudden madness, Falco, or do you think the victim had upset her particularly?'

'Well, something probably triggered her action. Not at the Games. A previous incident, because there was quite a lot of planning involved. She had dressed herself up as a priestess, and gone to the Grove equipped with sacrificial implements.'

'Do you think she and the man travelled there together?'

'Doubt it. He would have wondered about the religious accoutrements. A woman of standing would not normally travel out of Rome alone, though. She got there somehow. She must have had transport, if not a companion.'

'For a woman of standing, discreet transport is no problem. Half the scandals in Rome rely on it. So she took herself to the Games and confronted the man, fully intending to kill him? There can be no mitigating circumstances – yet now what, Falco? The crazed killer is simply returned to her family? Sent home in the same discreet transport, presumably! And allowed to continue her normal life?'

'Well, the Master said they are going to guard her,' I said dryly. 'If it was her husband she killed, perhaps all they have to do is ensure she never remarries. Though no doubt if she does, they will issue the new chap with a warning never to turn his back when she's slicing smoked meat.'

'Oh wonderful! Was that rude old man we passed earlier at the Master's house a relative coming to beg the Arvals to sanction the cover-up?'

'Seems likely.'

'Well, I think it's disgraceful if they get away with it.'

Since he had been born into the top circle where such cover-ups were permissible, I refrained from comment. What was to gain by publicising this woman's tragedy? A trial and execution would only be an added misery for her relatives. They could afford drugs to calm her and guards to restrain her. Plenty of perfectly ordinary Aventine families have batty old aunts who are kept well away from the kindling axe.

I walked with Aelianus to the senator's house to make sure that no muggers jumped him, then made my own way over the Aventine. Several times on the dark journey, I thought I heard footsteps following me, but I saw no one. In Rome, at night, all sorts of suspicious noises can make you nervous once you let yourself start hearing them.

XVI

The next day was the last in May. I looked it up in my calendar of festivals, an abomination that I now had to consult on a regular basis like a dutiful procurator. Today I could have voted or been a juror in a criminal case – had anybody wanted me. No one did, and so the last day of the month just seemed to slip away quite pleasantly. Anyone can be a responsible citizen when most of the world thinks he is still abroad.

I watched the day go. I was suffering belated weariness after sailing home. And I was uneasy. Acting as Procurator of Poultry had taken over my life. A major festival of Juno Moneta fell tomorrow (nagged the calendar). My place would be there. Even attending this junket would be a first for me, let alone serving as nursemaid to a set of geese. The geese were to exhibit their annual tasteless triumphalism over a sample of supposedly guilty watchdogs, poor stray curs who would be rounded up and ritually crucified. It was not my idea of a genteel nod to history.

Today, however, I was loafing at home, left in charge of young Julia while Helena dodged off somewhere. When, like a pompous head of household checking up on his wife's social life, I asked for details she just looked at me with a guileless expression that meant she was being devious. Whatever it was, she took Nux as a chaperon, plus enough bread rolls for a good lunch, her private note-tablet and stylus, and several sponges; then I spotted her hiding my best hammer under her cloak. I doubted she was visiting a girlfriend to discuss embroidery designs.

'Helena, is it possible, companion of my heart, that you are hiding something from me?'

'You do not want to know, darling!' Helena assured me.

94

'Enjoy your day.' Her parting tone was kindly and brave, like a farmer who has delivered his favourite horse to the knacker with a full nosebag.

I would have spent my time in men's activities – Forum, baths, shops, tracing Petronius to whichever wine bar he had chosen that day for his break. Having Julia with me hampered that. But I did visit Pa's warehouse at the Saepta Julia in order to broach Maia's money problems; he was out. Even Petro had made himself invisible, though his comrades at the patrol-house reckoned he was working.

'Sounds too diligent.'

'Maturity comes to everyone, Falco.'

'If that's happened to Lucius Petronius, he needs a surgeon right away!'

'No, somebody just happened to mention lettuce in his hearing – not thinking about his wife's lover, of course.'

'Oh no! He went off in a sulk?'

'Touchy tyke.'

Still carrying the baby, I went to the Forum anyway. Julia loved the crowds. The sleazier they were, the more she gurgled appreciatively. My family would say, at least there were no doubts about her fatherhood.

At the back of the Temple of Castor was the bath-house I frequented. I took a risk. Glaucus, the austere proprietor, had a strict entrance policy. His establishment was intended to be a haunt for serious professional men. He banned women. Nor did he tolerate pretty boys or the paederasts who lusted after them. To my knowledge, nobody had ever been mad enough to turn up with a one-year-old baby before. We got past the doorkeeper on the wings of sheer novelty. Brazen daring carried me through the changing room and I was heading for the gymnasium when I heard the rasp of Glaucus being sarcastic to some unfortunate he was training with weights; I chickened out and decided to keep fit another day.

I slunk through the baths as fast as I could, then looked in on the masseur, a gigantic bully from Tarsus with legendary manipulative powers. He was slapping about Helena Justina's father. I took Julia in and we sat on the side bench where the next customer was supposed to wait in terror. The masseur glared at the baby, but was too nonplussed to comment.

I grinned as I inspected Decimus. 'Thanks for dinner the other night. You managed to scrub off the ink, I see!'

'The child developed a lot while you were away. You might have warned me.'

'She learned to stand on the ship. She was beside the rail in brisk weather when she first tried it. I could have saved myself years of trouble by letting her tumble over the side – but I knew she was your favourite grandchild.' She was also his only one.

'So you made a quick grab?' Losing Julia would truly have broken his heart. I made another quick move, as Julia picked up a water scoop and prepared to hurl it at the huge, sweating masseur. The senator chortled, good going since he was already contorted in a hideous grimace under a barrage of slaps between the shoulders. I decided that the masseur believed in tribal individualism rather than senate-led democracy. He was certainly taking out his personal aggression on the Camillus physique.

Decimus and I were cronies here, exchanging secrets. 'Has Helena Justina said anything to you about some venture into property?'

'Nobody tells me anything,' her noble father complained. 'They just keep me to lie on one of the eating couches to prevent the dining room looking empty. What's she buying?' he asked nervously.

'Could be a house.'

'She may allow me to hear about it, once she has a whole row of them.' He paused while the man from Tarsus casually attempted to wrench his left arm from its socket. 'I told Aulus to see you today.'

'About his corn-ear friends again? I thought he had accepted their story – that the man he found dead was just an unlucky victim of a wife in a bad mood?'

'Wouldn't you like to know who the couple were – and what drove her to do it?'

'Yes, I would. Aulus seemed less curious when I left him last night.'

'Well, I told him he ought to find out.'

I grinned through the steam. 'I never had you down as a schemer, senator! Is he to acquire the facts in order to show the Brothers he is scrupulously keeping quiet – with the aim of securing votes?'

'Good gods, that would be blackmail!' exclaimed Decimus in mock-shock.

'I can't wait for your election-night party.'

At that moment in prowled Glaucus. He swelled with indignation at the sight of little Julia. She waved both her arms at him eagerly.

'Hey, Glaucus! This one wants a session with the dumb-bells.'

'I've told you already about that dog of yours, Falco! Now you try this –'

I was on my feet. 'Just bringing your most excellent client a glimpse of his only grandchild, Glaucus –'

'No children!' Glaucus stabbed his finger into my chest. It was almost as effective as a spear point in the breastbone. 'This is your last warning!'

I had reached the doorway. 'We're going.'

Glaucus glared at Julia, appalled. 'Is this a *girl* baby?'

'Boy!' Decimus assured him urgently. 'Julius, isn't it, Falco?'

Glaucus moved. He knew us. It looked as if he was intending to check. I grappled Julia to me protectively. She was fighting to break free as strongly as Hercules. 'Anybody looks up my son's tunic, I kill him, Glaucus – no argument. It probably goes for a daughter as well, of course, though I may find out if the fellow is wealthy first, for her sake . . .'

'*Out!*' roared Glaucus.

We left.

I popped my head back. 'By the way, Glaucus, next time you allow in that bastard Anacrites, ask him to tell you how he made use of your "Trainer's Cheat" move when we were on our holidays!'

Even when you're fleeing in defeat, remember to place a few stakes in pits to trap your enemy.

*

I went to see Maia.

Ma was there. They had both been out together to make arrangements for the memorial stone for Famia. For some reason the visit to the mason had entailed wearing heavy veils, which were now pushed back on their necks. They were sitting together in a pair of women's armchairs, with their hands folded over their girdles, looking thoughtful.

They were not much alike in facial features; Maia took after Pa's side of the family, as I did. Their bolt-upright stance and frowning expressions nonetheless marked them as close relatives. Somebody or something had affected both of them the same way.

'What's happened? If it's to do with money, I've told you – don't worry.'

'Oh it's money,' Maia snapped briskly. 'Famia usually forgot to pay his funeral club dues, I gather.'

'He never forgot!' Ma commented. 'He drank it all.'

'That was after I was visited by the landlord, who took it upon himself to warn me – for my own good – of the perils of falling behind with the rent.'

'Watch him!' muttered Ma.

'Mother and I were just talking about me paying a social call on my sweet friend Caecilia Paeta, to take my mind off it.'

'You need to get out,' I replied warily. Both my sister and my mother were watching me with a special glint. It might be friendly, but I doubted it. Ma pinched her mouth. She had a way of saying nothing which was worth three scrolls of rhetoric. 'Don't string me along – who's Caecilia and why are you after her?'

'Caecilia is a crab-faced snoot,' said Maia, now dragging her veil from around her neck and flinging it aside. 'She is one of the women I met at the Palace the other afternoon. Your little Gaia's mother, specifically.'

I handed the baby to Ma, who was always good at keeping Julia quiet. 'So why the planned expedition?'

'Nosiness,' laughed Ma.

Maia looked more prim. 'I keep thinking about what you and Helena said, about the girl being scared of her family.

Since Gaia and my Cloelia made friends, I did exchange words with the mother at the time. She obviously wanted to avoid contact, but that's enough for me – being brass-necked. I can follow this up for you, Marcus.'

'Well thanks, but I thought Helena was intending to visit her –'

'Helena's doing something else.'

'Oh you know about that?' It was worth a try.

'Sworn to secrecy,' said Maia, with an evil flash of teeth.

'I heard,' said my mother severely, 'that Helena has involved herself with Gloccus and Cotta!' Who in Hades were they? They sounded like cheap erotic poets.

'Anyway, Marcus, it's lucky you've come,' Maia rushed on. 'I'll let you share my little adventure. It's not far to go. These folks of Gaia's are living on the Aventine now – it was one thing the snooty mother allowed herself to discuss with me. Because the grandfather used to be Flamen Dialis, hogged the role for years apparently, they had always had possession of the official house called the Flaminia.'

'That's on the Palatine?'

'Yes. Horribly isolated place to bring up a family. It's all temple compounds and imperial suites up there.'

'Must have driven them mad,' was Ma's opinion.

Maia grinned. 'Caecilia Paeta told me that her husband and his sister lived there from childhood; they could remember no other home. Apparently it's a sore subject that everyone had to up sticks and move house unexpectedly when the Flaminica died.'

'Was her death recent?'

'I got that impression. Anyway, they have now taken a house on the Ostia Gate side of the hill. Caecilia was complaining to me that it was run down and unsatisfactory.'

I pulled a silly face. 'And will Caecilia be delighted to see you, Maia darling, if you track her down?'

Maia smiled at me. 'We'll have to ask her, won't we?'

Ma and I exchanged glances, willing to go along with any plan that made my sister behave like her old self, at least temporarily. My mother took charge of Julia for me. In no time I found myself marching over the Aventine with Maia,

99

and after a few wrong turns while we found the address, we were surveying the house of the family Laelius. I was not impressed. Maia and I immediately agreed that as prospective buyers or tenants, even if we were desperate, we would never even have given it a once-over.

Who chose this place? The ex-Flamen himself, grief-stricken for his newly dead wife – or at least for the loss of his position on her death? His son, Gaia's father? His errand-running son-in-law, the Flamen Pomonalis? Accepting that his household might be as liberal as my own, was it his womenfolk? Daughter? Daughter-in-law?

No. It had to be a realtor. Wincing at the gloomy place from down the street, I knew this was some housing market hack's idea of a residence for a retired high priest. A massive grey portico that must be causing street subsidence. High, narrow windows and mean roofs. A pair of tall urns either side of the forbidding doorcase; both empty. A property with no attractive features, situated in a dull area, over-looking nothing much. A large, cold building on the dank side of the street, it must have lodged like a permanent fixture on the agent's list for a decade. Few people with enough money to afford such an edifice would have such poor taste as to accept it. But a Flamen Dialis, turfed out of his state residence, fresh from a funeral, unworldly and desperate to be rehoused, must have seemed to the agent like a gift from the Olympian gods. The proverbial soft touch. A punter in a hurry, with absolutely no idea . . . and too sure of himself to take real expert advice.

'I hope he's not there,' muttered Maia. 'I deduce I will not care for him.'

'Right. Judging by his attitude to my goslings, he's what Ma would call a nasty old basket.'

We were not given a chance to test this theory. When we managed to persuade a door porter to answer our knocking, he told us there was nobody home at all. The man kept us out on the porch; he agreed to go and make enquiries for us, though I wondered how, because he had assured us the entire family had gone to a funeral. Even the Flamen Dialis (as the porter still called him despite his retirement) was attending the ceremony.

Maia raised her eyebrows. 'The Flamen Dialis is never allowed to see a body, but he can go to funerals,' I whispered, showing off my arcane knowledge, as we stood nervously alone on the threshold like untrustworthy trinket-sellers who were about to be sent packing. 'Just as well he has gone. He would never have liked hearing that you had palled up with Caecilia.'

'He won't like hearing we were here today at all then,' Maia said. She made no attempt to keep her voice down. 'I fancy Caecilia will receive a lecture about mingling with unsuitable company. Encouraging rough callers. Allowing common connections for the dear special little girl.'

'Caecilia sounds all right after all.'

Maia laughed ruefully. 'Don't believe it, Marcus. But the Flamen won't know it was no choice of hers that I sought her out at home.'

'Are you saying he mistreats her?'

'Oh no. I just reckon his word is law and his opinions are the only ones ever allowed to be voiced.'

'Sounds like our house, when Pa lived there,' I joked. Maia and I were both silent for a moment remembering our childhood. 'So the Flamen is bound to be rude, autocratic, and unfriendly – but do we believe he wants his precious little Gaia dead?'

'If he shows his face I'll ask him that.'

'You'll *what*?'

'Nothing to lose,' said Maia. 'I'll tell him as one mother to another, I want to ask Caecilia Paeta what has caused her sweet little girl – the dear new friend of mine – to be so unhappy and to take such a curious step as to approach my brother the informer with such a ridiculous tale.'

Perhaps it was fortunate after all that the porter then returned to confirm there was no one at home to speak to us. He was now accompanied by a couple of reinforcements. It was clear they were intended to persuade us to leave quietly. I would like to say that was what we did, but I had Maia with me. She hung around, insisting on leaving a message for

101

Caecilia Paeta to say that she had called.

While she was still harassing the porter, a woman appeared in the rather dark atrium that we could just glimpse over his shoulder. She looked about the right age to be Gaia's mother, so I asked, 'That your friend?'

As Maia peered in and shook her head, the young woman was surrounded by a group of females who must be her attendants; they all moved as one out of view again. It seemed a strangely choreographed little scene, as though the maids had swept up their mistress and she succumbed to being whisked away.

'Who was that?' Maia demanded bluntly, but the porter looked vague and pretended he had seen no one.

After we left, the odd glimpse stayed with me. The woman had had the air of a member of the family, not a slave. She had walked towards us as if she was entitled to come and speak to us – yet she seemed to let the maids change her mind for her. Well, I was probably making too much of it.

Maia allowed me to escort her home again and I collected Julia. When we left my sister's house, outside in the street a group of little girls was playing a Vestal Virgins game. These were not pampered babies in some careful patrician residence. The tough Aventine tots not only had a stolen water jug to carry on their heads, but had obtained some embers and had lit themselves a Sacred Fire on their own little Sacred Hearth. Unfortunately, they had chosen to recreate the Temple of Vesta rather close to a house with a very attractive set of wooden balconies, some of which were now on fire. As it was not on Maia's side of the street, I carried on walking in the traditional manner. I don't like getting young girls into trouble. Anyway, they had looked as if they would bash my head in if I interfered.

Around the corner, I did pass a group of vigiles sniffing for the smoke. My guess was they had had to endure rather a lot of tiny female arsonists since the Vestals' lottery was announced. The sooner the Pontifex Maximus pulled out a name, the better for everyone.

XVII

Fountain Court seemed quiet when Julia and I returned home. The sensible after-lunch drunks had collapsed on the side of the street with the dank shadows and old cabbage leaves. The daft ones opposite would have fiercely sunburnt foreheads, noses and knees when they woke up. A feral cat mewed hopefully, but kept well away from my boot. Disreputable pigeons were picking over what the down-and-outs had left them from the charred bread Cassius, our local baker, had chucked out when he shut up his stall for the day. Flies had found half a melon to torment.

There were empty stools outside the barber's shop. A thin pall of black smoke hung over one end of the street, reeking of burnt lamp oil; sulphurous fumes rose from the back of the laundry. I thought about checking how the goslings were, now they lived in the laundry yard, but Julia and I were weary after half a day doing nothing in particular. My neighbours were taking their usual siestas, which for most of those idlers meant all-day ones, so the man who walked up the street ahead of us stood out alone. I had seen him emerge from the funeral parlour, clearly repeating directions. I can't think why he had asked the undertakers for information, given the number of family mausoleums that end up containing urns with the wrong ashes due to those incompetents.

This fellow ahead of me was of average height, whiskery, hairy armed, brisk in his walk, dressed in a dark tunic and rather flappy calf-high boots. He checked outside the basket-weaver's lock-up as though he was going in there; then he skipped up the steps to the first floor apartment where I lived.

Whatever he wanted I was in no real mood for strangers, so

103

I stopped off to talk to Lenia. She was outside her business premises, in the part of the street she had commandeered for clothes-drying; the morning wash was twisting about on several lines in a slight breeze, and with an irritated expression she was listlessly straightening the most tangled wet garments. When she saw me, she gave up immediately.

'Gods, last day of May and it's too hot to move!'

'Talk to me, Lenia. Some beggar just went up to our house and I can't be bothered going to find out if he's someone who wants to annoy me.'

'Just now?' croaked Lenia. 'Some other beggar went up to look for you too.'

'Oh good. They can annoy one another while I have a rest down here.'

I leaned my backside against the portico. Lenia took Julia by both arms and practised walking her a few steps. Julia grabbed a dripping toga, with hands that had somehow grown more grubby than I had realised.

We heard a yell from the apartment.

'Who was your beggar?' I asked Lenia lazily.

'Young chap with purple trim on his tunic. Yours?'

'No idea.'

'Mine said he knew you, Falco.'

'Permanent look as if his breakfast is giving him gyp?'

'That's the pug-faced darling, by the sound of it.'

'Helena's brother. The one we don't care for. Sounds as if the man I followed home agrees.' The yelling continued. 'Helena isn't up there, as far as you know, Lenia?'

'Doubt it. She borrowed one of my washtubs. She'll drop it in when she comes home.'

'Know where she went with this tub?' I tried. Lenia just laughed.

There were a few more yells from opposite. I might have changed my mind and intervened, but someone else turned up to help with the heavy work, so I hid behind a wet sheet. It was Pa. As soon as he heard sounds of trouble, he rushed up the stairs to see the fun. He barged in and added his voice to the shouting, then Lenia and I watched him and Camillus Aelianus appear outside on the porch, grappling the man with the flappy boots. They were dragging him half on his knees, an arm apiece. Since they seemed to know what they were doing I just grinned to myself and let the officious pair get on with it.

They began forcing him down the steps, but soon found that holding him between them while they also descended was too difficult. As they all tumbled back to street level, inevitably they let him go. He made off. If he had come past me I might have shoved out a foot and tripped him, but his luck was in; he went the other way.

I winked at Lenia and sauntered across to the heroes who were offering mutual congratulations on the way they had saved my apartment from attempted robbery.

'I see you elected to show mercy,' I commented sarcastically, leading them indoors again. 'You let him go, very kindly.'

'Well we drove him off for you,' gasped Pa, who always took time to regain his breath after a fracas. Not that it ever stopped him, if he saw something stupid to join in. 'Jove knows what he thought he could lift from this place.' As a professional auctioneer, Pa lived amongst a treasure-trove of furniture and objects. He found our austere living quarters unsettling. Still, keeping our valuables in store at his ware-house meant Helena and I did not have to worry about losing them to some light-fingered Aventine low life. (That's assuming Pa himself kept his hands off our stuff; I had to check up on him regularly.)

'He was no thief,' I corrected quietly.

'He thought I was you, Falco,' Aelianus told me, sounding indignant. I was pleased to see his cheek was badly bruised. He tested it gingerly. The bones had stayed intact; well, probably.

'So you stopped a punch on my behalf! Thanks, Aulus. Good job you can handle yourself.'

'Who's this then?' demanded Pa, whose curiosity was notorious. 'Your new partner?'

'No. This is his brother, Camillus Aelianus, the next shining star in the Senate. My partner has very sensibly gone to Spain.'

'That should make it easy to combine your expertise,' Pa quipped. Justinus had no expertise for informing, but I saw no need to enlighten Pa that I had lumbered myself with an even more unsuitable colleague than Petronius or Anacrites. Aelianus might not yet have heard that his brother was setting up with me, because I saw him look askance. 'Were you expecting that riff-raff to drop in?' Pa then asked.

'Something like it, possibly. I reckon I was followed home last night – someone checking my address.'

'Gods!' exclaimed Aelianus, enjoying the chance to sound pious, while insulting me. 'That's rather thoughtless, Falco. What if my sister had been here today?'

'She's out. I knew that.'

'Helena would have bashed the intruder with a very heavy skillet,' Pa declared, as if it were his right to boast of her spirit.

'And made sure she tied him up,' I agreed, reminding the pair of their error. 'Then I could have found out who sent him to put the frighteners on.'

'Who do you think it was?' demanded Pa, ignoring the rebuke. 'You've only been back in the country about four days.'

'Five,' I confirmed.

'And you already managed to upset someone? I'm proud of you, boy!'

'I learned the art of upsetting people from you, Pa. I was the chosen target. But I think,' I said, making it pleasant for Aelianus, 'the rough message was really being sent to our friend here.'

'I never did anything!' Aelianus protested.

'And the message is *don't try it, either*,' I smirked. 'I suspect that you, Aulus, have just taken delivery of a hint to back off from offending the Arval Brothers.'

'Not those disasters?' groaned Pa in heavy disgust. 'Anything to do with the old religion makes my flesh creep.'

I pretended to be more tolerant: 'Fastidious father, you don't have a senatorial career to build from scratch. Poor Aelianus has to grit his teeth and enjoy cavorting about in a rustic dance waving ears of mouldy grain.'

106

'The Arval Brethren are an honourable and ancient college of priests!' protested their would-be acolyte. He knew it sounded feeble.

'And I'm Alexander the Great,' returned my father pleasantly. 'Those lads are ancient and as savoury as an old dog turd on the Sacred Way, waiting for you just where you plant your sandal . . . So what have you done to annoy them, Marcus?'

'We only asked too many questions, Pa.'

'Sounds like you!'

'You taught me to stir.'

'If this is the reaction, maybe you should stop, Falco,' suggested my beloved's brother, as if it had been all my idea.

'Don't let the bastards get away with it,' Pa counselled us. It was not his head the man had taken a swing at.

I opted for giving Aelianus the choice of whether we now backed down like good boys, reminding him that his father wanted him to obtain more evidence for political leverage; he decided to ignore his father, which – in the presence of my own – I could only applaud. Aelianus had been sent to see me by Decimus, but he now felt absolved from that duty and took his bruises home, where his mother was bound to blame his mishap on me.

Sometimes, dealing with the Camilli was even more complex than manoeuvring around my own relatives.

Pa snuggled up to the table where we normally ate, like a man who was hoping for a free dinner. He looked shifty. 'I got your message that you wanted to speak to me. Is this about Helena's project?' I was annoyed. If anybody else had given me this opener, I could have used it to discover what Helena had in hand. I resented Pa too much. 'Did she take up my tip about using Gloccus and Cotta, then?' *His* tip? My heart sank. 'Only I have heard since,' my father confessed uneasily, 'they may be going downhill a bit –'

Now this outfit really did sound dubious. 'I am sure,' I pronounced pompously, 'Helena Justina can sort out anyone who gives her trouble.'

'Right,' said Pa. He looked anxious. 'We should probably feel sorry for them.'

He jumped up. If he was leaving before he had tried to screw a meal out of me, he must be feeling even more guilty than usual.

I leaned on his shoulder and shoved him back on to the bench. When I told him I wanted to discuss help for Maia, he remembered a very urgent appointment; I made it plain he had to talk, or have his head stuffed in the door jamb. 'Look, we have a family crisis and it's down to us men. Ma can't do anything this time; she's already looking after Galla's brood financially –'

'Why should she? Bloody Lollius has not had a fight with a lion.' Now Famia was dead, Lollius probably ranked as the most horrendous of my brothers-in-law. He was a Tiber boatman, a foul bubble of riverbank scum. His one redeeming feature was his knack of keeping out of the way. It saved me having to think up new ways to be rude to him.

'Unfortunately not. But you know bloody Lollius is bloody useless, and even when he gives her any money Galla cannot be called a deft budget manager. Their children don't deserve to have been born to such terrible parents – but Ma drags the whole worthless crew through life as best she can. Look, Pa, Maia now has to find the rent, food, plus school fees for at least Marius, who wants a career in rhetoric – and she just found out that Famia never paid his funeral dues, so she even has to pay for a memorial to that scoundrel as well.'

Pa drew himself up, a broad, grey-haired figure with slightly bandy legs; forty years of fooling art purchasers helped him look convincing, even though I knew he was a fraud. 'I am not unaware of your sister's position.'

'We all know it, Pa – Maia most of all. She says she will have to work for that short-arsed tailor again,' I told him gloomily. 'I always thought the leery wretch had his eye on her.'

'Time he retired. He doesn't do much; he never did. He has all those girls who weave for him, and half the time they serve in the shop as well.' After a brief distraction while he felt jealous of the tailor's alluring young loom girls, Pa

108

became thoughtful. 'Maia would be perfect at running a business.'

He was right. I felt annoyed that he had first seen it – and Maia, who loathed Pa even more than I did, would have to be led extremely gently towards any idea which came from him. Yet we now had the answer, and to my surprise Pa actually volunteered to persuade the old tailor that he wanted to be bought out. Best of all, Pa offered to provide the cash.

'You'll have to make the fellow think it's his own idea.'

'Don't teach me how to do business, boy.' It was true that my father was extremely successful; I could not avoid knowing it. A brilliant talent for bluff had made him far richer than he deserved.

'Well, tomorrow is a public festival day, so you can shut up your shop –'

'I can't believe I heard that blasphemy! I never close for footling festivals.'

'Well do it this time and buzz off to strong-arm the tailor.'

'You coming with me?'

'Sorry; prior appointment.' I refrained from admitting I would have to manoeuvre fractious Sacred Geese. 'He won't let it go cheap, Pa.'

'Oh I've got funds – since you've spurned me!' (Pa had once offered to find me the money to support my bid for middle-rank status; there was no way he would ever appreciate that it was a measure of character when I earned the cash myself.) 'Leave this to me,' declared my incorrigible parent, throwing himself into being magnanimous as eagerly as he had once fled the family coop. 'You just enjoy yourself playing at being a gooseboy!' The bastard had just been waiting to thrill himself with this insult.

'Don't forget,' I retaliated: 'keep everything in your name for when some new chancer takes Maia's fancy. You don't want to wake up one day and find yourself financing Anacrites!'

Well, that brought him up short.

XVIII

Next day was the Kalends of June: there were celebrations for Mars and the Tempestates (goddesses of weather). It was also the festival of Juno Moneta. The day the geese were carried out in state to see the watchdogs crucified.

I prefer not to dwell on details of this bloodthirsty fiasco. Suffice it to say that when I came to make my report to the Palace as Procurator of the Sacred Poultry it would recommend extremely strongly that:

- To avoid cruelty to the animals and distress to very sensitive observers, the condemned watchdogs should be pacified with drugged meat before any attempt to nail them up.
- To prevent the Sacred Geese escaping from their ceremonial litter while acting as an audience, they too should be pacified with a dose of something, then tied down with jesses (which could be hidden beneath the purple cushions on which the geese traditionally sit).
- To clinch it, bars or a cage should be added to the litter.
- On the day before the Kalends, it should be the responsibility of the gooseboy to ensure that the wings of all Sacred Geese who would be taking part in the ceremony were adequately clipped so that they definitely could not fly away.
- Dogs from good homes (for instance, Nux) should be permitted to roam the Capitol in the control of authorised persons (say, me), without risk of being rounded up and held in custody under threat of being made part of the crucifixion ceremony.

- Innocent dogs who were accidentally apprehended should be returned to the charge of their authorised persons without having to be made the subject of a two-hour argument.
- The entire ritual of crucifying the 'guilty' guard dogs should be allowed to fall into abeyance as soon as possible. (Suggestion: to pacify die-hards, the cessation of this very ancient ceremony could be excused in our modern state as a compliment to the Celtic tribes, now that Gaul was a part of the Empire and the barbarians were no longer likely to attempt to storm the Capitol except in the form of tourists.)
- Every time the Procurator of Poultry attended the festival of Juno Moneta, he should be entitled to a serious drink allowance, at official expense, immediately afterwards.

XIX

Next day – four before the Nones of June, droned my calendar of festivals – happened to have no religious ceremonies assigned to it, and was a day on which legal transactions could occur.

I had an urgent message from Pa, to say he had persuaded the tailor to sell up, but the decision might prove temporary (or the price might go up) unless we pinned the man down and got his signature on a contract that very day. Pausing only to hope that when I folded my own informing partnership I would not be bludgeoned into it by an entrepreneur like my father, I fell to and took myself to my sister's house: Pa had decreed that convincing Maia she wanted to do what we had planned for her would be my task.

Her immediate reaction was suspicion and resistance. 'Olympus, Marcus, what's the hurry?'

'Your erstwhile employer may consult his lawyer.'

'Why – are you and Pa cheating him?'

'Of course not. We are honest lads. Everyone who deals with us says so. We just don't want to give him leeway to turn around and cheat us.'

'Everyone who deals with the pair of you, says "Never again!" This is my life you weasels are organising, Marcus.'

'Don't dramatise. We are giving you a healthy livelihood.'

'Can I not have at least a day to think this over?'

'We, the strong, benevolent males who are heads of your household, have done your thinking for you, as we are supposed to do. Besides, Pa says the next opportunity for legal business is days away, and we dare not wait. His legal assistant has drawn up a nice scroll and Pa wants to hear that you are happy for him to go ahead.'

'I don't want anything to do with Pa.'

'Excellent. I knew you would come round.'

Pa was right (I looked it up on my calendar). Thanks to the fine Roman attitude that lawyers are sharks who should be given as little encouragement as possible, there are usually only four or five days a month in which they are allowed to bamboozle clients. (Other nations might consider adopting this rule.) (Lawyers like it too, the lazy bums.) June offered particularly caring protection for the nervous citizen – though this was a trifle inconvenient if you were in league to do some bamboozling yourself. If we missed this chance, our next contract-signing day would be well after the Ides. I sent Marius to tell Pa that Maia was delighted.

My sister allowed Marius to leave but then, made even more contrary than usual by her bereavement, she changed her mind and wanted to scoot after him. Luckily, Marius was sharp enough to realise that to secure his future school fees, he must run very fast once he left the family home.

Helpfully too, Maia was intercepted by a visitor. As my sister bustled out of her front door with me tagging after her, we saw in the street the now familiar shape of the litter with the Medusa head boss that belonged to the Laelii. Considering that they wanted to avoid dealing with us, it was ploughing deep furrows between the houses of my family.

'Greetings, Maia Favonia!'

'Caecilia Paeta! Why Marcus, this is the mother of dear little Gaia Laelia.'

'Good heavens – well, she must come in at once, Maia darling –' (and I, your curious brother, must stay here to supervise . . .)

Caecilia Paeta was of slender build, dressed in rather heavy white clothes, with one dull metal necklace and nothing so irreverent as face paint to enliven her pallid complexion. Maia had claimed Caecilia squinted; in fact she suffered from severe short-sightedness, giving her that vague air of someone who misses anything more than three strides away and who pretends that nothing beyond her field of vision can really be happening. She had a thin mouth, a nose that looked better from the front than in profile, and a mass of under-nourished dark hair tied back in an old-fashioned style with a central parting.

She was not my type. (I had not expected she would be.) Of course, that did not prevent her being a woman other men would eventually warm to. (But probably not friends of mine.)

She looked nervous. As soon as a few listless pleasantries had been disposed of, she burst out, 'I know that you have visited our house. Don't ever tell Laelius Numentinus that I came here –'

'Why?' My sister was playing awkward. Maia had one eye on her door, still wanting to dash off after Marius so she could remonstrate with Pa. 'A girl has to go out and chat to her friends sometimes. A respectable matron should be trusted to have social contact. Are you telling us your father-in-law keeps you a prisoner?'

It was too much to hope that Caecilia had made a brave bid for freedom; she loved being safe in religious-flavoured oppression: 'We are a private family. When Numentinus was Flamen Dialis this was essential for the rituals, and he wishes to continue with the life he always knew. He is an old man –'

'Your daughter made an odd approach to my brother,' interrupted Maia bluntly. 'You are her mother. What do you think of her saying that someone wanted to kill her?'

'She told me too – and I then told her not to be so silly!' The woman appealed to Maia: 'Gaia Laelia is six years old. I was horrified to hear she had approached your brother –'

'This is my brother,' Maia finally remembered to inform her. I gave a polite salute.

Cecilia Paeta looked frightened. Well, informers have bad reputations. She may have been expecting a mean-eyed political reprobate. The sight of a normal, rather attractive fellow with spots of fish sauce down his tunic, being shoved down hard beneath his little sister's expert thumb, must have confused the poor woman. It often confused me.

'Gaia is rather over-imaginative. There is nothing wrong,' Caecilia said swiftly.

'So we have been told.' I found a snake-like grin. 'The Flamen Pomonalis insisted this to my wife, like a loyal and well-trained brother-in-law. Now you say it too. To feel absolutely certain, I would like to question Gaia herself again

– though the Pomonalis went to a great deal of trouble to inform us that she is much-loved and in no danger. So I imagine the same idea has been very thoroughly rammed into Gaia.' Caecilia's eyes did not blink. People who live in terror of tyrants do not flinch when threatened; they have learned to avoid annoying their oppressor.

'Is there,' I insisted, without much hope, 'any chance of me talking to Gaia?'

'Oh no. Absolutely not.' Aware that this sounded far too over-protective, Caecilia tried to soften it. 'Gaia knows what she told you was nonsense.'

'Well, you are her mother,' said Maia again wryly, like a mother who knew better. Still, even my hot-headed sister could be fair. 'She did seem thrilled with the idea of becoming a Vestal when she was talking about it to my daughter Cloelia.'

'She is, she is!' exclaimed Caecilia, almost pleading for us to believe her. 'We are not monsters – as soon as I realised something had made her unhappy I arranged for her to have a long talk with Constantia about what her life in the House of the Vestals would be –'

'Constantia?' I asked.

'The Virgin we all met at the Palace,' Maia reminded me grumpily.

'Right. Constantia is liaison officer for the new recruits?'

'She ensures the hopefuls hear the proper lies,' Maia returned with deep cynicism. 'She lays stress on the fame and respect Vestal Virgins receive – and forgets to mention drawbacks like living for thirty years with five other sexually deprived women, who all probably loathe you and get on your nerves.'

'Maia Favonia!' protested Caecilia, truly shocked.

Maia grimaced. 'Sorry.'

There was a silence. I could see Maia still writhing in frustration that she could not escape to run and deal with Pa. Caecilia seemed to have no clue how to continue or to break off this interview.

'Whose idea was it to put Gaia's name into the Virgins' lottery?' I asked, thinking about what had happened in my sister's family.

'Mine.' That surprised me.

'What does her father think?'

Her chin came up slightly. 'Scaurus was delighted when I wrote to make the suggestion.' I must have looked puzzled at the way she had expressed it; Caecilia Paeta added calmly, 'He no longer lives with us.'

Divorce is common enough, but one place I had not expected to find it was a house where every male was destined to serve as a flamen, whose marriage had to last for life. 'So where does Scaurus live?' I managed to sound neutral. Scaurus must be Gaia's father's name; it was his first hint of any personal identity and I wondered if that was significant.

'In the country.' She named a place that I happened to know; it was about an hour's drive past the farm my mother's brothers owned. Maia glanced my way, but I avoided her eye.

'And you are divorced?'

'No.' Caecilia's voice was quiet. I had the feeling she rarely spoke of this to anyone. The ex-Flamen Dialis would be outraged that she should. 'My father-in-law is strongly opposed to that.'

'Your husband – his son – was he a member of the priesthood?'

'No.' She looked down. 'No, he never was. It had always been presumed he would follow the family tradition, indeed it was promised at the time I married him. Laelius Scaurus preferred a different kind of life.'

'His break with family tradition must have caused great discontent, I imagine?'

Caecilia made no direct comment, though her expression said it all. 'It is never too late. There was always a hope that if we were at least only separated something might be salvaged – and there would be Gaia, of course. My father-in-law intended that she would be married in the ancient way to someone who would qualify for the College of Flamens; then one day, he hoped, she might even become the Flaminica like her grandmother . . .' She tailed off.

'Not if she is a Vestal Virgin!' Maia shot in. Caecilia's head came up. Maia's voice dropped conspiratorially. 'You defied him! You put Gaia into the lottery deliberately, to thwart her

116

grandfather's plans!'

'I would never defy the Flamen,' replied Gaia's mother far too smoothly. Realising she had given us more than she intended she prepared to sweep out. 'This is a difficult time for my family. Please, show some consideration and leave us alone now.'

She was on her way out.

'We apologise,' said Maia briefly. She might have argued, but she still wanted to be off on her own errand. Instead, she picked up the reference to it being a difficult time. 'We were, of course, sorry to hear of your loss.'

Wide-eyed, Caecilia Paeta spun back to stare at her. A rather extreme reaction, though grief can make people touchy in unexpected ways.

'Your family were attending a funeral when Maia came to visit you,' I reminded her gently. 'Was it somebody close?'

'Oh no! A relative by marriage, that is all –' Caecilia pulled herself together, inclined her head formally, and went out to the carriage.

Even Maia managed to wait until the woman had departed, so she could mouth at me, 'What's going on? That family is so sensitive!'

'All families are sensitive,' I intoned piously.

'You cannot be thinking of ours!' scoffed my sister – running off at last to hurl herself into a quarrel with Pa.

I went to see my mother, like a devoted boy.

It was a long time since I had driven Ma out to the Campagna to see Great-Auntie Phoebe and whichever she was currently harbouring of my unbelievable uncles: moody Fabius and broody Junius – though never the truly loopy one who had gone permanently missing, and of whom we were never supposed to speak. It would be easy to dump Ma at the family market garden for a long gossip, then to find something harmless to occupy myself.

I could, for instance, drive on a few miles to the place Caecilia Paeta had mentioned, and interview the estranged escapee father of little supposedly over-imaginative Gaia Laelia.

117

XX

'Helena Justina, a man who loves you ferociously is offering to jolt you for hours in a hot open cart, and then grope you in a cabbage field.'

'How can I resist?'

'You can surely leave Gloccus and Cotta on their own for just a day.'

Helena made no sign of hearing me mention the two names. 'Do you need me?'

'I do. I have to manage a mule, and you know how I hate that; I shall also require your sensible presence to control Ma. Anyway, if I don't produce you, Great-Auntie Phoebe will assume you have left me.'

'Oh why would anyone think that?' Helena knew how to deny it in a way I found faintly worrying.

'By the way sweetheart, Pa sent a message, in his devious style. He thinks you should know he has heard that Gloccus and Cotta are not all they were at the time he recommended them.'

Helena finally turned round from a pot she had been scrubbing with grit and vinegar. Her eyes blazed. Through set teeth she hissed, 'I really do not need anybody to tell me what Gloccus and Cotta are like. If I hear anyone else mention Gloccus and Cotta, I shall scream!'

It was from the heart. The picture at least had a chalk outline now. Pa had stuck her with a pair of his pet noodles; these boys had to be fixers in the building trade. I grinned and backed off.

It was now three days before the Nones of June, a festival of Bellona, Goddess of War: a deity to respect, naturally, but one with no direct poultry connections as far as I knew.

118

Another voting day, so it was handy to flee from the Forum before anyone grabbed me for jury service.

We made good time out to my relatives' disorganised patch of vegetable fields, where as usual the leeks and artichokes were struggling on their own, while the uncles busied themselves with lives of fervent emotional complexity. They were men of huge passions – grafted on to absolutely mediocre personalities. I stayed long enough to hear that dopey Uncle Junius had finally broken his heart over his doomed affair with a neighbour's flirty wife, and – after a terrible scene bang in the middle of the cress harvest – having failed to hang himself from a broken beam in the ox-harness room (which Great-Auntie Phoebe had repeatedly told him to mend), he had left home in a new huff over the ill-timed reappearance during a violent thunderstorm of his brother, Fabius, who had previously gone off in a huff over, I think, a crisis about what he did in life (since what Fabius actually did was to cause trouble in the lives of other people and then hang around apologising, his huff had been encouraged by everyone else). All much as usual. The two brothers had a lifelong feud, a feud so old neither of them could remember what it had been about, but they were comfortable loathing each other. I had not seen Fabius for years; he had failed to improve.

Ma took Julia from us and settled in to shake heads with Phoebe over the lads and their troubles. Nux came with me. Nux had become anxious and clinging after the episode on the Capitol where she was arrested by the priestly acolytes who were looking for doggies to crucify. In addition to that, a succession of nasty male curs had occupied our front porch recently, suggesting Nux was on heat; this too was making her behaviour unstable. I was annoyed; acting as midwife for my own child had been enough of a disturbing experience, one I was not keen to resume for a bunch of pups.

Helena knew I was checking up on the Laelius family, so once we dropped off Ma, she came on with me.

A hot June morning, ambling along with a mule who was tired enough to do as I instructed, feeling Helena's knee against my own, and Helena's lightly clad shoulder nuzzling my arm. Only the wet nose of Nux, squeezing between us from the back of the cart, spoiled what could have been an idyll.

'Well, here we are peacefully travelling together,' mused my beloved. 'Your chance to lull me into telling what my secret is.'

'Would not dream of it.'

'I expect you to try.'

'If you need to share your troubles, you'll come out and say so.'

'What if I really want you to squeeze the story out of me?'

'Child's stuff. You are far too serious,' I proclaimed piously. 'I love you because you and I never have to descend to such games.'

'Didius Falco, you are an aggravating swine.'

I smiled at her fondly. Whatever she was doing, I trusted her. For one thing, if she really wanted to deceive me, there was no way I would ever have noticed that anything was happening; Helena Justina was too clever for me.

I had my work. It tended to be a solitary occupation. She helped when it seemed appropriate – and sometimes when it was so dangerous I felt terrified that she was involved – but she deserved stimulus of her own. Even when our lives were separate, I would always seize any chance to extract her and take her apart so that we could lose ourselves . . .

Part of our early courtship had taken place in the countryside. It seemed a nostalgic treat to roll around with her while hard lumps of vegetation were sticking in our backs. Still, nostalgia is a dish for the young.

'*Ow!* Jupiter, let's just concede that we have a bed at home. Fun's fun – but we're grown up now.'

Helena Justina looked at me tenderly. 'Didius Falco, you will never be grown up!'

Nux, tied up to the cart, started to howl.

Anyway, it was later than it might have been when we found the farm. It was a neat smallholding that looked well run, though barely capable of supporting more than the people who were living there. They had rows of summer salad crops, occasional poultry pottering about in a soft fruit orchard, a couple of cows, and a large friendly pig. Two geese wandered out to greet us; I could have done without them.

The farm dogs sniffed out the presence of Nux within minutes. Tying her up would only have made her a sacrificial victim. I tied them up instead. Then I carried Nux, preserving her canine chastity however fiercely she tried to squirm. Helena said it would be good practice for when our daughter grew up.

This smallholding seemed designed as a Roman intellectual's retirement home, after the patronage ran out; from here he could write bucolic notes to his friends in town, praising the simple life where his table was set with just runny cheese and a lettuce leaf (while hoping some civilised visitor would bring him gossip, memories of sophisticated women, and a decent flask of wine). However, if Laelius Scaurus was, as I supposed, in his thirties, it seemed early for him to be giving up on city life.

We found a bent-backed aged retainer who pushed a hoe about. He looked happy to see us, but we got no sense out of him. All my prejudice against the country was rising fast. First my peculiar uncles, and now a rural slave who left his brains behind on a shelf when he went out of doors. Then things looked up. A girl appeared.

'Well!' I grinned at Helena. 'I can manage on my own now if you want to go and rest in the mule cart.'

'Forget it!' she growled.

The smallholding girl had a round face, with a big mouth, and swiftly emerging dimples. Her smile was willing; her figure fulsome; her nature friendly and open. Her eyes were dark and promising and her hair was tied up with blue ribbon. She wore a loose natural cream gown that had a few unravelled sections in the seams through which her burnished skin was clearly visible. Wherever could Scaurus have found her, leading his austere life as a flamen's son?

'He has gone to Rome.'

'Can't be parted from the Forum?' I asked.

'Oh he goes to and fro. Last time he sneaked a visit to his sister. This time he had a letter from his wife.' At least she knew about the wife. I would not have liked to think this shining young lady was the victim of cruel deception. 'He could have gone yesterday, but he held back because it was a legal day, and he was afraid they might make him sign something.'

'Like what?' I smiled. Her friendliness was extremely infectious.

'Oh I don't know.'

'And you are?' enquired Helena, rather sternly.

'I am Meldina.' Very nice. I managed to hold back the comment that she had a pretty name. It always sounds like a trite old pick-up line, however genuinely meant. I was in a difficult enough situation, trying to hold on to a skilfully wriggling dog who had hopes of a country romance.

From then on, I let Helena take on the questioning while I just controlled Nux and watched admiringly. (I mean – of course – only that I was admiring the skill of my dear girl's questioning.) 'How long has Laelius Scaurus lived out here?'

'About three years.'

'As long as that! And have you lived here all the time?'

'Mostly.' Meldina gave us an especially big smile. 'It's very nice out here.'

We all looked around. It was a picture of country perfection. If you were talking in terms of perspective, the foreground was particularly fine, due to the presence in it of Meldina's large-scale charms.

'Let me guess,' Helena said gently, in a tone that was unlikely to give offence: 'you would have been a Laelius family freedwoman?'

'Oh no!' Meldina sounded horrified. 'I had nothing to do with that lot. My mother was a freedwoman of his aunt's,' she corrected. This rather complicated definition implied that there had been no pressure on her to move here with Scaurus; freeborn herself, she had come of her own choice. Nonetheless, I wondered whether the aunt had encouraged her; such an attractive girl might have been too much of a favourite with Auntie's husband, maybe.

'Did you know Scaurus before he moved out to the country?' Helena was seeking to discover whether it was his friendship with Meldina that had caused Scaurus' estrangement from his wife.

'No, afterwards. Still,' smiled the girl (who never really stopped smiling), 'we are pretty settled now.'

'No chance of him divorcing his wife, presumably?'

'Never. His father has forbidden it.' As we thought.

'Excuse me asking all these questions,' Helena said.

'Oh that's all right. I'll talk to anyone.' What a refreshing attitude. I wondered how far Meldina's accessibility went. It seemed unlikely that she stinted much. Helena was giving me a stern look, for some reason. 'What did you want to see Scaurus about?' Meldina asked, also throwing a look my way. I was a man of the world; I could handle that. On the other hand, I might not be able to handle Helena after this incident.

'We wanted a word about his young daughter – little Gaia. We had an encounter with her that left us feeling concerned.'

'Funny little tot,' said Meldina, with a delicious frown. 'I've met her a few times. His aunt brings her out here to see him.'

The aunt had featured sufficiently for Helena now to fix on her. 'When you say his aunt, that wouldn't be Terentia Paulla, I suppose?' I was surprised by this, until reminded of a conversation at Helena's parents' house about this woman; she had been the sister of the late Flaminica: 'My grandmother knew her from the Bona Dea Festival,' Helena explained. 'Terentia is a Vestal Virgin isn't she?'

'That's the right aunt. But she's not a Virgin any more!' Meldina was giggling. 'Didn't you know? She retired at the end of her thirty years – then upset everyone by marrying!'

Retired Vestal Virgins could do that, in theory. It rarely happened since it was thought unlucky for a man to marry an ex-Virgin. Since she would probably be past childbearing age, a bridegroom would have to place a higher than usual premium on virginity to think it worthwhile. Any quick thrill from bedding a Vestal would be outweighed by then gaining a tyrant who came with thirty years' experience of ruling the roost.

'Good heavens!' exclaimed Helena, with spirit. 'Grandmother never told me that!'

'You are shielded from anything scandalous,' I intervened.

'Oh he can speak!' trilled Meldina.

'Far too much,' sneered Helena. 'I only bring him out with me to carry the lapdog. Well, retired Vestals are allowed to take husbands, but people do always look askance . . . I cannot say Grandmama liked Terentia much,' she tried.

'Oh didn't she?' The girl continued to look bright and helpful, though she was definitely deflecting the question this time. She was being loyal. To whom? I wondered.

Helena let it go and changed her approach. 'Meldina, did you know there is a plan for young Gaia Laelia to follow Terentia and become a Vestal too?'

'Yes, Scaurus said his wife came up with that.'

'He has given his consent?'

'I suppose so.'

'I just wondered if that was why he went to Rome today?'

'Oh no. His aunt wants him. He said it was to help with her affairs.'

Helena paused. 'I'm sorry; I must have misunderstood something. I thought you said Laelius Scaurus went to Rome after receiving a letter from his wife, not his aunt?'

Meldina's smile became broader than ever. 'Well, that's his lot all over, isn't it? His auntie wants him, but his wife wrote and told him that his father had decided Scaurus was not to know anything about it.' She grinned. 'Scaurus has gone to Rome to kick up a right stink!'

XXI

We stayed overnight with my relatives. The beauteous Meldina had promised that if Scaurus returned, she would send him to talk to us. She said this with a frightening air of certainty. I was used to being won over with much subtler manoeuvring but I could see that a man brought up in an atmosphere of repression might welcome a girl who was so firm. The poor wimp would feel secure.

Ma and Great-Auntie Phoebe were vying with each other in exclaiming dolefully that this might be the last time they ever saw one another. According to these two tough old birds, feeding a bone to Charon's dog in the Underworld was just a day away for each of them. Myself, I gave them both another decade. For one thing, neither could bear to depart life while Fabius and Junius were still providing them with disasters to deplore.

Fabius, the present homeboy, had been told about my new position as Procurator of the Sacred Poultry. 'Oh you must come and see what I am doing with our chickens, Marcus. This will interest you —'

My heart sank. While my Great-Uncle Scaro lived here, he too was full of crazy schemes and inventions, but Scaro had the knack of convincing you that when he showed you some weird piece of carved bone that looked like a pot-bellied pigeon, he had discovered the secret of flight. Any prototype produced by Fabius or Junius was bound to be of a more meagre dimension and their mode of expressing enthusiasm had all the vigour of a very old rag rug. Whichever one backed you up against a manger for a lecture, the result was torture.

My grandfather and Great-Uncle Scaro (both long passed away) had built the original hen yard, a large enclosure

125

which they had covered with nets and lined with coops, and where in good times they had nurtured upwards of two hundred birds. A woman and a boy lived alongside in a hut, but my uncles were the world's worst managers of staff (either seducing them, feuding with them, or totally neglecting them), and so the birds were badly managed too. Reduced to forty or fifty in total during the recent reign of Uncle Junius, the flock had lived pleasantly, hardly ever troubled by having eggs removed or birds killed for the family pot. Now that Junius had run off somewhere, Fabius had plans to change all that.

'I am fattening them for sale scientifically. We are going to be thoroughly organised.' Nothing about my uncle was scientific or organised, except when he went fishing. His note-tablets of tedious data on fishes caught, location and weather, variety, length, healthiness, and bait used took up a whole shelf in the kitchen food cupboard, forcing Phoebe to keep her pickles at the back of the bucket store. Otherwise, Fabius could hardly put on a pair of boots by himself; he would get stuck after the first one and worry what to do next.

Fabius now had a large clutch of hens in a dark building where they were individually confined, some in cribs along one wall, some in special wicker containers with a hole fore and aft for the head and the tail. They were lying on soft hay, but packed so that they could not turn round and use up energy. Here the hapless fowl were being crammed with linseed or barleymeal kneaded with water into soft pellets. I was informed it took just under four weeks to bring them up to a good marketable size.

'Is this regime cruel, Fabius?'

'Don't talk like a soft townee.'

'Well, be practical then. Is their flavour as good as the ones who run free?'

'People don't pay for flavour, you know. What buyers look at is size.'

This astuteness must be why the Romans thought so highly of their agricultural forebears. In mine, I was descended from true masters of the land. No wonder Ma, like that smelly old peasant Romulus, had escaped to the city life.

Against the constant clucking of the birds, Fabius relentlessly detailed his financial projections, which led him to the conclusion that in two years he would be a millionaire. After an hour of tosh, I lost my temper. 'Fabius, I have heard this before. If every get-rich scheme that came out of this family had worked, we would be a legend among the Forum banking fraternity. Instead, we just go downhill from year to year – and our reputation stinks.'

'The trouble with you,' said Fabius, in his maddeningly grave way, 'is that you never want to take a risk.'

I could have told him that my life was based on hazard, but it seemed cruel to boast when his own was grounded in hopelessness.

I always liked visiting the country. It reminded me why my mother had been so keen to get away that even marrying Pa had seemed worth it. It refreshed my view of the joys of city life. I always went home a true Roman: full of my own superiority.

XXII

The day before the Nones of June: the festival of Hercules the Great Custodian. A voting day.

At first, it looked as if Laelius Scaurus would not show. That's a common drudgery in the world of informing. I had spent half my life waiting for time-wasters who made no attempt to keep appointments.

Now the misery was aggravated by Helena's mockery: 'Meldina fooled you! She looked so desirable, grinning at you as she was bursting out of her tunic – she couldn't possibly be lying, could she?'

I went along with it. 'Seems she is so busy being a fertility goddess, she has no time to pass on simple messages.'

'Or maybe Scaurus is still stuck in Rome,' Helena conceded.

'Oh I expect he's back here. He just sees me as an interfering outsider: that's a family trait,' I said.

'And true, of course.'

Having seen both his pallid wife and his sumptuous girlfriend, I reckoned Scaurus would cut short his city visit. In his position, there were better pleasures on the farm. But I kept that to myself. I'm not stupid.

I hung about a while longer, discussing with Phoebe whether she could take in one of my young nephews, one of Galla's brood who needed to be lifted from Rome before life on the streets was the ruin of him. Ma sat in the cart, ready to go, pursing her lips and pronouncing that Galla would never agree to let Gaius leave home, even if it was for his own good. She had a point. I had already extracted his elder brother Larius and left him enjoying life as an artist at the Bay of Neapolis, so my sister now saw me as a child-thief. For some reason, Great-Auntie Phoebe had faith in my

aren't you?' It was too much to expect this dry stick to retort with the old *So my wife tells me* joke. 'I don't know if you managed to see your young daughter when you were in Rome?' I said.

'I saw all my family,' he answered me gravely. As a runaway son he was about as exciting as a bowl of cold dripping.

I decided to be blunt. 'I heard your aunt sent for you. Do you mind telling me why you had been summonsed?'

Scaurus looked up at the sky nervously. 'No, there can be no real objection –' I bet his father would have found one. 'My aunt, who is widowed, wishes me to be appointed as her guardian. I am Terentia Paulla's only surviving male relation.'

For information retrieval, usually a slog, this was quick going. Only yesterday we had heard that, on her retirement, Terentia Paulla had married. Today I learned that her husband had already passed away. It would be fun to think the man had had a seizure during the excitement of his wedding night with a Vestal – but more likely he was an old bird of ninety-three who went his way naturally. I was too delicate to ask Scaurus.

So now Terentia wanted Scaurus, her late sister's son, to act for her? In my family solitary aunts ran their own affairs, and did it with a grip of iron. My Aunt Marciana could zing beads along their wires on her abacus with a verve any money-changer would envy. But the law reckoned women were incapable of managing anything except the colours of their loom wool, so legally, especially where there was property, a woman was supposed to have a male friend or relative take charge of her. A woman who had borne three children became exempt (quite rightly, scoffed most of the mothers I knew). The aunt of Laelius Scaurus, being an ex-Vestal, presumably had no children. Once again, it seemed indelicate to speculate openly.

'You don't look too happy,' I commented.

Scaurus was frowning and looked ill at ease with my line of questioning. 'I daren't do it. I have never been emancipated from my father's patriarchal control.'

I already knew that his family was rent by quarrels; now the aunt's request added one more disruptive element. 'Your father is an ex-Flamen Dialis and he wishes to keep to the old rules. He will not change his mind?'

'No, never.'

'Could he look after your aunt instead of you? A guardian does not have to be a blood relative.'

'They hate one another,' said Scaurus, as if this was natural.

'No friendly freedmen she could turn to then?'

'That would be inappropriate.' Presumably because she had been a Vestal; some women were less squeamish about ex-slaves. A freedman had a duty to his patroness which could mean more, to be frank, than the affection felt by true relatives. Sometimes a freedman and his patroness were lovers, though of course I could not suggest that of a Vestal.

'So how did you sort it out, Scaurus?'

He hesitated. Perhaps he thought it was none of my business. 'My aunt will pursue the matter. I have to return to Rome in twelve days' time –'

'Twelve days?'

'The next time for legal action.' After Pa's urgency in sorting out my sister Maia, I should have remembered that. What Laelius Scaurus was planning with his auntie's connivance, however, turned out to be far more astonishing than our mere attempt to buy a business: 'An approach will be made to the Praetor to name me as *sui juris* – free to conduct my own affairs. If that fails, we shall petition the Emperor.'

I whistled. 'Fast going! Your aunt,' I said admiringly, 'seems to be more than capable, if she thought all this up.' He looked vague. I rather liked her idea: 'Pleading that she must have a male adviser is legal, reasonable and modest. If the issue goes to the Emperor, he has her interests at heart, since as Pontifex Maximus the Vestals are his direct responsibility. He must treat a retired one with heavy respect. As Pontifex, he out-ranks your father too.' I could see only one possible wrinkle. 'You don't suppose the Emperor will elect to act as your aunt's guardian himself?'

132

That would be seen as suitable, though it would not help Laelius Scaurus escape from his father's control – and it could mean the aunt acquired a guardian who would expect to be her heir too. Many did. And Vespasian was famously grasping.

Scaurus looked as if I was rushing him. 'If it happens, it happens.' A shade of humour propelled him on: 'The Emperor may feel that my aunt is a handful.'

'Ex-Vestals do tend to be forceful,' I sympathised. He was frowning again uneasily. Talking to him was like trying to clean cooking oil off a table. Every time I thought I was making headway the surface dried out to reveal the same old sheen. 'I take it she does not frighten you?' He looked as if she did. 'You're a grown man. There cannot be too much work or anxiety in running the lady's estates.'

'My aunt is very fierce.' Scaurus spoke woodenly. I guessed she was making a monkey of him in some way. But that was often the case when a patrician woman assigned her guardianship to some poor cipher who was then supposed to humour her.

'Bear up. Terentia Paulla must have great regard for you. Look, I hope you don't mind me asking this, but if you remain in your father's legal control you cannot yourself hold property. Does that mean somebody else owns the farm that you and the delightful Meldina occupy?'

'My aunt,' he confirmed, unsurprisingly. A pattern had emerged here. If I was any judge, the ex-Virgin and the ex-Flamen were enjoying a hot feud and were using poor Scaurus as one of their weapons. He was a limp foil to two tremendously strong characters.

What a terrible family. They made mine look perfectly normal.

I reminded myself that my interest was supposed to be in a child. I already believed little Gaia was also being used – by her parents, Scaurus and Caecilia, in their own struggle to thwart the old man's plans. Where did the aunt fit in there?

'I suppose Terentia Paulla must be delighted that your daughter is – fortune willing – to follow her career at the Vestals' House?'

An odd look crossed the face of the child's father. 'Actually, this is the one subject of difference between my dear aunt and me. I believe it would be an honour – and one in the traditions of my family – but my aunt for some reason is very strongly opposed.' He gave me a direct stare.

'Terentia objects? Why?'

'That is a long story,' said Scaurus. He had previously seemed like dough anyone could knead – yet he was as slippery as any other devious swine. 'And it is our family business, if you don't mind. I understand the Pontifex Maximus will conduct the lottery three days from now, so the matter will then be settled. Was that all you wanted to say to me, Falco? I promised Meldina I would not be away from home too long today.'

'You must have finished, Marcus!' shouted Ma from the cart. And so I took the hint. We bade Scaurus farewell. He drove south again to his luscious companion; we set off northwards towards Rome.

I gave Helena Justina a brief account of my interview. Her reaction was scathing: 'Save us from the intervention of loving aunts!'

'Your grandmother recognised a Virgin to avoid,' I agreed. I then listed for Helena all the caring actions of Terentia Paulla in her late sister's family – well, all the ones we knew about: 'Terentia was always at odds with her sister, the late Flaminica, over the Flaminica's having a lover; yet Terentia seems to have made a favourite of her sister's son. It can't be popular with his family. Three years ago she provided the means for Scaurus to leave home and live on her farm; by doing that she ensured he will never satisfy his father by joining a priesthood – and when he escaped he left his wife. If the family in Rome have heard about Meldina – who is connected to Terentia through her mother – it won't help. Terentia now courts more trouble by naming Scaurus as her guardian against his father's wishes. She is planning legal action, which at the very least will drag the ex-Flamen's name to public notice – we can guess how he will feel about a lurid *Daily Gazette* court report. If the action is successful, it may remove Scaurus from his father's authority.'

'Virgins who break their vows of chastity are buried alive,' Ma scoffed. 'It sounds as though this one should have been buried somewhere deep the instant she retired.'

'I have a feeling,' Helena answered, 'that whatever this woman has done or said – or whatever she is planning – may be at the heart of what was troubling Gaia Laelia.'

If she was right, a dreamy soul like Scaurus hardly seemed an adequate guardian of the lady's affairs. Nor did he inspire me in his role as father to a disturbed and rather isolated six-year-old. 'Well, we may have to accept that it is none of our business. Not one of these people is a paying client of mine.'

'When did that stop you?' muttered Ma.

'The little girl asked you for help,' Helena reminded me. Then she paused, looking thoughtful. I knew her well enough to wait. 'There is something madly wrong about that legal tale Scaurus spun you.'

'It sounded reasonable to me.'

'But for one thing.' Helena had made up her mind and was highly indignant. 'Marcus, it's complete nonsense – a Vestal Virgin is exempt from the rules of female guardianship!'

'Are you certain?'

'Of course,' Helena rebuked me for doubting her. 'It is one of their famous privileges.'

My mother's mouth tightened. 'Total freedom from male interference! The best reason for ever becoming a Vestal, if you ask me.'

'Of course,' said Helena, calming down as she became interested in the problem, 'it is always possible that the ex-Vestal in question has to have a guardian for special reasons. She may be disposing of her property in a brazenly profligate manner.'

'Or she may be a lunatic!' Ma chortled wickedly.

But Terentia Paulla sounded too good an organiser for that to be the case.

'So,' I pondered, with a certain amount of annoyance, 'Laelius Scaurus is either an unworldly booby who has utterly misunderstood something his aunt has said to him – or he has just bamboozled me with a pack of outright lies!'

But why should he do that?

I had let Scaurus go and we were too far down the road for me to drive back and challenge him. Besides, I really had to think about Gaia. Tomorrow was the Nones of June. In two days' time, as any conscientious procurator knew from consulting his calendar of festivals, would begin a period that was sacred to Vesta, including two great days of ceremony called the Vestalia. The women of Rome would progress to the temple to beg the goddess for favour in the coming year; there would be elaborate cleansing ceremonies for the temple and its storehouse. The start of these events this year was when the Pontifex Maximus had elected to draw lots for the next Virgin, after which it seemed likely that Gaia's fate would be fixed. Even if I did attempt to help her, I had only three days left. After that, the girl might well be removed from the oppression and strife of her family; but she would be sweeping up embers from the Sacred Hearth for the next thirty years.

Her father's aunt, who had carried out the duties for a full term, thought this a bad idea. Well, she should know.

XXIII

The Nones of June was dedicated to Jupiter, Guardian of Truth. Naturally, this was my favourite manifestation of the Best and Greatest of gods. Truth, in the life of an informer, is such a rare phenomenon. In case there were any ramifications for me in the festival, I made damned sure I stayed away from the big temples on the Capitol.

I had now been home from Africa for about ten days. I had expected that private clients who had need of an informer would have heard this with relief, and would start queuing up for my expert advice. Prospective clients thought otherwise.

There were three reasons to accept this calmly. Firstly, my supposed new partner, Camillus Justinus, was abroad and unable to share the task of rebuilding the business. If he offended his girlfriend's rich relatives in Corduba they might extract her and leave him so desolate he would go off on Herculean adventures for the next ten years. If Claudia's grandparents took to him too much, however, they might set him up as a married man, permanently growing olives in Baetica. Either way, if I ever saw him again, I would be lucky. But until I knew the result for certain, I was hampered in honing my business plan.

Secondly, I had rented an office in the Saepta Julia when I worked with Anacrites, but I dumped that when I dumped him. Once again my nominal office was my old apartment in Fountain Court, still occupied by Petronius Longus since his wife left him. Any person who needed to employ an informer was likely to have reasons to keep their private life unofficial on all fronts; they would be horrified to arrive for a consultation and find a large specimen of the official vigiles in his after-hours tunic, swigging a drink, with his feet up on the balcony parapet. I could not evict Petro. Instead I currently interviewed any clients who did turn up at my new apartment. Many a craftsman's lock-up in Rome is overrun by children; it may be fine if you only want to buy a bronze tripod with satyrs' feet, but people dislike being interviewed about their life-or-death problems while an energetic baby hurls porridge at their knees.

Thirdly, for the first time ever I could view all this without much urgent concern. Anacrites and I had achieved so much in our work for the Great Census that I had no pressing financial worries.

Yet that in itself was disturbing. I would need to get used to it. For the past eight years, since I had persuaded the army that it wanted to release me from legionary service, I had lived in fear of starvation and being thrown on the street by my landlord. I had once felt unable to marry, for dread of dragging others down with me. I had lived in filth. I lacked leisure and intellectual refinement. I had been forced into work that was dangerous and demeaning. So I drank, dreamed, lusted, complained, conspired, wrote gauche poetry, and did all that informers are reckoned to do by those who insult them. Then in Britain, on my first mission for Vespasian, I had met a girl.

For a man who sneered at snooty women, I had thrown myself into wooing Helena Justina with a wholeheartedness that appalled my friends. She was a senator's daughter and I was a street rat. Our relationship seemed impossible – a wondrous attraction to a fellow who liked challenges. She at first hated me: another lure. I even thought I hated her: ridiculous.

The story of how we came to live as we did now, so much more closely and companionably than most people (more, especially, than my turmoiled clients) would fill a few scrolls for your library. That Helena loved me was one mystery. That, even though she cared, she chose to endure my way of life was even stranger. We had lived for short periods in my old apartment, the one Petronius now filled with his mighty frame when he forced himself to return for a night's sleep under the leaky tiles. We had briefly shared a rental in a building that was 'accidentally' demolished by a crooked developer – fortunately when neither of us was at home. And now we lived in a three-room first floor sub-let, from which we had removed the obscene wall frescos and to which we imported our child's screams and our own laughter, but little else.

I had long harboured grandiose fantasies of owning a mansion – in a few decades, when I had time, money, energy, motive, and the name of a trustworthy real estate vendor (well, the last criterion ruled it out!). More recently Helena Justina had talked of acquiring somewhere spacious enough for us to share with her younger brother, whom we liked, and whose young lady (if she stuck with him) was as pleasant as we could hope for. I was not sure I liked anyone enough to endure a joint tenure of my home. Apparently, it was a closer possibility than I had thought.

'While we have the mule cart on hire,' Helena announced, looking only slightly sheepish, 'we could drive out tomorrow and look at this house I bought.'

'This is the house that I know nothing about, I suppose?'

'You know it is.'

'Right. If a man takes up with a formidable woman, he has to expect some curtailment of his domestic liberties. A whole house has been bought for me, without anybody telling me the street or the locality, showing me the site plan, or even, if I may be so coarse as to raise this, Helena, mentioning the price.'

'You will like it,' Helena assured me, sounding as if she had begun to doubt that she liked the place herself.

'Of course I will, if you chose it.' I was often firm. Helena had always ignored firmness, so it might have seemed pointless, but the statement made it clear who would be blamed if we were stuck with a bummer.

As we were. I could already tell.

Because of the daytime wheeled-vehicle curfew in Rome, after we took my mother home that evening we hitched the mule in Lenia's laundry and planned to rise very early in order to leave just before dawn. After a few hours' sleep at our apartment, I dragged myself awake the next morning only reluctantly. We put Julia and Nux in the back of the cart, still both asleep in separate baskets, and set off through the silent streets like defaulters doing a bunk.

'This seems to be the first disadvantage. Our house is miles outside town?'

'I was told that the distance is walkable.' Helena looked miserable.

'Time to own up, lady. Is that true?'

'You always said you wanted to live on the Janiculan Hill – with a view over Rome.'

'So I did. Very nice. I saw a superb gangster's house there once – mind you, he had excellent reasons for guarding his privacy.'

The house Helena had bought was the other side of the Tiber: secluded, you could say. If it had a view as she promised, I knew it must be an upland property. Every day when I returned home in the evening (I would obviously not bother nipping back just for lunch as I did now), the last part of the walk would be up a steep hill. I could manage that, I told myself. I had lived all my life on the Aventine.

'We can afford our own litter now,' Helena ventured nervously as we drove past the Theatre of Pompey and rattled over the Agrippan Bridge. This was already further out of the city than I normally enjoyed tramping.

'If you want a social life, we'll need one each.'

The house had tremendous potential. (Those deadly words!) Renovated – for it was suffering about twenty years of total neglect – it could end up truly beautiful. Airy rooms led from lofty corridors; attractive interior peristyle gardens separated pleasingly proportioned wings. There were good polychrome geometric mosaic floors in the principal rooms and hallways. Old-fashioned, slightly faded frescos posed interesting problems of whether to keep them or invest in more modern designs.

'It had no bath-house,' Helena said. 'There is a spring, luckily. I don't know how the previous owners managed. I thought it was essential to have our own facilities.'

I gulped. 'Gloccus and Cotta?'

'How did you guess?'

'They sound likely candidates for a job that can easily go wrong. I don't see them here.' I could, however, see their various piles of ladders, litter, and old lunch crusts. They also had a large trade plate advertising their services, which had pushed over the welcoming herm at the entrance gate. No doubt they would re-erect Hermes for us before they finally left.

I jest. The situation was clear to me. These were, without question, boys who left a trail of destruction in their wake. Snagging, in this contract, would mean employing a major contractor to put right everything that these smaller folk had done wrong – and all they had ruined which they should never have touched. There was nothing new or surprising in this situation. It is carefully worked out in the builders' guild. It is how they perpetuate their craft. Every time one comes in and ruins your home, the next in the chain is guaranteed work. Don't try to escape. They know every trick the luckless householder can pull. They are gods. Just leave them to get on with it.

'Gloccus and Cotta are never here,' Helena replied in a taut voice. 'That, I am forced to admit, is their big disadvantage. If I tell you I bought this house before we went to Africa –'

I smiled gently. 'We went in early April, didn't we? We were there nearly two months?'

'Gloccus and Cotta were supposed to build the bathhouse while we were away. It was a simple construction on a clean site and they had told me they were free to programme it in. It was to take twenty days.'

'So what happened, fruit?' She was so dismal it was easy to be kind to her; I could wind her up later, once she had provided the ammunition.

'I expect you can imagine.' She knew how I was playing this. Helena, who was a stalwart girl, took a deep breath and recounted the odyssey: 'They were late starting; their previous contract overran. They have to keep returning to Rome for more materials – disappearing for the rest of the

141

day. They need money in advance, but if you pay them up front as a courtesy they take advantage and vanish again. I gave them a clear list of what I wanted, but every item they supply is different from what I chose. They have broken the white marble bowl I ordered specially from Greece; they have lost half the tesserae for the hot-room floor – after the first half were firmly laid, of course, so the rest cannot now be matched. They drink; they gamble, and then fight over the results. If I come here to work on other parts of the house, they interrupt me constantly, either asking for refreshments or announcing that I have a problem with the design that they did not foresee – Do stop laughing.'

'What's the fuss about?' I was now openly doubled up with mirth. 'These seem like prime delights from the world of contracting – and what's more, Pa found them!'

'Don't mention your father!'

'Sorry.' I took a grip. 'We can sort this.'

Helena was beginning to show her panic and despair. 'Marcus, I cannot get anywhere with them! Every time I take them to task, they just admit they have let me down in an intolerable fashion, apologise cringingly, promise to apply themselves diligently from now on – then vanish from sight again.'

I had caught her eye. Relief at involving me was softening her tragedy. It was a mess, but now she could cry over it into my tunic braid. Just knowing that she could admit the truth to me was making her brave. 'Good thing you live with a man who never beats you, Helena.'

'Oh I am grateful for that. I would be happy if you restricted any teasing too.'

'Ah, no chance, sweetheart.'

'So I thought.'

Looking rueful, she let me caress her flushed cheek. She was wearing a dark red dress with a bevy of bracelets to hide her scarred forearm where a scorpion had bitten her outside Palmyra. Due to our early start that morning her fine dark hair was simply tucked in the neck of her tunic; I reached round and started pulling it loose. More relaxed, Helena leaned her head against my hand. I gathered her close and turned her round to survey the property.

It was the hour of the morning when the sun's heat first begins to strengthen as it fires up for a blazing day. We gazed at the fine two-storeyed house, with its satisfying rhythms of repeated arched colonnades below shuttered windows on the upper floors. The exterior façade was regular, and so fairly plain, with small red turrets on each corner and a porch with low steps and two thin pillars to break up the frontage.

A nervous white dove fluttered on to the pantiles; probably it had nested messily up in the warm roof space, though the roof in fact looked sound.

The grounds, in which the famous bath-house was not being built, hosted a terrace with stone pines and cypresses, unkempt topiary dotted through a sloped area, and near the house the usual box hedges and trellises. Gravelled paths, with most of the gravel missing, led in a determined way from gate to house and then wandered about the gardens, pausing now at the detached site of what Helena had planned as the bath-house. What the property lacked in pools and fountains would provide plenty of scope for a schemer like me to design and install them (and tear them out again after a child fell in). It was very peaceful here.

I twisted my belt around so the buckle would not dig into Helena as I held her tight against me, looking over her shoulder and nuzzling her neck. 'Tell me the story.'

She sighed. 'I liked it as soon as I saw it,' she said, after a moment, speaking quietly and with the direct honesty I had always adored in her dealings with me. 'I bought it for you. I thought it would delight you. I thought we would enjoy living here as a family. It was in decent condition, yet there was plenty we could do to make improvements in our own taste when we had time and the inclination. But I see it is a disaster. You cannot be so far from Rome.'

'Hmm.' I liked it too. I understood just what had made Helena choose this place.

'I can sell it again, I suppose. Build the bath-house, then pass it on as a "newly renovated home of character – fine views and own baths". Somebody else can discover that Gloccus and Cotta have failed to install a working soakaway.'

'And that the new hypocaust leaks smoke.'

Helena squirmed around to look at me in horror. 'Oh no! How can you tell?'

I shook my head sadly. 'When boneheads like Gloccus and Cotta install them, they always do, love. And they will leave the wall flues blocked up with rubble – and quite inaccessible –'

'No!'

'As sure as squirrels eat nuts.'

She covered her face and groaned. 'I can already see the scroll with the new owner's compensation claim.'

I was laughing again. 'I love you.'

'Still?' Agitated, Helena broke my hold on her and stepped back. 'Thank you very much – but that's avoiding the issue, Marcus.'

I caught her slender hands in mine. 'Don't sell it yet.'

'I have to.'

'We'll get it right first.' This suddenly seemed urgent. 'Don't jump too quickly. There's no need to –'

'We have to live somewhere, Marcus. We need space for a nursemaid for Julia, and help in the house –'

'Whereas this house needs a whole cohort of slaves; you would have to send a troop down into Rome every day just to shop at the markets – I like it. I want you to keep it while we consider what to do.'

Her chin came up. 'I should have asked you first.'

I looked around again at the gracious house in its sun-drenched grounds, overlooked by the worried white dove who could see we were people to reckon with. Somehow, it put me in a tolerant mood. 'That's all right.'

'Most men would say I should have consulted you,' Helena commented quietly.

'Then they know nothing.' I meant that.

'Nothing I suggest ever frightens you, or makes you lose your temper. You let me do whatever I like.' She sounded quite puzzled, though she had known me long enough not to feel surprise.

Doing what she liked had brought her to live with me. Doing what she liked had led us on greater adventures than

144

most men ever share with their dull wives.

I winked at her. 'Just so long as what you like is what you do with me.'

We stayed all day on the Janiculan. We walked round taking measurements and making notes. I made loose doors secure; Helena swept out rubbish. We talked and laughed a lot. If we were selling the place, it was theoretically a waste of our time. We did not see it that way.

Gloccus and Cotta, the keen bath-house contractors, never showed.

XXIV

I went over to Ma's house to tell her what I thought about the new house. (Helena came too, to hear what I said.) Trouble was waiting: the damned lodger was at home.

'Don't make a noise! Anacrites is off colour. The poor thing is having a wee snooze.'

That would have been fine, but warning us woke him up. He emerged eagerly, knowing that I would rather have left without seeing him.

'Falco!'

'Oh look; every perfect day has its low point, Helena.'

'Marcus, you're so rude! Good evening, Anacrites. I am sorry to hear that your wounds have been troubling you.'

He did look drawn. He had been suffering from a near-deadly head blow when he went out to Tripolitania, and the sword slashes he took while playing the fool in the arena were a further hindrance to his recovery. He had lost far too much blood in Lepcis; it had taken me hours to bind him up, and all through the trip home I had expected to find myself chucking his corpse over the side of the ship. Well, a boy can hope.

Ma fussed around him now while he tried to look brave. He managed; I was the one who nearly threw up.

He had forced himself to come off his couch still in his siesta wear – a bedraggled grey tunic and battered old slippers like something Nux might bring me as a treat. It was far from Anacrites' normal sleek gear: a hideous glimpse of the man behind the public persona, as unsuitable as a domesticated lynx. I felt embarrassed being in the same room as him.

He scratched his ear, then beamed. 'How is the new house?'

I would have given a good chest of gold to prevent him knowing my potential new address. 'Don't tell me you had your sordid operatives tail us there?'

'No need. Your mother always keeps me up to date.' I bet the bastard knew about the house before I did. Loyal to Helena, I bit that back.

Ma was bringing him invalid broth. At least that meant we all got some. It was stuffed with the vegetables she had pinched from the market garden yesterday.

'I am so well looked after here!' Anacrites exclaimed complacently.

I gritted my teeth.

'Maia was here today,' said Ma, as I wielded my spoon morosely. I saw Anacrites take an interest. Perhaps he was just being polite to his landlady. Perhaps he wanted to upset me. Perhaps he did have an eye on my newly available sister. (Dear gods!) Ma pursed her lips. 'I heard all about this plan you cooked up with your confederate.'

I decided not to mention that buying the tailor's business was my hated confederate's plan. My mother had guessed, I could tell. Whether she also knew it was Pa's money buying it for Maia I dared not even contemplate.

'It seems an ideal solution,' Helena backed me up firmly. 'Maia needs an occupation. Tailoring is what she knows, and she will thrive on the responsibility.'

'I'm sure!' sniffed Ma. Anacrites was keeping quiet in such a tactful way I could have rammed his broth spoon down his throat. 'Anyway,' my mother went on with great satisfaction, 'nothing may come of it.'

'It's all fixed, as far as I know, Ma.'

'No. Maia refused to agree unless she was given time to consider it. The contract was not signed.'

I put down my spoon. 'Well, I tried. The children need a future. She ought to consider that.'

Ma relented. She was a fierce defender of her grandchildren. 'Oh she's intending to do it. She just wanted to make it clear she does not jump when your father orders it.'

It was so rare for my mother to mention my father that we

147

all fell quiet. This really was embarrassing. Helena kicked me under the table, as a signal for us to leave.

'I say, Marcus,' Anacrites interrupted the awkward silence suddenly. 'I did find out what that lad you sent was asking.'

I replaced my backside on the bench from which I had lifted it tentatively. 'Someone I sent? What lad?'

'Camillus, what's his name?'

I glanced at Helena. 'I know two lads called Camillus. Camillus Justinus helped me rescue you from your due fate in Lepcis Magna – Anacrites, I presume not even you are so ungrateful as to forget him –'

'No, no. The other, this must be.'

'Aelianus,' Helena said coldly. Anacrites looked disconcerted. He seemed unaware that both Camilli were Helena's younger brothers and that he himself had actually cultivated Aelianus as a useful contact once. His head wound had affected the patterns of his memory.

I was annoyed. 'I never sent him or anyone else to see you, Anacrites.'

'Oh! He said you did.'

'Playing at mystery men. Have you forgotten you do know him? For some reason you and he were cuddled up like long-lost cronies last year at that dinner for the olive oil producers – the night you took your big crack on the head.'

Now Anacrites had definitely lost his bumptiousness. He chewed his lower lip. I had established in previous discussions that he remembered nothing about the evening he was battered. This troubled him. It was rather pathetic. For a man whose career involved knowing more about other people than they chose to tell even their mistresses and doctors, losing part of his own memory was a terrible shock. He tried not to show it, but I knew he must lie awake at night, sweating over the missing days of his life.

I had not been too cruel. He knew something about that night, because I had told him: he had been found unconscious, was rescued by me and taken to a safe house – Ma's – where he lay semi-comatose for weeks while she nursed him. But for her, he would be dead. You could say – though

I was carefully too polite to do it – he also owed his life to me. I had made sure his jealous rival at the Palace, Claudius Laeta, could not find him and help him into Hades. I had even tracked down those responsible for attacking him and, while Anacrites still lay helpless, I had brought them to justice. He never thanked me much for that.

'So I know him,' mused Anacrites, struggling to recover some feel for the past contact.

'You had been talking to him about what was going wrong in Baetica.' Helena took pity on him. 'At the time my brother had been living there, working with the provincial governor. He was only a passing contact of yours. You cannot be expected to recall it particularly.'

'He didn't remind me.' Anacrites still had a dark, disturbed look. He had held a discussion with a man who failed to disclose their previous relationship. There must seem a frightening lack of logic in that. I knew the reason, as it happened: Aelianus wanted to cover up a serious error of judgement on his own part. While delivering a document to the intelligence chief, he had let it fall into the wrong hands and be mangled. Anacrites had never found out, but once he saw that the Chief Spy had forgotten him, Aelianus would have happily played the stranger.

'Young tease!' I let Anacrites see me smirking. 'He's playing games,' I condescended to explain. ' I imagine he told you that one of the Arval Brethren has died in ghastly circumstances. Aelianus is annoying the cult by looking for a conspiracy.'

The conspiracy might be real, but if so I was annoyed that the young fool had alerted Anacrites. Aelianus and I were playing this game – and the spy would have to ask very nicely indeed before I let him join in.

'So what did Aelianus want?' Helena put to him.

'A name.'

'Really?'

'Stop acting, Falco,' Anacrites snorted. He was Chief Spy, as I had found out when we worked on the Census, because he did have some discernment.

I grinned and gave way. 'All right, partner. I suppose he

149

asked if you know who the dead Arval Brother is?'

'Right.'

'You have an identification?'

'None, when Aelianus raised it. The secretive Brethren had succeeded in keeping their loss under wraps. I was impressed!' he admitted, for once mocking himself gently.

'And did you and your cunning trackers then find out?'

'Of course.' Smug bastard.

'Well then?'

'The dead man was called Ventidius Silanus.' I had never heard of him. 'Mean anything?' prompted Anacrites, warily watching me.

I decided against bluff. I leaned back and threw open my hands frankly. 'It means absolutely nix.'

It was his turn to grin. 'Same here,' he confessed, and he too gave every appearance of speaking with a rare burst of honesty.

XXV

Rome was at her best. Warm stone, limpid fountains, swifts screaming at roof height; a resonance in the evening light that no other city I have ever visited seems to possess.

We had returned the mule cart to the hiring stable, so we were now on foot. As Helena and I walked home from Ma's house, both thinking in silence about our new Janiculan property, the streets on the Aventine remained lively without yet becoming dangerous. It was still light enough and hot enough for the day's commercial and domestic activities to be continuing, while the night-time whores and housebreakers had hardly begun to swarm. Even narrow alleyways were almost safe.

Julia Junilla lay asleep on my shoulder with a dead weight that reminded me of carrying cut turves for temporary ramparts in my army days. Ma always managed to tire the baby out. Nux trotted beside Helena, looking coy. Seven dogs of various shapes and sizes but all with one intent relentlessly trailed Nux.

'Our girl's definitely in season,' I commented glumly.

'Oh good – pups!' Helena sighed.

We lost a few followers outside a butcher's shop where scraps had been piled in the gutter. We would have lost Nux too, once she noticed what the curs were at, but Helena grabbed her as she nosed a particularly foul piece of discarded entrail. We dragged her off, paws scrabbling furiously on the lava slabs, then I picked her up and clamped her under my free arm. The dog howled for help from her sleazy admirers but they preferred slavering over bits of bloody bone and sweetbread.

'Forget them, Nux; men are never worth it,' commiserated Helena. I ignored the seditious girl-talk. I was

151

carrying the family treasure, and likely to lose my grip if I forgot to concentrate. Once again I remembered the army: anyone who had humped his quota of military equipment on a Marian Fork halfway round Britain – javelins, pickaxe, toolbag and contents, earth-moving basket, mess tins and three days' rations – could manage a baby and a dog for a few strides without raising a sweat. On the other hand, a military kettle does not thump you in the ribcage or try to slide off your shoulder; well, not if properly stowed.

In Fountain Court someone was having chargrilled escalopes for dinner – more charred than grilled, by the smell of them. Dusk had fallen now. Shadows of the looming tenements made the way treacherous. A solitary lamp burned on a hook outside the funeral parlour, not so much for the benefit of passers-by as to allow the unshaven staff to continue playing a game of Soldiers they had scratched in the dust. That tiny circle of light only served to make the narrow corridor of our street more dim and dangerous. Broken kerbstones harboured slithery vegetation on which it was easy to skid to a bone-breaking fall. We trod cautiously, knowing that every stride took our sandals into a morass of dung and amphorae shards.

Helena said that she would take charge of bathing the baby; we normally did this at the laundry, using any unwanted warm water after Lenia closed up. I decided to go upstairs and see Petronius. I had to tell him about the Janiculan house before he heard of it elsewhere.

His boots were lying askew under the table in the outer room; he was outside the folding doors, lazing in the last rays of sunlight on the balcony. This always gave me a jar. It was too reminiscent of my own bachelor life. I half expected to find some tasselled dancing girl sprawled in his lap.

He was having a drink. I could cope with that. He let me find myself a beaker and pour my own tipple.

'Been to your new house?' So much for telling him.

'Everyone in Rome seems to have known about it, except me!'

He grinned. He had reached the benevolent phase of dreaming on a bench after dinner. Remembering how easy it was not to bother preparing a platter for one, I guessed he had not had much dinner, in fact, but that just brought the dreamy phase forwards. 'So long as the rest of us liked the idea, why trouble you, my son?'

'Well, the plan is a dud. Helena now thinks we cannot live so far out of town.'

'Why did she buy the place then?'

'Probably the rest of you, who were in on the secret, forgot to point out the disadvantages.'

'Well is it a nice property?'

'Wonderful.'

We swallowed our drinks in silence for a while. I heard familiar women's voices down below at street level, but supposed it was Helena talking to Lenia. Lenia was probably sounding off about the latest horrors imposed on her by her ex-husband, Smaractus, the landlord who owned this block. I cradled my cup, thinking what an evil, insanitary, money-grubbing, tenant-cheating insult to humanity he was. Petronius had his head lolling far back against the apartment wall behind us, no doubt pondering hatreds of his own. His cohort tribune, probably. Rubella: an ambitious, unscrupulous, discipline-mad, tyrannical hard man who – according to Petro – could never wipe his bum with a latrine sponge without consulting the rules to see if a ranker was supposed to do it for him.

Footsteps scuffled outside. Petro and I both sat quite still, both suddenly tensed. You never knew here whether visitors were bringing you bad news or just a battering. *He* never knew if they were unwelcome manifestations of his own life and work, or some violent hangover from when I had lived here.

Someone came through the door into the room behind us. The steps were light and quick, even after mounting six flights of stairs. The person emerged through the folding doors. I was nearest; I stayed motionless, though ready to jump.

'Gods, you two are still a disreputable pair!' We relaxed.

'Evening, Maia.' We were not drunk, or even lightly dishevelled. Still, all my family liked to be unfair.

I wondered why my sister would be visiting Petronius. I

153

knew him well enough to tell when he was nervous; he was wondering the same.

Petro raised the flagon, offering. Maia seemed tempted, but then shook her head. She looked tired. Almost certainly she needed solace, but she had four children relying on her at home.

'Helena said you were up here slumming, Marcus. I can't stop; Marius is downstairs, inspecting that terrible dog of yours. He wants to know if there's a puppy yet. I'll murder you for this –'

'I am doing my utmost to keep Nux chaste.'

'Well, speaking of chaste maidens, I heard something today that I thought you would be intrigued to know,' said Maia. 'I was talking to one of the other mothers whose daughter is in the Vestal Virgins' lottery like my Cloelia. This woman happens to know Caecilia Paeta socially and had visited their house this afternoon. She's more welcome there than I am – but then her husband is some sort of Temple of Concord priest – well, I may be unfair to the man; perhaps he's a decent step-washer . . . Anyway, she told me she found all the Laelii running about in a fine tizz, and though they want to pretend publicly that there's nothing amiss, she knows why. Something has happened to Gaia Laelia.'

I sat up. 'Are you going to tell us?'

Maia had relished the tale up to this point. Now her voice stilled with genuine concern. 'They have lost her, Marcus. She has absolutely vanished. Nobody knows where the child is.'

XXVI

It was none of our business. At least, that was what we would be told by the Laelii. Anyway, there was little we could do at that late hour.

Petronius said he would escort Maia and her young son back home, not that Maia thought twice about the risk. Helena and I went straight to bed. All of us hoped, as you have to when a child is lost, that by morning everything would have resolved itself and Gaia would have turned up, leaving the adventure to become just one of those never-forgotten stories people retell every year around the fire at Saturnalia to embarrass the victim. But when a missing person is a child who has said that her family wants her dead, it evokes a bad feeling however calm you try to stay.

Next day, Maia went early to see her friend, the mother who had told her the news. Anxious herself, the woman had already called to see Caecilia Paeta, Gaia's mother. The child had not come home. The family were making light of it publicly.

Helena then visited the Laelius house with Maia – as matrons offering sympathy – but they were briskly rebuffed at the door.

Children lose themselves for all sorts of reasons. They forget the way home. They stay with friends without bothering to tell anyone. Occasionally, though, they have made sinister friends nobody knows about, and are lured to dangerous fates.

Children like to hide. Many 'lost' children are found again at home: stuck in a cupboard or head-down in a giant urn. Usually they have managed not to suffocate.

Sometimes girls are abducted for brothels. Petronius Longus muttered to me in an undertone, that in the disgusting stews where anything goes there would be a very unpleasant premium on a six-year-old from a good home, who was known to be a potential Vestal Virgin. As soon as Maia reported next morning that the child was still missing, he took it upon himself to put out an immediate all-cohort alert.

'You are my star witness, Falco. Description of the child, please?'

'Jupiter, how do I know?' Suddenly I felt more patient towards all the vague witnesses I had previously yelled at for giving me incompetent statements. 'Her name is Gaia Laelia, daughter of Laelius Scaurus. She is six years old; she's small. She was well dressed, with jewellery – bangles – and her hair fixed up –'

'That can be changed,' Petro said grimly. If she had been snatched by brothel-owners, disguising her was the first thing they would do.

'Right. Dark hair, dark eyes. Well-spoken, confident. Pretty –'

Petro groaned.

Perhaps against his better judgement, he decided to tell Rubella, his cohort commander, what was happening. He could not ignore the possibility that Gaia had been kidnapped to order. That would mean all the girls whose names were in the lottery might be potential targets too.

Rubella first told Petronius he was off his head. Despite that, the sceptical tribune immediately took himself to see the Prefect of the Urban Cohorts. At least the Fourth would be covered if there was any fallout later. Should the Prefect take this story seriously, his next step would probably be to ask the office of the Pontifex Maximus – the Emperor, of course – for a full list of the young girls in the lottery so all their parents could be warned. Since the Laelius family wanted to pretend this was a slight domestic problem that nobody need know about, I thought things were escalating dangerously. But in view of their social prominence, they would not be surprised that the story had been leaked.

*

Time counts. The Laelii were ignoring that. Even if little Gaia were just trapped in a store cupboard in her own home, they needed to hold a systematic search. They had to start now. Petronius and I could have instructed them how to go about it; we were frustrated by our inability even to approach those involved. But a Flamen Dialis was as close to the gods as you could get in human form, and a retired one could be just as arrogant. Laelius Numentinus had represented Jupiter on earth for thirty years. Both of us knew better than to tackle him. Petronius was too lowly a member of the vigiles, and his superiors had firmly told him to make no approach unless or until the Laelii directly requested help. As for me, I was the upstart in charge of the Capitoline geese – and Laelius Numentinus had made it plain what he thought of that.

It was now eight days before the Ides of June. Tomorrow the festival of Vesta would begin. Today had no sacred connections at all. As Procurator of Poultry, I had no demands on my time. When Helena and Maia returned, furious, from their abortive mission to offer sympathy at the Laelius residence, I was ready with a ploy to outflank that secretive family. It involved a visit to a very different house, one that was even more carefully closed to the public: the House of the Vestals at the end of the Sacred Way.

XXVII

It was not too far to walk, down from the Aventine via the Temple of Ceres, around the end of the Circus Maximus at the Cattle Market end, and into the Forum below the Capitol in the shadow of the Tarpeian Rock. We took the Sacred Way past the Basilica, turned under the Arch of Augustus between the Temples of Castor and Julius Caesar, and at about the mid-point of the Forum came to the Virgins' sanctuary. On our left the Regia, once the palace of Numa Pompilius, the second King of Rome, and now the office of the Pontifex; on our right the Temple of Vesta; beyond the temple, established between the Sacred Way and the Via Nova, the House of the Vestals.

Helena had escorted me, acting as a chaperon. We had brought Julia, though left Nux with Maia, who reluctantly agreed to safeguard her from the attentions of lecherous dogs. With us came Maia's daughter Cloelia, on condition that she never left our sight in case she had been marked by Gaia's abductors, should they exist. My plan was to consult the Virgin Constantia; Cloelia would be able to identify Constantia if I had to beard her when she was among the other respected ones solemnly engaged in their duties for the day.

I was wearing my toga. My late brother's toga, I should say. It had had a long life. Helena had wrapped it around me with much muttering that now I was respectable I must buy a new one. Being respectable would be expensive, apparently. But you do not approach a Virgin in a stained tunic with its neck braid hanging loose.

You may wonder why I did not simply call at the House of the Vestals and enquire if the lady would see me. There was no point trying. I knew she would not. Vestal Virgins are allowed to speak to people of rank in the course of their respected work. They will take in a consul's will for safe keeping, or appeal to the Prefect of the City in a crisis – but they have the same prejudices as anyone. Informers are way off their acceptable visitors' list.

Maia had looked at me very suspiciously when I suggested taking Cloelia. She suspected I wanted to pump her daughter for information. As we walked down to the Forum, I did tackle the child.

Helena gripped her hand. Clopping along in her rather large sandals (Maia expected her to grow into them), Cloelia looked up at me, expecting trouble. She had the Didius curls and something of our stocky build, but facially she resembled Famia most. The high cheekbones that had given her father's features a tipsy slant could, in Cloelia's finer physiognomy, make her strikingly beautiful one day. Maia had probably foreseen trouble. She could handle it, or at least make a fierce attempt. Whether her daughter would agree to be steered on a safe course was yet to be seen.

'Well, Cloelia; you have become a celebrity since I last saw you. How did you enjoy being taken to the Palace of the Caesars to meet Queen Berenice?'

'Uncle Marcus, Mother told me not to let you ask me a lot of questions, unless she was there.' Cloelia was eight, far more mature than Gaia had been, less obviously self-assured with strangers, but in my view probably more intelligent. I was no stranger, of course; I was just crazy Uncle Marcus, a man with a ridiculous occupation and new social pretensions, whom her female relations had taught her to scoff at.

'That's all right. You just may be able to help me with something important.'

'Well, I'm sure I don't know anything,' smirked Cloelia. She was a typical witness. Anything she did know would have to be screwed out of her. If Helena had not been watching with a disapproving glare, I might have tried the normal inducement (offering money). Instead, I could only grin gamely. Cloelia fixed her eyes ahead, satisfied that I was in my place.

159

'Suppose I ask the questions,' suggested Helena. 'What did you think of the Queen then, Cloelia?'

'I didn't like the scent she smelt of. And she only wanted to talk to the right people.'

'Who were they?'

'Well, not us, obviously. We stood out a bit. My mother's dress was much brighter than all the others; I had told her it would be. She did it on purpose, I suppose. And then I had to keep telling everyone my father works among the charioteers. Well, Helena Justina, you can imagine what they thought of that!' She paused. 'Used to work,' she corrected herself in a quieter voice.

I took her other hand.

After a moment, she looked up at me again. 'I can't be a Vestal now, you know. We had to be examined to ensure we were all sound in every limb – and they told us the other particular was that you have to have both parents alive. So you see, I don't qualify any longer. Neither Rhea nor I ever will. Anyway, it's probably better if I stay at home and help Mother.'

'True,' I said, feeling nonplussed as I often did. Maia's children were more grown up in some ways than our own generation. 'Tell me, Cloelia, did you meet the little girl called Gaia Laelia?'

'You know I did.'

'Just testing.'

'She was the one who might be selected.'

'By the Fates?'

'Oh Uncle Marcus, don't be so silly!'

'Cloelia, I don't mind if you believe state lotteries are fixed, but please don't tell anyone that I said so.'

'Don't worry. Marius and I have decided we won't ever tell anyone we even know you.'

'You think Uncle Marcus is a scamp?' asked Helena, pretending to be shocked. Cloelia looked prim. 'You and Gaia Laelia became quite friendly, didn't you?'

A scornful expression crossed my niece's face. 'Not really. She is only six!'

An easy one to miscalculate. For adults the little girls were a single group. But they ranged in age between six and ten, and within the hierarchies of childhood rolled enormous gulfs.

'But you did talk to her?' Helena asked.

'She was lonely. Once we could all see she had been singled out, none of the other girls would speak to her. Of course,' said Cloelia, 'after they thought about it, there were some who would have swarmed all over her. She could have been very popular. But then their mothers got sniffy and grabbed their precious darlings close to them.'

'Not your mother?'

'I dodged her.'

Helena and I exchanged a quick glance. We had slowed our pace through the Forum Boarium but we were now passing the Basilica Julia, fighting our way through the crowds that always milled on the steps in a haze of overused hair pomade.

I decided to be frank. 'Cloelia, as your mother has probably told you, something bad may have happened to little Gaia and what she talked about to you may help me help her.'

'We just played at being Vestal Virgins.' Cloelia had been ready for me. 'All she wanted to do was pretend to be fetching water from the Spring of Egeria and sprinkling it in the temple like the Virgins have to do. She just kept on playing the same game. I got really bored.'

'Before that, didn't she throw a little tantrum when she was sitting on the Queen's lap?'

'I don't know.'

'You didn't hear what it was about?'

'No.'

'Did you think Gaia was happy to be put forward as a Virgin?'

'I suppose so.'

'Did she say anything to you about her family?'

'Oh she wanted me to know how important they all were.' I waited. Cloelia considered. 'I don't think they have much fun. When my mother came to see if I was all right, Gaia saw her wink at me. Gaia seemed very surprised a mother would do that.'

'Yes, I met her own mother. She is very serious. I don't suppose Gaia said anything about wanting to run away from home?'

'No. You don't tell people you are going, or you get stopped.' Maia would be horrified to think Cloelia had thought about it.

'Right. So you don't think she was in any trouble at home?'

'I can't tell you any more,' Cloelia decided. The briskness with which she ended the interview was significant. Unfortunately, I could not push my eight-year-old niece up against a wall and yell at her that I knew she was lying. I was being glared at by Helena and I was too frightened of Maia.

'Well, thank you, Cloelia.'

'That's all right.'

'Maia is right,' said Helena, frowning at me sternly. 'You should have asked her permission to question Cloelia. I know how I would feel if it was Julia.' Cloelia nodded agreement, ganging up.

'Hold on, both of you. I'm not a total stranger. Now Famia is dead I am Maia Favonia's head of household –'

Helena laughed uproariously; so did Cloelia. So much for patriarchal power.

I knew when to shut up.

We had reached the Temple of Vesta anyway. Destroyed in the Great Fire in Nero's time, it had been quickly rebuilt, still on the ancient model: a mock round hut. In fact it was now a solid marble construction, standing on a high, stepped podium and surrounded by the famous columns and carved latticework. Smoke wreathed through a hole in the circular roof from the Sacred Fire below. At present the temple doors were open. Praetors, consuls and dictators would sacrifice before this flame upon taking up office, but a mere Procurator of Poultry would have to find a damned good excuse before he dared approach the sanctum.

Within the temple I knew there was never an image of Vesta, only the hearth representing the life, welfare and unity of the Roman state, shaded by a sacred laurel tree. Also

162

there was the Palladium, an obscure article said by some to be an image of Athene/Minerva though others doubted it; whatever it was, the Palladium acted as a talisman protecting Rome, and guarding it was one of the main tasks entrusted to the Virgins. Since the public was kept out by a walled enclosure, the chances of the precious talisman being spirited away by some light-fingered wrongdoer were slim. You could not sell it, anyway. Pa once told me that since nobody knew what it looked like, the Palladium had no value as collectable art.

The Vestals were attending to their chores as we arrived. They were one short in number of course, the position to be filled by tomorrow's lottery. Five of them, led by the pouchy-eyed Chief Vestal who looked as if she were having trouble with hot flushes nowadays, were here in their old-fashioned white woollen dresses, tied under the bust with girdles in Hercules knots that would never be unfastened by lovers, their hair bound up in bridal complexity and fastened with bands and ribbons. They had to tend the flame, since if it ever died it was an ill omen for the city; they would be scourged for the offence by the Pontifex Maximus, currently Vespasian, who was known for his strict views on traditional virtues. They also had to carry out daily purification rites, which would include sprinkling water from the Sacred Spring all round the temple. (One of them emerged carrying the ritual mop made from a horse's tail with which they performed this function.) Later they would be busy making salt cakes for religious purposes. They would say prayers and attend sacrifices, with veiled heads.

Each Vestal was attended by a lictor. Since even the Praetor's lictor was obliged to lower his ceremonial fasces if a Virgin approached, the Vestals' lictors were notoriously cocky. The maidens themselves might represent the antique simplicity of life enjoyed by a king's daughters back in the mists of time, but their modern guards were never slow in coming forward to stamp on your foot. These men were lounging in the enclosure, which it was possible to enter, though doing so caused suspicion even of a perfectly respectable procurator accompanied by his serene patrician wife and a demure female child. Inside the complex were an ostentatiously large shrine and the guarded entrance to the Vestals' House. It was perfectly clear I stood no chance of reaching the house or of bypassing the lictors to get into the temple. All I could do was to stand with my womenfolk, looking pious, while the Virgins paraded from the temple straight inside their menacing home. Cloelia kicked me when one of the younger dames passed by, to let me know that was Constantia.

Helena Justina marched boldly to the entrance gate and requested a formal interview. She even said she had information that touched on the forthcoming lottery. Her name was taken by an attendant in that bureaucratic manner that means *don't bother to stay at home waiting for a messenger*.

We stood around for a while like stale bread rolls after a party. Eventually we decided to leave, for a change making our way up the long stairway that led to the Via Nova in the deep shade of the Palatine. At the top of the steps I turned and looked back for a moment, because the view over the Forum is worth a breather any day. Suddenly Helena grabbed my arm. People were now coming out of a door in the back of the Vestals' House. A small group headed by a lictor had emerged, at the centre of which was the Virgin who must be on that day's rota to fetch water from Egeria's Spring for the House of the Vestals itself (to which no proper piped water had ever been led). Bearing on her head one of the special pitchers that the Vestals had to use, by good fortune today's water-carrier was Constantia.

As the white-clad maiden made her way along the well-trodden route, Cloelia grabbed Helena and me by the hand and towed us along after her.

XXVIII

Past the dust and commotion of the huge building site for the Flavian Amphitheatre and then beyond the massive plinth for the Temple of Claudius which Vespasian was also at last completing out of gratitude to his political patron, lay the Caelian Hill. This quiet, wooded haven looks south over the Capena Gate and the Circus Maximus. It is one of the most ancient, unspoiled parts of the city, the rocky hillside rich with springs. They were originally the province of water goddesses called the Camenae, but the nymph Egeria, saucy lass, rather usurped their dominance. Here is the famous grove where King Numa Pompilius consulted (his word for it) the darling nymph night after night while she (he alleged) dictated political edicts to him; here too is the spring named after his lovely, helpful muse, to which the Vestals daily traipse.

Egeria's Spring must have been extremely handy for the Palace of King Numa. He would not have had too long a stroll in his search for inspiration. (One more example, Helena explains to me, of a dumb but well-intentioned man in power being brought to greater glory than he ever deserved by a much more intelligent ladyfriend.) Egeria kept old Numa going strong to over eighty, anyway.

Constantia approached the ancient watering hole with the stately gait that her sisterhood cultivates. Carrying a water vessel on the head is supposed to improve the posture; it certainly draws attention to a full womanly figure in a way that is not supposed to happen with the damsels in white. Having a girdle tied in a Hercules knot right under a well-rounded bust is bound to draw attention to the bust. Generations of Vestals have probably been well aware of this. Constantia no doubt viewed such thoughts with disdain. She looked to be in her early twenties; she must have completed the first ten years of learning her duties and was now equipped to carry them out in a reverential – though slightly distracting – style.

While Constantia was filling the pitcher, Helena Justina took Cloelia by the hand and – with gestures to me to wait behind – they walked sedately forwards. Helena addressed the Virgin by name. The lictor immediately told Helena to get lost. Offered the threatening points of his ceremonial rods, she backed away.

Constantia, perhaps long practised, had ignored the small flurry as her petitioners were discouraged. Now the pitcher was full it was much heavier; she needed to concentrate. She swung it up on to her head, straight-backed and superior. I began to appreciate that the complex arrangements of braids worn by the Virgins might actually make a coiled mat to support their water jars and save them bruised heads. Eyes straight ahead like a tightrope walker, the Vestal moved to retrace her steps back to the Forum. She held her free arm very slightly apart from her body for balance, but mainly swayed gently as women in far-off provinces do as they visit wells outside their mud-hut villages, appearing to enjoy their carrying skills.

The stones around Egeria's shrine were green with slimy algae. Constantia seemed to be prepared for trouble. When her foot slipped, she regained her balance with commendable aplomb. Only a little water slopped out of her jar. It probably happened every day – and every day, Constantia probably looked just as annoyed when her ankle turned.

Helena was still standing nearer than I was. I think what she muttered to me afterwards, keeping it quiet from Cloelia with a genuinely shocked air, must have been a mistake. She surely misheard what Constantia had gasped as she skidded.

'Well, you believe what you like, Marcus. You are so innocent, I expect you would have thought Numa Pompilius was just a man who liked to work with a female secretary. Egeria proved to be efficient, and of course he never laid a finger on the nymph . . . But I could swear that when the venerable Virgin nearly turned her ankle, she winced and cursed.'

Little Cloelia looked up scornfully. 'Of course she did, Helena. She said "*Balls!*"'

XXIX

We trailed Constantia all the way back to the House of the Vestals, keeping at a safe distance in case the lictor got frisky with his rods. Helena, who could be sensationally persistent, went straight back to the door porter and asked if her request for an interview had been considered yet. Far too soon for an answer. Ladies who lead lives of traditional simplicity observe the traditional rules for correspondence too: they do not follow up messages until the feast has gone cold.

Constantia herself had an excuse: ferrying water from the shrine. But do not imagine the Virgins are so geared to simplicity they read letters from the public personally. They have a large staff, and it certainly includes secretaries.

No, of course I don't think they employ the secretaries to write their love letters. Saying that would be blasphemy.

We made our second attempt at going home. Leaving the enclosure on the Sacred Way side this time, we emerged on to the small Street of the Vestals opposite the Regia – once the grand Etruscan Palace of Numa Pompilius, afore-mentioned aficionado of nymphs. I shrugged off the swathes of my toga and slung that hot, hated garment over my shoulder casually.

The Regia had long ago ceased to be occupied domestically, and few traces now remained of whatever ancient buildings had once occupied the site. It was a sacred area, used for centuries by the College of Pontiffs. They know how to earmark good accommodation. Some consul had rebuilt everything in sight using his spoils of war, a plunder so magnificent he had been able to floor and wall the new edifice with solid white and grey marble. As a result, this strongly constructed area had survived the Great Fire when all the huge patrician houses further along the Sacred Way had been swept to destruction. Facing us now were the Temple of Mars, containing the spears that generals shook before departing for battle; an integral vestibule; and the Temple of Ops, the old-fashioned goddess of plenty, which only the Vestals and Pontifex Maximus were allowed to enter. To our right, at the far end of the complex, was a small porch, under whose columns we saw a disturbance.

A litter with an eagle on top and purple curtains was being lifted by bearers, who set off at a smart pace. Noisily tramping ahead went a phalanx of plumed helmets: Praetorian Guards. As they spread across the road, looking for more scope to knock passers-by aside, we knew we were witnessing the departure of the Emperor. Presumably, he had been there in his capacity as Pontifex, pootling around the priestly college on some religious business.

I would have thought nothing of it. But a crowd of hangers-on had been waiting for Vespasian to leave. As they now scattered, one man broke free of the rest; he was going at a fast lick. He saw me. A relieved expression lit his face. He slowed up.

'Falco! What a coincidence – I was sent out to find you. I thought it would take me half the day.'

I recognised him. I last saw him in Lepcis Magna, just a few weeks back. A calm, sensible slave, he attended the Emperor's envoy, Rutilius Gallicus. At present the last thing I wanted was a social invitation from the man who gave the order to send my brother-in-law to the lions. But nobody issues their dinner invitations from the Regia. This was about something else. As I suspected, the message for me was to see Rutilius urgently – on official business. There had to be a religious connection. However, I did not suppose it would involve geese or chickens.

Helena kissed me and said she would go back to see her parents at the Capena Gate before taking Cloelia home. I rushed across the road with the attendant, hoping to find Rutilius still at the Regia in order to avoid chasing around after him.

He was there. He was wearing full senatorial purple. With

169

a sigh, I resumed my toga as I approached.

His slave won a look of approval for finding me so speedily. I received a rather terse greeting. I knew this scenario. Vespasian and various officials had just held a meeting in the pontifical offices. Whatever the agenda, the action plan recorded in the minutes had been dumped on Rutilius Gallicus. Everyone else had now gone home for lunch, each congratulating himself on a successful discussion in which he dodged responsibility. My man from Libya was left in charge of some troublesome task.

I did not waste time or effort in sympathy. If he had sent for me, the next stage was as traditional and simple as the daily lives of the Vestals: the noble Rutilius would shed the burden; I would acquire it. Then *he* was going home for lunch. My eggs and olives would be fed to the dog tonight.

He started by looking around shiftily. Interviewing me at the Regia had not been his intention and he wanted to find somewhere suitable. Even in a place where every scroll was automatically stamped as confidential, an office would not do, apparently. Bad news.

He led me out into the courtyard, an odd, triangular-shaped area, and also coolly paved in white and grey marble slabs. Around it were various old rooms used for meetings, and scribes' nooks occupied by the guardians of the archives and annals which were stored here. Cut off from the bustle of the Sacred Way by a wall with a muffling colonnade, it was quiet, congenial, unhurried. I could hear occasional low voices and the light footfall of sandals on feet that knew the interior corridors.

In the centre of the courtyard was a large underground cistern, possibly an old grain silo from centuries ago when people actually lived in Numa's Palace. Rutilius led me here. Standing above it, as if inspecting the structure idly, we could talk without being approached or overheard. This was abnormal secrecy. My fears must be right: he had some ghastly job for me.

'Enjoying your return to Rome, Falco?' I smiled in silence. He could leave out the pleasantries. Rutilius cleared his throat. 'Congratulations on your social elevation!' I tucked my thumbs in my belt like a true plebeian. 'And Procurator of Poultry, too?' I nodded pleasantly; it was hardly an insult, even though my family all crumpled up in laughter whenever it was mentioned. 'You are a man of many talents; well, I realised that in Africa. Somebody told me that you also write poetry?' For one ghastly moment it looked as though he were about to confess that he scribbled too, and would I like to have a look at his notebooks some time?

I stopped smiling. Poetry? Nobody asked an informer about his intellectual life. Rutilius must be really desperate.

'We mentioned the other day that I am priest of the Cult of the Deified Emperors?'

'We did, sir. Sodalis Augustalis? Quite an honour.'

It was hard to see how he achieved it. A first generation rank-holder from the foot of the Alps, there must have been many a senator just as talented and much better known. His career, as I knew it, was a fair one with the usual civil and military service. Aedile; quaestor; praetor; consul. He had been governor of Galatia when the famous general Corbulo was swashbuckling around that arena. Nero had had Corbulo killed for being too good a soldier. Maybe the incoming Emperor, Galba, hoped to profit from any antagonism Rutilius felt towards Nero afterwards, and that was why he acquired his prestigious priesthood.

If so, Galba died too soon to enjoy any loyalty he tried to cultivate. But Rutilius also had personal connections with the legion Vespasian entrusted to his son Titus (the Fifteenth: my late brother's legion, so I knew just what a close-knit clique those braggarts were). When Vespasian became Emperor, Rutilius somehow pushed to the front, one of the first consuls of the reign. Nobody had heard of him. Frankly, I had taken no notice of the man either – until I met him out in Tripolitania.

What he did have was ambition. It made him a ferocious hard worker. He was stepping up the treads of power as niftily as a roofer with a shoulder hod of pantiles. This was the kind of official Vespasian liked: Rutilius Gallicus came with no awkward old debts of patronage. Galba was irrelevant; Rutilius had been made by the Flavians. He possessed energy and goodwill, and it was quite likely that whatever had been entrusted to him today he had volunteered for.

I knew I would not be granted the same option.

'I want to talk about a delicate issue, Falco. You are the first choice for the work.'

'I usually know what that means, sir.'

'It is not dangerous.'

'Surprise! So what is it?'

Rutilius remained patient. He understood these were my own pleasantries, a way to brace myself for today's unwanted supplicant and today's sour job.

'There is a problem, one you already know about.' He was brisk now. I liked him more. 'A child who was to be submitted to the Vestal Virgins' lottery tomorrow has disappeared.'

'Gaia Laelia.'

'Exactly. You can see the tricky elements – granddaughter of an ex-Flamen Dialis, niece of a Flamen Pomonalis. Apart from needing to find her for humanitarian reasons –'

'They do count, then?'

'Of course! But, Falco, this is extremely sensitive.'

'I won't suggest the lottery result is already decided, but let's say, sir: if Gaia Laelia were chosen, she would be regarded as highly suitable?'

'Her family background would certainly mean that the Pontifex would feel confident she is fully prepared for a lifetime of service.'

'That sounds like an official brief.' Rutilius for once grinned in sympathy. 'Rutilius, there is no need to dodge. You want me to find her?'

'Well, the Palace fixers are jumpy. The Urban Prefect raised the alarm.' Wrong. Lucius Petronius had done that. 'Her grandfather has now admitted to Vespasian that she is lost. Somebody learned of your interest. According to Palace records, you still work as a partner with a member of the

172

vigiles. The records are out of date, as always! We had an interesting discussion at the meeting I just attended about how you managed vigiles' support. Then Vespasian pointed out that your last known colleague was Anacrites, his own Chief Spy.'

'More shrieks of outrage ensued?'

'By that stage you had achieved some notoriety, yes.'

'So then you said, sir, that my current partner is Camillus Justinus so I no longer pirate my back-up from the ranks of public servants. This makes me a responsible hound who can safely be enrolled to sniff out lost Virgins?'

'I said, Falco, you had my utmost confidence as a discreet, efficient operative. You may like to know Vespasian agreed.'

'Thank you, sir. If I take this on, I will need entry to the Laelius house and permission to question the family.'

Rutilius groaned. 'I told them you would ask that.'

I gave him a straight stare. 'You would do the same.' He was silent. 'Rutilius, you would not be discussing the matter, had you failed to persuade your colleagues – including the Emperor – that it has to be done this way?'

He took a moment before answering. 'The Emperor left here on his way to inform Laelius Numentinus that you must be granted access.'

'Right.' I relaxed. I had been prepared for unacceptable conditions. This job had my interest; I would probably have taken it anyway. 'I am not being offensive. You know why I lay down these rules. The child will probably turn up at home. I need to carry out a proper search, which I admit will be intrusive. It has to be. The first place I look will be in their baskets of dirty underwear, and it will get worse from there on. Besides, if her disappearance is no accident, the most likely cause is domestic. It will be vital to question the whole family.'

'This is all understood.'

'I shall, as you say, be discreet.'

'Thanks, Falco.'

We had started to move towards one of the courtyard exits, heading for the elderly, foursquare arch of Fabius Maximus over the crossroads on the Sacred Way.

'Why,' I asked bluntly, 'are we being so careful with this family? Surely it is not just a matter of status?'

Rutilius paused, then shrugged. I felt he knew more than he had said. He gestured to our right as we emerged. 'Do you have the current address of the Laelii? Before Numentinus became Flamen Dialis and moved to the official residence, they used to live down there, you know – in one of the great houses that perished in Nero's Great Fire.'

'Jupiter! The Sacred Way – the best address in Rome? I know where their new place is, thanks; on the Aventine. A decent house – though hardly the same.'

'They were once a prominent family,' Rutilius reminded me.

'Obviously. This quarter was favoured by famous republicans: Clodius Pulcher, Cicero. And was there not a notorious house along here that was owned by a Scaurus – with those expensive red-black marble columns that ended up on the Theatre of Marcellus? My father is a specialist salesman and he always cites its record price: fifteen million sesterces it changed hands for once. Gaia Laelia's father has Scaurus as his cognomen; is that significant?'

Rutilius shrugged again. His noble shoulders were working hard today. 'There could well be a past connection. It is a family name, no doubt.'

I felt my eyes narrowing. 'Do the Laelii have money nowadays?'

'They must have some.'

'Will I be allowed to ask them?'

'Only if it is very obviously relevant. They may not answer, of course,' Rutilius warned. 'Please remember, you are not interrogating Census frauds today.'

I would have preferred that. Give me an honest cheat. Infinitely preferable to a devious and hypocritical so-called pillar of public life. 'One more thing, sir: time is of the essence. I need support. I would like to bring in my friend and ex-partner, Petronius Longus.'

'I thought you would say that too,' Rutilius confessed. 'Sorry; it is impossible. The Emperor decided that we should not involve the vigiles in direct contact with the

174

family. The troops are to be ordered to search the city for the child, but the old Flamen is adamant that he does not want the big boys invading his home. Remember, Falco, for most of his life, Numentinus was bound never to look on armed men or to witness fetters. Even his ring had to be made from a broken band of metal. He cannot change. The paraphernalia of law and order still affronts him. This is the situation: he refuses to let in the vigiles; you have been put forward as the acceptable alternative.'

'He may not accept me.'

'He will.'

Worst luck.

XXX

First, the house.

It looked as dreary as when I came here first with Maia. I felt today's errand was likely to be just as abortive. Visiting for the second time, now that I knew more about the family, I viewed their unappealing home with an even more gloomy sense of mistrust.

Somebody was leaving, just as I arrived. A litter emerged, ebony coloured, with heavily drawn grey curtains. It was not the one with the Medusa boss that the Laelii themselves used. A well-wisher, perhaps. Whoever it was, they appeared to be accompanied by their laundry: a short train of slaves followed, one with a bulging clothes hamper and others with smaller baggage items. I refrained from asking the escort who this was; off-putting lads with pug noses walked alongside the litter. They paid as much attention to checking that the half-doors were closed and the dark curtains kept tight as they did to surveying the street for menaces. Some husband who did not want his wife leaping out to buy too much from jewellery kiosks, I joked to myself.

After they left, I walked up to the house, thoughtfully. The porter's peephole was shuttered so I stood with my back to the front door as if waiting. Passers-by would suppose I had knocked and was waiting. Instead, I listened. This was a house where a young girl had gone missing. There should be panic inside. Every footfall on the front doorstep should make somebody rush to investigate.

Nothing.

I rang a bell which hung on its bracket so stiffly I had to wrench at it with a strength that seemed discourteous. Well, I am a delicate fellow. After an age of extra silence a

176

thin, pale porter answered – a different man from the one who had dismissed Maia and me. I recommended a light application of low-grade olive oil to the bell.

'Don't use fish oil. It stinks. You'll be plagued with cats.' He stared at me. 'My name is Didius Falco. Your master is expecting me.'

He was the kind of slave who only needed firm orders. Any burglar could have effected an entry just by speaking with bravado and a sweet accent. He had no idea what I wanted. I could have been any cheap confidence trickster about to offer the patrician householder a fake set of cheap Greek vases, stolen turnips, or this week's special in curses, guaranteed to rot your enemy's liver within five days or your money back.

I was wearing my toga again. It must have helped. The porter had no sartorial discernment or he would have seen that this garment had once belonged to the army's most disreputable centurion, and that the crumpled moths' delight now spent its idle time on a crude hook which had left a large poke in the wool, just where the swathe was so elegantly flung over my left shoulder.

Whoever he supposed I was, he set off to lead me straight to the old man. Now I was inside at last, I could sense the presence of a large staff. There had to be a steward or chamberlain yet the porter never thought of consulting a superior about me. It argued a lack of regular dealings with visitors. Still, this saved time.

As I followed my guide, I made rapid observations. After a standard curtained nook where the duty porter sat, we crossed a small hallway tiled in black and grey, then traversed a dark corridor. I could now hear the normal morning noises of a large house: brooms, voices giving domestic instructions. The voices were low, though not exactly hushed. I heard no laughter. No bantering old cooks or larking youths. No dog, no cat, no caged finches. The house was clean, though perhaps not spotless. No bad smells. No particularly pleasant ones either. Neither sandalwood boxes, potted white lilies, nor warm rose balsam bath oil. Either the kitchen was in another part of the house, or today's lunch must be cold.

We had first traversed the atrium. It was old-fashioned and open-roofed, with a small rectangular pool, dry at present. That was because – their first sign of humanity – the Laelii had builders in. Perhaps this was where Gloccus and Cotta bunked off to whenever Helena needed them. If so, here too they were conspicuously absent today, though they could have been sent away because of the trouble over Gaia.

The atrium surrounds had had their walls stripped for repainting, and on one side a small shrine was under construction, the kind of niche where families with well-tended pedigrees keep not just their Lares but ugly busts of their most elevated forebears.

I was taken to a side room. There the porter uncere-moniously left me. I began to smell incense: unusual in a private house. The porter had forgotten my name so I had to introduce myself. Luckily, I can do that. I could even name the person I was addressing. It had to be old man Laelius. He might be retired, but he found it impossible to let go. Even now, he wore the robes of his past office: the thick woollen toga praetexta, purple bordered and, according to ritual, woven by the hands of his late wife; and his apex, the conical cap with its ear-flaps and surmounting olive twig inter-twined with white wool.

I took him in quickly. Late sixties, thin-fleshed, wrinkled neck, slightly shaky hands, chin up, a haughty beaked nose to look down and a sneer that went back through five centuries of arrogant ancestors. I had seen him before some-where; presumably I recognised him from his role in past festivals. It surprised me that I remembered. Until I was landed with the Sacred Geese, I normally stayed in bed during such occurrences.

'Marcus Didius Falco, sir. You must be Publius Laelius Numentinus.' He gave me a hard stare, as if he had been the Flamen Dialis for so long it seemed an insult to be addressed by name. But whatever indulgence others granted him, I intended to stick to form. He had retired. The real Flamen Dialis was another man now. He could not complain. I had used his full three names. I used mine too, of course. At one level, we were equal: a democratic joke.

He was enthroned on an ivory stool with arms, like a magistrate. He had been sitting alone in that posture before I entered. Other people might have been reading or writing but he preferred the brooding stillness of a stone god.

The room was furnished with side tables and lamps and a small rug lay at his feet, which occupied a footstool. It could have been comfortable, but for the frosty atmosphere.

Helena Justina had brought me up to scratch on flamens when she and I had first talked about Gaia. Jove's priest lived a life so hedged around with restrictive duties he had no time to stray; that was the idea, no doubt. Representing the god, he was untouchable in the strictest sense. When he went out, adding a double cloak to his woolly uniform, he carried a sacrificial knife in one hand (which must have deterred unwelcome contacts) and in the other a long wand with which he kept the populace at a distance. He was preceded by a lictor, but also by criers at whose approach everyone had to lay aside their tasks, for not only was every day a holiday for the Flamen himself (nice life!), but he must never see others working.

There was more. He could not mount, or even touch, a horse. He might not leave the city (except in recent enlightened times, for a maximum of two nights, to carry out unavoidable family duties, if directly sanctioned by the Pontifex Maximus). He could wear no knots (his clothes were fixed with clasps); his rings were split; he was forbidden to name ivy because of its binding properties, or to walk under any pergola that was canopied with vines. If someone in bonds was brought to his house, the fetters were at once struck off and hurled down from the roof; if he encountered a criminal, that person could neither be scourged nor executed. Only a free man could barber a Flamen's beard; it must be cut with a bronze knife; the clippings and his nail trimmings were collected and buried beneath a sacred tree. The Flamen could not remove his tunic or head-dress during daylight, lest Jove glimpse his person.

He must avoid dogs (which explained why they had no guard dogs here), she-goats, beans, raw flesh or fermented dough.

There was probably more, but Helena had seen my eyes glaze over and had spared me. The restrictions seemed outrageous; they were designed to ensure the Flamen never let his mind wander, though he looked to me as if he had retained full control of his thoughts – and his rigid opinions too.

For all that, by virtue of his priesthood, this oddity would have sat in the Senate. Still, he probably fitted in among the other eccentrics and crazy men.

Here in his house, everything was arranged to suit his wishes. That did not include me. He looked at me as though I had scuttled out of a drain.

'I understand, sir, that the Emperor has cleared my path with you. Your granddaughter is missing, and I possess experience that may help find her. It is particularly important that you work with me, since you have expressed a wish not to have contact with the vigiles. I regret that. They could have helped save time – and time is vital in a case like this.'

'You were recommended as a specialist. Are you saying you are not up to the job?' His voice was thin, his tone edged with malice. I knew what I had here: a wicked old bastard. In families like mine, they wield no power and so can do no harm. This was nothing like my family.

'I shall do my best, sir. You will find it better than average. But success will depend on how much co-operation I receive.'

'And what do you offer?'

'A fast, discreet service – on my terms. The most likely solution is that Gaia has imprisoned herself accidentally somewhere in her own home. I have to search your house for hiding places that might attract a child. I have to look *everywhere,* though you have my assurance that what I see will be immediately forgotten if it is not relevant.'

'I understand.' His hauteur was chilly.

'I shall knock and wait before entering rooms. I shall give any occupants a chance to remove themselves. I shall work as quickly as I can.'

'That is good.'

'I do have to be allowed to speak to your family.'

'It is acceptable.'

'They need not answer any questions they regard as improper, sir.' I gave him a level stare. He was intelligent. He knew that refusing fair questions would be informative in itself. 'I should also like permission to talk to your staff. It is my intention to limit such interviews. But, for example, Gaia Laelia presumably was entrusted to a nursemaid?'

'There is a girl who looks after her. You may speak to the nurse.'

'Thank you.' I must be going soft. He did not deserve the restraint I was showing. Still, I could see he expected aggression. I was happy to surprise him.

'And what,' asked the ex-Flamen in a tense voice, 'are the questions that you wish to put to me?'

XXXI

I took out my note-tablet. I would make jottings occasionally, to look competent. Mostly I just held the stylus still
and listened, to show my impeccable tact.

'The investigation must begin with the facts of your
granddaughter's disappearance. You have expressed a
reluctance to raise the alarm or to involve the authorities.
Please tell me why.'

'There is no need. I recently gave instructions that Gaia
Laelia is never to go out alone.' After she came to see me,
presumably. 'The door porter would have stopped her – had
she tried.' I already knew that the door porter still cheerfully
left his station unattended.

'You first noticed her missing yesterday?'

'Ask her mother these details.'

'Very well.' I refused to be thrown. 'My sister is
acquainted with Caecilia Paeta –' I remembered not to land
Caecilia in trouble by admitting that I had met her when she
came secretly to Maia's house. 'I understand her to be
sensible.' Numentinus looked annoyed at me for comment-
ing. His eyes narrowed; like most people he encountered, I
felt that his daughter-in-law aroused mild contempt in him.
I was glad I had spoken. I wanted him to know I would
evaluate witnesses on my terms. 'Let us consider more
general issues. The vigiles have been asked to search the city
in case Gaia has been abducted. It is a complex task, but they
will do as decent a job as they can.' I was telling him it would
be near impossible to find her, unless the cohorts had some
clues. 'My own search starts here. If the child is deliberately
hiding, or if she has run away, what would make her do that?
Was she unhappy, sir?'

'She had no reason to be.'

'Her parents live apart. Did their separation distress her?'

'At first.' I was surprised he answered, but I suppose he had already realised this would be asked. 'My son left home three years ago. Gaia Laelia was an infant. She has accepted the situation.' More readily than the old man himself, probably.

'A parental separation might cause arguments that could have frightened her? But later she must have realised she remained in a secure and loving home.' Numentinus looked suspicious, as though he thought I was being ironic. 'Are you willing to answer questions about why your son, Laelius Scaurus, left?'

'No. Keep to the subject.' After that, I did not dare ask about the possibility of Gaia's parents divorcing, let alone the relationship between Scaurus and his aunt. I would have to tackle that with somebody, though. Somebody else.

'So Gaia settled down, still living here with her mother, and three years later her name has gone into the Vestals' lottery. I understand you are opposed to that?'

'My opinion is immaterial.'

'Excuse me. I simply wondered if there had been anger in the family home which might have caused a bad response in a sensitive child.' He made no answer. That chin came up again, warning me I strayed too far into an unwelcome area. 'Very well. Gaia Laelia's own reaction to her proposal as a Vestal is relevant, you will concede. A motive for her disappearance might be that she hates the prospect and fled to avoid it. Yet I am told by all sources that she was delighted. This, sir, is why I am inclined to believe that her disappearance is some childish accident.'

'She is a careful child,' he disagreed. No children are careful.

'And intelligent,' I said. There was no flicker of grand-fatherly pride. If I had been discussing Julia Junilla at home, either Pa or the senator would have been orating in full flood immediately. 'I met her, as you know. Which brings me unavoidably to this question: why would your grand-daughter seek out an informer and announce that her family was trying to kill her?'

The old man was ready, and full of contempt. 'Since it was untrue, I can offer no reason for her claim.'

I kept my voice quiet. 'Did you punish her when you found out?'

He hated having to answer. He knew if he did not tell me, the servants would. 'It was explained to her that she had erred.'

'Was she beaten?' I made the suggestion neutrally.

'No.' His lip curled as if disdaining the thought. I wondered. Still, Vestals have to be perfect in every limb. Her mother, wanting Gaia to remain eligible, would have protested against a beating, even if she dared not argue about much else.

'Was she confined to her room?'

'Briefly. She should not have left the house without permission.'

'When she left the house, where was her nurse?'

'Gaia had locked her in a pantry.'

Numentinus had expressed no emotion, but I let him see me smile slightly at Gaia's spirit and initiative before I continued in the same neutral tone as before: 'Was the same pantry used as a cell when Gaia disappeared yesterday?'

'No.'

'Who can best tell me what happened then?'

'Discuss it with my daughter-in-law.'

'Thank you.' I had finished with him. I might as well not have started. He knew that. He looked very pleased with himself. 'I shall just check your room, if I may, then you need not be disturbed here again.' I scanned everywhere quickly. Flat walls; no curtained arches; only small items of furniture – apart from one chest. 'May I look in the chest, please?'

Numentinus breathed; well, he seethed with annoyance. 'It is not locked.'

I half expected him to come and look over my shoulder. In fact, he sat like stone. I walked quickly to the great wooden box and lifted the lid. It was so heavy I nearly dropped it, but I recovered and held it, one arm braced. The chest contained scrolls and moneybags. I let the old man see me shift them aside enough to check that no child was hidden in the base, then I replaced the scrolls and bags as found, lowered the lid gently, and made sure I showed no visible interest in the contents.

'Thank you, sir.' The coinage did raise another issue, however. 'It is possible, I am afraid, that Gaia Laelia has been abducted by some criminal element, with a financial motive. Would your family be known as wealthy?'

'We live simply and very quietly.' Numentinus had answered only part of the question. I did not pursue it. After my Census work, I would soon sniff out his financial situation.

'This is a large house. I want to keep a record of rooms as I check them. You only moved here recently; did the agent provide a room plan, by any chance?'

'You may have it.' He clapped his hands. A slave appeared instantly from outside and was dispatched to the steward. 'That slave will accompany you in your search.' Supervision; I had expected it.

'Thanks. Was this house an outright purchase, or do you rent?'

I expected him to tell me he had bought the place, probably expressing horror that anyone should think such a family would be beholden to a landlord. 'I rent,' he said.

'Long term?' It must be, if he had the landlord's approval for the building work I had seen in the atrium. He nodded haughtily.

'I am grateful for your frankness. I hope the questions were not too painful. I shall see your daughter-in-law next.'

The slave was already back, saying the chart would be found for me.

'One final point, sir. I offer my sympathy for your late wife's death. I believe it was recent?'

'The Flaminica suffered from a tragic illness that came upon her last July.' Laelius Numentinus spoke out so abruptly I pulled up. It was the first time he had volunteered more than a minimal answer. Did he love his wife? 'There is no need – absolutely no need – for you to concern yourself with that. Her death was sudden, though nothing untoward.'

I had never supposed it was. I had only wanted to ask him if Gaia had been particularly fond of her grandmother, and perhaps troubled by her death. Instead I said nothing and followed the slave out.

XXXII

It took a while for me to be admitted to see Caecilia Paeta. I used the time to familiarise myself with the house plan; I marked off the room where I had seen the ex-Flamen, then covered two more while I waited. They were medium-sized reception rooms, very lightly furnished and probably not used. Given that the family had been here nearly a year, I was surprised how little progress they seemed to have made in settling in. Did they lack practical application, or had there been a reluctance to face the fact that they were staying?

The Flaminia, their official residence on the Palatine, would have been officially furnished. I had already noticed that what they owned here was old and of good quality – family pieces, probably – yet there was not much of it. Like many an élite family, these people appeared to have money, but less ready cash than they needed. Either that, or when they needed to re-equip they had been too caught up in their wrangles to find time to go shopping.

The reception room I was called to next was typical: too much bare space and no style. Caecilia Paeta was much as I remembered from her visit to Maia's house, though she looked more drawn. Several frightened maids had flocked to protect her from the immodesty of being interviewed by an informer. She sat hunched in a single basket-weave chair, pulling a light stole too tightly around her shoulders, while they squatted on stools or cushions in a circle around her and stared at the floor.

Once again, I kept my voice quiet and my manner calm, though not subservient. I would have to know much more about the situation here before I started throwing my weight about. But I could already feel the tension knotted around

187

this household. In the mother's silence as she faced me, I could sense the years of oppression that had crushed any spirit out of her.

What kind of life did she face? Abandoned by her husband who, if Numentinus had his way, would never be allowed to divorce her, she was denied the normal right to rejoin her own family and start afresh. Her father-in-law had probably thought little of her to begin with; bullies loathe their victims. When she failed to hold his son, it would seem logical to the tyrant to despise Caecilia more. Now she had lost her child.

'Don't give up hope.' I had not meant to be kind to her. She had not expected it, either. We shared a moment of uncomfortable surprise. 'Look, we won't waste time. I need to know everything that happened yesterday, up until it was noticed that Gaia was missing. I want you to describe the day.'

Caecilia looked nervous. When she spoke, it was in so quiet a voice I had to lean right forward to hear her. 'We all rose as usual, which was not long after dawn.' I could have guessed that. When your home is full of trouble, why waste good arguing time? 'The Flamen makes offerings to the gods before breakfast.'

'You eat together as a family? Who was present then?'

'All of us. The Flamen, me and Gaia, Laelia and Ariminius . . .' She paused, uncertainly.

'Ariminius is the Flamen Pomonalis, and Laelia is his wife? Your husband's sister? Anyone else there?' I asked, looking down at my tablet. I had thought I sensed something. Caecilia was so short-sighted, she could probably not see my expression, but tone of voice carries. Besides, the maids were watching and if I looked too keen on a particular question, their anxiety might communicate itself to her.

'Nobody.' I was sure she had hesitated.

'After breakfast you went your separate ways?'

'Laelia was in her room, I think. I had my household tasks.' So the daughter-in-law was their drudge while the daughter took her ease? 'Ariminius went out.' Lucky man.

'What about Gaia? Does she go to school?'

188

'Oh no.' Silly me.

'She has a tutor?'

'No. I have taught her the alphabet myself; she can read and write. Everything children in this household need to know, they learn at home.'

The priestly caste may be top notch on peculiar ritual; they are not famous for being erudite.

'So, please tell me about Gaia's day.'

'She sat quietly with the maids to begin with, helping them with their weaving at the loom.' I should have known that as well as believing in self-education, these were home-weaving cranks. Well, a Flamen Dialis has to insist that his Flaminica work her fingers sore preparing his ceremonial robes. I amused myself wondering about Helena's reaction, if I had come home with my new honour and suggested that a Procurator of Poultry ought to swank about in wife-sewn livery. 'After a while,' continued Caecilia, now speaking with more confidence, 'she was allowed to go into a safe inner garden and play.'

'When did you hear she was missing?'

'After lunch. That is an informal meal here, but of course I expected to see her. When Gaia did not appear, I accepted a story her nurse told, that Gaia had taken her food to eat by herself. She does that sometimes, sitting on a bench in the sun, or making herself a little picnic, still involved in play –' She suddenly looked at me sharply. 'I expect you think us a strange, strict family – but Gaia is allowed to be a child, Falco! She plays. She owns plenty of toys.' Not many friends to share them with, I guessed.

'I shall have to search her room shortly.'

'You will find that she lived in a dear little nursery, quite spoiled.'

'So she had no obvious reason to want to run away from home?' I demanded, without warning. Caecilia clammed up. 'No horrid new family crises?' I noticed a few restless movements among the waiting maids. They kept their eyes cast down. They had been well drilled, probably while I was kept hanging about before this interview.

'Gaia was always a happy child. A sweet baby and a

happy child.' The mother had retreated into a talismanic chant. Still, at least she was now showing some natural misery. 'What has happened to her? Will I ever see her again?'

'I am trying to find the answer. Please trust me.'

She was still agitated. I had no hopes of getting anywhere while she was surrounded by her female bodyguards. The maids were as much protecting me from the truth as protecting the lady from me. I pretended I had finished, then asked if Caecilia would now show me the child's room, saying I would like her to do this herself in case, under my guidance, she could spot anything different from normal that would act as a clue. She agreed to come without the maids. The slave who was supposed to escort me scuttled along behind us, but he was a loon and hardly ever kept up. He was already carrying the house plan for me, and I added my toga to burden him more.

Caecilia walked me along several corridors. Cooling down abruptly in just my tunic, I hooked my thumbs in my belt. I gave her time to relax too, then returned to the question she had avoided and asked gently, 'Something was wrong, wasn't it?'

She took a deep breath. 'There had been bad feeling, for various reasons, and Gaia has always been sensitive. Like any child, she assumed that all problems were her fault.'

'Were they?'

She jumped. 'How could they be?'

I said callously, 'I have no idea – since I don't know what these problems were!' She was determined not to tell me. Orders from the Flamen, no doubt. We paced along in silence for a while, then I pressed it: 'Was the trouble to do with your husband's aunt?'

Caecilia glanced at me sideways. 'You know about that?' She looked amazed. Too amazed. At the same moment we both realised we were somehow at cross-purposes. I made a mental note of the subject.

I said, 'Terentia Paulla sounds a force to be reckoned with.' She laughed, rather bitterly. 'Be frank. What's this aunt really playing at?'

Caecilia shook her head. 'It is all a disaster. Please don't ask any more. Just find Gaia. Please.'

We had reached the child's room.

It was of modest size, though the mother had correctly implied that the child hardly lived in a cell. Anyway, there was only so much space, so Caecilia ordered the slave that Numentinus had imposed on me to wait outside. The man did not like it, yet he took her instructions as though overruling the Flamen was not unknown.

I absorbed the scene. There was more jumble here than I had found anywhere previously. I had seen Gaia dressed in her finery; there was an open chest full of similarly dainty clothes: gowns and undergowns, small fancy-strapped sandals, coloured girdles and stoles, tot-sized cloaks. A tangle of beads and bracelets – not cheap fakes, but real silver and semiprecious hardstones – occupied a tray on a side table. A sunhat hung on a hook on the door.

For her amusement, Gaia possessed many a toy that my Julia would be happy to bang around the floor: dolls, wooden, ceramic and rag; feather- and bean-stuffed balls; a hoop; toy horses and carts; a miniature farm. They were all good quality, the work of craftsmen, not the whittled stumpy things that youngsters in my family had to make do with. The dolls had been sat in a line on a shelf. The toy farm was spread over the floor, however, with its animals arranged as if the child had just left the room temporarily while playing with them.

Looking down at the model farm that had been so meticulously displayed by her small daughter, Caecilia Paeta caught her breath, though she tried to conceal it. She folded her arms tight, gripping her body as if resolutely holding back her emotion.

I had stopped her on the threshold. 'Now, look around carefully. Is everything the way Gaia normally had it? Anything odd? Anything out of place?'

She looked, quite carefully, then rapidly shook her head. In the sea of treasures Gaia had owned, it would be difficult to spot disturbance. I entered the room and started a search.

191

The furnishings were less lavish than the child's personal possessions, and may even have come with the house. The oil lamps, rugs and cushions were minimal. There was a narrow child-sized bed in a specially designed alcove, covered with a chequered spread, and several cupboards, mainly built in. I looked in the bed and under it, then in the cupboards, where I found a few more toys and shoes and an unused chamberpot. A large wooden box, of fairly standard type and quality, contained a mirror, combs, pins, manicure tools on a big silver ring, and tangled lengths of hair ribbon.

Holding a solitary small ankle boot that I had found under the bed, I asked, 'Who buys all the toys?'

'Relatives.' Caecilia Paeta crossed the room and obsessively neatened the coverlet on the bed. She looked near to tears.

'Anyone special?'

'Everyone buys her things.' She gestured around, acknowledging that Gaia had had luxury lavished upon her. I could understand it: the only child in a moneyed family and, as I had seen, cute with it.

'You moved here when the Flaminica died. Does Gaia miss her grandmother?'

'A little. Statilia Paulla was fonder of my husband than anyone. She spoiled him, I'm afraid.'

'Even after he left home?'

Caecilia lowered her voice nervously. 'Please don't talk about him. His name is never mentioned now.'

'People do abscond,' I commented. Caecilia made no reply. 'How did Statilia Paulla react to the fact that her own sister Terentia had encouraged Scaurus to go, and had facilitated the move?'

'How do you think? It caused more trouble.' I could have guessed that.

I sighed. 'Does Gaia miss her father?'

'She sees him from time to time. As much as many children would.'

'If their parents were divorced, you mean? What about you? Do you miss him?'

'I have no choice.' She did not sound too upset.

192

'Had you any choice over marrying him in the first place?'

'I was content. Our families had old connections. He is a decent man.'

'But I take it you two were not passionately in love?'

Caecilia smiled faintly. It was not an affront, yet she appeared to regard the suggestion of passion as some odd quirk. Privately, I thanked the gods not all patrician girls had that upbringing. At least Caecilia did not seem to know what she was missing.

Plenty of Roman women of 'good' family are bedded by men they hardly know. Most bear them children, since that is the point of it. Some are then left to their own devices. Many welcome the freedom. They need not feign deep affection for their husbands; they can avoid the men almost totally. They acquire status without emotional responsibility. So long as acceptable financial arrangements are made, all that is demanded of them is that they refrain from taking lovers. Any rate, they should not flaunt their lovers openly.

I did not believe Caecilia Paeta had a lover. But how can you tell?

Still pressing to find Gaia, I tried a different tack: 'Does your husband's aunt, Terentia Paulla, have much to do with Gaia?'

Caecilia's expression became veiled again. I wondered if the subject might be even more tricky than I had already realised. 'Only since she retired from being a Vestal, of course. That was about a year and a half ago. She is very fond of Gaia.' It reinforced my impression that Gaia Laelia had been used in the family's endless emotional tugs of war.

'Yet she disapproves of Gaia becoming a Vestal?'

For once, Caecilia showed some natural acidity. 'Maybe she wants all the honour for herself!'

'Have you told her that Gaia has gone missing?' Caecilia looked uneasy. I was crisp. 'If Gaia felt close to her and has run away, she may turn up at Terentia's house.'

'Oh we would be told!'

'Where does Terentia live?'

'Her husband's house is twenty miles outside Rome.' Too far for a child to make the journey alone easily – though runaways have been known to cover astonishing distances. 'I shall need an address.'

Caecilia seemed flustered. 'There's no need for this – Gaia knew very well that Terentia is away from home at present.'

'Why? Is she in Rome?'

'She comes sometimes –'

I could not see why Caecilia was stalling. 'Look, I'm just considering people Gaia might run to.'

She still looked distressed. She had picked up a model bull from Gaia's farm and was twisting it in her fingers obsessively. I knew she must be lying about something, but I let her think I had swallowed it. 'Have you informed your husband that Gaia is gone?'

'I am not allowed to contact him.'

'Oh come! Not only is this rather important – but I do know you wrote to him only this week saying his aunt wished to see him.' Caecilia's head spun towards me. 'I have met your husband. He told me himself.'

'What did he say to you?' Caecilia gasped, rather too carefully. Was she afraid he might have criticised her conduct in their marriage?

'Nothing to alarm you. We talked mostly about a guardianship issue.'

She seemed horrified. 'I cannot discuss that.'

Since I thought the ridiculous tale Scaurus spun me was all nonsense, I felt startled. Was there another guardianship issue, not involving the ex-Vestal? I started getting tough. 'Laelius Scaurus came up to town this week to see his aunt and other members of the family. Now what's the truth about this?'

Caecilia shook her head extremely vigorously. 'It was just a family conference.'

'Something to do with Gaia?'

'*Nothing* to do with her.'

'Is Terentia Paulla causing trouble?'

'In fairness to her, no.'

'So what's the problem?'

'Nothing.' She was lying again. Why?

'Did this "nothing" make Gaia upset, do you think?'

'It was just something that had to be arranged, a legal matter,' sighed the mother. 'Terentia wanted my husband to be consulted; his father thought Scaurus should not be involved.'

'What do you think?'

'Scaurus was useless!' she complained, quite violently. 'He always is.' For a moment she sounded worn out by trying to cope. I could now understand why she might have accepted Scaurus' departure from Rome with some relief. After this brief glimpse of her frustration with him, she made an attempt to deflect me by saying, 'Many of Gaia's things here were presents from Aunt Terentia and Uncle Tiberius.'

I went with it. 'Uncle Tiberius? He would have been Terentia Paulla's husband? The one who died? Was that very recently?'

Another troubled look crossed Caecilia's pale face. 'Quite recent, yes.'

'That was why you needed the family conference, was it?'

I seemed to have caught her off-guard. 'Well, yes. It arose from his death.'

'When my sister first came here to call on you, most of the family were at a funeral – were you cremating Terentia's husband?' Caecilia's face confirmed it, though she looked hunted; perhaps she was remembering how angry the ex-Flamen had been about Maia visiting. 'Excuse me asking, but is it not unusual for a retired Vestal to marry?'

'Yes.'

'That's a bit terse! Was it another cause of conflict here?'

'Oh yes,' answered Caecilia, with a sudden release of emotion. 'Yes, Falco. It caused more conflict than you can ever realise!'

I waited for an explanation, but the drama had been enough for her. She wore a trace of defiance, as though she were glad she had spoken out – yet now she buttoned up. I thought of something that could explain a few things: 'When Vestals retire, they are often awarded large dowries by the Emperor, are they not?'

With her composure restored, Caecilia agreed quietly, 'Yes, Aunt Terentia was well endowed financially. But that was not the attraction for Uncle Tiberius. He was a very wealthy man himself.'

'So what *was* the attraction?' I ventured. Wrong move, Falco! Caecilia looked offended, and I backed off smartly. 'Now he's dead, does Terentia inherit?'

'Probably. I don't think she has even considered it. She has been far too taken up with other concerns.'

'Everything I hear about Terentia suggests she will have her financial situation well in hand – What concerns?'

'Just family business . . . What has this to do with finding Gaia, please?'

Caecilia was more intelligent than first impressions implied. She was learning how to dodge the questions. I could handle that. Noting which ones she ducked could prove useful.

An unplanned question came to me helpfully: 'Did you like Uncle Tiberius?'

'No.' It was swift and decisive.

I stared at her. 'Why was that?' I used a neutral tone first. Then, when she did not answer, I asked more dryly, 'Did he jump you?'

'He made advances, yes.' Her voice was tight. This was an unexpected development.

'Advances you rebuffed?'

'Of course I did!' She was angry now.

'Was this after he married?'

'Yes. He had been married to Aunt Terentia little more than a year – He was a loathsome man. He thought every woman was at his disposal – and unfortunately, he had the knack of persuading too many to believe it.'

When she fell silent, I saw she was trembling slightly. My thoughts were racing. Was the deceased just a regular sex pest fingering married women – or was he even worse? 'Caecilia Paeta, please don't distress yourself. I have to ask you a very unpleasant question. If that was the situation – is there any possibility the ghastly Tiberius ever tried to make advances to little Gaia?'

Caecilia took a long time answering, though she received the question more calmly than I had feared. She was a mother; fluttery in some ways, but she did not flinch from protecting her child. 'I was nervous about that. I did consider it. But no,' she said slowly. 'I know it happens, especially with young slaves. But when I thought about it, I was sure Uncle Tiberius had no interest in children.' She paused, then forced out with difficulty, 'I was afraid, in my heart, that it might become awkward later, when Gaia grew up – but he is dead, so there is no need to worry any longer, is there?' she concluded with relief.

'So Gaia certainly has not had to run away because of Uncle Tiberius?'

'No. She knows he is dead, of course. Falco, is that all you want from me?'

I reckoned I had tried her far enough. I had made more progress than I had expected, even if I did not yet understand the full significance of some of her answers. I felt the conversation had been especially harrowing for Caecilia. She must be under great pressure from Numentinus to keep family issues from me. We had been skirting more secrets than the old man would like.

'Yes, thank you. May I make a suggestion: Scaurus deserves to hear about Gaia. Send word to him today. And regarding Uncle Tiberius groping you, don't carry that alone either. Tell someone.'

She allowed herself to look grateful. As she fled the room, she gasped out, 'That's all right. I did.'

She was gone before I could ask her who her confidant was.

XXXIII

While I was in the vicinity, I searched the rest of the bedrooms on that corridor. A slave was sponging a floor and since my escort had been deliberately chosen by the old man to be useless, this woman left her bucket and told me who used each place; all were members of the family. It is always entertaining to explore other people's closets and sleeping quarters, especially when they have been given little warning that you will be popping along to do it. Burglars must have quite a few laughs. But of course, my lips are sealed. I had promised the ex-Flamen confidentiality, and he was not a man to cross.

Caecilia and the couple had large, decently equipped rooms. Caecilia had set hers out extremely neatly, as if she spent a lot of time alone there. Hiding from the family? Well, maybe she just had a very well organised lady's maid. The Pomonalis and his wife owned more clutter; from the boxes piled along one wall, it looked as if they had still not finished unpacking fully after the family's enforced house move. Ariminius used an unfortunate variety of hair pomade. I spread some on my hand and had great trouble removing the strong stink afterwards. It was crocus, but from its staying power could have been garlic.

I had to send for a crowbar to force open all the sealed boxes, if only to show I had been thorough. Since I had been told by Gaia that her family wanted to kill her, it was a nerve-racking task. I could be about to discover a hidden corpse.

So far, I hated the set-up yet found it hard to believe Gaia's story. This was a family in constant turmoil – yet with no evidence of real malice. I asked the escorting slave to find me the child's nurse. The man went off reluctantly.

'Not one to look for the joys in life.' I grinned at the fat

198

woman with the sponge. 'Have I finished here?'

'One more room around the corner.' Oh? Who could that belong to?

She waddled off ahead of me, willingly pointing out the extra bedroom. It was as large as the others, but subtly improved in décor. There were Egyptian rugs beside the high bed, instead of mere Italian wool. Female garments lay folded in a chest, though nothing was in the cupboards. A comb, with a few long grey hairs caught in its teeth, lay on a shelf beside a green glass alabastron that contained a sweeter perfume than the crocus goo that still accompanied me if I waved my hand about.

I looked at the slave. She looked back at me. She pursed her lips. 'We had people who used to stay here,' she announced, still meeting my eye rather pointedly.

'That sounds a bit peculiar,' I observed frankly. This one was a character. She nodded, admiring her own acting. 'Somebody told you to say that.'

'They lived out of Rome,' she added, as if just remembering her rehearsal. 'One of them died, and they do not come any more.'

'These mysterious visitors' names wouldn't have been Terentia and Tiberius?' She gave me a slow nod. 'And you are not supposed to talk about them to me?' Another nod. I looked around the room. 'You know, I think somebody has been here very recently!' Somebody who left in a hurry, departing the house in a carrying-chair only as I arrived today, I reckoned. So why were the Laelii so concerned to distract me from knowing that Terentia Paulla was a recent guest?

Unfortunately, that was the end of the pantomime. I did hope the slave would privately expand on it, but when I asked, she shook her head. Still, I can be grateful for an anonymous tip (and believe me, clues were so skinnily arrayed here that I was more generous than usual when I dipped into my arm purse). But the trouble with oblique hints like that is you can never work out what they mean.

'Any ideas what happened to the little girl?' I asked conspiratorially.

'I'd tell you if I had, sir.'

'Anyone here she is particularly friendly with?'

'No. She never has friends, that I know of. Well,' sneered my new source, 'not many would meet the right standards for the people here, would they?'

The male slave was returning, with a girl who must be Gaia's nurse.

'I'm surprised they let *you* in!' scoffed the floor-mopper to me, as she toddled back to work.

XXXIV

Gaia's nurse was an eye-catcher: a short, sturdily built, swarthy, hairy slave from somewhere unsavoury in the east. She probably worshipped gods with harsh, five-syllable names and cannibalistic habits. She looked as if she were descended from trousered archers who could ride horses bareback and shoot backwards sneakily. In fact, even if I were trying not to be unkind, facially she looked as if one of her own parents might have been a horse.

The looks belied her cowed nature. As a barbarian, she was a cipher. I did not need to witness her trying to supervise little Gaia to realise that any six-year-old with spirit could push this beauty about. Locking her in a pantry was too extreme; I bet Gaia Laelia could have ordered nursey to sit motionless on a thistle for six hours, and the girl would have been too terrified to disobey.

'I know nothing!' When she spoke, it was in an accent that the children in my family would have imitated happily for weeks, spluttering with hysterical laughter every time. Even lacking an audience, Gaia could probably imitate her cruelly. And reduce the nurse to sobs doing it.

She had been thrashed. They were new bruises. From the picturesque array, I guessed that after Gaia went missing yesterday, several people had tried to force this girl to answer questions, then when she produced no answers each had resorted to punishment. The nurse thought she had been brought here so that I could thrash her again.

'Sit down on that chest.'

It took her a long time to believe I meant it. This may have been the first time she had ever sat in the presence of the freeborn. I was under no illusions; she probably despised me for not knowing my place.

We were still in what had been described as the guest-room. I busied myself looking under the bed, even pulling it away from the wall and peering into the accumulated dust at the back of it.

'I am looking for Gaia. Something very bad may have happened to her and she has to be found quickly. Do you understand?' I dropped my voice. 'I shall not whip you if you answer my questions quickly and truthfully.'

The nurse glared at me with sullen eyes. Any trustworthiness in her nature had been beaten out of her long ago. She was spoiled as a witness – and spoiled as a child's nurse too, in my opinion.

Still, what did I know? My baby had never had one. The way we were going, I would never experience the anxiety of choosing, instructing, and no doubt eventually dismissing somebody to help with Julia. Some ill-trained, immature, uninterested foreigner for whom our baby represented a spoiled, rude Roman brat with spoiled, rude Roman parents, all of whom Fortune had spared from slavery and suffering for no obvious reason – unlike the conjectural nurse who would think herself, but for Fortune, as good as us. As, but for Fortune, she might well have been.

'Right.' I sat on the edge of the bed and stared at this one. 'Your name?'

'Athene.'

I sighed slowly. Who does these things? It was hard to think of anything more inappropriate.

'You look after Gaia. Do you like doing that?' A grim look in response. 'Does Gaia like you?'

'No.'

'Is the child allowed to beat you as the adults do?'

'No.' Well, that was something.

'But she locked you in a pantry the other day, I hear?' Silence. 'It sounds to me as though she is treated like a little queen here. I don't suppose that makes her very well behaved?' No reply. 'Right. Well, listen, Athene. You are in serious trouble. If Gaia Laelia has come to any harm, you – being her nurse – will be the first suspect. It is the law in Rome that if anyone freeborn dies in suspicious circumstances, the entire complement of slaves in the household is put to death. You need to convince me that you meant her no harm. You had better show you want this little girl rescued from whatever trouble she is in.'

'She's not dead, is she?' Athene seemed genuinely horrified. 'She's only run away again.'

'Again? Are you talking about the day you were locked up?' A nod this time. 'Gaia was coming to see me that day, and I sent her home afterwards. Has she ever suggested to you that she wanted to run away permanently?'

'No.'

'Does she confide in you?'

'She's a quiet one.' The Gaia I had met had spoken out confidently; somebody must have engaged her in conversation regularly.

I gazed at the girl, then sprang on her: 'Do you think someone in the family wants to kill Gaia?'

Her jaw dropped. Not an attractive sight. It was a new idea to Athene.

They kept their secrets well here. It was no surprise. They dealt in ritual and mystery. In my view, religion had nothing to do with it. The fanciful rites of the ancient cults, where only the favoured may communicate with the gods, are about power in the state. Easy to extend the same system to within the family. Every head of household is his own chief priest. Luckily we are not all expected to wear bonnets with olive prongs and ear-flaps. I'd sooner emigrate to a Cappadocian beanfield.

Athene really did not know Gaia had been afraid of being killed. The child had confided in me, a complete stranger, yet knew she must not risk telling her own nurse. Well, I could see a reason for that: the nurse answered to the family.

It's a myth that the slaves always know all the dark secrets in a household. They know more than they are supposed to, yes – but never everything. A successful slave-owner will release confidences selectively: you have to give away the scandals that are merely embarrassing, like adultery and bankruptcy and the time your grandmother wet herself in the best dining room, but keep absolutely silent about the impending treason charge, your three bastards, and how much you are really worth.

'Right, Athene; tell me about yesterday.'

With much prompting, I drew out the same story Caecilia had told about Gaia's morning: breakfast with the family; weaving; then play in a garden here at home.

'So when did you decide that you had lost her?' Athene gave me a sly look. 'Never mind when you really reported it.' I had seen that look a hundred times. Liars often give themselves away; it can be almost as if they are begging, or daring, you to find out the true story. 'Don't mess me about. When did you first notice?'

'Near lunchtime.'

'You mean, beforehand?'

'Yes,' admitted the girl sullenly.

'Why did you tell Gaia's mother the child had chosen to eat lunch by herself?'

'She does that!'

'Yes, but this time you knew you could not find her. You should have told the truth. Why did you lie? Were you frightened?'

Athene said nothing. I sympathised, but her behaviour had been illogical and dangerous.

'Why do you think Gaia likes to eat lunch alone?'

'To get away from them,' growled the nurse. It was her first sign of honesty. 'I just thought she had hidden herself somewhere. I thought she would turn up.'

'Might she hide to get you into trouble?'

'She never has done,' admitted the nurse grudgingly.

'I know she was unhappy,' I said. 'Was anybody cruel to Gaia? Tell me the truth. I won't tell them you said it.'

'Not cruel.' Perhaps not kind either.

'Did they punish her for wrongdoing?'

'If she had asked for it.'

'Like that day she locked you up and took the litter?'

'She should never have done that. She must have known it would cause a hurricane.'

'What happened when she came home?'

'The old man was waiting, and he gave her an earful.'

'Anything else?'

'She had to stay in her room and miss dinner. Afterwards, I was always supposed to stick with her all day and sleep in her room at night. She yelled at me too much when I tried that, so I made a bed outside the door.'

'They didn't beat her?'

Athene looked surprised. 'Nobody ever so much as smacked the child.'

'Did you?'

'No. I would be beaten for it.'

'So did you find her troublesome to control?'

Once again, the girl reluctantly admitted that things were not as bad as I might have supposed: 'Not normally.' She smiled grimly. 'People here do what they are told. If she had played me up too much, the old one would have told her it was not what their type do. "Better is expected of us, Gaia!" he would say.'

'So Numentinus rules by sheer force of personality?' She did not understand me. 'If you were meant to stick with Gaia all the time, why was she playing in the garden by herself yesterday morning?'

'I had to do something else. Her mother came by and said "Oh you can leave her to enjoy herself for a while." Then I had to help one of the other girls with a job she was doing.'

'What job?'

Athene looked vague. 'Can't remember.'

'Hmm. When you did go back to look for Gaia, there was no sign of her? But you kept quiet at first.'

'Not for long. I thought Gaia would be hungry. I went and lurked by the kitchen so when she came looking for a bite I could pounce on her.'

'Could she have been to the kitchen before you got there?'

'No. I asked them. They had kicked her out earlier when she kept bothering them for water to put in the jar she was playing with. I got shooed off too in the end, so then I had to go and own up to her mother.'

'A search was carried out?'

'Oh yes. They never stopped looking – well, not until you came. The Emperor descended on the old man and then we

205

all had orders to stop rushing around. We were told you were coming, and everything had to look calm.'

'I don't see why. They have nothing to be ashamed of in panicking over a lost child of that age. If it was my daughter and Vespasian dropped in, I would ask him to join the search party.'

'You've got some nerve!'

Briefly, I grinned. 'That's what he says.'

I felt there was not much more I could screw out of this bundle, so next I made her take me outside to the courtyard garden where Gaia liked to play.

XXXV

Twenty or so sparrows took off as we emerged. It suggested a lack of human presence previously.

We were in an interior peristyle, with slender columns on four sides forming shady colonnades; water canals added to the cool effect. I now knew from the plan that, by chance, I had first entered the house by a lesser door, one of three approaches (two doors and a short staircase) on different streets of the block. As I would expect in a house of this quality, used by people who thought they were superior, the property occupied its own *insula*.

The main entrance was out of action currently, due to the building work. The hod-carriers were not remodelling it, but had used the small rooms either side of the door as stores for their tools and materials, spilling over into the corridor, which they had completely blocked with spare ladders and trestles. I was amazed Numentinus stood for it; it just showed that the power of the construction industry eclipses anything organised religion has ever managed to devise. He had once been Jupiter's representative, but now a few cheap labourers could run rings around him, quite unafraid of his verbal thunderbolts.

Had the main entrance been in use, there would have been a fine view from the door, right through the atrium, to a glimpse of this garden's greenery – letting callers know what excellent taste and what an excellent amount of money (or what huge debts), the occupants possessed.

The peristyle had a formal layout. The surrounding columns were grey stone, carved with fine spiral decorations. The space within contained box trees clipped into obelisks and empty statue bases, which I was told were awaiting family busts. A central circular hedge surrounded a pool, drained so it showed the blue lining, in the centre of which reclined a metal ocean god with shaggy seaweed hair, forming a fountain, silent because of the drained works. Not much scope for a would-be Vestal Virgin to play in this drained basin.

'Where are the builders?' I asked Athene. 'They don't seem keen to finish. Have you got Gloccus and Cotta in?'

'Who? They were told to go today, because you were coming.'

'That was stupid. They could have helped me search. Builders like an excuse to do something that is not in their contract. Were they here yesterday morning?'

'Yes.'

'Did anybody think to ask them if they saw anything?'

'The Pomonalis did.' So somebody had shown initiative. He would be next on my list for interview.

'Did they say anything?'

'No,' returned the nurse, looking slightly shifty, I thought. Dear gods, she probably eyed up the labourers.

I walked out into the garden. There were signs it had been neglected but recently revived with emergency treatment. The clipped trees were bare in places, where they had been shaved too hard after growing lanky. I saw evidence that paths had been repaired. A low pierced wall had patches of new concrete and marks where ivy had been torn off it. I remembered that a Flamen Dialis is forbidden to see ivy. Foolish old man; he could have enjoyed it winding through his latticework and statuary now. Still, it had damaged the stonework, so perhaps the prohibition had some sense.

A gardener who cared had bothered to plant flowers. Gillyflowers and verbena scented the air. Statuesque acanthus and laurel made more formal contributions. Newly planted pots of ferns and violets were dotted about, dripping.

'Where does your water come from?' The nurse looked vague. Having no time to mess about, I worked it out for myself. 'Off the roof into the long containers –' In summer that would not produce enough. I poked around the pool and fountain. I found a lead pipe, leading to a raised cistern:

crude. Though the trickling sound produced would be pleasant, it would provide a very weak head in the fountain, and the cistern would need refilling constantly. It was currently empty; I hauled myself up a wall to inspect the contents and glimpsed the bottom before I lost my handhold and landed in a heap. Refills must be tipped in from off a ladder. 'How do they bring water here?'

'In buckets out of the kitchen.' I looked up the route on the chart. A narrow dogleg corridor led from one corner to the service area. That must drive the kitchen staff mad (I could see why they became irritable when Gaia's pleas to fill her Vestal's play equipment were added to their annoyances). Replenishing the garden tank would also be a deadly job for the carriers. It looked to me as though the builders had been brought in to connect water to the pool in some direct way. Once they had emptied it, they stopped making progress. Typical.

'And how does water reach the house? What's your source of supply?'

The nurse had no idea, but the slave who was tailing me finally spoke up and told me the house was linked to an aqueduct. The Aqua Appia or Aqua Marcia, that would be.

'Parts of the house look very old. Anyone know how they obtained water before the aqueduct was built?'

The escort slave helped me out again: 'The builders found an old well near the kitchen, but it had been filled in.'

'Completely? Wells make me nervous – can you get to it?'

'No, it's quite safe – all solid to floor level.'

'And is that the only one?' He shrugged. 'Right. Now, yesterday – where would Gaia have been playing?'

'By the pool here.'

It struck me that the dry basin did not make a very attractive alternative for the Spring of Egeria. Besides, the builders were supposed to have been here. Solitary little girls do not normally amuse themselves in imaginary games while muscular men in short tunics, with loud voices and raucous opinions, are moving to and fro with cement hods. Come to that, the louts do not enjoy constantly having to step around six-year-olds either.

The sparrows were back. They had discovered a large supply of crumbs. There was a smooth white bench with a marble table, both with sphinxes for legs, which it would be natural for workmen to take over for their regularly accessed lunch boxes. As I suspected: two used wineskins had been carefully hidden down against one of the bench legs because the lads could not be bothered to take their empties home with them. The sparrows hopped around in the dry pool, looking up at me as if asking where their drinking water and bath had gone.

'I really would not have thought a small girl would have been happy playing here.'

The escort slave piped up again: 'She goes over there.' He led me to one of the colonnaded corridors. Against the house wall was a small shrine. Apparently, Gaia would pretend this was the Temple of the Vestals. She would sprinkle water about, tend an imaginary fire, and pretend to be making salt cakes. I found a bunch of sticks, painstakingly tied together with wool in the form of a mop, which Gaia must use for pretending to clean out the temple, in imitation of the Virgins' daily rites.

'Do they let her have ingredients for the pretend salt cakes?'

'No. The Flamen does not like it.' Surprise!

I squatted down on my heels in front of the shrine. A lattice wall and a bank of oleander bushes hid me from most of the rest of the garden. Unless the nurse had stuck very close to her, Gaia could easily have stopped playing and sneaked off.

I heaved myself upright. Ignoring the two slaves, I set off to the nearest doorway out of the colonnade. I passed salons and anterooms bare of furniture. This was the least-used part of the house. More what a child would like. Private. Unobserved. With that ever-attractive atmosphere of a place nobody was supposed to go into without permission. But there was no sign of Gaia.

I kept walking.

On the plan, three sides of this house had streets marked beside them. There were shops and lock-ups leased to artisans; I would check later that they were all quite separate, with no access from the house, though I was certain the ex-Flamen would have insisted upon it. The fourth side had nothing shown, though the house extended slightly in two small wings.

As I thought. There was a rectangular outdoor area between the wings. It was larger than it looked on the plan. 'You could have told me there was another garden!'

'Gaia is not allowed to come here,' protested the nurse sullenly.

'Are you sure she obeys?'

Work was being carried out here too. When the Laelii took over, this part must have been a wilderness. It was supposed to form a small potager with square beds where lines of vegetable and salad crops could be grown for the house. Untended for years, giant parsley and asparagus fern were running riot. Some patches of ground had been cleared; one was now cleanly dug over, others still had stumps of perennial weeds sticking up. The whole central area ought to be shaded by a complex series of pergolas, supporting old vines.

There a disaster greeted me. 'Oh Jupiter, that's some hard pruning!'

The vines had been sliced right off a foot from the ground. Unbelievable. From the debris, I could see they had been until recently mature, healthy climbers, once well trained; new bunches had already formed among the bright green leaves. It was too late anyway to be cutting back vines, and the entire crop had now been lost. Mounds of limp vegetation were heaped everywhere. To me, with country ancestors, it was heartbreaking. I stepped out into the desecration, then could not bear to go on.

My mind was running on two different tracks. The Laelii would have to allocate slaves to help me here. All of this rubbish would have to be lifted, the mounds cleared right back to bare earth and the tangled branches forked over . . . But destroying those vines had been unforgivable.

'Did Numentinus order this?' Sensing my outrage, the slaves merely nodded. 'Dear gods!'

'He cannot walk under vines.'

'He can now! He stopped being the Flamen Dialis last year.'

I forced myself to restrain my anger and returned temporarily to the house.

XXXVI

Statilia Laelia and Ariminius Modullus, the ex-Flamen's daughter and her husband the Pomonalis, were together when I saw them.

I had managed to control my angry breathing by the time I was led into their presence. They were seated side by side on a couch, rather too deliberately for it to be natural. They seemed relaxed. That's about as relaxed as if they had both swallowed burning hot broth and had no water to cool their scorched mouths. If I had been sure a crime had been committed, they would immediately have become suspects.

I had only seen Ariminius from behind, when he came to Fountain Court, but I recognised his voice, affecting light conversation; at once, those slightly crude vowels I had overheard at my apartment jarred again. Face to face, he turned out to be an unassuming type with rather straight, untidy eyebrows and a mole near his nose. He was not wearing a flamen's pointed hat this time; he at least knew how to be normal when he was at home.

To my surprise, I did recognise his wife: she was the woman I had glimpsed briefly in the atrium when I first came here with Maia, the one who had been gathered up by a train of slaves and borne off before I could speak to her. The slaves were all here today again, clustered protectively round her even when her husband was present to supervise. Perhaps she was a nervous type. (Nervous of what?) Or was a flamen's daughter customarily afforded fierce chaperonage from men?

Statilia Laelia bore little resemblance to her brother Scaurus, except in manner. She had the same vague outlook as though nothing much would excite her and she would never exert herself in a cause. She was sitting with one knee crossed over the other, and did not shift from that position. She wore a plain white gown, with neither braid nor jewellery. Her hair was tied back but otherwise hung loose; frankly it looked less than clean, yet she wound strands of it between her fingers, near her mouth, all the time. Her lower lip tended to sag open slightly; when she did close up, her mouth was a tight little button.

'Thank you both for seeing me; I hope not to trouble you long.' I was slick with the smarm today. I appalled myself. 'I have managed to trace little Gaia's movements up until she was supposed to be playing in the peristyle garden. I believe her mother saw her there and said she could be left unsupervised, so that's a definite placing. Can either of you help me with what happened afterwards?'

They shook their heads. 'I was out, attending to business,' said Ariminius, firmly separating himself from the problem. 'You did not see Gaia after breakfast, did you, my love?' Laelia shook her head and twisted her hair some more.

The endearment had sounded formal. I wondered what kind of relationship they really had. Laelia seemed a limp specimen, but I was never fooled by such couples. They were probably at it like rabbits all the time. The fact they had no children meant nothing. I knew that was from choice. Alongside Ariminius' ghastly pot of crocus hair pomade in their bedroom, I had found a jar of the distinctive alum wax contraceptive that Helena and I used. It had been nearly empty, but an identical heavy jar with a film of clear wax sealing it had stood right alongside. They were not intending to run out.

'Thanks.' I decided to treat Ariminius as a sensible contact with whom I could share my thoughts. 'Look, I don't think Gaia stayed in the peristyle. She's not there now anyway; nowhere to hide. You have an area of rough ground behind the house, which I need to search. Can you let me borrow some sturdy slaves to turn over the weed piles and forage through the undergrowth?'

'Oh Gaia would not have gone there!' twittered Laelia.

'Maybe not. I have to search to be sure.'

'We can give you all the help you need. The outlook is

214

bad, isn't it?' asked Ariminius, looking at me searchingly. 'Tell us the truth, Falco. You think she may be –' He could not say it.

'You're right. The situation is desperate. When a child has been missing for a day and night, the odds double that she will not be found alive.'

'She would roam all over the place,' he told me, in a brisk, low voice. He was plainly ignoring Numentinus' wish to be circumspect. Laelia did not protest but shrank into his shadow, not contributing either. Whereas Gaia's mother had at least been driven by her fear for her child, Laelia was obeying family commands to stay silent – though she watched me closely. I felt her observation was almost malicious. She was curious what I would find out – and had a nasty little smile as she waited to see me thwarted.

'I can imagine what it was like living on the Palatine with an adventurous infant,' I commented to Ariminius.

'At least here the house is contained. Three sides face the street with secure doors and windows, and the area you mentioned at the back of the building has a high wall all around it.'

'But she has been known to run off. The nurse neglects her duties?' I suggested.

The Pomonalis sighed. 'She flirts with the workmen whenever she can.'

'Right. I don't want to be indelicate, but do you think it goes beyond flirting?' I did wonder if Gaia had seen something that shocked her.

Ariminius scoffed quietly. 'You have seen the nurse! But the men don't mind laughing with her – any excuse to stop their work.'

'And then Gaia slips away?'

'She means no harm,' Laelia cooed, like doting aunt. 'She just plays by herself.'

'A huge imagination, I gather?' The woman nodded. I asked quietly, 'And is that why she came to tell me someone wanted her dead?'

Both bristled. Both ignored the question fixedly.

'I think she really had been threatened,' I said.

Still no answer.

I looked pointedly from one to another, as if deciding whether the death threats came from either of them. Then I let it drop. 'There are various possibilities,' I told them coldly. 'Prime options are that – being unhappy for reasons that nobody wants to admit – Gaia ran away either to seek out her father or your Aunt Terentia. My view is, you should inform both of them, so they can look out for her.'

'Your view is noted,' said Ariminius. 'I shall discuss with the Flamen whether to tell Scaurus.'

'Terentia Paulla already knows the child is lost?'

'She does,' replied Ariminius – not revealing that the ex-Vestal had been staying here until only that morning. I in turn did not reveal that I was aware she had been a visitor.

'Other possibilities are that the child may be here, hiding or trapped; a full systematic search is my next move. The third option is that she has been abducted, possibly for financial gain.'

'We are not a wealthy family,' Laelia said, raising her eyebrows.

'That's a comparative term, of course. Where you see only mortgages, a starving robber might nonetheless hope to extract a fortune. Is money a problem?' I saw Ariminius shake his head, as much at his wife as at me. Although I had first thought him ineffectual, he now seemed to have a grasp of reality the others here lacked. Laelia just shrugged vaguely. I said to him, 'Well, please inform me immediately if anything like a ransom note arrives.'

'Oh yes.' Ransomers would probably address the ex-Flamen, but Ariminius was playing the man of decision again. At any rate, if he saw a large spider who could only run slowly he would perhaps think about ways he could step on it.

'The worst possibility, if indeed she has been abducted, is that she is brothel fodder by now.' I was being blunt deliberately. Shock tactics were the only weapon I had left. 'A potential Vestal Virgin would be seen as rich pickings.'

'Dear gods, Falco!'

'I don't mean to frighten anyone. But, you have to know.

That is one reason why the Emperor decided to take Gaia's loss so seriously. That is why I am here. That is why you have to be frank. The child is six. Wherever she is, she must be terrified by now. And I have to get to her fast. I need to know about any unusual occurrences – anyone seen hanging round – any aspect of her inclusion in the lottery that could affect her. She wanted to be a Vestal, but it was not universally popular, I understand?' I had borne around on the old tack again: their family feuds.

'Oh that was just Aunt Terentia!' Laelia assured me. Nervousness got the better of her and she giggled uncharacteristically. 'She was wicked about it – actually, she said enough women in this family had had their bedroom lives ruined.'

I managed not to look startled. 'She did not enjoy the celibate life herself, then?'

Laelia now regretted having spoken. 'Oh no, she was devoted to her calling.'

'She was a chaste Virgin – and afterwards she married. The sequence is not unknown. So, tell me about "Uncle Tiberius". Am I right that *his* boudoir life was, let's say, uninhibited?'

A glance was exchanged by the husband and wife. Ariminius had moved his foot against Laelia's; coincidence, perhaps. If it was a warning, it was not much of a kick.

'The man is dead,' he reminded me rather pompously.

'So all he deserves now are eulogies? Luckily we are past the funeral, so you can drop the sickening pretence that he was a worthy descendant of right-thinking republican heroes, and had unimpeachable moral standards.' I looked at Laelia. 'I gather he thought he should share his manly favours widely. Did he ever make advances to you?'

I was prepared for her to hide behind her husband, but she answered straight: 'No. Though I must say, I did not care for him.' It was very direct – too much so, perhaps, as though she had rehearsed it.

'You knew what he was like?'

This time her gaze did waver. Perhaps the man had groped her, yet she had never told her husband. I wished I could have talked to her without the Pomonalis present.

217

'You knew he had made himself unpleasant to Caecilia Paeta?' I insisted.

'Yes, I knew that,' Laelia answered in a low voice.

'It was you she confided in?'

'Yes.' I wondered briefly: if Caecilia had attracted the lecher but Laelia did not, was Laelia jealous?

'Did she tell you of her fears that he might one day go for Gaia?'

'Yes!' These affirmatives were snapping out now.

'Did anybody tell Laelius Numentinus?'

'Oh no.'

'You already had enough troubles in this family?' I asked dryly.

'How right you are!' returned Laelia, rather defiantly. That did not mean she would expound on what those troubles were. Ariminius, I noticed, looked distinctly uncomfortable.

'Did Terentia Paulla know what the man she had married turned out to be like?'

Laelia now sought support from her husband. He was the one taking decisions on what confidences to reveal – or what lies to tell. He said, 'Terentia Paulla knew what she was doing when she married.'

I gazed at him. 'How did she know?'

'Uncle Tiberius was a very old friend of the family.'

I paused. That, colleagues, is always an intriguing situation. Old friends of families are rarely what everyone pretends. They may well be like this one: dirty swine who can never keep their pricks under their tunics, men who bully the women into tolerating their abuse because quite simply no one ever complained before and it seems too late to say anything after so many years.

'So why, if his predilections were obvious, did an extremely holy woman who had just spent three decades living modestly ever want to marry him?'

'Only she can answer that!' cried Laelia harshly.

'Well, if I have no luck finding Gaia, I may have to talk to your aunt.' I noticed that caused a shock of panic, in at least Laelia. She hid it well.

218

Despite her disguised alarm, for once it was the wife and not her husband who came out with the official tale: 'Aunt Terentia prefers to see nobody at present. She is in mourning for her husband – and not in the best of health.' Mourning for her husband – or mourning her own stupidity in marrying a philanderer? Poor health – or just poor judgement?

'I shall try to spare her then. I met your brother,' I told Laelia. 'Do you get on with Scaurus?'

'Yes, we're very close.' I let that go too. I would not fancy having my sisters asked the same question.

'I believe you have seen him recently?'

'Not for anything special,' gasped Laelia, looking nervous at the question. Her shiftiness seemed to have something to do with her husband, as if he might not know.

'Wasn't there a family conference?'

'Minor legal issues,' Ariminius put in. Still watching Laelia, who was now feigning wide-eyed innocence, I remembered that Meldina, the girl at the farm, had mentioned that Scaurus had been to Rome recently 'to see his sister'. Once again, I yearned to interrogate Laelia without her husband. They seemed welded together, unfortunately.

'Issues arising from the death of Terentia's husband?'

Ariminius did not want to go down this route. 'Partly.'

'So Terentia was present?'

'Terentia Paulla is always welcome.'

Why, then, had the slave with the sponge and bucket been instructed to say that Terentia never came any more?

'This family conference must have been a lively occasion!' I remarked quietly. Laelia and Ariminius exchanged glances in which more was being said than I yet understood. 'By the way,' I enquired casually, 'what did your ever-so-friendly Uncle Tiberius actually die of?' When nobody answered I did not press the point, but asked, 'Was his wife with him when he died?'

Ariminius looked me straight in the eye. 'No, Falco,' he said gently, as if he knew why I was asking. 'Terentia Paulla was dining with her old colleagues at the House of the Vestals that night.'

The ultimate unshakeable alibi – had anybody needed one, of course.

I stared straight back at Ariminius. 'Sorry,' I said, not bothering to explain why.

'You know nothing about it, Falco.' The Pomonalis suddenly sounded tired. 'And this has nothing to do with finding Gaia.'

I pulled up.

He and his wife were involved in some deceit; I had no doubt of it. But he was right. A young child was in danger, and that took precedence. Finding Gaia was my job.

I asked Ariminius to supply me with slaves to assist, and then I set about completing a systematic search of the entire house and grounds.

XXXVII

It must have been early afternoon when we set to. With the help of a large contingent of slaves, the whole place was gone over within a few hours.

Ariminius Modullus hung about. I might have wondered if he knew something bad and was watching in case I got too close. I did not trust him, but he was straight about the search. He watched and listened when I first gave orders, then he joined in. He did seem to understand how urgent the situation was, yet in a perverse way he was starting to enjoy the action, as he collected a posse and began supporting my efforts to show them how they must look into every chest and hamper, then under, in, and behind anything that had even a crack of room to squeeze inside.

He liked having something to do. I always kept an eye out, but his co-operation took some of the strain off me. I was grateful. The responsibility of finding the child was a hard one. Not finding her would be a grim burden to live with. It would have been oppressive enough, even if I did not know she had asked for my help and I had refused her.

My bet was that since he married Laelia, Ariminius had sunk into apathy, living with such a strong figure as his father-in-law. By the end of the afternoon I actually went so far as to tell him, man to man, 'Numentinus has no patriarchal authority over you. You may respect him and the honoured position he used to hold in your priesthood – but you answer to your own father.'

'Grandfather, actually. He drools a bit, but he lets me do what I like.' He seemed almost human; still, before he joined the pointy-heads, he had been as common as I used to be. We were both born plebs.

'My advice is to leave here when this episode is over, and

become head of your own household.' When he looked uncertain, I remembered the drab side of being a plebeian and asked, 'Is funding a problem?'

To my surprise he said at once, 'No. I have money.'

'But living in the Flaminia was too attractive?'

He smiled wryly. 'I was ambitious once! But I shall probably not be promoted above Flamen Pomonalis now.' He did not say, *even with the ex-Flamen Dialis as my father-in-law*.

'I suppose you get sneered at by your in-laws for that?'

At first he was not intending to answer, then he squeezed out an affirmative. 'And there is my wife to consider.'

'But Statilia Laelia does not remain in her father's patriarchal control now she is married.'

'Not legally!' he said, with feeling.

'If her husband left to live independently, she would go with him – of course.'

Ariminius was silent. Interesting. 'At the moment,' he then said, like a man who had thought this out already, 'desertion would be a cruelty.' Desertion seemed a strong word to use for moving out of his father-in-law's house – though Numentinus was no ordinary father-in-law. Then I wondered if he meant more; if he left, would he shed the whole pack of them, wife and all? Would he want to leave Laelia behind?

Before I could ask him, he added, as if wanting to close the subject, 'It's a difficult time, Falco.'

'Really? There is a family secret, I gather.'

'Nothing escapes you.'

'I get to the truth in the end. I am beginning to suspect that I know what your secret is. So are you going to enlighten me?'

'It is not for me to tell. But it has nothing whatsoever to do with the child,' said Ariminius.

'Flamen Pomonalis, you had better be right – or if anything has happened to her, it will be on your conscience!'

We had started with the kitchen garden at the back of the house. We scoured every patch of ground, while the men used forks and two-pronged hoes to turn all the piles of rubbish. There had been a bonfire; I myself raked through its ashes while the slaves were making the final push into the area of wildest growth towards the far wall. I sent for a ladder (the builders had left plenty) and even climbed up and looked over that wall. There was a public baths beyond it, in a maze of streets. If Gaia had, somehow, scaled this barrier she would then have been away in the reaches of the Aventine that ran towards the Raudusculana Gate. But first she would have had a climbing feat ahead of her. Even I only managed to barge through the rampant undergrowth with a great many curses, scratches and a badly torn tunic; it seemed impossible for a child. The height of the wall when balanced on a precarious ladder placed on very rough ground was too off-putting. Not that I ever rule out anything absolutely. If she thought she was fleeing for her life, desperation could make anything feasible.

Next we probed and picked over the house. I divided the workforce and placed half in command of Ariminius; I started at the top with my men, he started at the bottom with his, and after crossing halfway we knew that every cranny should have been investigated not just once but twice.

There were large salons and small cubicles. An area which must have been far older than the rest of the property had all the rooms running into each other in an old-fashioned sequence, then there were other wings where tasteful modern reception rooms led off frescoed corridors. A damp basement consisted of about fifty cells for slaves; that allowed rapid searching. All they had in them were a few meagre treasures and hard pallets to sleep on. We lined up the slaves, army-style, each outside his or her own compartment, while we searched. That gave me a chance to ask every one if they knew anything or had seen Gaia yesterday after her mother sent the nurse to other duties.

'What duties were they, incidentally?' I checked routinely with Ariminius, but he only shrugged and looked vague. Giving instructions to women was a woman's business – or at least that was what he wanted me to think.

There are odd contents in most homes, though few so odd

as I saw here. In the ex-Flamen's bedroom, which was some way from the rest of his family, stood a casket of sacrificial cakes (in case of night starvation?) and the bed legs were smeared with clay – an accommodation that allowed a practising Flamen Dialis to escape the ancient prescription that he must sleep upon the ground. It was no longer necessary for Numentinus. Retirement meant nothing to the old man – though this seemed an affectation in his new house.

I could not have lived here. What passed for refinement in their lives made me turn up my fine long Etruscan nose: the ex-Flamen's library, for instance, contained nothing but scrolls of ritual nonsense, as oblique as the Sibylline Books. Throughout the house there were too many niches that had been set up as shrines, and the cloying stench of incense lingered everywhere. Looms for the women were lined up in a whole bank in a bare room, like the workshop of the most miserable tailor. The wine store was meagre. Even Helena and I, at our lowest ebb financially, had paid more attention to the quality of what went in our oil lamps. Shabbiness is one thing; lack of interest is pitiful.

I was not here to criticise their life. But if more people had done so in the past, and if its quality had been improved, just maybe there would have been less unhappiness. Then maybe the child would be safe at home.

We reached the point where there was only one ghastly place that we had not probed. My heart sank. I had hoped to avoid this. Still, it needed to be done. After checking with the plan, I led the way to a small cubicle in the kitchen area. A call for a volunteer met with silence, as I expected. I told Ariminius to pick out a slave who needed punishment, then I sent for buckets and gave orders to remove the wooden two-hole seat so we could excavate the lavatory.

It was impossible to reach down very far from ground level, so we put the protesting slave into the hole in a sling and passed him a long stick to probe the depths. We kept him down there an hour, until he seemed about to faint. We hauled him out just in time. The latrine had been very well constructed, with a shaft a yard and a half deep, but we found nothing, thank the gods.

Well, we found plenty. Nothing relevant.

We had done all we could. Short of tearing off the roof and battering holes in partitions, we had searched everywhere it was feasible to look. Ariminius lost himself, his earlier enthusiasm deflated by our failure. Receiving no further orders from him or from me, the slaves drifted off too. Even my escort conveniently forgot he had been ordered to stick with me.

There was nothing else I could do. I thought about sleeping here overnight, to listen to noises and absorb the atmosphere. But I had had enough of the dreary, stultifying aura of this unhappy home. I could not determine exactly what was wrong, but there were remnants of old miseries everywhere. I thought there was something worse too. Something terrible they were all hiding. I just hoped the Pomonalis had been right when he claimed it did not affect Gaia.

I walked for one last time into the peristyle garden. No one was there now. Holding Gaia's little twiggy mop, I strode slowly around the central area, then sat on the marble bench, leaning my elbows on my knees. I had not eaten all day. I was filthy and knocked about. Nobody here had ever thought of offering me refreshments or the facilities to clean up. I was long past being able to complain or say what I thought of them. Still, this was everyday fare for an informer. I was not yet so nicely respectable that I would shriek if I noticed my white tunic had turned nearly black and that, not to be too dainty about it, I stank.

Somebody came out behind me. I was too stiff and too depressed to move.

'Falco.' Hearing the voice of the ex-Flamen, I did force myself to turn around, though I would not rise for him. 'You have done well. We are grateful.'

I could not help sighing. 'I have done nothing.'

'It seems she is not here.'

I looked around again, helplessly. She was still at home. I felt convinced of it. My voice sounded husky. 'Forgive me for not finding her.'

'I am aware of how hard you have tried.' From him that was gratitude. Rather to my surprise he came and placed himself at the table where the workmen's crumbs had once been squabbled over by the sparrows. 'Do not think us harsh, Falco. She is a beguiling, sweet-natured little girl, my only grandchild. I prayed with all my heart that you would have found her today.'

I was too weary to react. But I did believe him.

I stood up. 'I'll find out whether the vigiles have discovered anything.' If so, it could only be bad news now. The old man looked as if he knew that. 'If she still fails to turn up, may I come back here tomorrow and see what else can be done?'

He pursed his lips. He did not want me here. Yet he inclined his head, allowing it. Maybe he really did love Gaia. Or maybe he sensed that this loss of the small child could be the incident that split apart his family when all else had failed to break his dominance.

'I know what you feel about the vigiles, sir, but I would like to bring in one officer, my friend Petronius Longus. He has vast experience – and is the father of young girls. I want to walk the ground with him, and see if he turns up anything I missed.'

'I would prefer to avoid that.' It was not quite a refusal, and I kept it in reserve. 'A woman is here to speak to you,' he then told me. 'You are wanted elsewhere.'

Nothing much seemed to matter to me at the moment, but I still had it in me to be curious. As I dragged myself to my feet and turned to leave the garden to find my personal visitor, the other curiosity prevailed.

'It had seemed to me,' I told Numentinus sombrely, 'the best hope of finding Gaia would be if she had mischievously crept into some hole from which she could not escape. But we seem to have disproved that.' Numentinus was walking slowly alongside me. 'The most likely alternative,' I commented, determined not to spare him now, 'is that she has run away because of family problems.'

I had expected the ex-Flamen to be furious. His reaction

turned everything I assumed on its head. He laughed. 'Well, we would all like to run away from those!' While I was getting over that, he tossed the suggestion aside with a sneer of contempt. 'Now you have lost my confidence, Falco, after all.'

'Oh I don't think I deserve that, sir! It's fairly plain something came to a head here after the death of Terentia Paulla's husband. Well, look at it – a man who was not even a blood relative, a family friend yes – but one who had been abusive towards your womenfolk –' Although they had told me Numentinus did not know, I reckoned he was well aware of it; at any rate, he showed no surprise now. 'Next minute, you are consulting everyone, including the widow – again, only a relative of your late wife's, and a woman with whom you yourself have been at odds regularly. Even your estranged son was in on the debate. He spun me a wild story about that! So tell me,' I insisted heatedly, 'for whom is the legal guardian really needed? And why, exactly?'

Shocked by my vehemence, Numentinus stayed silent. And he was not intending to answer me: he dodged it all. 'I cannot imagine what my son has said to make you think this way. It simply shows how unworldly he is, and proves me right to continue to hold him in my patriarchal power.'

'He wants to help his aunt. That seems commendable.'

'Terentia Paulla needs no help from anyone,' Numentinus uttered crushingly. 'Anybody who has told you otherwise is a fool!' He paused. 'Or completely mad,' he added, in a baleful voice.

I was too disheartened to protest or make further enquiries. What he said had a ghastly ring of truth.

I walked to the entrance hall they were using, and there at last my spirits rose slightly: the person who had asked for me was Helena. She was holding my toga, which somebody must have found and given to her, and she smiled gently. Obviously she had heard I had failed. There was no need to waste effort explaining.

I noticed she was rather well dressed, in a gleamingly clean white gown and a modest stole over her hair which looked suspiciously fanciful to arouse new dreads. She was wearing a gold necklace her father had given her when Julia was born. She was scented divinely with Arabic balsam and her face, on close inspection, had been lightly touched up with such skill in the use of the paint that it had to have been applied by one of her mother's maids or with the help of Maia.

The last thing I wanted now was the kind of social gathering that called for such titivation.

'Come along,' Helena grinned, seeing my horror. She sniffed at me. 'Nice unguents, Falco! You have such exquisite taste . . . A litter is waiting outside with a clean tunic for you. We can stop at a bath-house if you're quick.'

'I am in no mood for a party.'

'It's official: no option. Titus Caesar wants you.'

Titus Caesar sometimes did discuss state issues with me. I was not expected to take a chaperon. So what was this about?

Titus, in my opinion, had once nursed a partiality for Helena. As far as I knew it had remained hypothetical, though she had needed to leave Rome in a hurry to avoid awkwardness. She still avoided him, and would certainly never normally turn out rigged like this, in case it revived his ideas.

'What's the wrinkle, fruit?'

Helena was smiling. Full of joy at seeing her, I had already let myself start to sink into her power. 'Don't worry, my darling,' she murmured. 'I shall take care of you. I think, from what the messenger told me, our hosts will be wonderful Titus – and the fabulous Queen of Judaea.'

XXXVIII

No wise man can possibly answer the question: was Queen Berenice really beautiful? Well, not when any of his womenfolk are listening.

I wondered if my brother Festus, he who died the heroic or not-quite-so-heroic death in her country, had ever seen Titus Caesar's armful. I found myself overcome by a yearning to discuss with Festus what he thought of her. Not that I mean to imply that anything would have happened if Festus, a mere centurion of common origin and raffish habits, ever had seen her but, as is well known, Didius Festus was a lad.

Well, was she beautiful?

'Loud!' Ma would have said.

Achieved with sensitivity and high quality trappings, loudness has its virtues. I happen to believe there is a place for loud women. (Festus thought so too; for him, their place was in his bed.)

Let it not be suggested that I am dodging the issue through a bad brother who happened to have had a reputation for jumping anyone in long skirts. I just want to say, as I am quite happy to do even if Helena Justina should be on hand, that had my brother Festus seen Queen Berenice he would undoubtedly have risen to the challenge of trying to displace his élite commander (Titus Caesar, legate of the Fifteenth Legion when Festus served with them) – and that I personally would have enjoyed watching Festus have a go.

That's all. A man can dream.

Believe me, a man can hardly avoid it when he has spent hours supervising bucketfuls of grunge from the depths of a lavatory that must have been first used in republican times and rarely emptied since, then he walks into a room so full of exotic items that he can barely take them all in – not counting the dame in the diadem who is apparently feeding flattery to Titus as if it were huge pearly oysters in wine sauce. (Titus is lapping up her murmured endearments like a parched dog.) (The attendants have their eyes on stalks.) (Helena chokes.)

'Oh settle down, Falco. It's just a woman. Two eyes, one nose, two arms, a rather obvious bust, and perhaps not quite as many teeth as she must have owned once.'

I do not practise dentistry. I had not been looking at the Queen's teeth.

Luckily, we had just entered a suite in Nero's Golden House where the waterworks came in multiple quantities, with a luxuriant supply which was continually switched on. Liquefactious sheets of water slid down stair-fountains; fine spouts tinkled in marble shells. High ceilings absorbed some of the stray sound and swathes of rich drapery muffled the rest. Unintentionally, the mad imperial harpist had created a satirist's dream: in the Golden House, a sharp girl could be rude about a rival all the way across the room – indeed, right until the rival's oriental perfumes knocked her back a pace, trying not to sneeze.

With an upheaval of purple, Titus Caesar, all curls and chubby chops, rushed from a dais to welcome us. He was typical of the Flavians, thickset and almost stout, apparently an ordinary fit countryman, yet conscious of his dignity.

'Helena Justina – how wonderful to see you! Falco, welcome.'

Titus looked ready to burst with pride in his conquest – or at being conquered by such a wonder. Understandably, he was eager to show off his new royal girlfriend to a senator's daughter who once cold-shouldered him. Helena responded with a quiet smile. Had he known Helena well, Titus would have restrained his enthusiasm at that point. If she had smiled like that at me, I would have returned to my couch, rammed my knees together, clasped my hands, and kept quiet for the next hour in case I had my ears blasted.

Being the son and heir of an emperor, Titus assumed he was in charge here. Queen Berenice, if I am any judge, detected more complex undercurrents. She had followed him down to us, shimmering. A neat trick. Silken robes help. Then it's easy to do (Helena told me afterwards) if your sandals are difficult to walk in, so you have to sway sinuously in order not to fall over when traversing low steps.

Attendants placed us all informally on couches off the dais. The cushions were packed so hard with down, I nearly slid off mine. Like all architect-designed mansions, the whole place was dangerous; my boot studs had already skidded a few times on over-polished floor mosaics. There was so much to look at, I could not decide where to feast my eyes. (I refer to the exquisite paintwork – that on the walls and the ceiling vaults, of course.)

'Falco – you are very quiet!' chuckled Titus. He was reeking with happiness, poor dog.

'Dazzled, Caesar.' I could be polite. After today's efforts, however, I may have been openly flagging. Physically I was wrecked. I hoped it was temporary. I ached worryingly. Age was catching up. My hands and fingernails felt rough; the dry skin of my face felt stretched. Even after a fast steam and scrape in the baths, the contents of that lavatory were still arousing unpleasant nasal memories.

'Marcus is exhausted,' Helena told Titus, settling herself elegantly. Though a private lass, in company she sometimes produced a composure that startled me. I knew when to shut up, anyway. I was too tired, so she was crisply taking charge. 'He has spent all day searching for the little girl at the Laelius house. When I tracked him down for you, he was filthy and I am sure they had given him nothing to eat –'

Berenice responded at once to the cue. (So the rumours were true; she had taken over the domestic keys already . . .) Rubies flashed as she waved a languid hand to call for sustenance for me. Helena beamed thanks in her direction.

'No luck?' Titus asked me. He looked very keen for a reassuring answer.

'No sign of her, unfortunately,' Helena said. Trays of dainties had arrived. I started to pick at them; Helena weighed in like a food taster, then selected from the silver bowls and popped morsels into my mouth almost as fast as I

231

could deal with them. Fortunately, my well-wound toga stopped me slumping. Propped up in its hot woollen swathes, I succumbed to being tended like an invalid. This was nice. A comfortable palace. Helena did the talking. There was plenty for me to stare around at while I let her run the interview.

I wondered what the home life of the imperial family would be like nowadays: young Domitian, aping Augustus seizing Livia, had snatched a married woman and announced himself married to her; that was after seducing every senator's wife he could persuade to favour him – before his father came home and clipped his wings. Titus (once divorced, once widowed) had now been joined – perhaps unexpectedly – by his exotic royal piece. Vespasian had previously lived openly with an extremely astute freedwoman, Antonia Caenis, my late patroness (was it coincidence that Berenice had delayed her arrival in Rome until after the death of Vespasian's sensible, influential concubine?). There were a couple of very young female relations – Titus' daughter, Julia, and a Flavia. Vespasian himself had now decamped to live in the Gardens of Sallust in the north of the city, near his old family house. But even without the old man, communal breakfasts must be riveting affairs.

'I suppose your father must have considered whether to continue with the Vestals' lottery?' Helena was asking Titus.

'Well, we feel there is no choice about tomorrow. There are twenty perfectly good candidates –'

'Nineteen,' I mumbled, between mouthfuls.

'Gaia Laelia may yet be found safe and well!' Titus reproved me.

'One other little girl has had to be withdrawn,' Helena informed him calmly. 'Her father died.' Titus pulled up, seeing she knew more about this than he did. 'If the lottery is held,' Helena explained for the Queen's benefit, 'all the candidates must be present. It is essential that when the Pontifex Maximus selects a name, he can continue with the ritual: he must then take the girl by the hand, welcome her with the ancient declaration – and remove her at once from

232

her family to her new home in the Vestals' House.'

The Queen listened, making no comment, but watching with dark, heavily etched eyes. I wondered what she made of us. Had Titus told her who he had sent for? If so, how did he describe us? Did she expect this low-born man with tired limbs and chin stubble, bossed into easy submission by a cool creature who spoke to the Emperor's son like one of her own brothers?

Helena continued to include the Queen: 'We are talking about a symbolic ceremony in which the chosen girl leaves the authority of her own family, and abandons all her possessions as a member of that family, then becomes a child of Vesta. Her hair is shaved off and hung on a sacred tree – though of course, it is afterwards allowed to grow again; she dons the formal attire of a Vestal Virgin, and from that day begins her training. If the chosen child were not present when her name was called, it would be very awkward.'

'Impossible,' said Titus.

I chewed thoughtfully on a lobster dumpling. Tut, tut; the chef had left a piece of shell. I removed it with a pained expression, as if I expected better here.

'I thought Rutilius Gallicus was your commissioner in the search for Gaia Laelia?' Helena asked Titus, perhaps reproving him for interference. I caught the eye of the young Caesar and smiled faintly. Time was, he had had me on the hop whenever he summoned me to a meeting. Well, I was respectable now; I could bring along my talented, well-bred girlfriend to defend me like a gladiator's trainer choreographing a fight.

She had waved up an attendant with a wine flagon, but when the boy reached us, she took the vessel from him and poured my drink herself. The attendant looked startled. Helena flashed him a smile and he jumped back, unaccustomed to acknowledgement.

'Yes, well . . .' Titus was hedging. I had always reckoned he could be devious, so this was unlike him. I sipped the wine. Helena leaned forwards, as if waiting to hear what Titus had to say. Her flimsy stole had slipped down her back. Curled tendrils of her hair wafted on her neck. I

233

reached out my free hand and tugged one of the soft tendrils so she sat nearer to me again. In defiance of protocol, I put my arm around her.

'Some extra dimension, Caesar?' Now the authoritative tone was mine. I thought Berenice sharpened her gaze slightly, wondering whether Helena would accept my take-over. She did, of course. The refined and elegant Helena Justina knew that if she gave me any trouble I was going to tickle her neck until she collapsed in fits.

'This is rather sensitive, Falco.' It would be. I might be Procurator of the Sacred Geese, but I remained the fixer who was given all the rough jobs. 'I just want to beg you to do all you can.'

'Marcus will continue until he has found the child.' Long practised, Helena had worked free of my restraining arm.

'Yes of course.' Titus looked submissive. Then he looked at Berenice. She seemed to be waiting for something; he seemed embarrassed. He admitted, 'There has been some bad feeling about the Queen and me.'

I inclined my head politely. At my side, Helena took my hand. Surely, she cannot have imagined I would say something rude? The man was in love. It was sad to watch.

'Ridiculous!' scoffed Titus. In his eyes, Berenice could do no wrong and anyone who suggested there were problems was being unkind and irrational. He should have known better – as his father had done, when Berenice first tried her wiles on the old man himself.

The lovers were insulated here; they might have convinced themselves everything was fine. This would carry Titus through a great deal of public disapproval. But he would have to face the truth when Vespasian himself decided to bust up the love nest.

Murmurs of discontent must have already reached the romantic pair. 'As you may know,' Titus told me in a firm, formal voice, as if he were speech-making, 'the last time the missing child, Gaia Laelia, was seen publicly was at a reception which was given to allow all the young lottery candidates to meet Queen Berenice.'

'Gaia Laelia spent part of the afternoon on the Queen's

lap,' I said. 'I'm glad you raised this, Caesar – I understand there was some kind of commotion?'

'You are well informed, Falco!'

'My contacts are everywhere.' He thought about that. I regretted saying it.

'This may be important,' Helena said to Berenice, 'Can you tell us what the fuss was?'

'No.' Titus answered for the Queen. 'All the girl talked about was her pleasure in being selected – I mean, being subjected to the lottery.'

I was beginning to wonder if Berenice lacked Latin. However, this was the woman who, while sharing the Judaean kingdom with her incestuous brother, had once protested volubly against the barbarity of a Roman governor in Jerusalem; she was a fearless orator who had appealed for clemency for her people barefoot, though in danger of her life. She could speak out when she wanted to.

And now she did. Ignoring Titus studiously, she appeared to override his instructions to keep her mouth shut: 'The child was rather quiet. After I seemed to win her confidence, she suddenly exclaimed, "Please let me stay here. There is a mad person at home who is going to kill me!" I was alarmed. I thought the child herself must be crazy. Attendants came forward immediately and took her away.'

To her credit, the Queen looked disturbed by remembering the incident.

'Did anyone investigate her claims?' I asked.

'For heaven's sake, Falco,' snapped Titus. 'Who could believe it? She comes from a very good family!'

'Oh that's all right, then,' I retorted caustically.

'We made a mistake,' he admitted.

I had to accept it, since so had I. 'Gaia also talked at some length, that day and I believe on a subsequent occasion, to the Vestal Constantia,' I told him. 'Would it be possible for you to arrange officially for me to interview Constantia?'

He pursed his lips. 'It is thought preferable not to allow that, in case it should give the wrong impression. There must be no suggestion of any specific link between one particular child and the Vestals. We would not want to compromise the lottery.'

That clinched it for me. I had no doubts now: the lottery was not just compromised, it was a cold-blooded fix.

'With Gaia Laelia mysteriously missing, the reception has had unforeseen and rather unfortunate consequences,' Titus said. The food was starting to revive me, but I was still so tired I must have been slow. 'It has been seized on by scandal-mongers.'

Belatedly, I caught up. 'Surely the Queen is not being linked to the disappearance of a child she had only met once, and then formally?'

As soon as I said it, I could see the predicament. Slander need not be believable. Gossip is always more enjoyable if it looks likely to be untrue.

Berenice was Judaean. It was believed that Titus had promised her marriage. He may indeed have done so, though his father was unlikely ever to allow it. Ever since Cleopatra, Romans have had a horror of exotic foreign women stealing the hearts of their generals and subverting the peace and prosperity of Rome.

Titus spoke harshly. 'Madness!' Maybe. But an accusation that Berenice was a child-killer – or a Vestal Virgin abductor – was just the kind of ridiculous rumour that fools would want to believe. 'Falco, I want this girl found.'

For a moment, I did feel sorry for them. The woman had to go home again – but it ought to be for the proper reasons, not because of some sleaze dreamed up by political opponents. Instead, the Flavians would have to show that they understood what Rome required and that, if he were to become emperor one day, Titus was man enough to face his responsibilities.

To lighten the atmosphere, I said gently, 'If I do find Gaia safe and alive, and if it is too late for the lottery, I have just one request – can somebody else have the task of explaining to the weeping child that she will not be a Vestal Virgin after all?'

Titus relaxed and laughed.

*

Helena, who had been quietly munching the titbits while I talked, now jumped to her feet and pulled me after her. Visitors were supposed to wait until they were dismissed by royalty, but that did not bother her. Until I was made middle-class, it would not have bothered me either – so I reached back shamelessly for another lobster knick-knack. 'He needs to rest,' my beloved told Titus.

Titus Caesar rose, then came and clasped my hand. He had the good fortune to choose the non-fishy one. 'I am extremely grateful, Falco.' The one benefit of my new rank was that all my clients were perfectly polite to me. That did not mean the fees would arrive any quicker (or at all).

After his farewell to me, Titus had lifted Helena's hand. 'I am glad to see you here tonight.' He was speaking in a low voice. Helena looked nervous, though not as nervous as I was. 'I want you to explain something discreetly to your brother.'

'Aelianus?'

'He applied to join the Arval Brethren. Look; do let him know, they have nothing against him personally. He is well qualified. But there will have to be a period of readjustment after your uncle's unfortunate escapade.'

'Oh I see,' replied Helena in an odd tone of voice. 'This is a reference to unhappy Uncle Publius?' She meant the senator's brother, who some time before had unwisely plotted to destabilise the Empire and dethrone Vespasian. Misguided Uncle Publius was no threat now. He was out of it, his corpse rotting in the Great Sewer. I knew; I shoved him down there myself.

'You see what I mean?' asked Titus, eager for her acquiescence.

'Oh I do,' Helena answered. With a cool turn of her head, she offered her cheek for Titus Caesar to kiss, which he stalwartly did. Before I could stop her, she then leaned in like some old childhood friend who was about to kiss him back. Instead she added very, very gently, 'It was four years ago; my uncle is dead; the conspiracy was completely unravelled; and no question marks ever hung over my father's or my brothers' loyalty – Sir, what I see is just a feeble excuse!'

237

Titus had turned back to his lustrous lady love, pretending to make a joke of it. 'This is an exceptional couple!' Berenice looked as if she thought so too, though not for the same reasons. 'I love them both dearly,' Titus Caesar proclaimed.

I grabbed Helena's hand and tucked it firmly in my arm, pulling her back and keeping her close to me. Then I thanked Titus for his confidence in us, and took my defiant girl away.

She was extremely upset. I had seen it even before she answered. Titus, of course, had no idea. She would talk to me about it, although probably not for days. When she did speak, she would be raging. I could wait. I just kept my arm tightly around her while she controlled her immediate anger.

We walked together in silence for some distance. Since Helena was wrapped in her own thoughts, I could sink into mine. The pressure I felt upon me now was the same old dead weight. In addition to the domestic tragedy that I was trying to avert from the Laelii, my task had acquired much wider significance. This new burden, of saving Berenice from grief for Titus, was a tricky one.

So that was the ravishing Queen Berenice! If this had happened to my brother Festus, a scented notelet would have followed before he reached the street door.

Mind you, when Didius Festus visited fabulously beautiful women, he made sure that he went by himself.

XXXIX

In Nero's day, the entire ground floor of the Esquiline Wing of the Golden House had been given over to dining rooms. There were matched pairs, one half looking into a spacious courtyard, the complementary mirrored groups facing out over the Forum, where Nero installed a wildlife park but where Vespasian was now building his Amphitheatre. With his rather different lifestyle, Nero had needed not one elegant hall for feeding flatterers – his best being the famous Octagonal Room – but complex suites in threes or fives that would contain the wild parties he loved. It was amongst the labyrinth of these that we had seen Titus.

The Flavians were another breed from Nero. They conducted most official imperial business in the old Palace of the Caesars, high on the Palatine. It was said they intended to dismantle the Golden House soon. It represented not just hated luxury, but Nero's contempt for the people he had deliberately burned out and displaced in order to build it. The Flavians respected the people. At any rate, they would do, so long as the people respected them. But they were also frugal. While their predecessor's mad, gloriously ornate dwelling still existed, it did seem proper to them that Rome – in the person of the frugal Flavians – should make use of it. It had cost a great deal and Vespasian was hot on the value-for-money principle.

I had been here for private meetings before, and for one formal conference held in the Octagon. Titus often lurked here when he was off duty. He would call me in sometimes for a staid heart-to-heart.

The place was vast. Tall frescoed corridors ran in all directions. Most of the rooms were not too ostentatious sizewise, but they ran into each other in a bemusing honeycomb. There were peculiar backdoubles and dead ends, due to this wing having been hewn from the naked rock under the Oppian Hill. Unescorted, it would have been easy to get lost.

There was a casual atmosphere. Occasional Praetorian Guards had parked themselves in corridors, not least because Titus was their commander now. On the whole, nobody looked at visitors too closely, and it seemed possible to wander at will.

Somehow, you never did. Somehow your feet were guided out of the building quite rapidly and on what I was coming to realise was a well-worn path. The result was that despite the huge number of rooms, with their variety of exits and entrances, and despite the temptation to tiptoe into them to collect ideas for home décor, if two groups of people were visiting Titus on the same evening for the same purpose, although it hardly seemed feasible, they would actually end up face to face.

That was how Helena and I met Rubella and Petronius.

Those two big snide bastards were not pleased.

'Looks like we got to the buffet first,' I greeted them. I knew they would be hopping mad that the vigiles were firmly refused permission to investigate the Laelius house, whereas I had been called in specially. The gap between private informers and the vigiles would never close. 'Don't worry; I gave Titus Caesar a thorough briefing. You can just show your faces, then bunk off back to your patrol house.'

'Skip it, Falco,' growled my one-time partner Petro.

'All right. Owning-up time: I've failed to find any trace of the lost baby. How about you boys?'

'Nothing,' Rubella deigned to say. The Fourth Cohort tribune was a wide, tough, shaven-headed ex-centurion who practised the lowest degree of fairness and unpleasantness. In that, he was better than average. Fanatical ambition had hauled him up all the rungs in the vigiles; he really wanted to be a Praetorian. Still, so do lots of lads.

At his side Petronius looked taller, less wide in the body yet more powerful in the shoulder, quieter, a couple of pounds heavier because of his height, and far less intense. He was in brown leather, with a thong twisted round his head to hold down his straight hair during a tussle, triple-soled boots so heavy it made my feet tired just looking at them, and a night stick through his wide belt. He was a good-looking boy, my old tent-mate.

I gave him an ironical grin of approval. 'The luscious Berenice will love you!'

'As he said, skip it, Falco.' That came from Helena. She was still subdued over the unfair snub to her brother. I introduced her to Rubella, though he had worked out who she was.

'Falco is tired,' she announced. 'I am taking him home to recover from gawping at flashy Judaean pulchritude.'

'Have you given up the search?' Petro asked, sticking to the job in hand. He had a prudish streak. Alone with me, he would happily discuss leer-worthy women, but he believed it improper for women to know that that was what men did.

'Not me. How about you lot?'

'We'll find her if she's out on the streets. But will you, if she is still at home?'

Temporarily riled, I abandoned my plan of asking him to join me tomorrow. Obviously, the raucous members of the Fourth Cohort – and probably members of all the other six – were just standing around watching and waiting for me to make a mess of the task. I would disappoint them. But I needed to keep all options open: 'Don't let's quarrel when a child's life is at stake.'

'Who's quarrelling?'

Petronius was, but thinking about Gaia, I changed my mind again about tomorrow: 'Lucius Petronius, I just asked Numentinus for permission to bring you in, for the benefit of your experience.'

Petronius mimed an irritating bow. 'Marcus Didius, whenever you're stuck, just ask me to set you right.'

'For heaven's sake, stop playing about, you two,' Helena grumbled.

I shrugged, and prepared to leave. Rubella decided to take a hand. To him, normally, I was an interfering amateur whom he would like to lock in a cell until my boots rotted off. Tonight, since he always overruled Petro and since Petro was niggling, he chose amicable co-operation. 'Anything you need, Falco?'

'Thanks, but no thanks. It is a routine house search and the family is not being difficult. Well, not that I can see.'

'Found anything to help us?'

'I don't think so. The last time the girl was seen she was at home. She ought to be still there. There are no known external contacts –' Well, apart from me. I chose not to dwell on that. Rubella was suspicious as Hades. He would love to arrest me on a trumped-up charge of personal involvement. 'I have seen no sign that the Laelii are concealing a ransom demand. All the problems that I know about are family ones. That's going to be the answer.'

'They do have problems.' Rubella loved to repeat part of your briefing as though it was his own. I caught Petro's eye. He and I had always reckoned that persons in senior positions stole our ideas.

'Plenty. By the way – are either of you law-and-order experts able to tell me this about the rules for guardians?' I asked them. 'Could a son who was still officially in his father's control accept the job?'

'Oh yes.' It was Petro who answered. 'It's a civic duty. Like voting. Anyone who has come of age is entitled to do it, whatever his status otherwise. I thought you yourself would be standing guardian for Maia now, Falco.'

'Jupiter! I would hate to be the person who told Maia she had to report formally to me.'

Petro gave me an odd look, almost as though he felt I was abandoning my sister.

'So what's that to do with the missing girl?' Rubella asked.

'Gaia's father spun me some yarn. There was talk of legal pleas and all sorts – all for nothing, apparently. Either the father is up to something extraordinarily devious – or he is, as *his* father defines him, a complete idiot.'

'Where is this idiot?' Rubella mused.

I told him where Laelius Scaurus lived. 'I advised the family to inform him that Gaia was lost –'

'Oh we can do better than that,' smirked the tribune. 'If his darling daughter is in terrible trouble, we must bring the poor suffering man to Rome as quickly as possible – in fact, he can have an official escort of vigiles to clear the way for him!'

Refusing the assistance of the vigiles, as Numentinus would find, was unwise. Their cohort tribunes do not submit to rebuff.

I grinned. 'Dear me. Laelius Scaurus received an innocent, priestly upbringing. This will be a terrible shock. He will think you are arresting him.'

'So he will!' grinned Rubella evilly.

I had no idea what good this could possibly do, but anything unexpected can shake people up to good effect. To have the Fourth Cohort of vigiles explain his legal rights and responsibilities would certainly alarm Scaurus.

However, I was not sure I wanted to be in Rubella's shoes when this influential family complained with shrieks of outrage to the Prefect of the City that one of them had been subjected to an unfair arrest. The Laelii were more than just influential. They were being treated with elaborate care by the highest authorities – and I still did not know why.

XL

Incredibly, it was still eight days before the Ides of June. Dusk had fallen, but this was the same day that I rose at dawn and went to the House of the Vestals trying to meet Constantia, followed her to Egeria's Spring, was sent for by Rutilius Gallicus, and gained entrance to search the Laelius house. Now I had endured a visit to the Golden House as well. This was as long a day as I ever wanted to endure, but it was not over yet.

'You take the litter. Go home and rest,' said Helena. She sounded wan.

'Where's Julia?'

'I managed to find Gaius.' When my scruffy nephew could be deterred from totting in the backstreets, he made a dedicated nursemaid (if we paid him enough). 'I told him to sleep in our bed if we were late.'

'You'll regret that. He's never clean. What are you up to, as if I don't know?'

'I had better walk over to my father's house and break this news about my brother's fate.'

I went with her, of course.

The senator lent me his barber, and they gave me more to eat. While I was being cleaned up and pampered, I had a lot to think about. It did not really concern the Camilli and their dead traitor. For me, Publius Camillus Meto was a closed case. His relations, however, would never be free of him. Memories for scandal are long in Rome. A family could have scores of statesmanly ancestors, but biographers would dwell on their one ancient traitor.

When I rejoined the party, they were all absorbed in frantic debate over their new suffering. Aelianus saw me

244

appear in the doorway; he rose and led me to an anteroom, asking for a private word. The conversation in the salon behind him dropped slightly, as his parents and Helena watched him draw me aside.

'Aelianus, you have to ask your father for the details.' My situation had always been difficult; I badly wanted to avoid anybody finding out that I had disposed of Publius down a sewer.

'Father told me what happened. I was abroad. I came home and found my uncle gone, and what he had done settling on us like blight. Now I am stuck with the results, it seems. Falco, you were involved –'

'Anything beyond what your father has told you is confidential, I'm afraid.'

'So I am being shafted, yet I cannot be told why?'

'You know enough. Yes, it is unfair,' I sympathised. 'But a stigma was inevitable. At least there were no wholesale executions, or confiscation of property.'

'I always rather liked Uncle Publius.' That aspect must frighten his parents, though I did not tell Aelianus so. They feared he might yet follow his uncle in temperament. He too was restless and impatient with society. Like his uncle, Aelianus might lose patience with the rules and seek out his own solutions, unless he was handled just right in the next few years. An outsider. Latent trouble.

For a moment, I wondered whether this was the kind of trouble the Laelius family had gone through with Scaurus.

'Your uncle seemed quite hard to get close to.' To me, he had had a cold, almost gloomy outlook.

'Yes, but he was supposed to have lived a wild life; he spent all that time abroad; he lived on the edge. He had an illegitimate child too – and I heard that she was killed in peculiar circumstances.' Aelianus stopped.

'Sosia,' I said reproachfully. 'Yes, I know how she was killed.'

'She was just a girl. I don't really remember her, Falco.'

'I do.' I stared him out, as I fought back a tear.

Aelianus still wanted to press me for information. He was

out of luck. I was sinking under the effects of a long, depressing day. I had two choices now: to collapse and sleep, or to keep alert in the search for little Gaia by tackling some new activity. This was what I had been brooding on, while the barber grazed my neck. Lying still while I tried to avoid having my throat cut, my body had rested and my mind cleared. My thoughts had had time to concentrate, as they had not done all that afternoon while I was bound up in physical effort at the Laelius house.

Now I knew what was needed next. I also knew I required help. The best person would be Lucius Petronius, but in fairness to him I could not ask. He had already nearly lost his job over his dalliance with the gangster's daughter. What I planned was far too big a risk.

'So what's your advice to me, Falco?' Aelianus asked, surprisingly.

'Forget the past.'

'I have to live with it.'

'Build for the future. The Arvals were probably the wrong choice for you anyway: too much of a clique, too restrictive and backward looking. You don't want to dance around some grove where mad wives are killing their corn-wreathed husbands with sacrificial knives.' I remembered something I wanted to tackle him about. 'By the way, I hear you asked the Chief Spy to discover who the victim was?'

Aelianus had the grace to blush slightly. 'We were getting nowhere –'

'We? It was your puzzle, which you told me you were giving up anyway.'

'Sorry.'

'Right.'

'Anyway, Anacrites is useless, Falco. I never got an answer.'

'He told me instead. Ventidius Silanus is the man's name. Ever heard of him?' Aelianus shook his head. 'Nor me.' I gazed at him quietly. 'I was surprised you had approached Anacrites.'

'Well, it seemed the only hope. I had done all I could. I even thought of riding out along the Via Appia and looking at all the patrician tombs for evidence of a recent funeral. There was nothing. If that's where the urn went, all the funerary flowers and so forth have been swept up.'

He had really shown initiative. I hid my astonishment. 'You're lucky. The Chief Spy does not know.'

'Know what, Falco?'

I let him stew just long enough. 'But he could easily find out.'

'What do you mean?'

'I mean, the evidence is still sitting there in his pigeon-holes. I am amazed you should have risked reminding him. Of course, somebody else could do so.'

'You?' He was starting to notice my threats.

'You're in my power!' I grinned. Then I got tough. 'You were entrusted with a secret document, on which the fate of the Baetican oil industry, and perhaps the whole province of Hispania Baetica, hung. You let it fall into the hands of the very men named as conspirators. You allowed them the time and opportunity to alter it. Then, realising you had betrayed your trust, you pretended not to notice and handed in the corrupt scroll, in silence, to the Chief Spy.'

Aelianus was very still.

'Just like Uncle Publius really,' I taunted him. 'And we know what then happened to him – well, no; we have to imagine it.' I stopped, imagining all too vividly the stench of the traitor's gaseous and disintegrating body. 'Now listen hard: Anacrites is extremely dangerous. If you want a career – in fact, if you want any kind of future at all – don't tangle with him.'

The young man ran a dry tongue over drier lips. 'So what now, Falco?'

'Now,' I said, 'I have to attempt something that is sheer madness. But I am fortunate because you, Aulus, do owe me a large debt. So you – without any argument or hesitation, and certainly without telling your family – will be coming along to support me.'

'That is fair,' he acknowledged. He put a brave face on it. 'What is my task?'

'Just holding a ladder.'

He blinked. 'I can do that.'

'Good. You will have to be very quiet while I climb up. We cannot risk discovery.'

He looked more nervous. 'Is this something illegal, Falco?' Sharp fellow!

'About as illegal as it can be. You and I, trusty comrade, are about to break into the House of the Vestals.'

Aelianus knew it was bad news, but it took him a moment to remember precisely that for an offence against the Vestal Virgins, the penalty was death.

XLI

'I don't like this, Falco.'

'Hush. It's just a minor trespass.'

I had brought Aelianus to the end of the Sacred Way before his courage failed. He was huddling in a dark cloak, his idea of what to wear for murky work. I did not need to play dressing-up games; I had spent my working career under cover for real. It was best to look normal. I was still in my toga, a respectable procuratorial Roman.

Well, Festus used to swank in it. On me, for some reason, this old toga had always looked seedy and moth-eaten.

My idea was that we could pass along the streets like two relaxed dinner companions, deep in philosophical talk. If at any point later in the enterprise I was apprehended, wearing the toga should gain me valuable leeway. I would still be beaten to death, but I would be given time to apologise first. Unlike Maia's children enduring the shame of Famia, Julia Junilla would know when she grew up that her dear father might have shown disrespect to the Vestals, but he went down in style.

'We are going to get caught, Falco.'

'We will be if you don't shut up. Look as if you have a docket that entitles you to be here.'

Now my heart was pounding. The last time I felt this anxious, I had been working with Pa. In his company, there was good reason to feel terrified. Mind you, rampaging through the art world as the naughty Didius boys had been a doddle compared to this.

'Aulus, I'm not expecting you to come with me; you can stay on guard outside. I've done worse things. All I have to do is climb in, then prowl about until I find Constantia's bedroom door.'

'I can't believe the Vestals have name-tablets on their rooms.'

'I see you are the logical one in your family.'

We had left the senator's house (giving the porter a very oblique message about our future movements). We marched up to the Capena Gate, then turned right in front of the Temple of the Divine Claudius and left down the Via Sacra until we reached the Street of Vesta. We wheeled straight into the walled enclosure, which was not locked.

'Surprise!' muttered Aelianus.

'No, no; they have builders working here. Workmen never lock up other people's property.'

I could smell the scent from the Sacred Fire, as it wreathed up gently through the hole in the temple roof. It was too dark now to make out the thin trail. The temple's ornamental drum seemed to loom above us, larger than normal, with a pale white sheen. The Forum outside would soon become eerie. It would look deserted, but everywhere would be alive with sinister rustlings and shufflings. Love-making and other unsavoury deals would probably occur in here too. If the temple had been left open, dossers would warm themselves at the Sacred Hearth.

There would be patrols. They would come round and kick out vagrants. Once the creatures of the night took over Rome, we would be at risk from both them and those who guarded against them. We had to work fast.

Pallid lights flickered on the large Ionic shrine built against the entrance block. We could not risk a torch. I had not even brought one. The twinkly lamps on the shrine made it the best place to attempt entry. Anywhere else would be simply too dark. It would also mean we would be visible, if anyone came along.

I knew exactly where I was going to find a ladder. I had not been wasting time when I came here this morning. As in everywhere else I seemed to go these days, the contractors working on the Vestals' House after it was destroyed in the Great Fire had adopted a storage area, roping off a corner of the enclosure, probably without a by-your-leave. Nothing was sacred to them. I did borrow a lamp from the shrine in order to explore what the men had left for me. Struggling to be quiet, we edged out the nearest set of rungs. It moved freely at first, then as we angled one end away from the other stuff it seemed to grow heavier and more awkward.

We dropped it. I put my hand over the light.

Nothing.

Sucking at my scorched palm, I listened to the night-time sounds of Rome. Distant voices; faint wafts of desultory flute music; dear gods, an owl. More likely some gang's watchman, giving a signal to his mates. Perhaps early notice that their mark was now approaching; perhaps a warning about the vigiles.

Already wheels were rumbling on all the roads into town. The rumpus would grow louder as huge delivery wagons strove against one another in the rush to bring provisions in. Heavy goods and fresh produce; delicacies and household wares; marble and timber; baskets and amphorae; rich men's carriages. At least the racket might cover us if we had any more accidents.

Even though it was early June, the temperature had dropped with the coming of darkness. Cool air chilled my upturned face. Time to move.

Aelianus touched my arm; I breathed agreement. Together we lifted the ladder and transported it to beside the shrine. I bundled my toga and slung it over my shoulder. A well-sculpted haughty goddess watched me disapprovingly. Aelianus grinned and covered her up with his discarded cloak. He was worse than me.

I shinned up. The wall was too high. I might jump down on the other side with only mild sprains to hamper me, but I would have no means of escape. Cursing, I descended and whispered that we would have to bring another ladder, raise it, then I would sit astride the wall and heave the second one over to the other side. Professional roofers do it every day. I wished I had brought one with me to manage this.

It took a long time. Manoeuvring ladders is no joke. People who have never tried it just have no idea. Builders' ladders are crude – rough, thin trees as side members, with branches nailed too far apart to climb up easily – and they

251

tear your hands to shreds if you slip. If you want to test your ingenuity, brute strength, and calmness under pressure, try moving ladders in the dark, in silence, while thinking at every moment that your hour has come.

'Well done, Aulus. I'm going over. If you hear anybody coming, better remove the outside ladder. And keep quiet if a lot of lictors rush out here. Those layabouts don't care a damn where they poke their rods.'

'What do I do if anything goes wrong?'

'Run for your life.'

He was Helena's precious brother. I should have told him to go home.

XLII

Nobody seemed to be about.

I had descended into a corner of the garden area. Nearby, on the inner side of the gate, a handy lantern dangled from a hook. It was probably waiting for the Virgin who was on duty that night with responsibility for checking the Sacred Fire. I borrowed it.

If the Sacred Fire is ever allowed to go out due to inattention by one of the Virgins, the culprit is stripped and whipped by the Pontifex Maximus (in the dark, and from behind a modesty screen), then the Pontifex has to rekindle the flame using friction on fruitwood bark. Quite a performance. The Virgins are holy women who respect their ancient duties – but I had no doubt that if the flame should waver and dim at night, when no one was there as a witness, the duty Vestal just relit the embers from her lamp. Nervous that it might be missed, I decided to take it back.

I set off exploring, and within minutes my foot dropped into nothing, then I found myself plunged up to my knee in the cold water of an ornamental pool. I managed not to yell. With an effort I pulled out my sopping wet boot, shook off some strands of pondweed, and squelched back for the lamp.

Shielding the light, I picked my way around from the gate, this time along the ground floor of a long, quiet colonnade. The modest accommodation that had been destroyed in Nero's Great Fire was being remodelled, though there seemed to be the usual hitches, for the work was not advanced. Under the damp, dark lee of the Palatine Hill, the charred bulk of the residence was hung with scaffolding. Filthy with fine dust, the colonnades had their upper columns missing altogether, the lower ones currently replaced by temporary braces. Staircases were now just gaping holes in the masonry.

At the far end I found the skeleton of a large new hall under construction, approached by temporary framework steps, and apparently due to be flanked by six small rooms; it would represent a king's royal hut and six cells for his maidenly daughters, but even had it been complete the modern Virgins would never have slept here. Without doubt, their house contained numerous rooms for attendants – and fancy suites for each of them.

It was still quiet. Maybe the ladies all liked early nights. Their staff probably slipped out to taverns over towards the Circus Maximus if they wanted to carouse.

I retraced my steps, this time in the colonnade of the block that ran alongside the Via Nova. Here, there were more signs of occupation. I gently tested doors and windows, but they were all secure. Bound to be. Not so much to keep flighty Virgins in, as to keep out light-fingered construction workers who might purloin their jewellery.

Libel, Falco. Vestal Virgins never adorn themselves with necklaces.

CRINGING DISCLAIMER:
Any imputation of Vestals' vanity is retracted on legal advice.

I gathered they did wash their smalls: hearing a woman's voice humming, I walked out into the garden and peered up at the building above me. Light broke in a thin ray from an upper-storey window where the shutters were open – and where a string such as you may see any day above any Aventine backstreet hung, with long white ribbons drying in the night air. What you do not normally spot on washing lines are ribbons like the hair ornaments that the Vestals wear.

The tune being hummed was too cheerful to be hymnal, but I was contemplating a big surprise for one of the Empire's most serious, stately women, who had absolutely no reason to welcome an intruder on her windowsill. The risk was hers too. A Virgin suspected of breaking her vow of chastity faced death. A presumed lover would be stoned; she would be buried alive.

I was in a predicament, but the whole adventure was crazy. There was no going back. I tried standing in the shadows and letting out a low whistle to see what it produced, but the light-hearted hum just continued as before. I went and fetched the ladder which had brought me down over this side of the wall. I brought my toga too, though it was hardly a disguise.

The ladder was a very long one; upright, it swayed dangerously overhead. Inching the heavy contraption into place, I strained to make no sound as I lodged it carefully below the lit window. It took a few difficult moments to find a level place to stand it. Once I could let go, I collapsed against the rungs, breathing throatily. My heart raced. This certainly was the most stupid thing I had ever done.

I had climbed halfway up before disaster struck. My boot, still slimy from the pool, slipped on a rung. I managed to regain my footing, but made too much noise. I froze and clung on, motionless.

I thought all was well, until I heard the window open wider. Light flooded down. Looking up, I made out a woman's shape, with the stiff, high diadem all Vestals wore. I heard a stifled sound, which in other circumstances might have been giggling. Then a voice whispered facetiously, 'Oh darling, I thought you would never come!'

Joking. Well, I hoped she was.

Anyway, I had no time to argue, as the revered Constantia reached down with both arms, grabbed me by the back of my tunic, hauled me up over the windowsill and dragged me inside.

XLIII

'Nice place!'

'Thank you.'

'Constantia?' Vestals are generally known by only one name, though she presumably had two.

'That's me. And you?'

I tried to inject some formality. 'Marcus Didius Falco.'

'Oh Falco! I have been hearing about you. You're a chancer! What would you have done if I had screamed?'

'Pretended I was a shutter-painter on night work, and yelled very loud that it was you who had attacked me.'

'Well, it might have worked.'

'I won't test the theory. I hoped it was you up here. I've been standing in the garden trying to tell if the sweet soprano tones I could hear were the same ones that grunted "Balls!" this morning.'

'Oh you heard that,' she commented, matter-of-factly. 'Have the couch. Do excuse me while I slip off the uniform.'

Her slim fingers were unfastening the Hercules knot beneath her white-clad bosom. I gulped. For one startling moment, I thought I was about to be treated to a live impersonation of Aphrodite Undressing for the Bath. But as well as the spacious boudoir I had tumbled into, Constantia apparently had been allocated a dressing room where any slipping off of her white robes could be done decently. She saw me panic, though. Throwing me a wink, she vanished into the inner cubicle. 'Sit tight. Don't you go away!'

This wasn't the time for a brave boy to start crying for his mother. I perched on the couch as ordered. There was only one. I wondered where Constantia intended to sit when she came back.

It was an elegant piece of furniture in some exotic foreign hardwood, padded and covered with fine-woven wool. My boots discovered a matching footstool. My elbow sank sideways into a tasselled cylindrical bolster. Looking around, I saw that the room was a model of taste. Red and black architectural wall paintings, with roundels depicting simple urns. Light bronze tripods and lampstands. Discreet deerskin rugs. It was equipped with scroll-boxes that probably held romantic Greek novels. Well, you could not expect the girl to sit in here night after night, playing endless games of Soldiers against herself.

In no time I was rejoined by my hostess. I took a good look, while pretending not to. She knew I was inspecting her.

Closer to twenty than thirty, she was now looking a stunner in a flowing gown of mobile ochre material and dainty gold mules which showed her toes. Gripped under one arm were a decorated hand mirror and what looked like a cosmetics box. She had discarded the diadem and, as we talked, she untied various ribbons and shook out her traditionally plaited braids until her hair flowed loose. Gleaming in the lamplight, it was a rich chestnut, the long locks probably never cut since she first came to the Vestals' House.

Bending up one small foot under her, she dropped on to the couch at the other end, with space between us. She balanced the mirror on her knee. Then she proceeded to light a small brazier using the wick in one of the lamps.

'I see you're used to handling fire!'

Despite my pang of disquiet, the brazier was neither for witchcraft nor anything religious; it was to heat her curling iron. So there I was, illegally inside the House of the Vestals, watching a very much off-duty Virgin while she dipped her comb in a basin of water and restyled her hair.

'Yes, we are allowed relaxation,' she commented, at my bemused look. Her hands twisted the hot iron with great competence. 'Our free time is entirely our own. Nobody bothers us, so long as the Chief Vestal never notices any loud music or perfumes that have disturbingly erotic Parthian undernotes.'

'So the simple, celibate life doesn't bother you?'

Her eyes, which were mid-brown and well set, glinted. 'It has a few disadvantages.'

'Not many visitors?'

'You're my first, Falco!'

'Lucky me. My friend Petronius reckons all the Virgins must be lesbians.'

'Some may be.' Not this one, I decided.

'Or that really they have secret lovers scampering in and out all night.'

'Some may do.' She gave little away, but added some more suggestions: 'Or that we are all crabby, dried-up frights who want to dispossess men – or that simplicity of life means black teeth and body smells?'

'Yes, I believe those are other popular theories.'

'From time to time I expect they all apply. Why generalise? Any group of six people would contain all kinds of characters. What do you think, Falco?'

I thought a lot that I was not prepared to say. For instance, I liked the way she had made cheeky little ringlets to hang in front of her ears. 'You sound as if you were born on the wrong side of the Sacred Way. A token plebeian, right?'

Constantia shrugged. Her ringlets bobbed. Her accent was in fact perfectly neutral, but of course she would have been trained to speak acceptably. It was her outspoken, sprightly attitude that had given her away. 'You feel I don't fit in?' I nodded. 'Wrong, Falco. This is my career, and I am proud of it. Oh, I never expect to become Chief Vestal, but you won't find me skimping the duties or dishonouring the gods.'

'No doubt your salt cakes are impeccable.'

'Exactly. I am planning to open a cake stall after I retire.'

'I would have thought you would take the imperial dowry and get married?'

Constantia looked at me sideways as she twirled a lock of hair free from the iron. 'That will depend on what is on offer at the time!'

I thought not many men would feel up to taking on this lively character.

258

Applying her curler to the heat again, she wiped off smuts on a soft cloth then wound a new strand of hair around the metal bar.

'If you have the iron too hot, all your hair will snap off.' She gave me a look that made me retract. 'Well, so I have been told. I assume you have to be braided up again demurely tomorrow to attend the lottery?' Constantia paused, realising that this was what I had come to talk about. I handed her the mirror to check progress with her coiffure. 'I have been searching for the lost child.'

'But you failed to find her.' It was a blank statement, one that put me in my place.

'Ah, you know? I suppose as the virginal liaison point, you have been receiving hourly reports?'

'As well as almost hourly demands to discuss the issue with your girlfriend.' That came out as somewhat critical.

'Helena Justina is extremely persistent.'

'Now she has sent you?'

'No, she knows nothing about it. I intrude on women on my own account.'

'She will find out.'

'I shall tell her myself.'

'Will she be annoyed?'

'Why? She knows how much I desperately need to speak to you about Gaia Laelia. I climbed in the window after reasonable requests failed, not because I was looking for a cheap thrill.'

'More expensive than cheap, if you are caught, Falco.'

'Don't I know it! So why is there this obsessive secrecy about the high-flown Laelii?'

Constantia put aside her feminine dib-dabs and leaned towards me earnestly. Her gown was modestly pinned, yet I felt an odd quirk of alarm just at seeing a Virgin's pale bare neck above the gown's loose dark yellow folds. 'Never mind why, Falco.'

I was annoyed. She ignored it. 'All right; what about Gaia? I know she talked to you about becoming a Virgin – first at the reception for the Queen of Judaea. Her mother tells me, she was brought back afterwards too?'

259

'Yes.'

'So what worries did she want to talk about?'

'Only being a Virgin. I thought the dear little thing had a wonderful enquiring attitude. A most promising candidate. She consulted me about all the rituals. Naturally, I was as helpful as I could be.'

'I am consulting you now,' I growled. 'And you are not helping me.'

'Oh dear!' Her pout would not have disgraced any slightly tight tavern waitress flirting with a customer.

I restrained my annoyance. 'Gaia told me somebody in her family wanted to kill her. Jupiter, what in Olympus will it take to make anyone in authority listen and regard this as serious?'

'Nothing. She told me the same. I thought it was the truth.'

I leaned back on the couch, finally feeling that some mad nightmare might be ending. I breathed slowly. My troubles were not over, however. The Vestal in whose private apartment I was swanning reached over and stroked my forehead, then offered me wine.

She had a Syrian glass jug on a chased tray. She cannot have known I was coming to see her; it must be her regular nightcap. There was only one goblet. We agreed it would be unwise to send out for another one.

'What do you think?' she asked courteously as I sipped. 'I don't know the name, but I am promised it is good.'

'Very nice.' I did not recognise its vintage either, but whatever the grape and origin, it was more than acceptable. I would like to have tried it on Petro. In fact, I would have liked to show Petro this whole situation and watch him shoot off into a catalogue of howling incredulity. 'A gift from an admirer?'

'Honouring Vesta.'

'Very devout. So what did Gaia say?' I refused to be sidetracked. 'Which of them has threatened her?'

'Nobody will harm her. She is in no danger, Falco.'

'You know something!'

'I know she is now safe from anyone in her family. But I cannot say where she is. Nobody knows that. You have to discover the answer.'

'Why should I?' My temper was up now. 'I have already spent all day on this. I am exhausted, and baffled by the hindrances put in my way. What is the point? If I knew what Gaia was afraid of, I could find her more easily.'

'I don't think so, Falco.'

The girl continued plying me with wine, but I knew that old trick. Perhaps she sensed it, because she took the goblet from me and had a drink herself.

I grabbed the goblet back, then set it down smartly on its tray. 'Concentrate! I thought Gaia might have been troubled by the evil ways of nasty "Uncle Tiberius". Did she mention him?'

'Oh he was a filthy article,' Constantia admitted immediately.

'Then whyever would a retired Vestal like Terentia Paulla marry him?'

'Because he was rich?'

'A rich bastard.'

'He fooled Terentia into believing that he wanted her.'

'He was rich and she was foolish?'

'You are not going to give up?'

'No.'

'All right.' She had decided to give me something. It might not be everything (few women do that on a first acquaintance, after all; least of all sworn virgins). 'Terentia married him,' said Constantia, 'because he told her she was the one he had always really wanted. She was thrilled. She took him out of misplaced flattery, and a little spite perhaps – because he was the lover that her married sister had flaunted at her for years.'

XLIV

I folded my arms and stretched out my boots, crossing my ankles. I was now feeling desperately tired.

What would this have meant to Gaia? Yet more explosions in the family, that was certain. I now understood all too clearly what had been meant when I was told that 'Uncle Tiberius' had been an 'old friend' of the family.

I knew that Terentia Paulla had retired as a Vestal about eighteen months ago. She had been married for just under a year. This was June. Her sister, the ex-Flamen had said, had died in July last year. 'The Vestal's wedding and the Flaminica's death must have virtually coincided.'

'Probably so.' I sensed that Constantia now wanted to close up. Her bright eyes were watching me. I could live with that, if she liked the novelty of gazing at a handsome dog with tousled curls and an endearing grin – not to mention, of course, the faintly etched brow crease that hinted at my thoughtful, sensitive side.

She made a decent picture herself. She might look severe when she was attired in her religious robes, but she had regular features lit with obvious intelligence; off duty, she was a very pretty girl. As a centurion's daughter or a tribune's wife, she would have been the toast of any legion, and an inevitable source of problems among the men.

Thankfully, pretty girls present no problem to me.

'The Flaminica – Statilia Paulla, wasn't that her name? – died very suddenly, I heard. Do you happen to know what caused it?'

'Apart from fury at her sister's announcement of her marriage?' Constantia bit her lip. 'I do know, actually. She had a tumour. She had confided in the Chief Vestal – probably not just to share the tragedy, but to annoy her sister, who was not being made a confidante.'

'Had everyone in the family known about the Flaminica's long affair?'

'I should think so. Not little Gaia.'

'Does that mean even the Flamen knew?'

'It had always been accepted tacitly. Theirs was a marriage in form only.'

'He must have had feelings on the subject. When he talked about his wife was the only time I saw any signs of animation.'

'That,' said Constantia coldly, 'is simply because he blames his wife for dying and robbing him of his position.'

'You are very hard.' She made no reply. 'Was Gaia fond of her grandmother?'

'You mean, did the Flaminica's death upset her? I think the child was closer to Terentia. Terentia has made a big pet of Gaia. I gather she has even talked of making Gaia her heir.'

'What about Laelius Scaurus? I thought he was Terentia's favourite?'

'Yes,' said Constantia, playing with one of her ringlets. 'But he remains in his father's paternal control, so he cannot hold property.'

'What's the difference?'

'None, as things are. Gaia is also in the guardianship of her grandfather. But if Gaia were to become a Vestal Virgin, once she came to the House of the Vestals she – unlike her other relations – would be entitled to her own property. She could also make a will.'

This was intriguing. 'So then if Terentia died, and Gaia inherited, the loot would belong to her immediately and might eventually be left by her outside the family – whereas if Gaia *fails* to become a Vestal, anything Terentia leaves either to Gaia or her father will be controlled by Laelius Numentinus from the moment of probate.'

'While he lives. Then the position of head of household moves down to Laelius Scaurus.'

'Whom even his loving aunt may regard as a rather unworldly fellow to be put in control . . . But if he upsets his

263

father too much, Numentinus could disinherit him.'

'You seem very excited by this, Falco.'

I gave Constantia my best grin 'Well, it might explain many things. In their huge mansion stuffed full of slaves on the Aventine, the Laelii consider themselves to be living in genteel poverty.'

Constantia, a girl with a nature that I could take to, raised her eyebrows. 'Poor them!' she said scathingly.

'I am wondering now,' I pondered, 'whether somebody in her family has hidden Gaia away deliberately, to ensure she should *not* be selected in the lottery and made financially independent.'

'Drastic.'

'Money makes people lose their sense of reality.'

'Other things can do that.'

'Like what?' I asked – and this time when I gave her a grin, it was rather nicely returned.

'Love,' suggested Constantia. 'Or what passes for it in bed.'

Who knows what line of questioning might have developed next. Instead, just at that moment we heard steps tramping the corridor outside.

I leapt up and jumped over to the window on light feet. Constantia laid a finger on her lips. The footsteps went by, apparently only one person; Constantia, who seemed unfazed, may have recognised the heavy tread of one of her fellow inmates. Vestals tend to be solid women; to compensate for their lonely lives, they must be well fed.

The experience reminded me I should not linger. On her feet too, Constantia herself now whispered conspiratorially, 'I have enjoyed talking to you, but you ought to go. There is always a chance one of the others will come along for a hot toddy, or to borrow a novel and share a session of girl-talk.'

'Very nice! Thanks for your help, anyway. I'll be off down my ladder.'

She was scornful. 'Don't be ridiculous. Nasty splintery things –' However did she know that? 'Men should not go clambering around at high level after drinking wine. Come with me and I can let you out properly through the gate.'

When she opened her door on to the corridor, there was nobody about and it did seem sensible to walk softly in the shadows rather than climbing about like a thief. Rolling on the balls of my feet for quietness, I let myself be led through dimly lit corridors to ground level. There I went back to the ladder that was still at Constantia's window, and tidied it away on its side under the colonnade as if the workmen had just lazily left it there.

We crept down the dark cloister towards the exit gate. Suddenly there was a noise and a door opened. I never saw who came out. Constantia grabbed my hand. Then, with great presence of mind, she dragged me to a litter that was standing unattended in the vestibule; we both piled inside, pulling the curtains down.

I do realise that crude people will now be speculating wildly about what a keen Roman male might get up to while squashed very tight in a litter with a Vestal Virgin. Just calm down. She had a religious calling; I was faithfully devoted to my girlfriend; and anyway, the need for silence overrode everything else.

LV

No; honest, praetor. I never laid a finger on the girl.

XLVI

Mind you; I hope nobody ever asks me what that rude madam did to me!

XLVII

Jupiter. She was a disgrace.

XLVIII

Stifling my shock and readjusting my dignity, I looked out to check if the coast was clear.

I scrambled free, then turned back to examine the litter we had been hiding in. It was a dull black colour, with silver handholds on the poles and long charcoal-grey curtains. I had seen it before, when I first approached the house of the Laelii.

'I know the Vestals possess the right to ride in a carriage, but is this yours too, for when you travel incognito to buy knick-knacks and fashionwear?'

'No, it belongs to a visitor.'

'Now who would that be?'

'An ex-Vestal. Some stay here on retirement, well cared for in the tranquillity of the home they know. Others who decide to leave are always welcome back.'

Her grapple with me had left her unruffled, but she knew we were in danger here. She was trying to move me on. I stood my ground. 'Your visitor is a complete stranger to tranquillity! I know she left the Laelius house earlier today. This is Terentia Paulla, returning to the sisterhood?'

'The Chief Virgin is comforting her; she is desolate about the disappearance of little Gaia.'

'Is that so? I need to speak to her.'

'Do not intrude, Falco.'

'Don't balk me! Will I have to climb in through her window too?'

'No. You are going to walk out of the gate now.'

I knew I had pushed it far enough tonight. I let Constantia lead me to the door in the wall that led to the Temple of Vesta enclosure. My hair-raising adventure was reaching its end, quite successfully. Or so I thought, until my companion unlocked the gate for me.

Outside, near the temple, a group of lictors and other heavy types were clustered around a young man; I could see it was Aelianus. They must have only just apprehended him. He was responding with spirit: 'Officers!' he cried in his reassuringly patrician tones. 'I am so glad I ran into you. I just noticed that there is a ladder leaning up against the Vestals' House. It may have something to do with a rough-looking fellow I just saw running off. He went that way –' He gestured towards the Regia.

'Show us!' The watch guards were not completely convinced. More practical than I had hoped, they had the sense to keep him with them while they went to investigate. Still, he was a senator's son and had every right to stroll around Rome at night looking for a rumpus he could join in.

Constantia had pulled the door closed hastily before we were seen by anyone. Again, she used that word a Virgin should not know. Pulling a face, she gestured for me to follow her, whispering that she would show me the Via Nova exit.

'Is it locked?'

'I hope not.'

'Dear gods!' I was deeply apprehensive. I could cope with the mere fact of gliding about a residence that was strictly closed to men. I did not want to find myself in another dark corner where Constantia might jump me.

Somebody else was coming. Even Constantia was losing her nerve. I asked her for directions, then instructed her to hasten back to the security of her own suite. 'If I get arrested, you never saw me, and you know nothing about me.'

'Oh I wouldn't say that, Falco!' She was incorrigible.

'That's right. Be sensible.'

I had some trouble with the directions. Nobody is perfect. Constantia had seemed a thoroughly delightful character, no doubt absolutely packed with talent. She could probably have driven a chariot round and round the Circus, but as a navigator she was useless; she could not distinguish between left and right. Still, eventually I found the door she had described. Unfortunately, it was locked.

This was a door in the interior of the residential block, so there was no climbing out. Increasingly apprehensive now, I worked my way once more to the central garden area. Here too, the gate had now been secured by somebody. Keeping deep in the shadows, I sidled back for my ladder. All went well. I was extremely tired, but I took care how I lifted and carried it. More or less in silence, I made it back to where I first climbed over and set the ladder gingerly against the wall. Up I went, once again within sight of freedom.

Needless to say, when I reached the top, the ladder I had left beside the shrine on the other side was no longer there. No use hoping for help from Aelianus. He would have removed himself from this dangerous scene.

I could lower myself on to the shrine's roof, then drop carefully. I had done worse. Alternatively, I could sit astride the wall, and try to raise the inner ladder up enough to heave it over. I was still debating when I heard troops marching outside, coming towards the temple enclosure. I stepped down a few rungs again, keeping out of sight. Then somebody below on the ground behind me grabbed the back of my left calf.

Thinking it was Constantia about to grope me again, I turned to protest, only to find myself looking down into the ferocious scowls of three lictors. Normally they have nothing much to do; today was now their best day ever. For perhaps the first time in history they had caught an intruder. They were thrilled.

The man who had hold of me jerked my foot outwards. I fell off the ladder, luckily on top of him. It gave me a soft landing, though it seemed to annoy him.

My captors did then courteously allow me to put on my toga. I would be formally attired for my interview with the Chief Vestal. That's the interview I was now compelled to have, where she would sentence me to death.

XLIX

What a horrendous woman.

She looked as if she had been boiled in milk for too long. She was in full garb, with the white, purple-bordered veil that they wear at sacrifices, its two cords pinned under her double chin with her special Vestal's brooch. I recognised her outline and deportment from seeing her at the theatre and at festivals. One of the well-built, statuesque variety. One with truly Gorgonesque features. Religious devotion oozing from her. This time the sacrificial beast was a captured informer; that did seem to give her pleasure.

'A man! And what are you doing here?' she enunciated sarcastically.

I left Constantia out of it. She was watching. All the four lesser Virgins had appeared and were jostling behind their leader excitedly, owl-eyed; Constantia was conspicuous by the yellow hem hanging down under the white robe that she must have flung on top of her lounging wear.

'I merely wanted to ask some vital questions of Terentia Paulla,' I decided to say. Nobody present looked identifiable as Terentia. She had retired from her duties, so she was allowed to see men; anyway, she could say that I had never found her. Would that let me off?

Also present at my humiliation was a full set of lictors, and their other prize: Camillus Aelianus. 'This man, a respectable senator's heir, saw somebody lurking suspiciously, ma'am.'

'Is this the felon you saw?'

'Oh no. That was a tall, handsome, fair-haired man.' Good try.

'Thanks for exonerating me, young sir, but if you don't regard me as handsome, let me give you the name of a competent oculist.'

'You have defiled the House of Vesta.' Something about the slow, deliberate way the Chief Vestal made her pronouncements was beginning to draw my attention.

I suppose after my visit to Constantia I should have been prepared for anything. The Chief Vestal was a forty-year-old, iron-hard, prudish, dictatorial image of moral purity. And something else: Jupiter! She had the slack eyelids of a drear toper who had really been hitting the amphora. The rich evidence hung on her breath. On close inspection, anyone could detect that she was a hesitant, sozzled, soused, fuzzled, bung-licking, dreg-draining, secret Bacchanalian.

Why mince words? The Chief Vestal was a lush.

In the time it was taking for the woman's thoughts to broach the grape-clogged path from brain to speech, I managed to invent and try out various sickly protests about the official nature of my mission, the high level of support I could command, and the urgency of finding Gaia Laelia, through whatever unorthodox means it took. I made myself out to be, in this search, actually a servant of the Vestals. Reduced to the lowest depths, I even muttered that old sad plea about no harm having been done.

Indubitably, a waste of breath.

Then Aelianus came up with a winner.

'Ma'am –' His tone was meek and respectful. He knew how to play-act, apparently. I would never have thought it; he had always seemed so bad-tempered and prim. 'I am a mere observer brought to this scene by chance –' Overdoing it, Aulus! – 'but the man does appear to have an official mission; his need to collect information was urgent and desperate. His efforts on behalf of the small child are completely benign. If his motives were well meant, can I appeal to you? Am I not correct that if a Virgin meets a criminal she has, by ancient tradition, the power of interceding for his reprieve?'

'You are correct, young man.' The Chief Vestal surveyed Aelianus through those heavy lids. 'There is a condition, however, or the Vestals would be subject to constant harassment by convicts. It has to be proved that the meeting

273

between the criminal and the Virgin was a complete coincidence.' She turned back to me, triumphant with spite. 'Breaking into the House of the Vestals with ladders makes this meeting far from coincidental. Take him to the Mamertine Jail – the condemned cell!'

It had been a good try by Aelianus but I could see her point. Without more ado the lictors and their henchmen massed around me, and I was marched out.

'What an absolutely terrible woman!' Always be friendly to your guards. Sometimes they find you a better cell.

Her personal lictor leered at me. 'Lovely, isn't she?'

I barked my shin on a builder's trestle. 'Having some work done? Progress seems slow. Don't tell me Vespasian is reluctant to pay for it?'

'The Chief Vestal has a full set of working drawings for complete remodelling. She'll wait. She'll get exactly what she wants one day.'

'I'd like to see that.'

'What a shame!' they guffawed as they dragged me along the Sacred Way, knowing that I only had about one day's life left to me.

When we arrived under the Gemonian Stairs in the shadow of the Capitol, it took them hours to find and fetch the custodian, who was not expecting customers. All too soon, though, I was being installed in the dungeon which normally houses foreigners who have rebelled against Roman authority, that bare, stinking hole near the Tabularium from which the public strangler extracts his victims when they pay the final, fatal price for being enemies of Rome. My arrival dismayed the jailer, who normally makes a small fortune from showing tourists the cells where barbarians are so briefly dumped at the end of a Triumph. He would still admit the punters, but he realised that for the short time I was in occupation before I was exterminated, I would expect to share the fees. He went off gloomily, back to wherever he had been enjoying himself.

The Mamertine is a crude prison. Strong stone walls enclose irregular cells that used to form part of a quarry. Water runs through it. At least the jailer's lack of interest meant he just left me in the upper cell, not shoved down through the hole in the floor into the fearsome lower depths. It was pitch dark. It was chilly. It was solitary and depressing.

This was still, just about, the eighth day before the Ides of June. Behind me lay the longest day I could ever remember, and now I was facing death. I toyed with a few none-too-serious plans for escaping. Once I would have had a go. The problem with being the well-known equestrian Procurator of the Sacred Geese and Chickens was that I could never again merge into anonymity. If I did escape, either I would have no life, even on the Aventine, or I would be recognised by the public and thrown straight back in here.

In the absence of anything optimistic to contemplate, I rolled myself up in my toga and went to sleep.

L

Dawn straggled over the Palatine and the Capitol, ushering the seventh day before the Ides of June. At last. It had to be less tiring and depressing than the eighth. I hoped the journey to the Styx would be an easy one.

Had I been at home, my calendar would have reminded me it was the start of the Vestalia. Today Vespasian would hold the lottery for a new Virgin. Today, that is, but only after some frantic rejigging of the favourites list by clerks in the pontifical offices, to take account of the absence of Gaia Laelia. Today, perhaps, the Emperor would be told about me.

Perhaps not. I was history.

Light hardly managed to penetrate this hole. Running with water, the walls bore no messages from previous prisoners. No one could see enough to carve a plea for help. Nobody ever stayed there long enough. The stench was appalling. I woke stiff and cold. It was easy to feel terrified.

I left my mark by relieving myself in a corner. There was nowhere else. I was plainly not the first.

Helena would know by now exactly where I was. I wondered what her brother had done after I was dragged away. They would have compelled him to dictate a formal statement. Then what? He must have told his father what had happened. The Camilli knew. Helena must know. I would not be executed without a great deal of fuss first being made in the marble-floored halls of officialdom. Maybe the Sacred Geese would honk a bit in protest too.

Helena would go to Titus and throw herself on his mercy. She would do it, even though the last words she had spoken to him in the Golden House were deliberately rude. He was famously good-natured. The sight of her desperation would overcome any grudges he felt.

He had no power to help her. Nobody could extract me from this. I had offended against the Vestals. I was a dead man.

Somebody was rousing the jailer.

I woke myself up enough to take an interest. Whatever negotiations were required to gain admittance took ages. I wondered if the agent who had come on my behalf was short of money. Apparently not; he was just an amateur.

'Aelianus!'

'The last person you expected, I suppose?' He could be wry, like all of his family. 'I'm not just a spoiled brat, Falco. Well, I dare say, even you have good qualities that you hide under a cloak of modesty.'

'Being in a cell is bad enough without the punishment of other people's mordant wit. Back off, before I knock a hole in your head.'

More coins chinked, and though the jailer was curious, he condescended to leave us alone. Aelianus raised a small oil lamp, looked around and shuddered.

I kept talking to stop my teeth chattering. 'Well, it's pleasant of you to come visiting me in my trouble. You must be very frightened of your sister!'

'Aren't you?'

In the light of his one pathetic hand lamp, the young and noble Camillus appeared ill at ease; he had not realised that when the jailer left, he too would be locked in. He was in a nice clean tunic, dark red, with three lavish rows of squiggly neck braid.

'You look very smart. I like a man who enjoys casual fashion wear. Especially when he is visiting the death cell. A reminder of normality; such a thoughtful touch.'

'Always there with the repartee, Falco.' He was pale and tense, keyed up with some restless expectancy. This was out of place. I was the one who was facing a demanding day. Mine had a bier and an urn at the end of it. 'We went into this together,' he told me pompously. 'Obviously, I shall do my utmost to get you out of it. I brought you something.'

'I do hope so. The traditional gifts are a sword to kill the jailer and a large set of skeleton keys. A really well organised rescuer includes a passport and some cash.'

He had brought me a cinnamon pastry.

'Breakfast,' he murmured huffily, on seeing my face. I said nothing. 'If you don't want it, I can eat it for you.'

'I am telling myself I am just dreaming.'

'Falco, I have been working hard all night on your behalf. I hope it's fixed. Someone will be coming soon.'

'A stuffed vineleaf seller? A chickpea specialist?'

He was eyeing up the pastry. I snatched it and ate it myself.

I had barely wiped the crumbs from my chin with a corner of my toga when we felt muffled reverberations caused by heavy boots. Aelianus jumped up. I saw no urgency. Execution could take all the time in the world coming. There was no hope of delaying my date with Fortune, however. The jailer's ugly face appeared and I was fetched from my cosy cell to the cruel light of day.

Outside, at first I shuddered even more, before the faint warmth of the dawn sunlight in the Forum started to revive me. My eyes took time to readjust. Then I realised my honour escort was the best I could ever have requested: a small but spankingly turned-out detachment of the Praetorian Guard. 'Now that's class, Aulus!'

'Glad you like it. Here's our contact.'

Next minute I nearly regurgitated my flavoursome breakfast all over the Gemonian Stairs. Accompanying the tall fellows in the shiny plumed helmets, I saw Anacrites.

'Right!' He had some gall. He was actually giving orders. Well, as Chief Spy his official next-of-kin had always been the Guards. His remit was protecting the Emperor, just as theirs was. In the strict hierarchy of the Palace, Anacrites was on detachment to them – yet little was made of it and I had never known him exercise Praetorian rights. They certainly never invited him to their mess dinners. But then, who would? 'Chain him up!' He was really enthusiastic about hurting and humiliating me. 'Pile the fetters on. As many as possible. Never mind whether he can walk in them. We can drag him along.'

'May I,' I remonstrated while I was being trussed, 'be allowed to know whither I am to be dragged?'

'Just keep quiet, Falco. You have caused enough trouble.'

I glared at young Aelianus. 'Do something for me, lad. Ask your sister where my mother lives, and when this is all over, make sure you tell Ma that it was her treacherous lodger who delivered her last living son to his fate.'

'Ready?' Anacrites, ignoring me, for some reason addressed himself in an undertone to Aelianus. 'I can get him there, but you'll have to do the talking, Camillus. I don't want this fiasco ever showing up on my personal record!'

Sheer amazement coloured my view of this queer situation.

'Right, lads. Follow me. Bring this disgraceful felon up to the Palatine.'

I had had a nice sleep and been treated to breakfast. I just went along with it.

As I was hauled in front of the Temple of Concordia Augusta, where the Arval Brothers held their elections, it was still far too early for most people. The Forum lay deserted, apart from one drunk sleeping it off on the steps of the Temple of Saturn. The streets contained debris from the night before, rather than any promise of the day to come. A mound of crushed garlands half blocked our way as we marched under the Arch of Tiberius to the Vicus Jugarius. Loose petals stuck in one of my boots, and as I kicked out to get rid of them the Guards almost lifted me bodily and carried me along.

I imagined we were heading for the administration area of the Palace. This turned out to be incorrect. Had we gone up the Arx or the Capitol I might have feared that the plan was to hurl me down on the traitors' route, from the top of the Tarpeian Rock. Whatever torture was intended must be more refined.

We seemed to approach a private house. All the Palatine had been in public ownership for many years. Augustus had had the good fortune to be born there in the days when anybody rich could own a private home on the best of the Seven Hills; he then acquired all the other houses and used the whole Palatine for official purposes. In among the temples stood his own abode, a supposedly meagre piece of real estate where he had claimed he lived very modestly; nobody was fooled by that. There was another extremely smart dwelling, the preserve of the imperial women, which bore the name of the dowager Empress Livia. And there was the Flaminia – the official residence of the currently serving Flamen Dialis – an ordinary house to look at, though affected by odd ritual covenants such as that fire might never be carried out of it, except for religious purposes.

Suddenly, Anacrites whipped a toga around his thin shoulders. Aelianus donned one too. Then they wheeled into the Flaminia while the Praetorians carried me after them, shoulder high, like the main roast at a feast.

The scene which ensued was curious. We were admitted at once to the presence of the Flamen and his stately wife. I was set on my feet, hemmed in by Guards. Various white-clad attendants lined the walls of the room respectfully. Scented oil wafted from a patera after some libation to the gods.

The Flamen wore hand-woven robes identical to those I had seen Numentinus parade in, topped off by the bonnet with the olive prong. He was holding his sacrificial knife, in its case, and his long pole to keep folk at a distance. His wife also carried her knife. She wore a thick gown of antique styling, with her hair bound up even more intricately than the Vestals. To match his leather hat she had a conical purple one, covered with a veil. She was, I knew, bound by almost as many restrictions, including one that said she must never climb more than three steps (lest someone see her ankles). She may have been an attractive woman, but I felt no temptation to ogle her.

The Flamen Dialis appeared to be slightly nervous. He at least had the advantage that he knew the plan.

The priestly couple sat enthroned on curule chairs, the backless folding items with curved legs that were formally used as a symbol of office by senior magistrates. A third had been placed near the Flamen. Alongside on this third seat was a familiar figure: Laelius Numentinus, though for once *he* was not wearing priestly robes. Perhaps a visit to the home of his successor had finally prevailed on him to abandon his lost glory. He was bare-headed. White hair surrounded a bald pate. I felt a shock of recognition. I glanced quickly at Aelianus. He too now saw that this was the haughty elderly man we had both witnessed leaving the house of the Master of the Arval Brethren when we went there to report the corpse. The man we thought had gone there to persuade them to maintain their silence about the killing – the man we assumed to be a close relative of the murderess.

There was no time to wonder. They all seemed to be expecting us. We had packed into the room with little formality. I was still held by the Guards. Anacrites tried to merge into the wall fresco, looking like a very dead still-life duck. Young Aelianus stepped forward. At a nod from the Flamen, he made a short prepared speech. It was much like the plea for mercy that he made to the Chief Vestal last night. With time to consider what he was doing, he had become more hesitant, but he acquitted himself decently.

Before replying, the Flamen Dialis leaned towards Numentinus as if to confirm his agreement. They exchanged a low murmur, then this time they both nodded. The Praetorians stepped aside from me. The Flamen Dialis struck a pose and affected to notice me. He started and covered his eyes theatrically. Assuming a sudden air of horror, he cried in a loud voice, 'A man in chains! Strike them off in accordance with the ritual!'

I believe that sometimes criminals are freed formally from fetters by sending for a blacksmith who cracks open the links. That must be a satisfying form of release. But Anacrites had always been a cheapskate. (It was not his fault. Shortage of resources went with his job.) He had originally secured the fetters with a padlock, and on the Flamen's word, he undid them carefully with the proper key, so they could be kept for re-use.

The ironmongery was then carried from the room and we all waited in silence until we heard the racket as it was hurled off the Flaminia's roof. There were metallic scuffles

281

afterwards, as the links were gathered up frugally. Anacrites winked at the Praetorians, who gave a smart salute in unison then removed themselves, their boots thumping scratchily on the floorboards. The Flaminica winced. Perhaps it was a ritual that she went on her knees and applied the beeswax herself. Perhaps she was just a careful housewife with a respect for antique carpentry.

'You are a free man,' confirmed the Flamen Dialis.

'Thank you,' I said to everyone.

As I rubbed my bruised limbs, the new Flamen spoke gravely from the curule chair. 'Marcus Didius Falco, I have decided you should receive an explanation of certain matters.'

He asked his attendants to leave the room. He and his wife, together with Numentinus, remained. So did I. So, at a gesture from the Flamen, did Camillus Aelianus. He came and stood alongside me. He looked pleased with himself and I did not begrudge him that.

Out of unwilling respect for the other man who had helped save my life, I said, 'I would like Anacrites to hear this too.' He was allowed to stay. He kept well back, looking humble. Well, as humble as it is possible to be if you are a lousy-natured spy.

The Flamen Dialis addressed Aelianus and me. 'You two have been attempting to discover the identity of the Arval Brother who was murdered in the Sacred Grove of the Dea Dia.'

We said nothing.

'His name was Ventidius Silanus.'

Less experienced than me, Aelianus was on the verge of bursting out that we already knew as much. I gripped his arm unobtrusively.

It was Laelius Numentinus, staring ahead of himself fixedly, who then volunteered to tell us what I had privately guessed: 'Ventidius Silanus was married to Terentia Paulla, my late wife's sister.'

It seemed courteous not to comment; it would have been difficult to do so tactfully at first. I breathed slowly, then somehow ignored the scandalous aspects and said in a

282

deferential tone, 'We offer our commiserations, sir.' I breathed again. 'That gives us a lot to think about. However, with respect, it does not alter the urgent need to find your little granddaughter. I hope you will still accept help to search for her?' Numentinus inclined his white head stiffly. 'Then I shall go home quickly now to see my wife. When I have washed off the stench of prison, I shall return to your house and continue where I left off yesterday.'

Nobody said the obvious: according to what the Master of the Arval Brethren had let Aelianus and me believe, Terentia Paulla, wife to the late Ventidius, was a crazy murderess.

Did that mean that this madwoman had also killed little Gaia?

LI

Outside the Flaminia, we three pulled up to catch our breath.

I offered my hand to Anacrites. We clasped arms like military blood brothers.

'Thanks. You saved my life.'

'So we are quits, Falco.'

'I shall always be grateful, Anacrites.'

I gazed at him. He gazed at me. We would never be quits.

I clasped hands with Aelianus too and then, since he was in effect my brother-in-law, I embraced him. He looked surprised. Not as surprised as I was to find myself doing it. 'This was your idea, Aulus? You organised everything?'

'If a ploy fails once, just repeat it with more verve.'

'Sounds like the wonderful nonsense that informers spout!'

Aelianus grinned. 'Anacrites suggested I was doing so well at this, I ought to continue working with you. When you have taught me a few things, he says there might be an opening in the security service with him.'

He could have told me this in confidence later, which is what I would have done in his shoes. Anacrites and I glared at each other. We could both see that Aelianus had deliberately said it in front of both of us. He was not the pushover we both had taken him for.

Anacrites tried to make light of it. 'I'm letting you have him first, Falco.'

'But you'll take advantage of the experience I give him? I train him, then you pinch him?'

'You owe me now.'

'Anacrites, I owe you zilch!' I turned to Aelianus. 'As for you, you reprobate, let's not pretend you want to set aside your purple stripes and go slumming.' Aelianus did not really

284

believe I had anything to teach him; if he joined me, his only desire would be to show me how to do my job by effortlessly surpassing me. 'I am supposed to be in partnership with your brother – when he deigns to show his face.'

Aelianus grinned. 'He pinched my girl – I'll pinch his position!'

'Well, that's fair,' I commented, quoting him on another subject.

After a moment we were all laughing.

We calmed down.

'That was a facer about Ventidius,' I said. We all walked slowly towards the Circus side of the Palatine where a path wound down.

'Have you been told the whole story now, I wonder?' Anacrites mused. He was not so dumb sometimes.

'Doubt it. Just enough to keep us off their backs. It does explain a lot. The ex-Vestal married a man who turned out to be a lecher – and so shameless that he even tried it on with one of her own female relatives – Caecilia Paeta, her nephew's wife; Caecilia told me herself. The rest now fits: Terentia presumably heard about it. Perhaps Caecilia told her, or the other one – Laelia, the ex-Flamen's daughter. So Terentia runs wild and slays Ventidius in the Sacred Grove, bloodily cutting his throat and saving the drips as if he were the white beast at a religious sacrifice.'

Aelianus took up the story: 'To the Arval Brothers this must have been a double horror. The corpse was a terrible sight – I can vouch for that – but it must also have seemed that night as if every cult in the old religion was touched by the scandal: the Arvals themselves, the Vestals, and even the College of Flamens –'

'Right,' I said. 'The dead man was an Arval and it happened in the Sacred Grove; the killer was a Vestal. Ventidius had been the lover of the previous Flaminica. That seems to have been common knowledge in Rome. Certainly most women knew. Then, to cap it all, the whole bunch is related to the child who has been picked out as the *next* Vestal.'

'So that was why a cover-up was so readily agreed?' suggested Anacrites. 'Influence?'

We stopped, on the heights just by the carefully preserved (that is, entirely rebuilt) supposed Hut of Romulus.

'Looks like it. Numentinus was definitely nagging the Arvals about something; he was at the Master's house the next night, and they did not sound too pleased about it. They were even less pleased about us,' I said. 'Everything would probably have worked very smoothly, if Aelianus and I had not started to poke about. The corpse was spirited away and a funeral held very quietly. Terentia is to be looked after and guarded, eventually no doubt at her own home though my guess is that as a first move she has been taken in by Laelius Numentinus, perhaps out of some regard for his dead wife. She has been living in a guestroom, though when I turned up to search she had to be packed off hastily to the Vestals' House, out of the way. As one of their own, the Virgins would agree to tend her.'

'Would her presence explain why Numentinus did not want the vigiles to come in after the child disappeared?' Anacrites asked.

'You heard about that?'

'I keep in touch,' he bragged.

'The vigiles might have sniffed out the scandal. And this explains the nonsense Laelius Scaurus told me about his aunt wanting a legal guardian. As an ex-Vestal, she would not need one, but arrangements are essential now. She must have been declared *furiosa* – not to be prissy, a raving lunatic. Somebody has to be her custodian.'

'Can she choose her own?' Aelianus asked.

'If she has moments of lucidity, why not?'

'But is she still dangerous?'

'After the way Ventidius was killed, she must be. That was not just an angry wife, lashing out with the nearest cooking knife. You cannot say it was a sudden act that she will never repeat. She planned it; she took the implements to the Grove; she dressed up in religious style; she murdered the man, and then carried out an extraordinary sequence of actions with his blood –'

286

Aelianus shuddered. 'Remember the cloth I saw covering the dead man's face? Now I know about the rituals involved, I think it must have been one of those veils priestesses wear when they attend a sacrifice.'

'And Vestals,' I said.

'Vestals,' said Anacrites, picking holes as usual, 'never actually cut throats.'

'Looks like this one learned to do it, once she got herself a husband.'

'A warning to all of us.'

'Oh?' I asked coldly, thinking about Maia. 'Are you considering marriage then, Anacrites?'

He just laughed, the way spies love to do, and looked mysterious.

Anacrites left us when we reached the Aventine. For one thing, he was going to ingratiate himself with Ma, pretending that the rescue of her bonny boy had been all his own idea. I could set her straight. Not that my mother would listen to me when she could choose to believe Anacrites instead.

He had another plan too: 'While you go back to the Laelius house, Falco, I'll trot along to the House of the Vestals and see whether any sense can be extracted from Terentia Paulla.'

'The Virgins won't let you in.'

'Yes they will,' he replied, gloating. 'I'm the Chief Spy!'

I took Aelianus with me, but when we came to Fountain Court I asked him to join the early morning queue at the stall Cassius the baker ran, to buy some breakfast rolls. I wanted to go up ahead of him and see Helena on my own. He understood.

Helena must have stayed up all night. She was sitting in her wicker chair, beside the baby's cradle, holding Julia as if she had been feeding her. They were both fast asleep.

Very gently, I lifted the baby from Helena's arms. Julia awoke, wondering whether to cry or chortle, then greeted me with a loud cry of 'Dog!'

'Olympus, her first word! She thinks I'm Nux.'

Startled by the baby's exclamation, Helena roused herself. 'She knows the dog. Her father is a stranger. I am disappointed, though. I have been trying so hard to teach her to say "Aristotelian Philosophy" – Where have you been, Marcus?'

'Long story. Starts in the House of the Vestals and ends in the death cell at the Mamertine.'

'Oh, nothing to worry about then . . .'

I sat Julia in her cradle. Helena was on her feet and clasping me to her with relief. I clung back, as if she was the only floating spar in the ocean, and I was a drowning man.

'I thought I would never see you again!'

'Me too, fruit.'

After a long time she leaned back, sniffing. For a moment I thought she was crying, but it was straight detective work.

'Sorry. I must stink of jail.'

'You do,' she said, using a special voice. 'And of something else. I know you like to try out promising skin lotions, my darling, but since when have you dabbed iris oil behind your ears?'

I must have been still rather tired. 'That would be what the Virgin Constantia wears off duty, I fear.'

'Really.'

'Cloying, but persistent. Survives even a night's incarceration in the filthiest jail. Don't be annoyed. I don't chase after women.'

'You don't need to. I gather they chase after you! And they catch you, I can tell.'

How fortunate that Helena's dear brother arrived at that moment, releasing me from this awkwardness. He seemed to know what was wanted. As an assistant, Camillus Aelianus was shaping up in superb style.

I washed. We took in food and water. I kissed Helena goodbye; she turned her head away, though she just about let me near her. Nux, who had no qualms about my loyalty, ran up barking and hopefully brought me the rope that I used as her lead sometimes. I accepted the plea, in order to show Helena that I responded to love.

As we descended the stairs to the street, I saw Maia

approaching. She was dressed demurely in white, with her curls fairly well taped down. She was holding hands with Cloelia, also kitted out like a religious offering.

'Marcus! We are just going to watch the lottery. We decided we may as well witness the flummery. There may be fascinating refreshments we think, don't we, Cloelia?'

'Did you find Gaia?' Cloelia asked me, frowning at her mother's frivolity.

'Not yet. I am going back to search again.'

'Cloelia wants to tell you something,' Maia said, graver now.

'What's this, Cloelia?'

'Uncle Marcus, has something bad happened to Gaia?'

'I hope not. But I am very worried. Do you know anything that might help?'

'She told me not to tell. But I think I ought to mention it now. Gaia has an aunt she thinks is mad. The aunt said she would kill Gaia. Gaia told her mother and her grandfather but nobody seemed to believe her. Does that help you?'

'Yes. Thank you, Cloelia; it helps a lot. Was there anything else?'

'No, Uncle Marcus.'

Petronius Longus had come out of the laundry, on his way to work, and had walked across. 'Maia! Want somebody to come with you today? I know you can't expect support from this unreliable brother of yours.'

'No thanks,' Maia told him coolly. 'I was married for years. I am quite used to dealing with family business on my own.'

She left. Petro scowled.

'Rubella has sent some of our lads to fetch that Scaurus,' said Petro in a level tone. 'He should be with you later this morning, Falco.'

'Usual story,' I told him. 'Mad aunt. Case solved – but unfortunately, no body.'

'If it's a case with a body, there's no hurry.' The vigiles have to have a brutal outlook. 'So it's a mad aunt? I'm not surprised. With their snobbery and strict marriage requirements, the priestly colleges are inbred to the point of utter lunacy. It's well known.' Petro looked Aelianus up and down. He did not even bother to be rude to him. He just said to me, 'Let me know when you are ready to call in the specialists.'

'It's all right,' I sneered back. 'We are not expecting any fires.' He hated being regarded as just part of the fire brigade.

Taking Aelianus and the dog, I set off for the final time to the house of the Laelii.

LII

The scent of incense seemed stale today, like so many of the occupants' relationships.

Drawn magically by the hint of trouble to gawp at, the builders had returned, bringing even their project manager, that mythical figure who normally just fails to order materials on time and who can never be contacted because he is always at some other, more important site.

In order to justify watching and listening to everything, the men were busily finishing the shrine in the atrium. The lower two-thirds of the shrine took the form of a cupboard with double doors, which were now receiving their final polish; the top section represented a temple, with ornately carved Corinthian columns at each side. Already someone had placed there the dancing Lares and Penates, poor little bronze gods who would have their work cut out bringing good fortune to this miserable household. On the shelves of the cupboard below were kept lamps and vases, and a selection of religious implements: spare flaminical hats, sacrificial vessels, jugs and bowls. Together on one side were items which must have been kept as a memorial of the late Flaminica: her conical purple hat and her sacrificial knife.

I lifted out the knife. It had a thick handle, in the form of an eagle's head, and that special design, with a broad stumpy blade made of bronze, both sides of which were slightly curved, almost trowel-shaped.

'There is no sheath,' commented Aelianus. I knew what he meant.

'Lost it,' said one of the workmen. 'Must have happened when they moved house. Terrible stink when they couldn't find it. Of course,' he said, self-righteously, 'we got the blame.'

'But you had nothing to do with it?' I knew they had not.

Aelianus handled the knife, being extremely cautious. It was finely sharpened, as it had to be in use. 'You would think cutting animals' throats was no job for a woman.'

'Oh you soon get used to it.' We turned, startled, to see Statilia Laelia watching us. 'My mother told me. She used to joke that you could tell a sacrificing priestess anywhere; they develop strong forearms.'

'I had always assumed that an assistant actually slew the beasts for the Flaminica,' I said.

Laelia smiled. 'Women are far less squeamish than you think, Falco.'

She turned away. Then she spun back. 'Juno! Is that a dog?' Nux wagged her tail. 'We cannot have that here, Falco!'

'I have brought this dog to conduct a further search for Gaia. Anyone who has a ritual objection can go out for the day. The dog stays.'

Laelia bustled off, probably to complain to her husband or her father. Nux sat down on the atrium floor and scratched herself.

Aelianus gingerly replaced the knife. 'Somebody has given this a splendidly good clean, Falco.'

'Got it to come up nicely, haven't they?' the workman agreed.

Unlike us, he did not know that what had been cleaned off was probably the blood of the murdered Ventidius Silanus.

We took Nux to little Gaia's bedroom. I let her sniff around, then showed her one of the child's shoes. Nux lay down with her head between her paws, as if she was waiting for me to throw it.

'This won't work,' scoffed my new assistant. He had a lot to learn. To start with: knowing when to shut up.

I gave Nux the shoe, which she agreed to carry while I led her downstairs and into the peristyle garden. The workmen were now mucking about with the pool, but they happily abandoned that and came to watch me. I led the dog around the colonnade. Nux liked that. She sniffed all the columns with interest. I turned her loose. She dropped the shoe and bounded off to explore the bags where the workmen were keeping their lunch.

I called her back. She came, sauntering reluctantly. 'Nux, you are hopeless. Helena is a better sniffer dog than you. I wish I had brought her.'

'You want a proper hunting hound for this,' Aelianus sneered.

'Know anybody who owns one?'

'Plenty.'

'Here in Rome?'

'Of course not. People hunt in the country.'

'Well then, keep quiet until you can offer something useful.'

I showed Nux the clump of twigs bound together that Gaia had played with while pretending to clean out the Temple of Vesta. Puzzled, Nux shook it about in her teeth then let it fall, waiting for a different game.

One of the workmen remarked, 'The little sprat had a better mop than that. I made her one with real horsehair, like those the Vestals really use.'

Where was it?

I left Aelianus to talk to the men about the day Gaia disappeared. I could trust him with that. Presumably if they had anything useful to say, they would have offered it when the alarm was first raised.

I led my hopeless bloodhound to the other garden. Off the leash the scruffy bundle of fur wandered about, digging potholes, sniffing leaves, and looking back at me to see what behaviour I wanted. I was still holding Gaia's shoe, so I hurled it as far as I could into the undergrowth in the distance. Nux ran off and vanished. I sat on a bench, waiting for her to get bored.

No gardeners were about today. I was completely alone.

Sometimes you have no idea what progress you are making with a case. Sometimes it all seems to be sorted, yet you find yourself niggled by the feeling that what looks straightforward cannot be that simple. I kept wondering what I had missed here. There were gaps in the story, gaps so well disguised that I could not even see where they existed, let alone try to fill them. I knew I was on the wrong tack. I just could not see why I felt that way.

It was still early morning, but now much warmer than when I was hauled out of the Mamertine. Blue sky was gradually deepening in colour above me. Bees explored what long strands of herbage remained. A blackbird foraged among upended pots, wildly tossing aside unwanted leaves. I took one of those moments when I ought to have been busy, but hoped letting the quietness seep into my spirit might refresh me and bring me a bright idea. What could I do, anyway? I had searched yesterday as thoroughly as I knew how.

A woman came out from the house to my right. Someone I had never seen before. She was alone. A tallish, slim, middle-aged female, wearing grey in several layers, long full skirts and a graceful stole. She came straight to me and joined me on the bench. I noticed she wore a wedding ring.

'You must be Falco.' I made no reply, but glanced sideways uneasily, hoping for back-up.

She had a face, bare of paint but probably well tended, which had gone past youth; her skin was still firm and her movements were easy. Grey eyes watched me with a bold, challenging air. She was unafraid of men. My guess was, she had never been afraid of anything. But then, courage is a form of lunacy. And of course, the woman who had killed Ventidius Silanus must have been both courageous and completely mad.

LIII

Oddly enough, she looked perfectly sane.

Her eyes still considered me, lucid, serene, visibly intelligent. Women who have completed successful careers acquire a certain address. She was used to taking decisions, speaking out, leading the ceremonial.

Maybe it depends on your starting point. Maybe we are all mad in our own ways. Mind you, not many of us could slash the throat of another human. Not off the battlefield; not in cold blood.

'I understand you took a considerable risk last night, Falco, in order to speak to me.' I moved my head in assent. She was definitely the ex-Vestal, Terentia. 'Some informer! You never found me, never came near me.'

'No, I apologise.'

'I suppose you saw the other chit instead.' I looked mystified. 'Constantia. You know who I mean.'

'Yes, I saw her.'

'What did you think?'

'A talented young woman. She should go far.'

'Or to the bad!' humphed Terentia. 'A latter-day Postumia!'

'Postumia?'

'Don't you know your history? She was tried for unchastity; she had dressed too elegantly, and spoken too freely and wittily. The Pontifex Maximus acquitted her of the sexual charge, but Postumia was warned to behave more becomingly, to stop making jokes and to dress less smartly.'

'I am shocked.'

'You are a clown, Falco. Someone else came badgering me this morning,' Terentia grumbled. 'That dreadful man Anacrites.'

'Did you see him?'

'Certainly not. I left by the other door and came straight here. I do not communicate with spies.'

So much for Anacrites' self-confidence! 'He will follow you here.'

'Probably.'

She looked less mad than my own aunts, most of whom are contentious harridans with a tendency to throw burning hot skillets around. All the same – well perhaps because of my dear aunties – I did not relax.

'May I talk to you?' I asked meekly. 'I am not a spy, merely a Procurator of the Sacred Geese, ma'am.'

'My name is Terentia Paulla, as you well know.' I thought to myself that proper lunatics were supposed to believe themselves to be Julius Caesar. Mind you, this one issued orders like a dictator, right enough. 'As for you,' she said, 'I imagine that after your escapade at the Vestals' House, you will find it expedient to resign from your curation of the poultry.'

'No, no; I'll stand my ground. I have learned to enjoy the post.'

'Vespasian will sacrifice your sinecure in the next round of public spending cuts.'

'I agree that's a possibility.'

'I shall suggest it to him myself,' said Terentia, in the full hauteur of an ex-Virgin. Well, that would save me bestirring myself. I was starting to feel very glad Maia's daughter would not become a Virgin. We would not want Cloelia coming back to us in thirty years' time as rude and provocative as this.

With my bright new credentials under attack, I decided to turn tough. 'If it is not impolite to ask, why did you marry Ventidius?'

'It is impolite. Because he asked me. He was an attractive, urbane, amusing man, with a great deal of money too. He had been, as I am sure you know, my sister's lover for a very long time.'

'You were not afraid of upsetting your sister?'

'I dare say I intended it.' I tried not to look shocked. I

could see why Helena's mother, Julia Justa, that most rational and socially restrained of women, had spoken of Terentia with dislike. The ex-Virgin was not just awkward; she actively enjoyed being unlikeable. 'My sister paraded her conquest shamefully and laid rather too much emphasis on telling me the details, pointing out how her bedroom activities contrasted with my own chaste life. She forgot that my vowed thirty years would end one day. Statilia Paulla was ill. She was not aware that I knew it, but when our betrothal was announced I realised I would not be depriving her of her lover for long.' Terentia paused. 'Still, it should have been longer than it was.'

'Her illness advanced very rapidly?'

'No, Falco. She opened her veins in her bath. My sister killed herself.'

She was quite matter-of-fact. Was this the unfeeling out-spokenness of a crazy woman, or simply that, like an extremely sane one, Terentia saw no purpose in messing me about? Any rate, it meant there had been yet another crisis, yet another tragedy, disrupting this terrible family. I began to understand why the ex-Flamen spoke as he did of his wife's death; she would presumably have died anyway, but she had deprived him of his own position before time, and deliberately.

'So then,' Terentia continued softly, 'I married Ventidius. I had no choice.'

'Why?'

'Well, don't you see? I thought I could control him. My sister had managed it before she became ill.'

'I don't follow.'

'He was a very old friend of the family –'

'The very friendly "Uncle Tiberius" – so I heard,' I said dryly. Terentia shot me a look of distaste. I survived.

'Ventidius needed to be closely watched,' she explained. 'He would have been around all the time –'

'On the prowl?'

'Precisely. I knew Numentinus would certainly not break with Ventidius after Statilia's death, not after he had tolerated the man's behaviour before. He refused to see there was now a danger to the girls. What a fool. He could not see how necessary it had become for him to act.'

'Necessary, why?'

'You know that.'

'Because Ventidius started to eye up Caecilia?'

'Caecilia and, to a far greater extent, Laelia.'

'Caecilia admits that she had to rebuff Ventidius. Laelia denies he ever touched her.'

'Then,' said Terentia crisply, 'Laelia lied to you.'

'Modesty, no doubt,' I murmured, thinking that a Vestal would approve of that.

'Don't be ridiculous! Statilia Laelia has good reasons for everything she does.'

'She needs to lie?'

'Oh we all need to do that!' For a moment, Terentia looked tired.

'So,' I mused, 'you knew about Ventidius moving in on the other two? Who told you, may I ask?'

'Laelia told me that Caecilia had confided in her. She took more pleasure in the telling than she should have done. Before that, I had myself already warned him to leave Laelia alone. He had been playing about with her for some time; she is very immature – and she took it very seriously. Scaurus, her brother, had found out and told me in the end. Ventidius enjoyed thinking he had the privilege of bedding more than one generation.'

'So he made a long-term play for Laelia – successfully? I find it hard to believe.'

'You misjudge everyone, Falco.' After crushing me to her own satisfaction, she settled to explanations again. 'Laelia probably allowed it quite readily, I am afraid. She was always difficult. But I stopped it, once I knew.'

'So Laelia was promiscuous?'

'Not widely; she never had much opportunity. The children of a Flamen Dialis are brought up in isolation.'

'I can see that would have made her easy meat for an ever-present family friend. Why was she always difficult?'

'Why?' Terentia seemed astonished that I had asked. 'How should I know why? That was just how it was.

Children are born with inherent, strong-willed streaks of character.' Strong-willed was the last word I would have used for the ex-Flamen's pasty daughter. Again, I reminded myself that I was hearing all this from a supposed mad-woman. 'Her mother was too busy spoiling Scaurus to notice – unless perhaps Statilia simply felt powerless to deal with Laelia. The boy and girl were a strange, secretive couple, too often left in their own company. Sometimes they squabbled violently, sometimes they were dangerously quiet, heads together like little conspirators.'

'Being the offspring of a Flamen, they were kept from other children – and to some extent, I suppose, from adult company too?'

'It was fatal, in my opinion,' said Terentia cryptically.

'They never learned normal behaviour?'

'No. They seemed to buckle down to their religious duties well as infants, but they developed a ridiculous sense of their own importance which could do neither any good.'

'They both seem rather vague now,' I commented.

'They both have uncontrollable tempers when thwarted. They brood. They lash out. They lack tolerance and restraint. Some children never need companionship to make them sweet natured. Look at Gaia; yet she is an only child, brought up utterly solitary too.'

'A little spoiled materially?' I suggested.

'Blame Laelia,' Terentia said, in a clipped tone. 'No sense of decency. She constantly buys presents without reference to Caecilia, and sneaks them to Gaia. Once Laelia has given clothes or toys to the child, it is hard to remove them again.'

'So Laelia loves her little niece Gaia?' Laelia, it struck me, was the real aunt here; Terentia a great-aunt. 'Is it consistent, or might she turn on the child?'

'Laelia's love is a volatile emotion,' Terentia commented. Still, she was mad. How could she evaluate emotion?

'Would she threaten Gaia with violence just as easily as spoiling her?'

Terentia made a slight gesture of assent – as if congratulating me on at last seeing the truth. 'As for Laelia, we did our best. When she reached marriageable age, I

299

suggested Ariminius – a complete change, fresh blood. He was flattered to be asked to join a family of such standing. It has to be said, he is very good with Laelia.'

I had interviewed Ariminius and his wife together, at their choice – his, maybe? He must have been deliberately guarding against indiscretions by the woman. I had certainly missed any suggestion that Laelia had been willingly playing about with 'Uncle Tiberius'.

'They seem to have a good marriage,' I interposed in defence of the Pomonalis, not revealing that I realised he wanted to move on.

'You are easy to bluff!' sneered Terentia. 'From a man who comes with a seal of approval from a more than usually efficient emperor, I expect better. Ariminius has reached his limit. He has had enough. He is asking for a divorce.'

Yes, that fitted his remarks yesterday afternoon when he was searching for Gaia with me. 'He has spoken of a yen for independence.' In fact he spoke of 'desertion', I now recalled. That would fit leaving an unstable wife. So just how unstable was Laelia? 'I thought a flamen had to stay married for life? You can't mean Ariminius will give up being a member of the priestly college?'

'I do mean that. Now you see why I have been trying to arrange formal guardianship. If there is a divorce, Laelia comes back into her own family. Numentinus is growing old and cannot be relied on indefinitely.'

'Scaurus told me you wanted him to act for *you*!'

She stared at me. 'Me? Why should I need that?' It seemed wise not to answer. 'Oh really! The boy is an imbecile.'

'I understood that you were very fond of him, Terentia Paulla.'

'Fond? Fond is not the word. Both those children were brought up ignorant and in need of control. Scaurus is irredeemably foolish and I try to protect him from public shame.'

Now this was the kind of madness I could understand: a woman who had apparently been declared *furiosa* convincing herself, and trying to convince me, that her very protectors

300

were in need of care! Yes, it was time for a serious rethink.

'Terentia Paulla, your nephew looks like the only one here who has shown some initiative – I mean, by refusing to be drawn into the family traditions, and by leaving home.'

His loving aunt beat the side of her hand against her other fist impatiently. 'Nonsense. The evidence is right in front of you, Falco. Whatever has he told you about this question of guardianship? Why spin you such a stupid story? All he had to say was the truth: that he came to Rome on legal business. *He* knew the whole matter has to be confidential, and by the time he saw you, his father and I had decided he was incapable of taking on the burden of his sister. He had also been clearly told to keep quiet. Instead, he dreams up some complicated fantasy that even you will soon see through –'

'So Scaurus is a bit dim?'

'Dim? My poor nephew really needs a guardian himself. When I had talked to him about his sister, I realised he was useless and I packed him off home. It leaves us with no solution, but there are hopes of Ariminius.'

I thought for a moment. 'Why not help Ariminius to a divorce, with a very large settlement if possible, and ask him to be Laelia's guardian? He could still do it. And he can be capable in a crisis. I'm sorry,' I added. 'I realise it might have to be your money in the settlement, and you might not enjoy giving it over to Laelia.'

'My idea,' said Terentia, with relish, 'is to use my husband's money after I inherit! Ventidius caused this. He owes some return to the family. His wealth can make Ariminius Modullus happy, and provide for Laelia's future care.'

'And what about Scaurus? Is his lack of brainpower why he never became a flamen?'

'Of course. The highest posts were open to him in theory. Appointing him would have been a shambles. Even his father had to admit that. Scaurus would never remember the rituals – even if he could summon the will to try. Caecilia Paeta thought, when they were first married, that she could help him through it, but in the end even she lost heart. Rituals have to be carried out exactly.'

'Ah the old religion!' I groaned. 'Appeasing the gods by the mindless repetition of meaningless words and actions, until the divine ones send good crops just to win themselves some peace from the mumbling and the smell of burning wheatcake crumbs!'

'You blaspheme, Falco.'

'I do indeed.' And I was proud of it.

Terentia decided to ignore my outburst. 'My nephew's wife, like my niece's husband, could only endure so much. Ariminius will look after himself when he is ready; he has reason enough to leave, after all.' I wanted to ask what she meant, but she was in full flow, unused to interruptions. 'Three years ago, Caecilia was breaking down; she had to be relieved of the burden of her marriage but Numentinus would not face the problem. I put Scaurus on the farm to keep him out of harm's way, and a sensible girl of mine looks after him.'

'The lovely Meldina?' I leered.

'You have the wrong idea again, Falco. Meldina is happily married with three children. To persuade her to do this, I have to accommodate her husband and family as well.'

'Ah! Excuse me, but does Numentinus play no part at all? You appear to have assumed responsibility; does the rigid ex-Flamen really accept you managing his children for him?'

'He watches feebly, complaining. His children are a great disappointment to him – so instead of attempting to put matters right, he absorbs himself in honouring the gods. As Flamen Dialis, he had an excuse: every hour of his time was occupied with his duties to Jupiter. My sister was no better. In a serious crisis, they both used to chew bay leaves and put themselves into a trance until somebody else had sorted it out. Thank goodness, as a Vestal I could command authority.'

Everything Terentia Paulla said could be true – or it could be some maniacal distortion of the truth. Was she really a dedicated saviour of these hopeless people, or was her constant fanatical interference beyond belief? An intolerable strain from which they could not shake themselves free?

I kept reminding myself, the Arval Master had implied

302

that this woman had run mad and cut down her husband like a blood sacrifice. The more she talked, in that angry yet well-controlled tone, the easier it was to believe that she could easily have killed her husband if she had decided it was necessary – and yet the harder it became to envisage her turning the death into a stagy tableau, conducted in a crazy trance.

Surely she would have wanted it quick, clean and neat? Instinct said she would have made the crime itself undetectable – or at least concealed the perpetrator. If ever a killer had the intelligence and the nerve to get away with it, that was Terentia Paulla. Even if she had done it and, in her haughty way, had chosen to admit the deed, I reckoned she would have waited beside the body, then made her confession brisk and businesslike. The scene described by the Master of the Arvals, where a raving bloodstained woman was apprehended, then coaxed into confessing, did not fit at all. Nor did his description of a pathetic creature who would be taken into care match the cool woman talking to me here.

'So what about Gaia?' I asked her carefully.

'Gaia is the one shining star amongst this family. From who knows where – my family most likely, and even perhaps from her mother's side – Gaia has acquired intelligence and strength of character.'

'Yet you are very unwilling to see her follow you into your own profession as a Vestal?'

'Perhaps,' said Terentia, for once very quietly, 'it is time one member of this family grew up to lead a normal life.'

I felt a reply would be intrusive.

'I would like to see some changes, Falco. Gaia will be dutiful, whatever role in life she undertakes.' She paused. 'Then, as a Vestal, I must consider my order. I cannot knowingly approve of her selection. The potential for scandal is too great. She is a wrong choice for Vesta – and the burden on Gaia herself would be intolerable too, if a ghastly murder in her close family ever became public knowledge.'

'The lottery will be taking place now,' I said. 'She's out of it. If somebody has hidden her away to avoid her selection, she can be safely released.'

'Nobody did that. Nobody has deliberately harmed her either,' Terentia assured me.

'I'd like to ask Gaia how she felt about that.'

'Once the danger was known, I was on hand to protect her.' Protect her from whom? 'She has to be found first. That, if I may remind you, Falco, is your prime responsibility.'

I decided to chance it. 'According to my own young niece, Gaia Laelia has a mad aunt who has threatened to kill her.'

Terentia showed no reaction. She was going to pursue the cover-up to the very end if she could.

I tried again. 'Gaia told me, and she told the Vestal Constantia, that somebody in her family wanted her dead. Forgive me,' I said gently. 'I have to take that seriously, especially as she has a relative who was murdered recently. It could be assumed that the killer has in fact struck twice.' Still no reaction. 'Terentia, the Master of the Arval Brethren let me believe that Ventidius Silanus was slain by his wife.'

'He's a fool.' Terentia Paulla gazed at the sky with her head back. She leaned forwards, with her face in both hands, rubbing her eyes. Were they the eyes of a deranged woman? Or merely one who was sinking under a morass of male incompetence? She growled to herself, a low, desperate noise at the back of her throat, yet I felt strangely unafraid.

'If the Master is right, how courageous you are!' she suggested sarcastically after a moment. 'Sitting here alone with me . . . I have killed neither Ventidius nor Gaia. I love the child dearly, and she knows it. I am merely the stubborn, benevolent sister of her grandmother, who has been trying to protect her.'

I watched the woman carefully. She must be under great stress. The questions I was now asking would tax anyone, even the innocent. Especially the innocent. Terentia knew she could not simply accuse me of an informer's impertinence. So she had been dragging out for me what she believed to be the truth, much of it embarrassing to repeat to any stranger. If I accepted the Master's hint, she was accused of a dreadful crime. If Terentia Paulla was the type to break out and run crazy, this was the time for it to show.

304

She looked back at me with arrogance, anger, and high feminine scorn. She wanted to rage at me, probably to strike me. But she did nothing.

'It was somebody else,' she said. 'Somebody else killed my husband. Apprehended and bloodstained, she raved at the Master that she was the dead man's wife, and the Master believed her at the time. Men are so unobservant and easily suggestible. Besides, if you know anything about marriage, her claim seemed perfectly feasible. Later, of course, pretending that a wife had killed him seemed a good way to deter you and that Camillus boy from poking your noses in. But she was simply a past victim of Ventidius, whom he had dropped – at my insistence – and who went wild when she felt rejected.'

'Not you, then?' I confirmed softly.

'No, it was not me. I could never, ever do any such thing.'

Of course, all cornered killers say that.

Sadly, I nodded, letting Terentia know that I would not be coerced into protecting the real killer. Not while there was any doubt about the fate of little Gaia.

Then two things happened.

My dog came to look for me. Nux suddenly rushed out of the far undergrowth barking, though her yelps were muffled by what she was carrying in her mouth. She brought it to me: a piece of clean white wood, a new stave, to which had been nailed long strands of horsehair to make some kind of brush.

And from the house stepped Aelianus. He looked startled when he saw Terentia, but what he had to say was too urgent to put off.

'Falco, you ought to come.' I was already on my feet. 'The vigiles have just delivered Scaurus here, and everyone is going absolutely wild. It seems more than just a quarrel. If they aren't stopped, I think somebody is going to be killed.'

I picked up the dog and ran.

LIV

The furore was occurring in the atrium. Very traditional. The centre of a true Roman house. The hearth, the pool (still dry, in this instance), and the household gods.

There were people everywhere. The first one I recognised was Anacrites. He was vainly attempting to shepherd slaves and builders away from the fuss, while they tried to push past him and ogle. Aelianus joined in, shoving the crowd back down a corridor.

'Anacrites! Quickly – what's happening?'

'Madness! The vigiles brought the son –'

'Scaurus?'

'Yes. I had just arrived and was attempting to gain admittance to see the ex-Vestal –' His eyes lingered upon Terentia. 'The old man had come to argue with me. When he saw his son, apparently under arrest, Numentinus seemed to have expected it. He was furious. He went at Scaurus, berating him, saying that Scaurus had only had to do what he had been told, and everything could have been sorted out. I don't know what Scaurus' orders were –'

'To keep quiet!' Terentia elaborated. Then she fumed, 'Numentinus could have done the same.'

Anacrites obviously guessed who she was, and still thought she was the lunatic who had killed Ventidius. He looked nervous; I no longer was. I had no time to explain. 'Then a woman rushed in,' he told me. 'The son yelled at her – he was demanding, what had she said to get him brought here like this? She went hysterical –'

'Falco –' Terentia began urgently.

'It's Laelia – yes, I understand.' I gave her a straight look. I needed to hear no more. I shoved the dog into Anacrites' arms. If Nux bit him, so much the better. I rushed ahead into the atrium. Terentia Paulla was close on my heels.

They were all there. Numentinus appeared to have had some kind of seizure. Caecilia Paeta was bending over the elderly man, trying to fan his face with her hands. Ariminius was on the floor. He had blood all over him, though I could not see where he was hurt. He was alive, though curled up and gasping; he needed help, and in the next few minutes.

A couple of vigiles were trying to drag Scaurus to safety while his sister Laelia wielded the late Flaminica's sacrificial knife. Laelia must have snatched it from the shrine. I cursed myself for having ever left it there. Athene, Gaia's horse-faced nurse, was making a brave attempt to hold Laelia back; she must share the duties of caring for and guarding the lunatic. In great danger herself, she was nonetheless hanging on although Laelia was fighting her off with obscenities and violence. As I approached, Laelia started beating the nurse, luckily with her free hand, not the one that held the knife. Athene acquired yet more bruises on top of those she had had when I interviewed her, yet she doggedly took the punishment.

Every time his sister lunged near enough to Scaurus, she stabbed at him wildly. Instead of retreating, Scaurus was waving his arms at her, and yelling. He was fuelling her agitation. It almost looked deliberate.

One of the watch fastened both arms round Scaurus from behind and would have carried him off backwards, but a fierce knife stroke from Laelia slashed into the man's forearm and he let go, cursing and pouring with blood. Another vigilis rushed to support his wounded colleague and pull him away from danger.

Caecilia Paeta now saw what was happening. With a scream, she left the old man and ran to her husband, crying at Scaurus to stop before he was killed. Oblivious, Scaurus only concerned himself with goading his sister. She looked radiant, exultantly jeering at him, and encouraging him to risk himself on the wide sweeps of the wicked bronze knife. She tossed Athene to one side; the poor girl fell heavily and as I broke through the crowd I signalled her to keep away.

Caecilia had caught at the front of Scaurus' clothing,

trying to deter him from approaching his crazy sister. With great determination, his still-loyal wife hung on to him and held him back. Nobody else seemed willing to help.

'Dear gods, what a mess!'

I keep a dagger in my boot. Half the time I never use it, and it would not achieve much now. I was the only person here who would have any sort of weapon, except possibly Anacrites, and he was still in poor health, unreliable in a ruck. This was a household of priests; for them, swords were what antique heroes hung up in temple sanctums prettily adorned with laurel twigs. Even the vigiles, as civil troops, are unarmed. So it was up to me.

Laelia was now really raving. Apart from Athene's and Caecilia's efforts, only his sister's uncontrolled mania had saved Scaurus from real harm. Nobody dared approach her, but she had no aim and only half an intention. Flecks of froth showed around her mouth. A manic grin was transfixed on her flushed face. She was dancing from foot to foot, swinging the knife to left and right. So far, she appeared not to want to harm herself, but I felt that could come at any moment.

I, of course, am a correct Roman. I do not fight women. This was a problem. I would have to disarm Laelia, and then rapidly overpower her. Her grip on the knife was so tight her knuckles shone white.

I leapt across the hall, vaulting the dry pool, to where the workmen had stored their equipment. I snatched up a piece of rough wood that they probably used as scaffolding. Sensing a new situation, Laelia started screaming repeatedly. Other people were shouting. Scaurus suddenly stopped struggling, so Caecilia let go of him.

Scaurus threw open his arms as if to embrace Laelia.

Abruptly she stood still. 'Cutting his throat was not enough,' she told Scaurus. Her calm was even more unnerving than her previous violence. She could have been explaining why she had changed the daily bakery delivery. Everyone else froze in horror. 'The man's entrails should have been examined for omens. The liver should have been offered to the gods.'

I started walking towards her. 'So it was you who killed

Uncle Tiberius?' I asked, trying to distract her. 'Why did you do that, Laelia?'

She turned in my direction. 'He stopped wanting me. Aunt Terentia made him stay away – he should not have listened to her. I held the bowl!' she exclaimed. Something that had always bothered me began to make sense.

'I realise how hard it must have been.' I was managing to move in closer. 'Ventidius had thrashed around trying to escape. He fell outside, through the wall of the tent. He landed on the grass. The rest must have been extremely awkward –' I kept stepping forward gently. I was nearly there.

'You know, don't you?' Laelia demanded of me. 'It's not like sacrificing an animal, is it? Anyway, the priest has assistants. Tiberius was lying on the ground. It was very difficult to put the bowl under his throat –'

It was impossible for one to manage. At the ritual sacrifice of Ventidius Silanus, *two* people must have officiated. As realisation dawned it must have shown on my face. While Laelia was watching me, Scaurus decided to get to her.

'Keep away,' I warned him urgently. Laelia's gaze flickered wildly between us; Scaurus hesitated. The people watching had fallen very quiet, and were at last all standing still. 'Leave it to me, Scaurus.'

Laelia turned to me and said clearly, 'I could not have done it. I was never taught how – but my brother had been trained in what a flamen has to do, so he knew. Scaurus said, if the knife is sharp, it's easier than you think!'

Scaurus came at her ahead of me. He grabbed her wrist. As everyone kept telling me, the man was an idiot. He had grabbed the wrist nearest to him – not the one holding the knife. Laelia spun, actually pivoting more easily because her other arm was held. She brought round her free hand, trying to carve a stroke across his neck. She was hopeless too. She drew blood from his shoulder but he leapt back out of harm's way.

Suddenly I was free to act. Safely at arm's length, I brought the stave down on Laelia's knife hand as hard as possible. The weapon jerked from her grasp and skidded away across the hall mosaic. She hardly seemed to feel it. She was going from us now; her mind was visibly wandering.

I got to her. I had turned the stave, as if intending to hold her at bay with it. I managed to extend one end beyond Laelia just as Scaurus bent and retrieved their mother's sacrificial knife. I was ready for him. I flung an arm around Laelia and dragged her back away from him. Nobody else seemed to have any idea of the danger she was in. She knew least of all; that made it even more dangerous.

Sobbing wildly now, Laelia grabbed at the stave suddenly and hampered my movements. While I shook her off, somebody whipped past me in a blur of grey. Terentia Paulla stepped past her mad niece just as Scaurus, her equally mad nephew, squared up to kill Laelia.

'You!' cried Terentia, in complete exasperation. 'It was bad enough thinking that your ridiculous sister killed him – but you helped her!'

'He was an animal,' said Scaurus.

I hurled Laelia as far from me as possible and turned to protect Terentia. There was no need.

The furious ex-Vestal let fly at her nephew with a straight-armed, right-handed punch that came all the way from the shoulder. I heard his jaw crack. His head jerked back. Scaurus looked at the ceiling abruptly. Then he went down.

LV

Everyone fell on the various victims.

I muttered in an undertone to Terentia, 'Dare I ask where you learned the knock-out blow? From one of the Vestals' lictors, preparing you for married life with Ventidius?'

'Instinct!' she snapped. 'I can supervise here. Now, Falco – find Gaia!'

She turned to where Anacrites was still standing with my dog in his arms. Unusually for her, Nux had retained her interest in a trophy. Her white teeth firmly gripped the little horsehair mop – surely the one the builder had made for Gaia.

Feeling stupid, Anacrites put the dog down, and she ran to sit in front of me, wagging her unhygienic stump of tail against the floor mosaic.

'What is it, Nux?'

I bent down and took the mop from between her jaws. Being Nux, she clung on for some time, growling happily and shaking her find while I tugged it free. She started to bark.

'Good girl.' When she saw that I was now prepared to notice her, she began running round in wide circles in front of me. I followed. Nux took off and streaked back the way we had come from the garden. Whenever she reached the corner of a corridor, she stopped and barked. It was a harsh, high, piercing noise, meant to hold my attention. Nothing like her normal pointless woof.

I had left everyone behind as I strode after my excited pet. She nosed her way along passageways and through doorways, looking back sometimes to check that I was still with her. 'Good girlie! Show me, Nux.'

Out into the kitchen garden went the dog. Past the seat

311

where so little time ago I had been talking to Terentia. Through the newly dug beds, under the despoiled pergolas, into the brambles and tangled creepers that ran back to the high wall.

Yesterday we were supposed to have searched everywhere, even here. Slaves with scythes had hacked at the creepers. I had trodden down parts of the undergrowth myself. I had told some of the helpers to crawl into the thickets.

Not good enough, Falco. There was a place where an angle of the boundary wall turned away. Bushes shielded it from obvious view nowadays, but it had once had a purpose. In fairness to me, I had seen someone else exploring this area yesterday. But it is never safe to rely on other people. In a real emergency, you must double-check every inch of ground yourself. Never mind if your helpers grow fractious because it looks as if you do not trust them. Never mind if you exhaust yourself. Nobody else is truly trustworthy. Not even when, like you, they know a child's life is at stake.

Nux was going crazy now. She had reached a small clearing, where stonework had defied the encroaching undergrowth. This might be where Nux had found the mop. Gaia had definitely been playing here. Somehow, she had even managed to make herself a fire. Perhaps she spent hours rubbing sticks together to do it; more likely she took some embers from the burning garden rubbish nearer the house. The ashes of her mock Vestal fire, cold now, of course, formed a neat circle. They were quite clearly different from the great mounds of garden clippings, and if anyone had shown me these yesterday, I would have tracked down the child there and then.

I spotted a kitchen pitcher, lying on its side.

Nux ran to the pitcher, sniffed at it, then ran past and lay down with her nose between her paws, whining frantically.

'Well done, Nuxie; I'm coming –'

I could see what had happened. Little hands had pulled back a curtain of weeds to discover an old flight of four or five shallow stone steps. Ferns grew in crevices and green slime lurked on the lower slabs. Anyone familiar with springs would realise that this had once been a source of water, though it must have been an inconvenient distance from the house. Even a six-year-old girl, if she was bright and capable, would work out what she had found; then, forbidden to trouble the kitchen staff, she might try to see if she could fill her pitcher here. The steps led to the head of a well shaft. When it went out of use, it must have been boarded over. Over the years, the boards had rotted. So when Gaia tried to move them or walk on them, some gave way and fell into the shaft. Gaia must have gone down with them.

I knelt at the edge. I leaned over too far and a sharp rattle of stones frightened me; the edge was crumbling perilously. All I could see was darkness. I called out. Silence. She had drowned or been killed by the fall. Nux began to bark again, with that terrible sharp yowking noise. I gripped the dog and held her. Under her warm ribcage I could feel her breath panting as fast as mine. My heart was breaking.

'*Gaia!*' I yelled down the echoing shaft.

And then from the impenetrable darkness a faint whimper answered me.

LVI

I was still debating how to get help when a voice nearby cried my name.

'Aulus! Over here – quickly.'

My new partner might be a spoiled, surly senator's son, but he knew how to stick with the most urgent job in hand. Alone of the crowd in the atrium he had bothered to follow me. I heard him curse as he crashed towards me through the bushes, snagging his tunic or scratching himself on thorns.

'Gently,' I warned in a low voice, before I turned back and called down, 'Gaia! Don't move. We're here now.'

Aelianus had reached me. He took in the situation rapidly, pointed downwards with his index finger to ask if that was where the child was, then silently grimaced.

'We need help,' I groaned. 'We need Petronius Longus. Only the vigiles are equipped for this. I want you to go and fetch them. I'll stay with the child and try to keep her calm. Tell Petro the situation –' I was crouched back at the shaft, examining it. 'Say this: the well looks deep; the child sounds a long way down; she is alive, but very weak. I reckon she has been down there over two days. Someone will have to go down to her. It looks a pig's arse.'

'Very difficult?' interpreted Aelianus primly.

'We need ropes primarily, but also any other useful equipment the vigiles can come up with.'

'Lights,' he suggested.

'Yes. Above all, we need the stuff fast.'

'Right.' He was moving off.

'Aulus, listen – I want you to go yourself. Don't be sidetracked at the house.'

'I won't go that way,' he said. 'Leg me up. I'll shin over this wall. Then I'll be in the street and straight off.'

'Good thinking. You're almost at the Fourth Cohort headquarters.' I started giving him directions while we tackled shunting him up and over the tall wall at the end of the property. He was no lightweight. Next time I chose a partner I would go for a thin, half-starved one.

'Jove! Falco, this job of yours seems to consist entirely of climbing into and out of places . . .' After a few groans and complaints he was off. I heard him thump down on the other side, then his footsteps at once ran off. He was certainly athletic. He must exercise somewhere, some rich boys' gym with a high joining fee and a fitness instructor who looked like a Greek god slathered in dripping.

I should have known somebody else would not miss out on a crisis: Anacrites was the next to turn up. I showed him the layout, told him not to cause panic, and asked him to go back indoors and fetch torches.

'And ropes, surely, Falco.'

'If you can find any. Not much hope of it as a Flamen Dialis is forbidden to see anything that indicates binding. But ask the builders to bring out any wood they have that could be used for supports.'

He pottered off. Sometimes he was sensible. In an hour or two he might find me an oil lamp and a piece of string.

I sat down by the well, Nux fretting beside me; I began to talk in a reassuring voice to the invisible Gaia. 'Don't answer, sweetheart. I'm just talking to you so you know that I'm still here. People have gone to fetch equipment so we can lift you out.'

I was starting to wonder how we could do that. The more I viewed the situation, the more difficult it looked.

I heard the welcome voice of Petronius Longus on the far side of the wall just as Anacrites returned. It had seemed an age. Soon the vigiles were raising ladders. Anacrites shouted out to them, then he joined me. We were about two feet below ground level, on the last step. He had brought out a couple of flares, ready lit, and one short length of filthy rope that the builders had been using for some half-hearted purpose. Straight away I tied one of the torches to the end of the rope and tried lowering it down the well. I had to stand, leaning forwards above the shaft. Anacrites lay out flat beside me, peering over into the murk.

'The side walls are in bad condition. Keep going,' he urged. The flickering light revealed only a small area. When the rope was all played out we still had not seen Gaia. 'Not good news,' muttered Anacrites in a low voice to me. He sat up again, but he stayed there, ready for another go. His tunic was covered with dirt. Ma would have a good flap over that when he went home. Still, he could say he had been out with her rascal son.

Petronius had come up behind me, almost silently. He gave no greeting. He made no jokes. He walked to the far side, looking down from above us. He whistled once, very quietly to himself; then he stood still, assessing the problem. Some of his men lined up with him. Aelianus appeared too. He passed me more rope, which I knotted on to the torchline. I continued lowering it slowly while the others watched.

'Stop there,' ordered Anacrites, now flat on his face again.

I stayed my hand. He scrambled even nearer to the edge, leaning out as far as he dared. Petro muttered a warning. Aelianus bent to a crouch, ready to grab hold of Anacrites by his belt if he slipped. Anacrites shifted, splayed on the ground. Foolishly perhaps, he reached out across the shaft and supported himself against a side wall.

'I can see something.' I paid out a couple more inches of rope. 'Stop – you'll hit her.'

'Pass it this side,' said Petro. I pulled the rope back up slightly and leaned over to give him the free end, keeping one hand on the taut length. When Petro had taken hold, I let go gently.

'Whoa – it's swinging madly – wait! Right. More slack – yes, she's there. She is not moving. The boarding has lodged and she's clinging on.'

'All right, Gaia – we can see you now!'

'No. Too late. The torch has gone out.'

Anacrites pushed off from his suspended position and we hauled him back. He scrambled to his feet, white-faced. He looked around the group of us and shook his head. 'It's a miracle she stuck at that point – and that she has managed to stay there. One false move and the whole lot will slip down further. I couldn't see how deep it goes.'

Petronius came to life.

'We have to try – is that agreed?' He did not, in fact, wait for an answer. He was going to make the best attempt, whatever anyone else felt. 'Right lads; this is a bearer and brattice job.' He was talking to his men. 'We want anchor points for the ropes, and the head of the shaft will need lining too. I'm not sending anyone down there only to have the hero and the girl both swept away by shit and rubble from up top. Time we spend stabilising the head of the shaft won't be wasted.'

The problem was physical, logistic, a teamwork task. It was natural that the vigiles took over. They had the expertise for reaching inaccessible places in a hurry. They dealt with fires and with collapsed buildings. I had laboured in a mine once, in Britain, but it had been surface worked. Even there, proper experts had designed and installed the props in the seams.

Various materials had been turning up from the moment Petro himself appeared. Without fuss his men set to, planning how to tackle the work, fetching gear from beyond the wall, sending off for more. Anacrites, who had now made himself legate in charge of lighting, said he was going indoors to look for covered lanterns. That would keep him out of our way. I started measuring the length of the ropes the vigiles had brought, and testing their strength. Aelianus watched, then helped me.

'Sailcloth!' one of the vigiles exclaimed. 'Quicker than woodwork for lining the shaft.'

'Got any?' asked Petro, rather scathingly, I thought.

'In the stores. Easy to fetch while the balks are being fixed at the shaft head.'

'If not, just bring esparto mats,' Petro decided. He had always been receptive to ideas and quick to adapt. 'We only have time to cover the first few feet in any case. And we can't risk disturbing too much loose material that may drop on the child.'

317

From time to time, everyone halted. Silence would descend. One of us would stand above the well and call down encouragement to Gaia. The little girl had stopped answering.

When Anacrites came back, I heard women's voices with him. Bad news. He had been forced to bring Caecilia Paeta, who was demanding to see where her daughter was. Terentia had come with her, and the nurse, Athene. Without anybody needing to issue orders, those of the vigiles who were not involved in the immediate task of building a braced platform above the shaft, moved into a discreet cordon, keeping the visitors back. The vigiles were used to gawpers getting in their way. Their response could be brutal, though when occasion called they could fend off the interest with surprising tact.

I went over to the women. 'It's all right. Caecilia Paeta is very sensible.' For once this ploy worked. At my announcement Caecilia, who had been growing hysterical, decided to quieten down. 'Listen. I'll take you near and you can call out to tell Gaia that her mother is here. Try not to sound frightened. Try to reassure her. But keep her calm. She really must not become agitated, in case she moves about – do you understand?'

Caecilia drew herself up. She nodded. Her estranged husband had just been exposed as a murderer; her mad sister-in-law was beyond help; she was trapped in the house of a tyrannical father-in-law; even Terentia, the other force in her life, was a bully. Gaia Laelia was all the poor woman had to console her. I would not blame her if she lost her nerve and wept and wailed, but I could not risk allowing her to do so.

I kept a tight grip on her. The men paused, though it was clear they hated to be held up. Caecilia stood where I told her, a spot where she could really see little of the well. She trembled slightly. Maybe she had more imagination than I would once have given her credit for. She called Gaia's name. After one feeble attempt she tried again, more loudly and firmly. 'I am close by, darling. These kind men will soon have you out of there.'

She forced herself to maintain a strong voice, though tears

318

were streaming down her face. Forget exalted birthrights and religious callings. At least what we had now was a real mother fearing for the life of a real small child. If we could, by some miracle, rescue the child alive, things in future might be better for both of them.

One of the men at the edge of the shaft raised an arm to us. 'I heard her! Keep still, little one! We're coming. Just keep still.' He and his colleagues immediately returned to their work.

Caecilia Paeta turned to me. Her eyes showed that she understood just how slim were our chances of removing Gaia safely. Too horrified to ask my opinion, she made no sound. I would have preferred her to plead and twitter. Silent bravery was hard to take. I led her back to Terentia.

'Go to the house. This is bound to take some time. We are being careful at every stage; you can see why. We will tell you if anything happens.'

'No,' said Caecilia. She folded her arms, pulled her stole tight around her, and just stood. 'I will stay near Gaia.' Even Terentia looked surprised by this unexpected determination.

I stood with them for a moment. 'Everything all right at the house now?'

'My niece and nephew have both been sedated and put under guard,' Terentia reported quietly. 'Ariminius had his wound dressed, and the doctor is waiting here in case he is needed again.'

'Hadn't the old man collapsed too?'

'As usual, Laelius Numentinus managed to recover as soon as the crisis was over,' said Terentia with asperity.

'You have everything in hand, I see.'

'But you will have to do what's needed here!' commented the ex-Vestal, nodding towards the well and politely acknowledging that she was not all-competent.

I left the women and rejoined my colleagues.

A basic platform had been thrown up across the well-head. We could work off it safely. It would not give way. Boots would grip on the wood. Heavy timber beams had been set up to act as anchors for the ropes. More ropes had been brought and woven through the edges of esparto mats, the thick grass material that the vigiles used to smother fires. These had been hung down inside the shaft where the sides were most unstable and where there was bound to be most disturbance once the rescue got under way.

I noticed that more and more members of the Fourth Cohort kept coming in over the boundary wall. This was the current big event. Hard men have notoriously soft hearts where young children are concerned. They stood back, very quiet, with the patience of those who understood what they were watching, and who knew that the outlook was grim.

A rope sling had been created. Petronius, who had stood aside while his experts arranged the framework, now took command. He would supervise the actual drop. I knew he would have gone down himself if possible. We all looked at him.

'I'm too big.' It was a call for a volunteer.

I had been a silent observer, but I stepped forward now. 'I'll go.'

'This is for us, Falco.'

'It's just a job for an idiot,' I answered. 'Somebody tough but not too heavy or too large.'

'Are you fit?'

'I'll do.' Besides, I owed Gaia something. I slapped his arm. 'I'd like to know you are on one of the ropes.'

'Naturally.' Lucius Petronius offered me the harness, but first he said, 'There is something you may not have thought about.'

I sighed. 'No, I do realise. The shaft is too small. The boarding she is lying on blocks the shaft anyway. It is impossible to be lowered past her. If I am to stand any chance of grabbing her once I'm close enough, I have to go down head first.'

'Bright boy!' Petro began fixing straps around each of my ankles. 'Well, Marcus, my old friend, I hope you are wearing a loincloth or when we turn you upside down you can prepare yourself for some very bawdy jokes.'

'Dear gods. Send one of your rankers then to make the ex-Vestal move further away! I haven't worn a loincloth since I was a year old.'

I pulled my tunic well between my legs and made a flap to tuck into my belt. I thought about pinning it, but sticking a crude brooch pin in that sensitive area somehow failed to appeal to me.

'Right.' Petro spoke quietly. I had seen him in this character before; outwardly, he ignored how bad the situation was, but I trusted him. 'This is the plan. We put the lantern down first, so you should have light ahead of you. It won't be much, but a torch would probably set fire to you. The air may be bad; we don't want to add smoke. We think three ropes should hold you. The third will be around your waist for safety, fixed to the harness, and will be kept loose. All the ropes will be anchored. We have plenty of men to hang on to the slack ends.' He gripped me by both shoulders. 'You will be safe. Trust me.'

'Isn't that what you say to all those girlfriends of yours?'

'Stop playing about. We'll try not to drop you.'

'You had better not,' I said. 'If you do, you can explain everything to Helena.'

'In that case, I'll jump down the bloody hole straight after you, I think.'

'You always were a pal.'

'Your arms will be free, but let us do the work to start with. Save your strength for when you reach the girl. The blood will have rushed to your head by then. Just grab her, shout to tell us, then hang on.'

Aelianus came forward and asked to be on rope duty. So did Anacrites. Well, well. Always be nice to your partners. One day you may find yourself suspended upside down over a bottomless hole, with three of the friendly fellows hanging on to the ropes and controlling your fate.

LVII

I have always hated wells.

The worst part was being first positioned. Upright, I could have climbed in, easing myself gradually into the shaft. Head down, there was a moment when I just had to drop. Had I not already collected quite enough nightmares to haunt me, this would have been the one that woke me screaming for years afterwards.

They did their best to manoeuvre me safely over the edge. After I was fed past the timbers, the bad moment came when I felt the helping hands let go of me, and my weight tensing the ropes around my ankles. I swung out of control as they first took the weight. I would have screamed with terror but I was too busy stopping myself being scraped against the side wall. I heard a lot of desperate noise above me, then they regained control. I had my arms out to brace myself and control lateral movement. I kept trying to move my feet apart too, forgetting they were taking my weight. The descent was fairly smooth, but if they let me slip unexpectedly, my palms were badly grazed. I swore. In my head. We should have brought in stevedores for this part. At this rate, I was about to find out how a sack feels when it has been carelessly spilt open on the docks.

They steadied. Thank the gods for that. They were learning. I might have been learning too, learning to trust them. In that position, frankly, you never do.

Slowly now they let me down.

Despite the light we had sent down first, it was virtually pitch black. I felt like a trussed goat, but without the support of a spit. Petro was right. The blood had drained from my feet and legs. I was far too hot. My ears throbbed. My eyeballs were straining. My arms felt swollen. My hands felt

322

huge. Sweat began to trickle down my chest inside my tunic and down my face, straight into my eyes.

It was difficult to look down. I kept my head level, except for occasional attempts to see whether I was near the child.

The ropes felt as if they were stretching. Best not to think about that. I tried not to think about anything.

I was so far down, those above had no chance of controlling me. Frequently I bashed against the sides. I used my hands as best I could, but that sent loose material skittering below me. The atmosphere was dank, and sometimes my palms slipped on slime. If there was any sound from Gaia, I was too preoccupied to hear her.

They had stopped lowering. I was stuck. Panic rose, as I hung motionless. I forced myself to keep calm and still.

'Falco!' Petronius. 'If you can shout, call "Down" or "Up"!' His voice seemed muffled, yet it echoed around me. My anxiety increased. Soon I would be so frightened I would be absolutely useless.

'Down!' Nothing happened. They had not heard me. After a moment they started to drop me further anyway. Thanks, lads. If I ever yelled 'Up' would they hear that?

Suddenly I thought I heard a whimper. Faint light glimmered at last. I knew they had managed to position the lantern right opposite Gaia. As I tipped my head back, my skull hit something. Dear gods – the boards!

I reached out blindly. My hands found something. I clawed into cloth; pulled; felt weight; was kneed in the eye; clung on.

Around me noise roared. I had dropped right into the fallen boards and dislodged them. They were now tumbling down the shaft. For a moment, I felt as if I was going with them. Dirt and timber showered down below us. Noise thundered. I thought I heard water splash. Shouts came faintly from somewhere I could not place. Of course the light went out.

Everything settled. I stopped spinning, more or less. My left leg felt half dragged from its hip where Petro and the others must have been trying to help still me. The harness was by now cutting deep into my shoulders and waist; they must have used the safety rope. I was in agony – but now hard against my chest was the weight of a child. I had felt cold limbs. Her hair had brushed my cheek. I gripped her clothing fast, forcing my hands inwards to keep her tight against me, sticking out my elbows to protect her from being crushed against the rough sides of the well.

'Up! *Up!*'

If the descent was ghastly, the ascent was even worse. It was the longest few minutes I had ever lived. The lads must have pulled as hard as possible. They must have raised me as fast as they dared. It seemed endless. I was unable to brace myself, but repeatedly swung against the stony shaft. It was unbelievably painful. I could feel that the ropes were now definitely stretching.

'Stop!'

She had moved. I lost my grip.

As she slipped, somehow I regained my hold on her. But she was now much lower, held against my neck and not my chest. No way could I move her. Any moment I would lose her. I dared not adjust my grip in case she fell again. I just clung on, even sinking my teeth into her dress where I felt cloth in front of my face.

I could not shout now. The others decided to start pulling me up again anyway.

From above, I heard Petronius – nearer – speaking quiet but tense reassurance. Perhaps he could see me now. It sounded as though he was soothing the child. He may have been calming me. I fixed my attention on his voice and waited for death or rescue. Either would be suitable. Either would be a relief.

When hands grabbed my ankles, I jumped so much it nearly ruined everything. Rough timber scraped my spine. Suddenly I was jerked so fast I would have lost Gaia for certain, only by then other people had taken her. I remembered to unclench my teeth. All parts of my own body were being gripped ferociously, lest I fell back down.

I must have been safe because I heard Petro grunting, 'Full moon below!' Yes. The worst had happened. I was now being tortured by my tunic, which had worked free, stifling me and exposing all my nether parts.

The jokes started coming thick and fast. 'Is that what all the fuss has been about? A lot of women have been very loyal, I must say –'

'You'd shrink a bit if you'd been through what he just has!'

I didn't care. They had brought me out. These strong, insulting bastards were wonderful. I was swung like a sandbag, caught, hauled sideways, dropped gently on to earth. Air hit me. Bright June sun blinded me. The ropes loosened. The pain grew worse as my blood returned too fast to its accustomed channels. I could hear Nux barking hysterically; then she must have escaped from whoever was holding her because next minute a hot tongue was passionately licking my face.

I wrenched violently sideways – and, yes, glimpsed the child. She was white-skinned, her clothes filthy, her dark hair tangled. The vigiles were rubbing her limbs furiously; then they bundled her into a blanket, one swept her up and he set off at a run towards the house – so they thought she was alive.

They had lain me down on my side. Somebody was violently massaging my own shins and calves. Suddenly I became aware of my agony. I was so cold I had lost all feeling below my waist. My feet were free. People were dragging my boots off to attend to the entrenched weals made by the supporting ropes.

I could rest. I could stop being frightened. As I gasped for breath, my brain stopped fearing it would burst.

'Gaia –'

'She's alive. She's gone to the doctor. Well done.'

I closed my eyes. The world stilled gradually.

'Do you want anything, Falco?'

'Peace. Merit amongst my equals. Restraint from the gods. The love of a good woman – that's a particular woman, by the way. The Blues to beat the bloody Greens into Hades. A home with its own bath-house. A dog who doesn't smell. A pork rissole with rosemary and pine nuts, and a large beaker of red wine.' I waited for one or another to tell me that

I talked too much. They must all have collapsed with exhaustion too.

'I'm sure we can do you the rissole,' offered young Aelianus after a moment. He sounded tired and remote.

'And the drink,' said Petronius in an interested voice.

'We could fetch his woman for him,' said Anacrites, also rather more friendly than his norm. 'Assuming she wants to come.'

I rolled on my back and looked at the three of them. They were all sitting on the turf around me. Despite the jibes, they looked devastated. Their hands, where they had paid out the rope, were lolling limply on their knees, red raw. Their heads hung. Their faces wore the drained and haggard look of men in shock who had been far too close to another's near death. They stared back, unable to do more.

'Thanks, partners,' I said tenderly. 'I'm glad you didn't leave me down there. I would never have wanted to be on your consciences.'

'Think nothing of it,' said one of them, smiling. I cannot even remember now which of them it was.